THE LIVING PRISON

"Have you ever talked to Incarceron, Maestra? In the darkest night when everyone else is asleep? Prayed and whispered to it? Begged it to end the nightmare of nothingness? That's what the cell-born do. Because there is no one else in the world. It is the world."

Finn bit his lip and pushed the hair from his eyes, knowing they were wet and not caring. "I had no one but the Prison, and the Prison has a heart of stone. But gradually I began to understand that it was huge and that I lived inside it, that I was a tiny, lost creature, that it had eaten me. I was its child and it was my father, vast beyond understanding. And when I was sure of that, so sure that I was numb with silence, the door opened. . . ."

CATHERINE FISHER

SCHOLASTIC INC.
New York Toronto London Auckland
Sydney Mexico City New Delhi Hong Kong

Published in Great Britain by Hodder Children's Books, 2007

ISBN 978-0-545-40034-3

12 11 10 9 8 7 6 5 4 3 2 1   11 12 13 14 15 16/0

Printed in the U.S.A.   75

First Scholastic printing, September 2011

Designed by Nancy R. Leo-Kelly
Text set in Adobe Garamond

To Sheenagh Pugh
brilliant poet, wise webmistress.

INCARCERON

CRYSTAL EAGLE, DARK SWAN

1

Who can chart the vastness of Incarceron?
Its halls and viaducts, its chasms?
Only the man who has known freedom
Can define his prison.

　　　　　　　　　—*Songs of Sapphique*

Finn had been flung on his face and chained to the stone
slabs of the transitway.

His arms, spread wide, were weighted with links so heavy,
he could barely drag his wrists off the ground. His ankles were
tangled in a slithering mass of metal, bolted through a ring in
the pavement. He couldn't raise his chest to get enough air. He
lay exhausted, the stone icy against his cheek.

But the Civicry were coming at last.

He felt them before he heard them; vibrations in the ground,
starting tiny and growing until they shivered in his teeth and
nerves. Then noises in the darkness, the rumble of migration
trucks, the slow hollow clang of wheel rims. Dragging his head
around, he shook dirty hair out of his eyes and saw how the
parallel grooves in the floor arrowed straight under his body.
He was chained directly across the tracks.

Sweat slicked his forehead. Gripping the frosted links with

one glove he hauled his chest up and gasped in a breath. The air was acrid and smelled of oil.

It was no use yelling yet. They were too far off and wouldn't hear him over the clamor of the wheels until they were well into the vast hall. He would have to time it exactly. Too late, and the trucks couldn't be stopped, and he would be crushed. Desperately, he tried to avoid the other thought. That they might see him and hear him and not even care.

Lights.

Small, bobbing, handheld lights. Concentrating, he counted nine, eleven, twelve; then counted them again to have a number that was firm, that would stand against the nausea choking his throat.

Nuzzling his face against the torn sleeve for some comfort he thought of Keiro, his grin, the last mocking little slap as he'd checked the lock and stepped back into the dark. He whispered the name, a bitter whisper: "Keiro."

Vast halls and invisible galleries swallowed it. Fog hung in the metallic air. The trucks clanged and groaned.

He could see people now, trudging. They emerged from the darkness so muffled against the cold, it was hard to tell if they were children or old, bent women. Probably children—the aged, if they kept any, would ride on the trams, with the goods. A black-and-white ragged flag draped the leading truck; he could see its design, a heraldic bird with a silver bolt in its beak.

"Stop!" he called. "Look! Down here!"

The grinding of machinery shuddered the floor. It whined in his bones. He clenched his hands as the sheer weight and impetus of the trucks came home to him, the smell of sweat from the massed ranks of men pushing them, the rattle and slither of piled goods. He waited, forcing his terror down, second by second testing his nerve against death, not breathing, not letting himself break, because he was Finn the Starseer, he could do this. Until from nowhere a sweating panic erupted and he heaved himself up and screamed, "Did you hear me! Stop! *Stop!*"

They came on.

The noise was unbearable. Now he howled and kicked and struggled, because the terrible momentum of the loaded trucks would slide relentlessly, loom over him, darken him, crush his bones and body in slow inevitable agony.

Until he remembered the flashlight.

It was tiny but he still had it. Keiro had made sure of that. Dragging the weight of the chain, he rolled and wriggled his hand inside his coat, wrist muscles twisting in spasm. His fingers slid on the slim cold tube.

Vibrations shuddered through his body. He jerked the flashlight out and dropped it and it rolled, just out of reach. He cursed, squirmed, pressed it on with his chin.

Light beamed.

He was gasping with relief, but the trucks still came on. Surely the Civicry could see him. They must be able to see him!

The flashlight was a star in the immense rumbling darkness of the hall, and in that moment, through all its stairs and galleries and thousands of labyrinthine chambers he knew Incarceron had sensed his peril, and the crash of the trucks was its harsh amusement, that the Prison watched him and would not interfere.

"I know you can see me!" he screamed.

The wheels were man-high. They shrieked in the grooves; sparks fountained across the paving. A child called, a high shout, and Finn groaned and huddled tight, knowing none of it had worked, knowing it was finished, and then the wail of the brakes hit him, the screech in his bones and fingers.

The wheels loomed. They were high above. They were over him.

They were still.

He couldn't move. His body was a limp rag of terror. The flashlight illuminated nothing but a fist-thick rivet in an oily flange.

Then, beyond it, a voice demanded, "What's your name, Prisoner?"

They were gathered in the darkness. He managed to lift his head and saw shapes, hooded.

"Finn. My name's Finn." His voice was a whisper; he had to swallow. "I didn't think you were going to stop . . ."

A grunt. Someone else said, "Looks like Scum to me."

"No! Please! Please get me up." They were silent and no one

moved, so he took a breath and said tightly, "The Scum raided our Wing. They killed my father and they left me like this for anyone who passed." He tried to ease the agony in his chest, clenching his fingers on the rusty chain. "Please. I'm begging you."

Someone came close. The toe of a boot halted next to his eye; dirty, with one patched hole.

"What sort of Scum?"

"The Comitatus. Their leader called himself Jormanric the Winglord."

The man spat, close to Finn's ear. "That one! He's a crazed thug."

Why was nothing happening? Finn squirmed, desperate. "Please! They may come back!"

"I say we ride over him. Why interfere?"

"Because we're Civicry, not Scum." To Finn's surprise, a woman. He heard the rustle of her silk clothes under the coarse travelcoat. She knelt and he saw her gloved hand tug at the chains. His wrist was bleeding; rust made powdery loops on his grimy skin.

The man said uneasily, "Maestra, listen . . ."

"Get bolt-cutters, Sim. Now."

Her face was close to Finn's. "Don't worry, Finn. I won't leave you here."

Painfully, he looked up, saw a woman of about twenty, her hair red, her eyes dark. For a moment he smelled her; a drift of soap and soft wool, a heart-stabbing scent that broke into his memory, into that black locked box inside him. *A room. A room with an applewood fire. A cake on a china plate.*

The shock must have shown on his face; from the shadow of her hood she looked at him thoughtfully. "You'll be safe with us."

Finn stared back. He couldn't breathe.

A nursery. The walls stone. The hangings rich and red.

A man came hastily and slid the cutter under the chain. "Watch your eyes," he growled. Finn dropped his head on his sleeve, sensing people crowding around. For a moment he thought one of the fits he dreaded was coming over him; he closed his eyes and felt the familiar dizzying heat sweep his body. He fought it, swallowing saliva, gripping the chains as the massive cutters sheared them open. The memory was fading; the room and the fire, the cake with tiny silver balls on a gold-bordered plate. Even as he tried to keep it, it was gone, and the icy darkness of Incarceron was back, the sour metallic stench of oily wheels.

Links slid and rattled. He heaved himself upright in relief, dragging in deep breaths. The woman took his wrist and turned it over. "This will need dressing."

He froze. He couldn't move. Her fingers were cool and clean, and she had touched him on his skin, between the torn sleeve and the glove, and she was looking at the tiny tattoo of the crowned bird.

She frowned. "That's not a Civicry mark. It looks like . . ."

"What?" He was alert at once. "Like what?"

A rumble miles off in the hall. The chains at his feet slithered. Bending over them the man with the cutters hesitated. "That's odd. This bolt. It's loose . . ."

The Maestra stared at the bird. "Like the crystal."

A shout, behind them.

"What crystal?" Finn said.

"A strange object. We found it."

"And the bird is the same? You're sure?"

"Yes." Distracted, she turned and looked at the bolt. "You weren't really—"

He had to know about this. He had to keep her alive. He grabbed her and pulled her to the floor. "Get down," he whispered. And then, angrily, *"Don't you understand? It's all a trap."*

For a moment her eyes stared into his and he saw their surprise fractured into horror. She jerked out of his grip; with one twist was up and screaming, "Run! Everyone run!" But the grids in the floor were crashing open; arms came out, bodies were heaved up, weapons slammed down on the stone.

Finn moved. He flung the man with the cutters back, kicked the false bolt off, and wriggled out of the chains. Keiro was yelling at him; a cutlass flashed past his head and he threw himself down, rolled, and looked up.

The hall was black with smoke. The Civicry were screaming, racing for the shelter of the vast pillars, but already the

Scum were on the wagons, firing indiscriminately, red flashes from the clumsy firelocks turning the hall acrid.

He couldn't see her. She might be dead, she might be running. Someone shoved him and thrust a weapon into his hand; he thought it was Lis, but the Scum all wore their dark helms and he couldn't tell.

Then he saw the woman. She was pushing children under the first wagon; a small boy was sobbing and she grabbed him and flung him in front of her. But gas was hissing from the small spheres that fell and cracked like eggs, its sting making Finn's eyes water. He pulled out his helm and dragged it on, the soaked pads over nose and mouth magnifying his breathing. Through its eye grid the hall was red, the figures clear.

She had a weapon and was firing with it.

"Finn!"

It was Keiro, but Finn ignored the shout. He ran for the first truck, dived under it, and grabbed the Maestra's arm; as she turned he knocked the weapon aside and she screamed in anger and went for his face with her nailed gloves, the spines clawing at his helm. As he dragged her out, the children kicked and struggled with him, and a cascade of foodstuffs was tossed down around them, caught, stowed, slid efficiently into chutes down the grids.

An alarm howled.

Incarceron stirred.

Smooth panels slid aside in the walls; with a click, spotlights of brilliant light stabbed down from the invisible roof, roaming back and forth over the distant floor, picking out the Scum as they scattered like rats, their stark shadows enormous.

"Evacuate!" Keiro yelled.

Finn pushed the woman on. Next to them a running figure was drilled with light and evaporated soundlessly, caught in mid-panic. Children wailed.

The woman turned, breathless with shock, staring back at the remnants of her people. Then Finn dragged her to the chute.

Through the mask his eyes met hers.

"Down there," he gasped. "Or you'll die."

For a moment he almost thought she wouldn't.

Then she spat at him, snatched herself out of his hands, and jumped into the chute.

A spark of white fire scorched over the stones; instantly, Finn jumped after her.

The chute was of white silk, strong and taut. He slid down it in a breathlessness that tipped him out at the other end onto a pile of stolen furs and bruising metal components.

Already hauled to one side, a weapon at her head, the Maestra watched in scorn.

Finn picked himself up painfully. All around, the Scum were sliding into the tunnel, encumbered with plunder, some hobbling, some barely conscious. Last of all, landing lightly on his feet, came Keiro.

The grids slammed shut.

The chutes fell away.

Dim shapes gasped and coughed and tore off masks.

Keiro removed his slowly, revealing his handsome face smeared with dust. Finn swung on him in fury. "What happened? I was panicked out there! What took you so long?"

Keiro smiled. "Calm down. Aklo couldn't get the gas to work. You kept them talking well enough." He looked at the woman. "Why bother with her?"

Finn shrugged, still simmering. "She's a hostage."

Keiro raised an eyebrow. "Too much trouble." He jerked his head at the man holding the weapon; the man snicked back the trigger. The Maestra's face was white.

"So I don't get anything extra for risking my life up there." Finn's voice was steady. He didn't move, but Keiro looked over at him. For a moment they stared at each other. Then his oath-brother said coolly, "If she's what you want."

"She's what I want."

Keiro glanced at the woman again, and shrugged. "No accounting for taste." He nodded, and the weapon was lowered. Then he slapped Finn on the shoulder, so that a cloud of dust rose from his clothes. "Well done, brother," he said.

2

We will choose an Era from the past and re-create it.
We will make a world free from the anxiety of change!
It will be Paradise!

—*King Endor's Decree*

The oak tree looked genuine, but it had been genetically aged. The boughs were so huge that climbing them was easy; as she hitched up her skirt and scrambled higher, twigs snapped and green lichen dusted her hands.

"Claudia! It's four o'clock!"

Alys's screech came from somewhere in the rose garden. Claudia ignored it, parted the leaves, and looked out.

From this height she could see the whole estate; the kitchen garden, glasshouses, and orangery, the gnarled apple trees in the orchard, the barns where the dances were held in winter. She could see the long green lawns that sloped down to the lake and the beechwoods hiding the lane to Hithercross. Farther to the west the chimneys of Altan Farm smoked, and the old church steeple crowned Harmer Hill, its weathercock glinting in the sun. Beyond, for miles and miles, the countryside of the Wardenry lay open before her, meadows and villages and lanes, a blue-green patchwork smudged with mist above the rivers.

She sighed and leaned back against the trunk.

It looked so peaceful. So perfect in its deception. She would hate to leave it.

"Claudia! Hurry!"

The call was fainter. Her nurse must have run back toward the house, because a scatter of pigeons flapped up, as if someone was climbing the steps by their cote. As Claudia listened, the clock on the stables began to strike the hour, slow chimes sliding out into the hot afternoon.

The countryside shimmered.

Far off, on the high road, she saw the coach.

Her lips tightened. He was early.

It was a black carriage, and even from here she could make out the cloud of dust its wheels raised from the road. Four black horses pulled it, and outriders flanked it; she counted eight of them and snorted a silent laugh. The Warden of Incarceron was traveling in style. The blazon of his office was painted on the coach doors, and a long pennant streamed out in the wind. On the box a driver in black and gold livery wrestled with the reins; she heard the rattle of a whip clear on the breeze.

Above her a bird cheeped and fluttered from branch to branch; she kept very still and it perched in the leaf cover near her face. Then it sang; a brief creamy warble. Some sort of finch, perhaps.

The coach had reached the village. She saw the blacksmith

come to his door, a few children run out of a barn. As the riders thundered through, dogs barked and the horses bunched together between the narrow overhanging houses.

Claudia reached into her pocket and took out the visor. It was non-Era and illegal, but she didn't care. Slipping it over her eyes she felt the dizzying second as the lens adjusted to her optic nerve; then the scene magnified and she saw the features of the men clearly: her father's steward, Garth, on the roan horse; the dark secretary, Lucas Medlicote; the men-at-arms with their pied coats.

The visor was so efficient she could almost lip-read as the coachman swore; then the posts of the bridge flashed past and she realized they had reached the river and the lodge. Mistress Simmy was running out to open the gates with a dishcloth still in her hands, hens panicking before her.

Claudia frowned. She took off the visor and the movement made the bird fly; the world slid back and the coach was small. Alys wailed, "Claudia! They're here! Will you come and get dressed!"

For a moment she thought she wouldn't. She toyed with the idea of letting the carriage rumble in and climbing down from the tree and strolling over, opening the door, and standing there in front of him, with her hair in a tangle and the old green dress with the tear in its hem. Her father's displeasure would be stiff, but he wouldn't say anything. If she turned up naked he probably wouldn't say anything. Just "Claudia. My dear." And the cold kiss printed under her ear.

She swung over the bough and climbed down, wondering if there would be a present. There usually was. Expensive and pretty and chosen for him by one of the ladies of the Court. Last time it had been a crystal bird in a gold cage that trilled a shrill whistle. Even though the whole estate was full of birds, mostly real ones, which flew and squabbled and chirruped outside the casements.

Jumping off, she ran across the lawn to the wide stone steps; as she descended them, the manor house rose in front of her, its warm stone glowing in the heat, the wisteria hanging purple over its turrets and crooked corners, the deep moat dark under three elegant swans. On the roof doves had settled, cooing and strutting; some of them flew to the corner turrets and tucked themselves into loopholes and arrow slits, on heaps of straw that had taken generations to gather. Or so you'd think.

A casement unclicked; Alys's hot face gasped, "Where have you been! Can't you hear them?"

"I can hear them. Stop panicking."

As she raced up the steps the carriage was rumbling over the timbers of the bridge; she saw its blackness flicker through the balustrade; then the cool dimness of the house was around her, with its scents of rosemary and lavender. A serving girl came out of the kitchens, dropped a hasty curtsy, and disappeared. Claudia hurtled up the stairs.

In her room Alys was dragging clothes out of the closet. A silken petticoat, the blue and gold dress over it, the bodice quickly laced. Claudia stood there and let herself be strapped and fastened into it, the hated cage she was kept in. Over her nurse's shoulder she saw the crystal bird in the tiny prison, its beak agape, and scowled at it.

"Keep still."

"I am still!"

"I suppose you were with Jared."

Claudia shrugged. Gloom was settling over her. She couldn't be bothered to explain.

The bodice was too tight, but she was used to it. Her hair was fiercely brushed and the pearl net pinned into it; it crackled with static on the velvet of her shoulders. Breathless, the old woman stepped back. "You'd look better if you weren't scowling."

"I'll scowl if I want to." Claudia turned to the door, feeling the whole dress sway. "One day I'll howl and scream and yell in his face."

"I don't think so." Alys stuffed the old green dress into the chest. She glanced in the mirror and tucked the gray hairs back under her wimple, took a laser skinwand out, unscrewed it, and skillfully eliminated a wrinkle under her eye.

"If I'm going to be Queen, who's to stop me?"

"He is." Her nurse's retort followed her through the door. "And you're just as terrified of him as everyone else."

It was true. Walking sedately down the stairs, she knew it had always been true. Her life was fractured into two; the time when her father was here, and the time he was away. She lived two lives, and so did the servants, the whole house, the estate, the world.

As she crossed the wooden floor between the breathless, sweating double row of gardeners and dairywomen, lackeys and link-men, toward the coach that had rumbled to a halt in the cobbled courtyard, she wondered if he had any idea of that. Probably. He didn't miss much.

On the steps she waited. Horses snorted; the clatter of their hooves was huge in the enclosed space. Someone shouted, old Ralph hurried forward; two powdered men in livery leaped from the back of the coach, opened the door, snapped down the steps.

For a moment the doorway was dark.

Then his hand grasped the coachwork; his dark hat came out, his shoulders, a boot, black knee breeches.

John Arlex, Warden of Incarceron, stood upright and flicked dust off himself with his gloves.

He was a tall, straight man, his beard carefully trimmed, his frockcoat and waistcoat of the finest brocade. It had been six months since she had seen him, but he looked exactly the same. No one of his status need show signs of age, but he didn't even seem to use a skinwand. He looked at her and smiled graciously; his dark hair, tied in the black ribbon, was elegantly silvered.

"Claudia. How well you look, my dear."

She stepped forward and dropped a low curtsy, then his hand

raised her and she felt the cold kiss. His fingers were always cool and slightly clammy, unpleasant to touch; as if he was aware of it, he usually wore gloves, even in warm weather. She wondered if he thought she had changed. "As do you, Father," she muttered.

For a moment he remained looking at her, the calm gray gaze hard and clear as ever. Then he turned.

"Allow me to present our guest. The Queen's Chancellor. Lord Evian."

The carriage rocked. An extremely fat man unfurled from it, and with him a wave of scent that seemed to roll almost visibly up the steps. Behind her Claudia sensed the servants' collective interest. She felt only dismay.

The Chancellor wore a blue silk suit with an elaborate ruffle at the neck, so high she wondered how he could breathe. He was certainly red in the face, but his bow was assured and his smile carefully pleasant. "My lady Claudia. The last time I saw you, you were no more than a baby in arms. How delightful to see you again."

She hadn't expected a visitor. The main guestroom was heaped with the half-sewn train of her wedding dress all over its unmade bed. She'd have to use delaying tactics.

"The honor is ours," she said. "Perhaps you'd like to come into the parlor. We have cider and newly baked cakes as refreshment after your journey." Well, she hoped they did. Turning, she saw three of the servants had gone and the gaps in the line had closed swiftly behind them. Her father gave her a cool look, then walked up the steps, nodding graciously along the row of faces that curtsied and bobbed and dropped their eyes before him.

Smiling tightly, Claudia thought fast. Evian was the Queen's man. The witch must have sent him to look the bride over. Well, that was fine by her. She'd been preparing for this for years.

At the door her father stopped. "No Jared?" he said lightly. "I hope he's well?"

"I think he's working on a very delicate process. He probably hasn't even noticed you've arrived." It was true, but it sounded like an excuse. Annoyed at his wintry smile she led them, her skirts sweeping the bare boards, into the parlor. It was a wood-paneled room dark with a great mahogany sideboard, carved chairs, and a trestle table. She was relieved to see cider jugs and a platter of the cook's honeycakes among a scatter of lavender and rosemary.

Lord Evian sniffed the sweet scents. "Wonderful," he said. "Even the Court couldn't match the authenticity."

Probably because most of the Court's backdrop was computer-generated, she thought sweetly, and said, "At the Wardenry, my lord, we pride ourselves that everything is in Era. The house is truly old. It was restored fully after the Years of Rage."

Her father was silent. He sat in the carved chair at the head of the table and watched gravely as Ralph poured the cider into silver goblets. The old man's hand shook as he lifted the tray.

"Welcome home, sir."

"Good to see you, Ralph. A little more gray about the eyebrows, I think. And your wig fuller, with more powder."

Ralph bowed. "I'll have it seen to, Warden, immediately."

The Warden's eyes surveyed the room. She knew he wouldn't miss the single pane of Plastiglas in the corner of the casement, or the prefabricated spiderwebs on the pargeted ceiling. So she said hastily, "How is Her Gracious Majesty, my lord?"

"The Queen's in excellent health." Evian spoke through a mouthful of cake. "She's very busy with arrangements for your wedding. It will be a great spectacle."

Claudia frowned. "But surely . . ."

He waved a plump hand. "Of course your father hasn't had time to tell you about the change of plans."

Something inside her went cold. "Change of plans?"

"Nothing terrible, child. Nothing to concern yourself about. An alteration of dates, that's all. Because of the Earl's return from the Academy."

She cleared her face and tried to allow none of her anxiety to show itself. But her lips must have tightened or her knuckles gone white, because her father stood smoothly and said, "Show His Lordship to his room, Ralph."

The old retainer bowed, went to the door, and creaked it open. Evian struggled up, a shower of crumbs cascading from his suit. As they hit the floor, they evaporated with minute flashes.

Claudia swore silently. Something else to get seen to.

They listened to the heavy footsteps up the creaking stairs, to Ralph's respectful murmurs and the rumble of the fat man's hearty enjoyment of the staircase, the paintings, the urns from China, the damask hangings. When his voice had finally faded in the sunlit distances of the house Claudia looked at her father. Then she said, "You've brought the wedding forward."

He raised an eyebrow. "Next year, this year, what's the difference? You knew it would come."

"I'm not ready . . ."

"You've been ready for a long time."

He took a step toward her, the silver cube on his watch chain catching the light. She stepped back. If he should drop the formal stiffness of the Era, it would be unbearable; the threat of his unveiled personality turned her cold. But he kept the smooth courtesy. "Let me explain. Last month a message came from the Sapienti. They've had enough of your fiancé. They've . . . asked him to leave the Academy."

She frowned. "For what?"

"The usual vices. Drink, drugs, violence, getting serving girls pregnant. Sins of stupid young men throughout the centuries. He has no interest in education. Why should he? He's the Earl of Steen and when he is eighteen he will be King."

He walked to the paneled wall and looked up at the portrait there. A freckled cheeky-faced boy of seven looked down at them. He was dressed in a ruffled brown silk suit, and leaning against a tree.

"Caspar, Earl of Steen. Crown Prince of the Realm. Fine titles. His face hasn't changed, has it? He was merely impudent then. Now he's feckless, brutal, and thinks he is beyond control." He looked at her. "A challenge, your future husband."

She shrugged, making the dress rustle. "I can deal with him."

"Of course you can. I've made sure of that." He came over to her and stood before her, and his gray gaze appraised her. She stared straight back.

"I created you for this marriage, Claudia. Gave you taste, intelligence, ruthlessness. Your education has been more rigorous than anyone's in the Realm. Languages, music, swordplay, riding, every talent you even hinted at possessing I have nurtured. Expense is nothing to the Warden of Incarceron. You are an heiress of great estates. I've bred you as a queen and Queen you will be. In every marriage, one leads, one follows. Though this is merely a dynastic arrangement, it will be so here."

She looked up at the portrait. "I can handle Caspar. But his mother . . ."

"Leave the Queen to me. She and I understand each other." He took her hand, holding her ring finger lightly between two of his; tense, she held herself still.

"It will be easy," he breathed.

In the stillness of the warm room a wood pigeon cooed outside the casement.

Carefully, she took her hand from his and drew herself up. "So, when?"

"Next week."

"*Next week!*"

"The Queen has already begun preparations. In two days we set off for Court. Make sure you're ready."

Claudia said nothing. She felt empty, and stunned.

John Arlex turned toward the door. "You've done well here. The Era is impeccable, except for that window. Get it changed."

Without moving she said quietly, "How was your time at Court?"

"Wearisome."

"And your work? How is Incarceron?"

For a fraction of a second he paused. Her heart thudded. Then he turned and his voice was cold and curious. "The Prison is in excellent order. Why do you ask?"

"No reason." She tried to smile, wanting to know how he monitored the Prison, where it was, because all her spies had told her he never left the Court. But the mysteries of Incarceron were the least of her worries now.

"Ah yes. I nearly forgot." He crossed to a leather bag on the table and tugged it open. "I bring a gift from your future mother-in-law." He pulled it out and set it down.

They both looked at it.

A sandalwood box, tied with ribbon.

Reluctant, Claudia reached out for the tiny bow, but he said, "Wait," took out a small scanning wand, and moved it over the box. Images flashed down its stem. "Harmless." He folded the wand. "Open it."

She lifted the lid. Inside, in a frame of gold and pearls, was an enameled miniature of a black swan on a lake, the emblem of her house. She took it out and smiled, pleased despite herself by the delicate blue of the water, the bird's long elegant neck. "It's pretty."

"Yes, but watch."

The swan was moving. It seemed to glide, peacefully at first; then it reared up, flapping its great wings, and she saw how an arrow came slowly out of the trees and pierced its breast. It opened its golden beak and sang, an eerie, terrible music. Then it sank under the water and vanished.

Her father's smile was acid. "How very charming," he said.

3

*The experiment will be a bold one and there
may well be risks we have not foreseen. But
Incarceron will be a system of great complexity
and intelligence. There could be no kinder or
more compassionate guardian for its inmates.*

—*Project report; Martor Sapiens*

I t was a long way back to the shaft, and the tunnels were low. The Maestra walked with her head bent; she was silent, her arms hugging herself. Keiro had put Big Arko to watch her. Finn stayed right at the back behind the wounded.

In this part of the wing, Incarceron was dark and mostly uninhabited. Here the Prison rarely bothered itself to stir, putting its lights on infrequently and sending few Beetles out. Unlike the stone transitway above, these floors were made of a metallic mesh that gave slightly underfoot; as Finn walked he saw the gleam of a rat's eyes where it crouched, dust falling on its metal scales.

He was stiff and sore, and as always after an ambush, angry. For everyone else the pent-up tension had burst; even the injured chattered as they stumbled, and their loud laughter had the energy of relief in it. He turned his head and looked back. Behind them the tunnel was windblown and echoing. Incarceron would be listening.

He couldn't talk and he didn't want to laugh. A bleak stare at a few joking remarks warned the others off; he saw Lis nudge Amoz and raise her eyebrows. Finn didn't care. The anger was inside, at himself, and it was mixed with fear and a hot, scorching pride, because no one else had had the guts to be chained like that, to lie there in all that silence and wait for death to come rolling over him.

In his mind he felt the huge wheels again, high above his head.

And he was angry with the Maestra.

The Comitatus took no prisoners. It was one of the rules. Keiro was one thing, but when they got back to the Den he'd have to explain her to Jormanric, and that turned him cold. But the woman knew something about the tattoo on his wrist, and he had to find out what that was. He might never have another chance.

Walking, he thought about that flash of vision. As always it had hurt, as if the memory—if it was one—had sparked and struggled up from some deep, sore place, a lost pit of the past. And it was hard to keep it clear; already he had forgotten most of it, except the cake on a plate, decorated with silver balls. Stupid and useless. Telling him nothing about who he was, or where he had come from.

The shaft had a ladder down its side; the scouts swarmed over first, then the Prisoners and the warband, lowering goods and the wounded. Last of all Finn climbed down, noticing how the smooth sides were cracked here and there where shriveled black ferns broke out. Those would have to be cleared, otherwise the Prison might sense them, seal off this duct, and reabsorb the whole tunnel, as it had last year when they'd come back from a raid to find the old Den gone, and only a wide white passageway decorated with abstract images of red and gold.

"Incarceron has shrugged its shoulders," Gildas had said grimly.

That was the first time he had heard the Prison laugh.

He shivered, remembering it now, a cold, amused chuckle that had echoed down the corridors. It had silenced Jormanric in mid-fury, had made the hairs on his own skin prickle with terror. The Prison was alive. It was cruel and careless, and he was Inside it.

He leaped down the last rungs into the Den. The great chamber was as noisy and untidy as ever, the warmth of its blazing fires overwhelming. As people clustered anxiously around the plunder, pulling the grain sacks open, tugging out food, he pushed through the crowd and made straight for the tiny cell he shared with Keiro. No one stopped him.

Inside, he latched the flimsy door and sat on the bed. The room was cold and smelled of unwashed clothes, but it was quiet. Slowly, he let himself lie back.

He breathed in, and inhaled terror. It came over him in a wave, appalling; he knew the hammering of his heart would kill him, felt cold sweat ice his back and upper lip. Until now he had kept it at bay, but these shuddering heartbeats were the vibrations of the giant wheels; as he jammed his palms into his closed eyes he saw the metal rims looming above him, lay in a screeching fountain of sparks.

He could have been killed. Or, worse still, crushed and maimed. Why had he said he would do it? Why did he always have to live up to their stupid, reckless reputation?

"Finn?"

He opened his eyes.

After a moment, he rolled over.

Keiro was standing with his back to the door.

"How long have you been there?" Finn's voice cracked; he cleared his throat hastily.

"Long enough." His oathbrother came and sat on the other bed. "Tired?"

"That's one word for it."

Keiro nodded. Then he said, "There's always a price to pay. Any Prisoner knows that." He looked at the door. "None of them out there could have done what you did."

"I'm not a Prisoner."

"You are now."

Finn sat up and rubbed his dirty hair. "You could have done it."

"Well, yes, I could." Keiro smiled. "But then, I'm extraordinary, Finn, an artist of theft. Devastatingly handsome, utterly ruthless, totally fearless." He tipped his head sideways, as if waiting for the snort of scorn; when it didn't come he laughed and pulled off his dark coat and jerkin. Unlocking the chest, he dropped the sword and firelock in, then searched among the heap of clothes and dragged out a red shirt flamboyantly laced with black.

Finn said, "Next time you, then."

"Have you ever known me not take my turn, brother? The Comitatus have to have our reputation pounded into their thick heads. Keiro and Finn. The fearless. The best." He poured water from the jug and washed. Finn watched wearily. Keiro had smooth skin, lithe muscles. In all this hell of deformed and starved people, of halfmen and pock-beggars, his oathbrother was perfect. And he took great care to stay that way. Now, pulling the red shirt on, Keiro threaded a stolen trinket into his mane of hair and looked at himself carefully in the fragment of mirror. Without turning he said, "Jormanric wants you."

Finn had been expecting it; even so it chilled him. "Now?"

"Right now. You'd better clean up."

He didn't want to. But after a moment he poured out fresh water and rubbed at the grease and oil on his arms.

Keiro said, "I'll back you about the woman. On one condition."

Finn paused. "What?"

"That you tell me what this is really all about."

"There's nothing . . ."

Keiro threw the ragged towel at him. "Finn Starseer doesn't

32

sell women or children. Amoz yes, or any of the hard cases. Not you."

Finn looked up; Keiro's blue eyes gazed straight back.

"Maybe I'm just getting like the rest of you." He dried his face in the gritty rag, then, not bothering to change, headed for the door. Halfway there Keiro's voice stopped him.

"You think she knows something about you."

Ruefully, Finn turned. "Sometimes I wish I'd picked someone less sharp to watch my back. All right. Yes. There was something she said . . . that might . . . that I need to ask her about. I need her alive."

Keiro moved past him to the door. "Well, don't sound too keen or he'll kill her in front of your face. Let me do most of the talking." He checked for listeners outside and looked back over his shoulder. "Scowl, and stay silent, brother. It's what you're good at."

THE DOOR to Jormanric's cell had the usual two bodyguards in front of it, but a wide grin from Keiro made the nearer grunt and step aside. Following his oathbrother in, Finn almost choked on the familiar sweet stench of ket, its intoxicating fumes heavy in the air. It caught in his throat; he swallowed, trying not to breathe too deeply.

Keiro elbowed through the pairs of oathbrothers, right to the front, and Finn trailed after his flashy red coat among the drab crowd.

Most of them were halfmen. Some had metallic claws for hands, or plastic tissue in patches where the skin had gone. One had a false eye that looked exactly like a real one, except that it was blind, the iris a sapphire. They were the lowest of the low, enslaved and despised by the pure; men whom the Prison had repaired, sometimes cruelly, sometimes just on a whim. One, a dwarfish, bent man with wiry hair, didn't step out of the way fast enough. Keiro floored him with one blow.

Keiro had a peculiar hatred for the halfmen. He never spoke to them, and barely acknowledged they existed, rather like the dogs that infested the Den. As if, Finn thought, his own perfection was insulted by their existence.

The crowd fell back, and they were among the warband. The Comitatus of Jormanric was a shambling and feckless army, fearless only in its own imagination. Big and Little Arko; Amoz and his twin, Zoma; the frail girl Lis, who went berserk in fights; and her oathsister, Ramill, who never said a word. A crowd of old lags and brash big-mouthed boys, sly cutthroats, and a few women expert in poisons. And, surrounded by his muscle-bound bodyguard, the man himself.

Jormanric, as always, was chewing ket. His few teeth worked automatically, scarlet with the sweet juice that stained his lips and beard. Behind him his bodyguard chewed in unison.

He must be totally immune to the drug, Finn thought. Even if he couldn't do without it.

"Keiro!" The Winglord's voice was a drawl. "And Finn the Starseer."

The last word was heavy with irony. Finn scowled. He pushed past Amoz and stood shoulder to shoulder with his oathbrother.

Jormanric sat sprawled in his chair. He was a big man, and the carved throne had been made especially for him; its arms were notched with raid tallies and stained with ket. A slave known as the dog-slave was chained to it; he used them to taste his food for poison, and none of them ever lasted long. This one was new, taken on the last raid, a huddle of rags and tangled hair. The Winglord wore a metallic warcoat and his hair was long and greasy, plaited and knotted with charms. Seven heavy skull-head rings were squeezed on his thick fingers.

He eyed the Comitatus with a hooded glare.

"A good raid, people. Food and raw metal. Enough for everyone's share to be plentiful."

A buzz from the room. But *everyone* meant only the Comitatus; the hangers-on would live on the scraps.

"And yet not as profitable as it might have been. Some fool annoyed the Prison." He spat out the ket and took another piece from the ivory box at his elbow, folding it carefully into his cheek. "Two men were killed." He chewed slowly, eyes fixed on Finn. "And a hostage was taken."

Finn opened his mouth, but Keiro trod firmly on his foot. It was never a good idea to interrupt Jormanric. He spoke slowly, with irritating pauses, but his appearance of stupidity was deceptive.

A thin sliver of red spittle hung on Jormanric's beard. He said, "Explain, Finn."

Finn swallowed, but Keiro answered, his voice cool. "Winglord, my oathbrother took a great risk back there. The Civics could easily not have stopped or even slowed. Because of him we have enough food for days. The woman was a whim of the moment, a small reward. But of course the Comitatus is yours, the decision yours. She means nothing, one way or the other."

The *of course* was a silken sarcasm. Jormanric didn't stop chewing; Finn couldn't tell whether the needle-stab of such a veiled threat had even registered.

Then he saw the Maestra. She was standing at the side, guarded, chains linking her hands. There was dirt on her face, and her hair was coming undone. She must have been terrified, but she stood tall, her gaze on Keiro and then, icily, on him. He couldn't meet that scorn. He looked down, but Keiro nudged him and at once he forced himself upright, outstaring them all. To seem weak, to look doubtful here, was to be finished. He could never trust any of them, except Keiro. And then only because of the oath.

Standing arrogantly he returned Jormanric's glare.

"How long have you been with us?" the Winglord demanded.

"Three years."

"Not an innocent anymore, then. The blankness has gone

from your eyes. You no longer jump at screams. You no longer sob when the lights go out."

The Comitatus tittered. Someone said, "He hasn't killed anyone yet."

"About time he did," Amoz muttered.

Jormanric nodded, the metal in his hair clinking. "Maybe that's so." His eyes watched Finn, and Finn stared straight back, because this was a bleary mask the Winglord wore, a bloated, slow disguise over his shrewd cruelty. He knew what was coming now; when Jormanric said, almost sleepily, "You could kill this woman," he didn't even blink.

"I could, lord. But I'd rather make some profit. I heard them call her Maestra."

Jormanric raised a ket-red eyebrow. "Ransom?"

"I'm sure they'd pay. Those trucks were heavy with goods." He paused, not needing Keiro to tell him not to say too much. For a moment the fear shivered back, but he fought it down. Any ransom would mean Jormanric would take a share. Surely it would sway him. His greed was legendary.

The cell was dim, its candles guttering. Jormanric poured a cup of wine, tipped a splash down for the small dog-creature, and watched it lap. Not until the slave sat back, unharmed, did he drink himself. Then he raised his hand and turned it outward to show the seven rings. "Do you see these, boy? These rings contain lives. Lives I stole. Each one of them was once an enemy, killed slowly, tormented in agony. Each one of them is trapped here in a loop around my fingers. Their breath, their energy, their strength, drawn out of them and held for me, until I need it. Nine lives a man can live, Finn, moving from one to another, fending off death. My father did it, I'll do it. But as yet I only have seven."

The Comitatus eyed one another. At the back women whispered; some strained to see the rings over the heads of the crowd. The silver skulls shimmered in the drug-laden air; one winked at Finn, crookedly. He bit his dry lips and tasted ket; it was salty as blood, made blurs swim in the corners of his eyes. Sweat soaked his back. The chamber was unbearably hot; high in the rafters rats peered down, and a bat flicked out and back into the darkness. Unnoticed, in one corner, three children dug in the pile of grain.

Jormanric heaved himself up. He was a huge man, a head higher than anyone else. He looked down at Finn. "A loyal man would offer this woman's life to his leader."

Silence.

There was no way out. Finn knew he would have to do it. He glanced at the Maestra. She looked back, pale, her face gaunt.

But Keiro's cool voice broke the tension. "A woman's life, lord? A creature of moods and folly, a frail, helpless thing?"

She didn't look helpless. She looked furious, and Finn cursed her for it. Why couldn't she sob and beg and whimper! As if she sensed him, she dropped her head, but every inch of her was stiff with pride.

Keiro waved a graceful hand. "Not much strength for a man to covet, but if you want it, it's yours."

This was too dangerous. Finn was appalled. No one teased Jormanric. No one made him look ridiculous. He wouldn't be so far gone on ket not to feel that thrust. If you want it. If you're that desperate. Some of the warband understood. Zoma and Amoz exchanged covert smiles.

Jormanric glowered. He looked at the woman and she glared back. Then he spat out the red weed and reached for his sword.

"I'm not as choosy as preening boys," he snarled.

Finn stepped forward. For a moment he wanted only to drag the woman away, but Keiro had his arm in a grip of iron and Jormanric had turned to the Maestra; his sword was at her neck, the sharp point whitening the delicate skin under her chin, straining her head upward. It was over. Whatever she knew, Finn thought bitterly, he would never find it out now.

A door slammed at the back.

An acid voice snapped, "Her life is worthless, man. Give her to the boy. Anyone who lies down before death is either a fool or a visionary. Either way, he deserves his reward."

The crowd parted hastily. A small man strode through, his clothes the dark green of the Sapienti. He was old but upright, and even the Comitatus moved aside for him. He came and stood by Finn; Jormanric looked down at him heavily.

"Gildas. What does it matter to you?"

"Do as I say." The old man's voice was harsh; he spoke as if to a child. "You'll get your last two lives soon enough. But she"—he jerked his thumb at the woman—"won't be one of them."

Anyone else would be dead. Anyone else would have been hauled out and hung down the shaft by his heels while rats ate his insides. But after a second Jormanric lowered the sword. "You promise me."

"I promise you."

"The promises of the Wise should not be broken."

The old man said, "They won't be."

Jormanric looked at him. Then he sheathed the sword. "Take her."

The woman gasped.

Gildas stared at her irritably. When she didn't move, he grabbed her arm and pulled her near. "Get her out of here," he muttered.

Finn hesitated, but Keiro moved at once, pushing the woman hastily through the crowd.

The old man's grip, fast as a claw, caught Finn's arm. "Was there a vision?"

"Nothing important."

"I'll be the judge of that." Gildas looked after Keiro, then back. His small black eyes were alert; they moved with a restless intelligence. "I want every detail, boy." He glanced down at the bird-mark on Finn's wrist. Then he let go.

Instantly Finn pushed through the crowd and out.

The woman was waiting out in the Den, ignoring Keiro. She turned and stalked in front of Finn back to the tiny cell in the corner and he motioned the guard away with one jerk of his head.

The Maestra turned. "What sort of Scum hole is this?" she hissed.

"Listen. You're alive . . ."

"No thanks to you." She drew herself up; she was taller than he was, and her anger was venomous. "Whatever you want from me, you can forget it. You murderers can rot in hell."

Behind him, Keiro leaned on the doorframe, grinning. "Some people have absolutely no gratitude," he said.

4

Finally, when all was ready, Martor convened the council of the Sapienti and asked for volunteers. They must be prepared to leave family and friends forever. To turn their backs on the green grass, the trees, the light of the sun. Never again to see the stars.

"We are the Wise," he said. "The responsibility for success is ours. We must send our finest minds to guide the inmates."

At the appointed hour, as he approached the chamber of the Gate, they say he murmured his fear that it would be empty.

He opened the door. Seventy men and women were waiting for him. In great ceremony, they entered the Prison.

They were never seen again.

—Tales of the Steel Wolf

That evening the Warden held a dinner for his honored guest.

The long table was dressed with a magnificent service of silver, the goblets and plates engraved with linked swans. Claudia wore a dress of red silk with a lace bodice and sat opposite Lord

Evian, while her father at the head of the table ate sparingly and spoke quietly, his calm gaze moving over the nervous guests.

All their neighbors and tenants had obeyed the summons. And that's what it was, Claudia thought grimly, because when the Warden of Incarceron invited, there was no refusal. Even Mistress Sylvia, who must be nearly two hundred, flirted and made mincing conversation with the bored young lord next to her.

As Claudia watched, the young lord carefully stifled a yawn. He caught her eye. She smiled at him sweetly. Then she winked and he stared. She knew she shouldn't tease him; he was one of her father's attendants, and the Warden's daughter would be far above him. Still, she was bored too.

After the endless courses of fish and peacock and roast boar and sweetmeats, there was dancing, the musicians up in a candle-lit gallery above the smoky hall. Ducking under the raised arms of the long line of dancers she wondered suddenly if the instruments were accurate—surely violas were from a later period? That came of leaving details to Ralph. The old retainer was an excellent servant, but his research was sometimes hurried. When her father wasn't here, she didn't care. But the Warden was precise about detail.

It was well after midnight when she finally saw the last guests to their carriage and stood alone on the steps of the manor. Behind her, two link-boys waited sleepily, their torches guttering in the breeze.

"Go to bed," she said without turning.

The glimmer and crackle of the flames faded. The night was quiet.

As soon as they were gone, she ran down the steps and under the arch of the gatehouse to the bridge over the moat, breathing the deep stillness of the warm night. Bats flitted over the sky; watching them, she tugged off the stiff ruff and the necklaces, and from under the dress she stepped out of the stiffened petticoats and dumped them with relief into the old disused privy below the bank.

Much better! They could stay there till tomorrow.

Her father had retired earlier. He had taken Lord Evian up to the library; perhaps they were still there, talking money and settlements and discussing her future. And afterward, when his guest was gone and all the house was silent, her father would pull back the black velvet curtain at the end of the corridor and open the door of his study with its secret combination, the one she had tried for months to work out. He would disappear in there for hours, perhaps for days. As far as she knew, no one else ever entered the room. No servant, no technician, not even Medlicote, the secretary. She herself had never been in.

Well, not yet.

Glancing up at the north turret she saw, as she'd expected, a tiny flame in the window of the topmost room. She walked quickly to the door in the wall, opened it, and climbed the stairs in the dark.

He thought of her as a tool. A thing he had made . . . bred, was his word. She tightened her lips, her fingers groping over the cold greasy wall. Long ago she had come to know his ruthlessness was so complete that to survive she would have to match it.

Did her father love her? As she slowed for breath on a stone landing she laughed, a quiet amusement. She had no idea. Did she love him? She certainly feared him. He smiled at her, had sometimes picked her up when she was small, held her hand on grand occasions, admired her dresses. He had never denied her anything, had never struck her or been angry, even when she'd had tantrums and broken the string of pearls he'd given her, or ridden off for days to the mountains. And yet as far back as she could remember the calmness of his cold gray eyes had terrified her, the dread of his displeasure hung over her.

Beyond the third landing the stairs were cluttered with bird droppings. They were certainly real. She picked her way through, groped along the corridor to the bend, climbed another three steps, and came to the iron-barred door. Grasping the ring, she turned it softly and peered in. "Jared? It's me."

The room was dark. A solitary candle burned on the sill, its flame guttering in the draft. All around the turret, the windows had been rolled back, in a disregard of protocol that would have given Ralph kittens.

The observatory roof rose on steel beams so narrow, it

appeared to float. A great telescope had been wheeled to face the south; it bristled with finderscopes and infrared readers and a small flickering monitor screen. Claudia shook her head. "Look at this! If the Queen's spy sees this, the fines will cripple us."

"He won't. Not after the amount of cider he sank tonight."

At first she couldn't even find him. Then a shadow at the window moved and the darkness resolved into a slender shape that straightened from the viewfinder. "Take a look at this, Claudia."

She felt her way across the room, between the cluttered tables, the astrolabe, the hanging globes. Disturbed, a fox cub streaked to the sill.

He caught her arm and guided her to the telescope. "Nebula f345. They call it the Rose."

When she looked in, she could see why. The creamy explosion of stars that filled the dim circle of sky opened like the petals of a vast flower, millennia of light-years across. A flower of stars and quasars, worlds and black holes, its molten heart pulsing with gaseous clouds.

"How far away is it?" she murmured.

"A thousand light-years."

"So what I'm looking at is a thousand years old?"

"Maybe more."

Dazzled, she withdrew her eye from the lens. When she turned to face him, tiny flickers of light blurred her sight, played over his tangle of dark hair, his narrow face and spare figure, the unlaced tunic under his robe.

"He's brought the wedding forward," she said.

Her tutor frowned. "Yes. Of course."

"You knew?"

"I knew the Earl had been expelled from the Academy." He moved into the candlelight and she saw his green eyes catch the glimmer. "They sent me a message this morning. I guessed this might be the result."

Annoyed, she brushed a pile of papers off the couch onto the floor and sat wearily, swinging her feet up. "Well, you were right. We've got two days. It's not going to be enough, is it?"

He came and sat opposite her. "To finalize tests on the device, no."

"You look tired, Jared Sapiens," she said.

"So do you, Claudia Arlexa."

There were shadows under his eyes and his skin was pale. Gently she said, "You should get more sleep."

He shook his head. "While the universe is out there wheeling over me? Impossible, lady."

She knew it was the pain that kept him awake. Now he called the fox cub and it came and jumped on his lap, rubbing and butting his chest and face. Absently he stroked its tawny back.

"Claudia, I've been thinking about your theory. I want you to tell me about how your engagement was arranged."

"Well, you were here, weren't you?"

He smiled his gentle smile. "It may seem to you as if I've been here forever, but I actually came just after your fifth birthday. The Warden sent to the Academy for the best Sapient available. His daughter's tutor could be nothing less."

Reminded of her father's words, she frowned. Jared looked at her sideways. "Did I say something?"

"Not you." She reached out to the fox but it turned away from her, tucking itself tidily into Jared's arm. So she said sourly, "Well, it depends which engagement you mean. I've had two."

"The first."

"I can't. I was five. I don't remember it."

"But they betrothed you to the King's son. To Giles."

"As you said, the Warden's daughter doesn't get second best." She jumped up and prowled around the observatory, picking up papers restlessly.

His green eyes watched her. "He was a handsome little boy, I remember."

Her back to him, she said, "Yes. Every year after that the Court painter would send a little picture of him. I've got them all in a box. Ten of them. He had dark brown hair and a kind, sturdy face. He would have been a fine man." She turned. "I only really met him once. When we went to his seventh birthday party at Court. I remember a boy sitting on a throne too big for him. They had to put a box for his feet. He had big brown eyes. He was allowed to kiss me on the cheek, and he was so embarrassed." She smiled, remembering. "You know how boys go really red. Well, he went scarlet. All he could mumble was, 'Hello, Claudia Arlexa. I'm Giles.' He gave me a bunch of roses. I kept them till they fell to pieces."

She went to the telescope and sat astride the stool, hitching her dress up to her knees.

The Sapient stroked the cub, watching Claudia adjust the eyepiece and gaze through it. "You liked him."

She shrugged. "You'd never have thought he was the Heir. He was just like any other boy. Yes, I liked him. We could have gotten along."

"But not his brother, the Earl? Not even then?"

Her fingers turned the fine dials. "Oh him! That twisted grin. No, I knew what he was like straightaway. He cheated at chess and tipped the board over if he was losing. He screamed at the servants, and some of the other girls told me things. When my . . . when the Warden came home and told me Giles had died so suddenly . . . that all the plans would have to be changed, I was furious." She sat up and turned quickly. "What I swore to you then still goes. Master, I can't marry Caspar. I won't marry him. I detest him."

"Calm down, Claudia."

"How can I!" She was on her feet now, pacing. "I feel as though everything's crashed in on me! I thought we'd have time, but a few days! We have to act, Jared. I have to get into the study, even if your machine is untested."

49

He nodded. Then he lifted the cub off and dumped it on the floor, ignoring its snarl of dismay. "Come and look at this."

Beside the telescope the monitor flickered. He touched the control and the screen rippled with words in the Sapient tongue of which he had never, for all her pleading, taught her a word. As he scrolled through it a bat whipped through the opened room and vanished back into the night. Claudia glanced around. "We should be careful."

"I'll shut the windows in a moment." Absently Jared stopped the text. "Here." His delicate fingers touched a key and the translation appeared. "Look. This is a fragment of a burned draft of a letter written by the Queen, retrieved and copied by a Sapient spy in the Palace, three years ago. You asked me to find anything that might support your absurd theory—"

"It's not absurd."

"Well, your unlikely theory, then, that Giles's death was—"

"Murder."

"Suspiciously sudden. Anyway, I found this."

She almost pushed him aside in her eagerness. "How did you get it?"

He raised an eyebrow. "Secrets of the Wise, Claudia. Let's just say a friend in the Academy went searching in the archives."

As he went to the windows she read the text eagerly.

> . . . As for the arrangement we spoke of before, it is unfortunate, but great changes often require great sacrifices. G has been kept aloof from others since

> his father died; the people's grief will be real but
> short-lived and we can contain it. It barely needs
> saying that your part will be beyond value to us.
> When my son is King I can promise you all I . . .

She hissed in annoyance. "Is that it?"

"The Queen has always been very careful. We have at least seventeen people in the Palace, but evidence for anything is rare." He slid the last window down, closing out the stars. "That took a lot of finding."

"But it's so clear!" Eagerly she read it again. "I mean . . . grief will be real . . . When my son is King . . ."

As he came over and lit the lamp she looked up at him and her eyes were bright with excitement. "Master, it proves she killed him. She murdered the King's Heir, the last of the Havaarna dynasty, so that his half brother, her own son, could have the throne."

For a moment he was still. Then the flame steadied and he looked up at her. Her heart sank. "You don't think so."

"I thought I taught you better than that, Claudia. Be rigorous in your argument. All this proves is that she intended her son to be King. Not that she did anything about it."

"But this G—"

"Could be anyone with that initial." Remorselessly he stared her down.

"You don't think that! You can't . . ."

"It's not what I think that matters, Claudia. If you make an accusation like this, you need proof so complete, there can be no question of any doubt." He eased himself into a chair and winced. "The Prince died in a fall from his horse. Doctors certified it. His body lay in state in the Great Hall of the Palace for three days. Thousands filed past it. Your own father . . ."

"She must have had him killed. She was jealous of him."

"She never showed any sign of that. And the body was cremated. There's no way of telling now." He sighed. "Don't you see how this will look, Claudia? You'll just be a spoiled girl who doesn't like her arranged marriage and is willing to rake up any sort of scandal to get out of it."

She snapped, "I don't care! What—"

He sat up. "Quiet!"

She froze. The fox cub was on its feet, ears pricked. A whisper of draft gusted under the door.

Instantly they both moved. Claudia was at the window in seconds, darkening the glass; turning, she saw Jared's fingers on the control panel for the sensors and alarms he had fitted on the stairs. Small red lights danced.

"What?" she whispered. "What was it?"

For a moment he didn't answer. Then his voice was low. "Something was there. Tiny. Perhaps an eavesdropping device."

Her heart thudded. "My father?"

"Who knows? Maybe Lord Evian. Maybe Medlicote."

They stood a long time in the dimness, listening. The night was still. Somewhere a distant dog barked. They could hear the faint baas of the sheep in the meadow beyond the moat, and an owl, hunting. After a while a rustle in the room told them the cub had curled back up to sleep. The candle guttered and went out. In the silence she said, "I'm going into the study tomorrow. If I can't find out about Giles, at least I can learn something about Incarceron."

"With him in the house . . ."

"It's my last chance."

Jared ran long fingers through his untidy hair. "Claudia, you must go. We'll talk about this tomorrow." Then all at once his face was white, his hands flat on the table. He leaned over and breathed hard.

She came around the telescope quietly. "Master?"

"My medication. Please."

She grabbed the candle, shook it back into light and cursed the Era for the hundredth time.

"Where . . . I can't find it . . ."

"The blue box. By the astrolabe."

She groped, grabbing pens, papers, books, the box. Inside was the small syringe and the ampules; fitting one on carefully, she brought it to him. "Shall I . . . ?"

He smiled gently. "No. I can manage."

She brought the lamp closer; he rolled his sleeve up and she saw the innumerable scars around the vein. He made the injection carefully, the microinfuser barely touching the skin, and as he replaced it in the box, his voice was calm and steadier.

"Thank you, Claudia. And don't look so scared. This condition has been killing me for ten years and it's in no hurry. It will probably take another ten to finish me off."

She couldn't smile. Times like this terrified her. She said, "Shall I send someone . . . ?"

"No, no. I'll go to bed and sleep." Handing her the candle, he said, "Be careful how you go down the stairs."

She nodded, reluctant, and crossed the room. At the door she stopped and turned. He stood as if he had been waiting for that, closing the box, the dark green of the Sapient coat with its high collar glinting with strange iridescence.

"Master, that letter. Do you know who it was written to?"

He looked up unhappily. "Yes. And it makes it even more urgent that we get into his study."

The candle flickered as she breathed in dismay. "You mean . . ."

"I'm afraid so, Claudia. The Queen's letter was addressed to your father."

5

*There was a man and his name was Sapphique.
Where he came from is a mystery. Some say he
was born of the Prison, grown from its stored
components. Some say he came from Outside,
because he alone of men returned there. Some
say he was not a man at all, but a creature
from those shining sparks lunatics see in dreams
and name the stars. Some say he was a liar and
a fool.*

—*Legends of Sapphique*

"You have to eat something." Finn scowled down at the woman. She sat facing resolutely away from him, her hood over her face.

She didn't say a word.

He dumped the plate and sat on the wooden bench next to her, rubbing his tired eyes with the palms of his hands. Around them the noise of the Comitatus at breakfast rang and clattered. It was an hour after Lightson when the doors that were not broken had sprung open with that great crack of sound it had taken him years to grow used to. He looked up at the rafters and saw one of the Prison's Eyes watching curiously; the small red light stared unblinkingly down.

Finn frowned. No one else took any notice of the Eyes, but he loathed them. Getting up, he turned his back on it. "Come with me," he snapped. "Somewhere quieter."

He walked quickly, not turning to see if she followed. He couldn't wait any longer for Keiro. Keiro had gone to see about their share of the plunder because Keiro always saw to those things. Finn had realized long ago that his oathbrother was almost certainly cheating him, but he could never bring himself to care that much. Now, ducking under an archway, he came out at the top of a wide staircase that curved elegantly down into darkness.

Out here the noise was muted and echoed strangely in the cavernous spaces. A few scrawny slave girls hurried past, looking terrified, as they always did when one of the Comitatus even glanced at them. From the invisible roof vast chains hung in loops like great bridges, each link thicker than a man. In some of them the uber-spiders had nested, creaming the metal with sticky web. Half a desiccated dog hung head-down from one cocoon.

When he turned, the Maestra was there.

He stepped forward, his voice low. "Listen to me. I had to bring you. I don't want to hurt you. But back there, in the transitway, you said something. You said you recognized this."

Dragging back his sleeve, he held his wrist out to her.

She flicked one disdainful glance at it. "I was stupid to feel sorry for you."

Anger rose in him but he held it down. "I need to know. I have no idea who I am or what this mark means. I don't remember anything."

Now she did look at him. "You're a cell-born?"

The name annoyed him. "That's what they call it."

She said, "I have heard of them but have never seen one before."

Finn glanced away. Talking about himself disturbed him. But he sensed her interest; it might be his only chance. He sat down on the top step, feeling the cold chipped stone under his hands. Staring out into the dark, he said, "I just woke up. That was all. It was black and silent and my mind was totally empty and I had no idea who or where I was."

He couldn't tell her about the panic, the terrible screaming panic that had surged up and made him beat and bruise himself against the walls of the tiny airless cell.

Couldn't say that he had sobbed himself into a vomiting fit; that he had cowered in the corner shaking for days—the corner of his mind, the corner of the cell, because each was the same and each was empty.

Perhaps she guessed; she came and sat by him, her dress rustling.

"How old were you?"

He shrugged. "How do I know? It was three years ago."

"About fifteen then. Young enough. I've heard some of them are born insane, and already aged. You were lucky."

The barest sympathy. He caught it despite the harshness of her voice, remembered her concern before the ambush. She was a woman who felt for other people. That was her weakness and he would have to play on it. As Keiro had taught him.

"I was insane, Maestra. Sometimes I still am. You can't imagine how it is to have no past, no idea of your name, where you came from, where you are, what you are. I found I was dressed in a gray overall with a name printed on it, and a number. The name was FINN, the number 0087/2314. I read those numbers over and over. I learned them, scratched them on the stones with sharp fragments, cut them in letters of blood on my arms. I crawled around the floor like an animal, filthy, my hair growing long. Day and night were lights that came on and went off. Food slid in on a tray through the wall; waste went out the same way. Once or twice I made an effort and tried to scrabble through the hole, but it snapped shut too quickly. Most of the time I lay in a sort of stupor. And when I slept, I dreamed terrible dreams."

She was watching him. He sensed she was wondering how much was true. Her hands were strong and capable; she worked hard with them, he could see, but she had reddened the nails too. Quietly he said, "I don't know your name."

"My name doesn't matter." She kept her gaze level. "I've heard of these cells. The Sapienti call them the Wombs of Incarceron. In them the Prison creates new people; they emerge as infants or adults, whole, not like the halfmen. But only the young ones survive. The Children of Incarceron."

"Something survived. I'm not sure it was me." He wanted to tell her about the nightmares of fractured images, the times he woke even now in a panic of forgetfulness, groping for his name, where he was, until Keiro's quiet breathing reassured him. Instead he said, "And there was always the Eye. At first I didn't know what it was, only noticed it in the night, a tiny red point glowing near the ceiling. Slowly I realized it was there all the time, came to imagine it was watching me, that there was no escape from it. I began to think there was an intelligence behind it, curious and cruel. I hated it, squirmed away, curled up with my face against the damp stones not to see it. After a while, though, I couldn't stop glancing around to check it was still there. It became a sort of comfort. I got scared it would go away, couldn't stand the thought of it leaving me. That was when I started to talk to it."

He had not told even Keiro this. Her quietness, her closeness, that smell of soap and comfort, he must have known something like them once, because they drew out his words, hard now, reluctant.

"Have you ever talked to Incarceron, Maestra? In the darkest night when everyone else is asleep? Prayed and whispered to it? Begged it to end the nightmare of nothingness? That's what the cell-born do. Because there is no one else in the world. It is the world."

His voice choked. Careful not to look at him she said, "I have never been that alone. I have a husband. I have children."

He swallowed, feeling her anger puncture his self-pity. Perhaps she was working on him too. He bit his lip and pushed the hair from his eyes, knowing they were wet and not caring. "Well, you are lucky, Maestra, because I had no one but the Prison, and the Prison has a heart of stone. But gradually I began to understand that it was huge and that I lived inside it, that I was a tiny, lost creature, that it had eaten me. I was its child and it was my father, vast beyond understanding. And when I was sure of that, so sure that I was numb with silence, the door opened."

"So there was a door!" Her voice was edged with sarcasm.

"There was. All the time. It was tiny and it had been invisible in the gray wall. For a long time, hours perhaps, I just watched the rectangle of darkness, fearing what might come in, the faint sounds and smells from beyond. Finally I summoned up the courage to crawl to it and peer out." He knew she was looking at him now. He gripped his hands together and went on steadily. "The only thing outside the door was a tubular white corridor lit from above. It ran straight in either direction, and there were no openings in it, and no end. It narrowed eternally into dimness. I dragged myself up—"

"You could manage to walk, then?"

"Barely. I had little strength"

She smiled, humorless. He hurried on. "I stumbled on till my legs wouldn't hold me, but the corridor was as straight and featureless as before. The lights went out and only the Eyes watched me. When I left one behind I found another ahead, and that comforted me, because stupidly I thought Incarceron was watching over me, leading me to safety. I slept where I fell that night. At Lightson there was a plateful of some bland white food by my head. I ate it and walked on. For two days I followed that corridor until I grew convinced I was walking on the spot, getting nowhere, that it was the corridor that was moving, streaming past me, that I was on some terrible treadmill and would walk forever. Then I slammed into a stone wall. I beat on it in despair. It opened, and I fell out. Into darkness."

He was silent so long she said, "And found yourself here?"

She was fascinated, despite herself. Finn shrugged. "When I came around I was lying on my back in a wagon with a pile of grain and a few dozen rats. The Comitatus had picked me up on one of their patrols. They could have enslaved me or cut my throat. The Sapient was the one who talked them out of it. Though Keiro takes the credit."

She laughed harshly. "I'm sure he does. And you never tried to find this tunnel again?"

"I tried. I've never succeeded."

"But to stay with these . . . animals."

"There was no one else. And Keiro needed an oathbrother; you can't survive here without one. He thought my . . . visions . . . might be useful, and maybe he recognized I was reckless enough for him. We cut our hands and mixed blood and crawled under an arch of chains together. It's what they do here—a sacred bond. We guard each other. If one dies, the other takes revenge for him. It can never be broken."

She glanced around. "He's not a brother I would choose. And the Sapient?"

Finn shrugged. "He believes my flashes of memory are sent by Sapphique. To help us find the way out." She was silent. Quietly he said, "Now you know my story, tell me about the skin-mark. You spoke of a crystal . . ."

"I offered you kindness." Her lips were tight. "In return I'm kidnapped and likely to be murdered by a thug who believes he can store lives up for himself. In silver rings!"

"Don't joke about that," Finn said uneasily. "It's dangerous."

"You believe it?" She sounded astonished.

"It's true. His father lived for two hundred years . . ."

"Total rubbish!" Her scorn was absolute. "His father may well have lived to old age, but probably because he always took the best of the food and clothing, and left any danger to his stupid followers. Like you." She turned and glared at him. "You played on my compassion. You're still doing it."

"I'm not. I put myself at risk to save you. You saw that."

The Maestra shook her head. Then she caught his arm and before he could pull away, pushed the ragged sleeve up.

His dirty skin was bruised but unscarred.

"What happened to the cuts you made?"

"They healed," he said quietly.

She let go of his sleeve in disgust and turned away. "What will happen to me?"

"Jormanric will send a messenger to your people. The ransom will be your weight in treasure."

"And if they won't pay it?"

"Surely they will."

"If they won't?" She turned. "What then?"

Unhappy, he shrugged. "You end up a slave here. Processing the ore, making weapons. It's dangerous. Little food. He works them to death."

She nodded. Looking straight out into the dark emptiness of the stairway, she took a breath and he saw its mistiness in the cold air. Then she said, "In that case we make a deal. I get them to bring the crystal and you release me. Tonight."

His heart thumped. But he said, "It's not that easy . . ."

"It is that easy. Otherwise I give you nothing, Finn Cellborn. Nothing. Ever."

She turned and her dark eyes watched him steadily. "I am the Maestra of my people and will never submit to Scum."

She was brave, he thought, but she had no idea. In less than an hour Jormanric could have her screaming to give him anything he wanted. But Finn had seen that too often, and it sickened him.

"They must bring it with the ransom."

"I don't want them to have to. I want you to take me back

to where you found me, today, before lockup. Once we get there—"

"I can't." He stood up abruptly. Behind them the clang of the signal bell sent a flock of the sooty doves that infested the Den flapping out into the dark. "They'd skin me alive!"

"Your problem." She smiled sourly. "I'm sure you can invent some story. You're an expert."

"All I've told you is true." Suddenly he needed her to believe him.

She put her face close to him and her eyes were fierce. "Like the hard-luck tale at the ambush?"

Finn stared back. Then he dropped his gaze. "I can't just free you. But I swear, if you get me this crystal, you'll get home safely."

For a moment the silence was icy. She turned her back on him and hugged herself. He knew she was about to tell him. Her voice was grim.

"All right. A while ago my people broke into a deserted hall. It had been bricked up from the inside, maybe for centuries. The air was foul. When we crawled in we found some clothes gone to dust, some jewelry, a skeleton of a man."

"So?" He waited, intent.

She looked at him sidelong. "In his hand was a small cylindrical artifact made of crystal or heavy glass. Inside it is a hologram of an eagle with open wings. In one claw it holds a sphere. Around its neck, like yours, it wears a crown."

For a moment he couldn't speak. Before he could draw breath she said, "You must swear my safety."

He wanted to grab her hand and run with her, now, back to the shaft and climb up and up to the transitway. But he said, "They have to pay the ransom. I can't do anything now—if we tried, we'd both be killed. Keiro too."

The Maestra nodded wearily. "It will cost everything we have to make my weight in treasure."

He swallowed. "Then I swear to you—on my life, on Keiro's life—that if they do, no harm will come to you. That I'll make certain the exchange is honest. That's all I can do."

The Maestra drew herself up. "Even if you were once cell-born," she breathed, "you are fast becoming Scum. And you're as much a prisoner here as I am."

Without waiting for his answer, she turned and swept back into the Den. Slowly, Finn rubbed a hand around the back of his neck, feeling the damp of sweat. He realized his body was a knot of tension; he made himself breathe out. Then he froze.

A dark figure was sitting ten steps down the dark stairs, lounging against the balustrade.

Finn scowled. "Don't you trust me?"

"You're a child, Finn. An innocent." Keiro turned a gold coin over thoughtfully between his fingers. Then he said, "Don't swear on my life again."

"I didn't mean . . ."

"Didn't you?" With a sudden jerk his oathbrother stood,

strode up the steps, and stood face-to-face with him. "Fine. But remember this. You and I are joined by sworn contract. If Jormanric finds out you're double-crossing him in any way, we both end up as the last of his pretty little rings. But I don't intend to die, Finn. And you owe me. I brought you into this warband, when your head was empty and you were stupid with fear." He shrugged. "Sometimes I wonder why I bothered."

Finn swallowed. "You bothered because no one else would put up with your pride, your arrogance, and your thieving ways. You bothered because you saw I would be as reckless as you. And when you take on Jormanric you'll need me at your back."

Keiro raised a sardonic eyebrow. "What makes you think—"

"You will one day. Maybe soon. So help me in this, brother, and I'll help you." He frowned. "Please. It means a lot to me."

"You're obsessed with this stupid idea that you came from Outside."

"Not stupid. Not to me."

"You and the Sapient. A pair of fools together." When he didn't answer, Keiro laughed harshly. "You were born in Incarceron, Finn. Accept it. No one comes in from Outside. No one Escapes! Incarceron is sealed. We were all born here and we'll all die here. Your mother dumped you and you can't remember her. The bird-scar is just some tribemark. Forget it."

He wouldn't. He couldn't. He said stubbornly, "I wasn't born here. I can't remember being a child, but I was one. I can't remember how I got here, but I wasn't bred out of some artificial womb of wires and chemicals. And this"—he held up his wrist—"will prove it."

Keiro shrugged. "Sometimes I think you're still out of your head."

Finn scowled. Then he stalked back up the stairs. At the top he had to step over something crouched there in the dark. It looked like Jormanric's dog-slave, straining at the end of its chain to reach a bowl of water that some joker had placed just out of reach. Finn kicked the bowl nearer and strode on.

The slave's chain clanked.

Through its tangle of hair, its small eyes watched him walk away.

6

It was decided from the beginning that the location of Incarceron should be known only to the Warden. All criminals, undesirables, political extremists, degenerates, lunatics would be transported there. The Gate would be sealed and the Experiment commence. It was vital that nothing should disturb the delicate balance of Incarceron's programming, which would provide everything needed—education, balanced diet, exercise, spiritual welfare, and purposeful work—to create a paradise.

One hundred and fifty years have passed. The Warden reports that progress is excellent.

—Court Archives 4302/6

"That was so delicious!" Lord Evian wiped his plump lips with a white napkin. "You really must let me have the receipt, my dear."

Claudia stopped tapping her nails on the cloth and smiled brightly. "I'll have someone copy it for you, my lord."

Her father was watching from the head of the table, the crumbs of his ascetic breakfast of two dry rolls gathered neatly in a pile on the side of his plate. Like her he had finished at least half an hour ago, but his impatience was hidden with iron control. If he was impatient. She didn't even know.

Now he said, "His Lordship and I will ride out this morning, Claudia, and take a brief lunch at one p.m. exactly. Afterward we will resume our negotiations."

Over my future, she thought, but only nodded, noticing the fat lord's dismay. He couldn't be such a fool as he seemed or the Queen wouldn't have sent him, and though he tried hard, a few shrewd comments had slipped out. But he was hardly a rider.

The Warden was aware of that. Her father had a grim humor.

As she stood he rose with her, meticulously polite, and drew the small gold watch from his pocket. The timepiece gleamed. It was beautiful, digitally accurate, and totally out of Era. It was his one eccentricity, the watch and the chain and the tiny silver cube that hung from it.

He said, "Perhaps you'd touch the bell, Claudia. I'm afraid we've kept you long enough from your studies."

She went quickly to the green tassel by the hearth and he added without raising his head, "I spoke to Master Jared in the garden earlier. He looked very pale. How is his health these days?"

Her fingers froze a fraction from the bell. Then she pulled it firmly. "He's well, sir. Very well."

He put the watch away. "I've been considering. You won't need a tutor after your marriage, and, besides, there are several

Sapienti at Court. Perhaps we should allow Jared to return to the Academy."

She wanted to stare at him in horror in the dim mirror, but that would have been what he expected. So she kept her face bright and turned lightly. "As you wish. I'd miss him, of course. And we are in the middle of a fascinating study of the Havaarna Kings. He knows everything there is to be known about them."

His gray eyes watched her closely.

If she said another word her dismay would show and it would decide him. A pigeon fluttered on the tiles outside.

Lord Evian creaked to his feet. "Well, if you do, Warden, I assure you some other family will snap him up. Jared Sapiens is renowned through the Realm. He could name his fee. Poet, philosopher, inventor, genius. You should hold on to him, sir."

Claudia smiled in pleasant agreement but inside she was startled. It was as if the greasy man in the blue silk suit knew what she couldn't say for herself. He smiled back, his small eyes bright.

The Warden's lips were tight. "I'm sure you're right. Shall we go, my lord?"

Claudia dropped a curtsy. As her father followed Evian out and turned to close the double doors, he met her eyes. Then the doors clicked shut.

She sighed in relief. Like a cat eyes a mouse, she thought. But all she said was, "Now, please."

Instantly paneling slid back; maids and men raced out and

began removing cups, plates, candelabra, centerpieces, glasses, napkins, kedgeree dishes, fruit bowls. Windows snapped open and burned-out candles relit; the roaring fire in the log-filled hearth vanished without a whiff of charred wood. Dust vaporized; curtains changed color. The air sweetened itself with potpourri.

Leaving them to it, Claudia hurried out. She crossed the hall decorously holding her skirts, then raced up the curved oak staircase and dived through the concealed door on the landing, passing instantly from contrived luxury into the chilly gray corridors of the servants' quarters, bare walls roped with wires and cables and powerpoints, small camera screens and sonic scanners.

The back stairs were stone; she pattered up and opened the quilted door, and stepped out into the luxurious, Era-perfect corridor.

Two steps took her across to her own bedroom.

The maids had already cleaned it. She double-locked the door, flipped on all the security blocks, and crossed to the window.

Green and smooth, the lawns were beautiful in the summer sunshine. The gardener's boy, Job, was wandering about with a sack and a spiked stick, stabbing stray leaves. She couldn't make out the tiny music implant in his ear, but his jerky movements and sudden struts made her grin. Though if the Warden saw him, he'd be sacked.

Turning, she slid back the drawer of her dressing table, took out the minicom, and activated it. It flashed on and showed her a distorted echo of her own face, grotesque in curved glass. Startled, she said, "Master?"

A shadow. Two vast fingers and a thumb came down and lifted the alembic away. Then Jared sat down before the hidden receiver.

"I'm here, Claudia."

"Is everything set? They ride out in a few minutes."

His thin face darkened. "I'm concerned about this. The disc may not work. We need trials . . ."

"No time! I'm going in today. Right now."

He sighed. She knew he wanted to argue, but despite all their precautions, someone might be listening; it was dangerous to say too much. Instead he murmured, "Please be careful."

"As you've taught me, Master." For a brief second she thought about the Warden's threat against him, but this wasn't the time. "Start now," she said, and cut the link.

Her bedroom was dark mahogany; the great four-poster hung with red velvet, its tester embroidered with the black swan singing. Behind it was what looked like a small garde-robe set into the wall, but as she walked through the illusion it became an en-suite bathroom with every luxury—there were limits even to the Warden's strictness on Protocol. As she stood on the toilet seat and peeped out of the narrow window, sunlit dust swirled in motes about her.

She could see the courtyard. Three horses were saddled; her

72

father was standing by one, both gloved hands resting on the reins, and with a suppressed whoop of relief she saw that his secretary, the dark watchful man called Medlicote, was climbing onto the gray mare. Behind, Lord Evian was being heaved into the saddle by two sweating stable hands. Claudia wondered how much of his comic awkwardness was an act, and whether he'd been prepared for real horses rather than cybersteeds. Evian and her father were playing an elaborate and deadly game of manners and insults, irritation and etiquette. It bored her, but that was how things were at Court.

The thought of a future lifetime of it turned her cold.

To hide from it she jumped down, and tugged off the elaborate dress. Underneath she was wearing a dark jumpsuit. For a moment she glanced at herself in the mirror. Clothes changed you. Long ago, King Endor had known that. That was why he had stopped Time, imprisoned everyone in doublets and dresses, stifled them in conformity and stiffness.

Now Claudia felt lithe and free. Dangerous, even. She stepped back up. They were riding through the gatehouse. Her father paused and glanced toward Jared's tower. She smiled secretly. She knew what he could see.

He could see her.

Jared had perfected the holo-image in the long nights of sleeplessness. When he had shown her herself, sitting, talking, laughing, reading in the window seat of the sunny tower, she had been fascinated and appalled.

"That's not me!"

He'd smiled. "No one likes to see themselves from the outside."

She had seen a smug, pert creature, her face a mask of composure, every action considered, every speech rehearsed. Superior and mocking.

"Is that really how I am?"

Jared had shrugged. "It's an image, Claudia. Let's say it's how you can appear."

Now, jumping down and running back into the bedroom, she watched the horses pace elegantly over the mown lawns, Evian talking, her father silent. Job had vanished, and the blue sky was mottled with high clouds.

They'd be gone at least an hour.

She took the small disc from her pocket, tossed it, caught it, put it back. Then she opened her bedroom door and peered out.

The Long Gallery ran the length of the house. It was paneled in oak and lined with portraits, books in cabinets, blue vases on pedestals. Above each door the bust of a Roman emperor gazed sternly down from its bracket. Far down at the end sunlight made brilliant slanting lozenges across the wall, and a suit of armor guarded the top of the stairs like a rigid ghost.

She took a step, and the planks creaked. The boards were old, and she scowled, because there was no way to turn that off. There was nothing she could do about the busts either, but as she passed each painting she touched the frame control and darkened them—after all, there were almost certainly cameras in some of them. She held the disc gently in her hand; only once did it give a discreet bleep of warning, and she already knew about that, a crisscross of faint lines outside the study door, easily dissolved.

Claudia glanced back down the corridor. Far off in the house a door banged, a servant called. Up here in the muffled luxury of the past, the air was fragrant with juniper and rosemary, pomanders of crisp lavender in the laundry cupboard.

The study door was recessed in shadow. It was black, and looked like ebony; a bare panel, except for the swan. Huge and malevolent, the bird stared down at her, neck stretched in spitting defiance, wings wide. Its tiny eye glinted as though it were a diamond or dark opal.

More likely a spyhole, she thought.

Tense, she lifted Jared's disc and held it carefully to the door; it clamped itself on with a tiny metallic click.

The device hummed. A small whine emerged from it, changing tone and pitch frequently, as if it chased the intricate combination of the lock up and down the scales of sound. Jared had gone into patient explanations as to how it worked, but she hadn't really been listening.

Impatient, she fidgeted. Then froze.

Footsteps were running up the stairs, lightly pattering. Perhaps one of the maids, despite orders. Claudia flattened herself into the alcove, cursing silently, barely breathing.

Just behind her ear, the disc gave a soft, satisfied snap.

At once she turned, had the door open, and was inside in seconds, one arm whipping back out to snatch the disc.

When the maid hurried by with the pile of linen, the study door was as dark and grimly locked as ever.

Slowly, Claudia withdrew her eye from the spyhole and breathed out in relief. Then she stiffened, her shoulders tight with tension. A curious, dreadful certainty swept over her that the room behind her was not empty, that her father was standing at her back, close enough to touch, his smile bitter. That the horseman she had seen leave had been his own holo-image, that he had outguessed her as he always did.

She made herself turn.

The room was empty. But it was not what she'd expected.

For a start it was too big.

It was totally non-Era.

And it was tilted.

At least she thought so for a moment, because the first steps she took into its space were strangely unsteady, as if the floor sloped, or the perspective of the bare gray walls rose to odd angles. Something blurred and clicked; then the room seemed to gently even out, become normal, except for the warmth and the sweet faint scent and a low hum she couldn't quite identify.

The ceiling was high and vaulted. Sleek silver devices lined the walls, each winking with small red lights. A narrow illumination strip lit only the area directly below it, revealing a solitary desk, a neatly aligned metal chair.

The rest of the room was empty. The only thing marring the perfect floor was a tiny speck of black. She bent down and examined it. A scrap of metal, dropped from some device.

Astonished, still not quite sure she was alone, Claudia gazed around. Where were the windows? There should be two—both orieled casements. You could see them from outside, and through them a white pargeted ceiling and some bookshelves. Often she'd wondered about climbing up the ivy to get in. From outside, the room had looked normal. Not this humming, tilted box too big for its space.

She paced forward, gripping Jared's disc tightly, but it registered no warnings. Reaching the desk, she touched its smooth, featureless surface and a screen rose up silently with no visible controls. She searched, but there was nothing, so she assumed it was voice-operated. "Begin," she said quietly.

Nothing happened.

"Go. Start. Commence. Initiate."

The screen stayed blank. Only the room hummed.

There must be a password. She leaned down, placed both hands on the desk. There was only one word she could think of, so she said it.

"Incarceron."

No image. But under the fingers of her left hand a drawer rolled smoothly open.

Inside, on a bed of black velvet, lay a single key. It was intricate, a spun web of crystal. Embedded in the heart of it was a crowned eagle; the royal insignia of the Havaarna Dynasty. Bending closer, she looked at its sharp facets that glittered so brilliantly. Was it diamond? Glass? Drawn by its heavy beauty she bent so close her breath misted on its frostiness, her shadow blocking the overhead light so that the rainbow glints went out. Might it be the key to Incarceron itself? She wanted to lift it. But first she ran Jared's disc cautiously over its surface.

Nothing.

She glanced around once. Everything was quiet.

So she picked up the key.

The room crashed. Alarms howled; rays of laserfire shot up from the floor, ringing her in a cage of red light. A metal grille slammed over the door; hidden lights burst on and she stood frozen in the uproar in terror, her heart slamming in her chest, and in that instant the disc jabbed a pepperpoint of red pain urgently into her thumb.

She glanced down at it. Jared's message was breathless with terror.

He's coming back! Get out, Claudia! Get out!

7

*Once Sapphique came to the end of a tunnel
and looked down on a vast hall. Its floor was a
poisoned pool of venom. Corrosive steams rose
from it. Across the darkness stretched a taut
wire, and on the far side a doorway was visible,
with light beyond it.*

*The inmates of the Wing tried to dissuade
him. "Many have fallen," they said. "Their
bones rot in the black lake. Why should you be
any different?"*

*He answered, "Because I have dreams and
in those dreams I see the stars." Then he swung
himself up onto the wire and began to cross.
Many times he rested, or hung in pain. Many
times they called on him to return. Finally,
after hours, he reached the other side, and they
saw him stagger, and vanish through the door.*

*He was dark, this Sapphique, and slender.
His hair was straight and long. His real name is
only to be guessed at.*

—*Wanderings of Sapphique*

Gildas said testily, "I've told you many times. Outside exists. Sapphique found a way there. But no one comes in. Not even you."

"You don't know that."

The old man laughed, making the floor sway. The metal cage hung high over the chamber and was barely big enough for both of them to squat in. Books on chains dangled from it, surgical instruments, a swinging cascade of tin boxes stuffed with festering specimens. It was padded with old mattresses from which wisps of straw fell like an irritating snow onto the cooking fires and stewpots far below. A woman looked up to yell in annoyance. Then she saw Finn and was silent.

"I know it, fool boy, because the Sapienti have written it." Gildas pulled a boot on. "The Prison was made to hold the Scum of humanity; to seal them away, to exile them from the earth. That was centuries ago, in the time of Martor, in the days the Prison spoke to men. Seventy Sapienti volunteered to enter the Prison to minister to its inmates, and after them the entrance was sealed forever. They taught their wisdom to their successors. Even children know this."

Finn rubbed the hilt of his sword. He felt tired and resentful.

"No one has entered since. We know about the Wombs too, though not where they are. Incarceron is efficient; it was designed to be. It doesn't waste dead matter, but recycles everything. In those cells it grows new inmates. Perhaps animals too."

"But I remember things . . . bits of things." Finn gripped the cage bars as if to hold on to his belief, watching Keiro cross the floor of the hall far below, arms around two giggling girls.

Gildas's gaze followed his. "You don't. You dream Incarceron's mysteries. Your visions will show us how to Escape."

"No. I remember."

The old man looked exasperated. "Remember what?"

He felt foolish. "Well . . . a cake. With silver balls and seven candles. There were people. And music . . . lots of music . . ." He hadn't realized that until now. He was oddly pleased, until he caught the old man's eye.

"A cake. I suppose it may be a symbol. The number seven is important. The Sapienti know it as the sigil of Sapphique, because of the time when he met the renegade Beetle."

"I was there!"

"Everyone has memories, Finn. Your prophecies are what matter. The visions that descend on you are the great gift and strangeness of the Starseer. They're unique. The people know that, the slaves and the warband, even Jormanric. It's in the way they look at you. Sometimes they fear you."

Finn was silent. He hated the fits. They came suddenly, dizzy sickness and blackouts that terrified him, and Gildas's relentless interrogation after each one left him shivering and sick.

"One day I'll die from one," he said quietly.

"It is true few cell-born live to be old." Gildas's voice was harsh, but he looked away. Buckling the ornate collar over his green robe he muttered, "The past is gone; whatever it was, it doesn't matter anymore. Put it out of your head or it will drive you to madness."

Finn said, "How many other cell-born have you known?"

"Three." Gildas tugged the plaited end of his beard free irritably. He paused. "You're rare beings. I spent my life searching before I found you. A man rumored to be cell-born used to beg outside the Hall of Lepers, but when I finally coaxed him to speak I realized his mind had gone; he babbled about an egg that talked, a cat that faded out to just a smile. Years later, after many rumors, I found another, a worker of the Civicry in the Ice Wing. She seemed normal enough; I tried to persuade her to speak to me of her visions. But she never would. One day I heard she had hanged herself."

Finn swallowed. "Why?"

"They told me she had gradually begun to believe a child followed her, an invisible child that clutched her skirts and called her, woke her at night. Its voice tormented her. She couldn't shut it out."

Finn shivered. He knew that Gildas was watching him.

The Sapient said gruffly, "Finding you here was a chance in a million, Finn. Only you can guide my Escape."

"I can't . . ."

"You can. You're my prophet, Finn. My link with Incarceron. Soon now you'll bring me the vision I've waited a lifetime for, the sign that my time has come, that I must follow Sapphique and seek the Outside. Every Sapient makes that journey. None have succeeded, but none have had a cell-born to guide them."

Finn shook his head. He'd heard this for years and it still scared him. The old man was obsessed with Escape, but how could Finn help him? How could flashes of memory and the skin-tingling, choking lapses into unconsciousness help anyone?

Gildas pushed past him and grasped the metal ladder. "Don't talk about this. Not even to Keiro."

He climbed down and his eyes were on a level with Finn's feet before Finn muttered, "Jormanric will never just let you go."

Gildas glared up through the rungs. "I go where I want."

"He needs you. He rules the Wing because of you. On his own he—"

"He'll manage. He's good at fear and violence."

Gildas descended one rung, then pulled himself up, his small wizened face lit with sudden joy. "Can you imagine how it will be, Finn, one day, to open a hatch and climb out of darkness, out of Incarceron? To see the stars? To see the sun!"

For a moment Finn was silent; then he swung down on a rope past the Sapient. "I've seen it."

Gildas laughed sourly. "Only in visions, fool boy. Only in dreams."

He clambered with surprising agility down the diagonal of lashed ladders. Finn followed more slowly, the rope's friction warm through his gloves.

Escape.

It was a word that stung him like a wasp, a sharpness that pierced his mind, a longing that promised everything and meant nothing. The Sapienti taught that Sapphique had once found a way out, that he had Escaped. Finn wasn't sure if he believed that. The stories about Sapphique grew in the telling; every itinerant storyteller and poet had a new one. If a single man could have had all those adventures, tricked all those Winglords, made that epic journey through the Thousand Wings of Incarceron, he must have lived for generations. The Prison was said to be vast and unknowable, a labyrinth of halls and stairs and chambers and towers beyond number. Or so the Sapienti taught.

His feet hit the ground. Glimpsing the snake-green iridescence of Gildas's robe as the old man hurried out of the Den, Finn ran after him, making sure that his foil was in its sheath and that he had both daggers in his belt.

The Maestra's crystal was what concerned him now.

And getting it was not going to be easy.

The Chasm of Ransom was only three halls away, and he crossed the dark empty spaces quickly, alert for spiders or the inbred shadowhawks that swooped high in the rafters. Everyone else seemed to be there already. He heard the Comitatus before he came through the last archway; they were shouting and howling insults across the abyss, their scorn ringing back from the smooth unclimbable slabs.

On the far side the Civicry waited, a line of shadows.

The Chasm was a jagged crack across the floor, a sheer face of black obsidian. If a stone was dropped down it, no sound ever came up. The Comitatus considered it bottomless; some even said that if you fell into its depths, you fell right through Incarceron into the molten heart of the earth, and certainly heat rose from it, a miasma that made the air shimmer. In the center, split off by whatever Prisonquake had formed the abyss, rose a needle-thin rock called the Spike, its flat platform cracked and worn. From each side a bridge of scorched metal rusted and dark with pig-grease led there. It was a neutral place that belonged to no one, a place for truces and parleys, of hesitant exchange among the hostile tribes of the Wing.

At the unfenced edge, from which he often had troublesome slaves thrown screaming down, Jormanric lounged on his throne, the Comitatus around him, the small dog-slave crouched at the end of its chain.

"Look at him," Keiro's voice whispered in Finn's ear. "Big and thick."

"And as vain as you."

His oathbrother snorted. "At least I've got something to be vain about."

But Finn was watching the Maestra. As they led her in, her eyes glanced quickly at the crowd, the rickety bridges, her people waiting in the shimmering air beyond. Over there, just for a moment a man cried out, and at the sound her face lost its

85

composure; she tugged away from her guards and screamed, "Sim!"

Finn wondered if that was her husband. "Come on," he said to Keiro, and pushed forward.

Seeing them, the crowd moved back. *It's in the way they look at you*, Finn thought bitterly. Knowing that the old man was right made him angry. He came up behind the Maestra and grabbed her arm. "Remember what I said. No harm will come to you. But are you sure they'll bring this thing?"

She glared at him. "They won't hold anything back. Some people know about love."

The jibe stung him. "Maybe I did once."

Jormanric was watching them, his dull eyes barely focused. He jabbed a ringed finger at the bridge and yelled, "Get her ready!"

Keiro pulled the woman's hands behind her and shackled them. Watching, Finn muttered, "Look. I'm sorry."

She held his gaze. "Not as sorry as I am for you."

Keiro smiled archly. Then he looked to Jormanric.

The Winglord heaved himself up and strode to the Chasm edge, glaring out at the Civicry. The greasy chainmesh creaked as he folded his great arms across his chest. "Listen, over there!" he thundered. "You get her back for her weight in treasure. No more, no less. And that means no alloy and no junk."

His words rang in the steaming heat.

"First, your word there'll be no treachery." The reply was cold with fury.

Jormanric grinned. Ket-juice glistened on his teeth. "You want my word! I haven't kept my word since I was ten and knifed my own brother. You're welcome to it."

The Comitatus sniggered. Behind them, half in shadow, Finn saw Gildas, his face sour.

Silence.

Then, from deep in the shimmering heat haze came a clang and a thud. The Civicry were hauling their treasure across to the Spike. Finn wondered what they had—ore certainly, but Jormanric would be hoping for gold and platinum and most precious of all, micro-circuitry. After all, the Civicry were one of the richest groups in the Wing. That had been the reason for the ambush.

The bridge shuddered. The Maestra grasped the rail to steady herself.

Finn said quietly, "Let's go." He glanced behind himself. Keiro had drawn his sword.

"I'm here, brother."

"Don't let the bitch go till you get every last ounce," Jormanric rasped.

Finn scowled. Pushing the Maestra in front, he began the crossing.

The bridge was a web of woven chainwork; it swung with every step. Twice he slipped, once so hard that the whole structure swayed crazily and nearly tipped the three of them into the abyss. Keiro swore; the Maestra's fingers gripping the metal links were white-knuckled.

Finn did not look down. He knew what was below; nothing but blackness and heat that rose and scorched your face, bringing strange drowsy fumes it was unwise to breathe.

As she inched forward, the Maestra's voice came back to him, hard and cold. "If they don't bring . . . the crystal? What then?"

"What crystal?" Keiro asked slyly.

Finn said, "Shut up." Ahead in the dimness he could see the Civicry—three men, as agreed, waiting by the weighing platform. He edged up close behind the Maestra. "Don't even try to make a run for it. Jormanric will have twenty weapons trained on you."

"I'm not a fool," she snapped. Then she stepped onto the Spike.

Finn followed, taking a deep breath of relief. It was a mistake. The fumes of the heat haze choked his throat; he coughed.

Keiro pushed past him, sword drawn, and grabbed the woman's arm. "On this."

He shoved her onto the weighing platform. It was a vast aluminum construction, dragged here in pieces and reassembled with immense difficulty for occasions like this, though in all Finn's time with the Comitatus he had never seen it used. Jormanric didn't usually bother with ransoms.

"Look hard at the marker, friend." Keiro turned silkily to the Civic leader. "Not such a lightweight, is she?" He grinned. "Perhaps you should have kept her on a stricter diet."

The man was stocky, muffled in a striped coat, bulky with concealed weapons. Ignoring Keiro's taunt he came and glanced at the needle on the rusting dial, exchanging a swift, snatched look with the Maestra. Finn recognized him from the ambush. The one she'd called Sim.

The man gave Finn a filthy glare. Taking no chances, Keiro pulled the Maestra back and held his dagger to her neck. "Now pile it on. And don't try anything."

In the moment before the treasure began to be poured, Finn wiped sweat from his eyes. He swallowed again, trying not to breathe too hard, wishing desperately he had tied something over his mouth and nose. Faint, horribly familiar, the spots of redness began to swim before his eyes. Not now, he thought frantically. Please.

Not now.

Gold was slithering and rattling. Rings, cups, plates, elaborate candlesticks. A bag was upended and silver coins cascaded out, forged probably from the ore smuggled by traders; then a deluge of delicate components robbed from dark and unfrequented parts of the Wing—broken Beetles, Eye-lenses, a Sweeper with its radar mangled.

The needle began to move. Watching it, the Civicry dumped a sack of ket and two small pieces of the precious ebony wood that grew somewhere in a stunted forest even Gildas had only heard rumors of.

Keiro grinned at Finn.

As the red needle edged across, a heap of copper wire and Plastiglas went on, a handful of crystal filaments, a patched helm, and three rusted foils that would certainly snap at the first good blow.

The men worked hurriedly, but it was clear they were running out of goods. The Maestra watched tight-lipped, Keiro's knifepoint whitening the skin under her ear.

Finn's breath was ragged. Prickles of pain sparked behind his eyes. He swallowed and tried to whisper to Keiro, but he had no breath and his oathbrother was watching the last sack—of useless tinware—being placed on the heap.

The needle swung over.

It stopped short.

"More," Keiro said quietly.

"There's nothing more."

Keiro laughed. "You love the coat you're wearing better than her?"

Sim tore the coat off and flung it on. Then, with a glance at the Maestra he tossed his sword and firelock after it. The other two men did the same. They stood empty-handed and each of them watched the needle quiver.

It didn't quite make the mark.

"More," Keiro said.

"For God's sake!" Sim's voice was harsh. "Just let her go!"

Keiro glanced at Finn. "This crystal. Is it there?"

Dizzy, he shook his head.

Keiro smiled icily at the men. He pressed the blade; a glistening trickle of dark blood edged it. "Beg, lady."

She was very calm. She said, "They want the crystal, Sim. The one you found in the lost hall."

"Maestra . . ."

"Give it to them."

Sim hesitated. It was only for a second, though through his nausea Finn saw it strike the Maestra like a blow. Then the man put his hand into his shirt and pulled out an object that caught a glimmer of light, so that a brief rainbow rippled in his fingers. "We've found out something," he said. "Something it does . . ."

She stopped him with a look. He tossed the crystal slowly down onto the pile.

The needle touched the mark.

At once Keiro shoved the woman away. Sim grabbed her arm and pulled her onto the second bridge. "Run!" he yelled.

Finn crouched. Saliva welled in his throat as he picked up the crystal. Inside it an eagle spread wide wings. It was the same as the mark on his wrist.

"Finn."

He looked up.

The Maestra had stopped and turned, her face white. "I hope it destroys you."

"Maestra!" Sim had her arm but she shook him off. Gripping the chains of the second bridge, she faced Finn and spat words at him.

"I curse the crystal, and I curse you."

"There's no time," he said hoarsely. "Just go."

"You've destroyed my trust. My compassion. I thought I could tell truth from lies. Now I'll never dare show kindness to a stranger again. For that I can never forgive you!"

Her hatred scorched him. Then, as she turned away, the bridge lurched.

The abyss swung crazily. In a second of frozen horror the Maestra screamed and he gasped, "No!" staggering one step toward her. Then Keiro had hold of him and was shouting and something was cracking and as if the pain in his head had slowed them down he saw the chains and rivets that held the bridge snapping and jerking out, heard Jormanric's great howl of laughter and knew this was treachery.

The Maestra must have realized too. She stood upright.

She gave him one look, her eyes to his; then she was gone, she and Sim and the others were gone, down and down, and the bridge was a crazy contraption slamming and shedding wrecked ironware in a clattering uproar against the side of the cliff.

Screaming echoes faded.

Crumpling to his knees, Finn stared, appalled. A wave of nausea shuddered through him. He clutched the crystal, and through the roaring in his ears heard Keiro say calmly, "I should have guessed the old rogue would do that. And a lump of glass doesn't look much for all your trouble. What is it?"

Then Finn knew, in a second of sour clarity, that he was right, that he must have been born Outside; knew it because he held in his hand the one object that no one in Incarceron for generations had ever seen or would even guess the purpose of, and yet it was familiar to him, he had a word for it, he knew what it was.

It was a key.

Darkness and pain roared up and swallowed him.

He fell into Keiro's firm grip.

Underground,
the Stars are Legends

8

The Years of Rage are ended and nothing can be the same. The war has hollowed the moon and stilled the tides. We must find a simpler way of life. We must retreat into the past, everyone and everything, in its place, in order. Freedom is a small price to pay for survival.

—King Endor's Decree

Finn felt himself fall for a thousand miles down the abyss before he crashed onto a ledge. Breathless, he raised his head. All around, darkness roared. Beside him, leaning back against the rock, someone was sitting.

Finn said instantly, "The Key . . ."

"At your side."

He groped for it in the rubble, felt its smooth heaviness. Then he turned.

A stranger sat there. He was young and had long dark hair. He wore a high-collared coat like a Sapient's, but it was ragged and patched. He pointed to the rock face and said, "Look, Finn."

In the rock was a keyhole. Light shone through it. And Finn saw that the rock was a door, tiny and black, and in its transparency stars and galaxies were embedded.

"This is Time. This is what you must unlock," Sapphique said.

Finn tried to lift the Key, but it was so heavy he needed both hands, and even then it shook in his grasp. "Help me," he gasped.

But the hole was closing, swiftly, and by the time he got the Key steady, there was nothing left but a pinhole of light.

"So many have tried," Sapphique whispered in his ear. "Have died trying."

⊲◦◦◦⊳

FOR A second Claudia was stock-still with despair.

Then she moved. She shoved the crystal key into her pocket, used Jared's disc to make a perfect holocopy of it nestled in the black velvet and slammed the drawer shut. Fingers hot with sweat she took out the box prepared just for this emergency and flipped out the ladybugs. They flew, landing on the control panel and the floor. Then she clicked the blue switch on the disc to red, swung, and aimed it at the door.

Three of the laserlights fizzed and died. She slid through the gap they left, flinching from imaginary bolts of weaponry. The grille was a nightmare; the disc chuntered and clicked, and she howled at it in desperation, sure it would break down, run out of power, but slowly a white-hot hole melted in the metal as the atoms scrambled and re-formed.

In seconds she was through it, had the door open, was in the corridor.

It was silent.

Amazed, she listened. As the study door clicked shut behind her, the panic alarms were sliced off as if they rang in some other world.

The house was peaceful. Doves cooed. And below, she heard voices.

She ran. Up the back stairs, right to the attics, then down a passageway through the servants' garrets to the tiny store-room at the end; it stank of wormwood and cloves. Diving in she groped hastily for the mechanism that opened the ancient priesthole, her fingernails scraping grime and spiderwebs and then, yes, there! The latch barely wide enough for her thumb.

As she jabbed it, the panel grated; she flung her weight on it, heaved it, swearing, and it shuddered open and she fell in.

Once she had it shut and her back against it, she could breathe.

Before her, the tunnel to Jared's tower ran into darkness.

⊰○○○⊱

FINN LAY crookedly on his bed.

He lay there a long while, gradually becoming aware of the noises of the Den outside, of someone running, of the clatter of dishes. Finally, groping with his hand, he found that a blanket had been laid carefully over him. His shoulders and neck ached; cold sweat chilled him.

He rolled over and looked up at the filthy ceiling. Echoes of a long scream were ringing in his ears, the tingling of alarms and panicking, flashing lights. For a sickening moment he had the sense that his vision had stretched into a long dark tunnel leading away from him, that he could step into it and grope his way toward the light.

Then Keiro said, "About time."

Blurred and distorted, his oathbrother came and sat on the bed. He made a face. "You look rough."

Finn's voice, when he tried it out, was hoarse. "You don't."

Slowly he focused. Keiro's mane of blond hair was tied back. He wore Sim's striped coat with far more panache than its owner ever had, a wide studded belt slung around his hips, a jeweled dagger strapped to it. He spread his arms. "Suits me, don't you think?"

Finn didn't answer. A wave of anger and shame was rising somewhere in him; his mind squirmed away from it. If he let it in, it would drown him. He croaked, "How long? How bad?"

"Two hours. You've missed the shareout. Again."

Carefully Finn sat up. The seizures left him dizzy and dry-mouthed.

Keiro said, "It was a bit more severe than usual. Convulsions. You jerked and struggled, but I held you down and Gildas made sure you didn't injure yourself. No one else took much notice; they were too busy gloating over the treasure. We carried you back."

Finn flushed with despair. The blackouts were impossible to predict, and Gildas knew of no cure, or so he said. Finn had no idea what happened after the hot, roaring darkness engulfed him, and he didn't want to know. It was a weakness and he was bitterly ashamed of it, even if the Comitatus held him in awe. Now he felt as if he had left his body and had come back to find it sore and empty, that he was aslant inside it. "I didn't have them Outside. I'm sure of it."

Keiro shrugged. "Gildas is desperate to hear about your vision."

Finn looked up. "He can wait." There was an awkward silence. Into it he said, "Jormanric ordered her death?"

"Who else? It's the sort of thing that amuses him. And it's a warning to us."

Grim, Finn nodded. He swung his feet off the bed and stared down at his worn boots. "I'm going to kill him for that."

Keiro raised an elegant eyebrow. "Brother, why bother? You got what you wanted."

"I gave her my word. I told her she'd be safe."

Keiro watched him a moment, then said, "We're Scum, Finn. Our word means nothing. She knew that. She was a hostage; if they'd gotten hold of you, the Civicry would probably have done the same, so think no more about it. I've told you before, you brood over things too much. It makes you weak. There's no room for weakness in Incarceron. No mercy for a fatal flaw. Here it's kill or be killed." He was staring straight ahead and there was an odd sourness in his voice that was new to Finn. But when he turned his smile was sharp. "So. What's a key, then?"

Finn's heart thumped. "The Key! Where is it?"

Keiro shook his head in mock wonder. "What would you do without me?" He held up his hand and Finn saw that the crystal was dangling from one hooked finger.

He snatched at it, but Keiro jerked it away. "I said, what's a key?"

Finn licked paper-dry lips. "A key is a device that opens."

"Opens?"

"Unlocks."

Keiro was alert. "The Winglocks? Any door?"

"I don't know! I just . . . recognize it." He reached out hastily and grabbed it, and this time, reluctantly, Keiro let it go. The artifact was heavy, woven of strange glassy filaments, and the holographic eagle in its heart glared at Finn majestically. He saw that it wore a fine collar shaped like a crown around its neck, and tugging back his sleeve he compared it with the fading blue marks in his skin.

Over his shoulder Keiro said, "It looks the same."

"It's identical."

"But it means nothing. In fact, if anything, it means you were born Inside."

"This didn't come from Inside." Finn nursed it in both hands. "Look at it. What material do we have like this? The workmanship . . ."

"The Prison could have made it."

Finn said nothing.

But at that moment, just as if it had been listening, the Prison turned all the lights off.

WHEN THE Warden softly opened the observatory door the wall-screen was lit with images of the Havaarna Kings of the Eighteenth Dynasty, those effete generations whose social policies had led directly to the Years of Rage. Jared was sitting on the desk, one foot propped on the back of Claudia's chair, the fox cub in his arms; she was leaning forward and reading from a pad in her hand.

". . . *Alexander the Sixth. Restorer of the Realm. Created the Contract of Duality. Closed all theatres and public forms of entertainment* . . . Why did he do that?"

"Fear," Jared said dryly. "By that time any crowd of people was seen as a threat to order."

Claudia smiled, her throat dry. This is what her father must see; his daughter and her beloved tutor. Of course he would know perfectly well that they knew he was here.

"Ahem."

Claudia jumped; Jared looked around. Their surprise was masterly.

The Warden smiled a cold smile, as if he admired it.

"Sir?" Claudia stood up, her silk dress uncreasing. "Are you back already? I thought you said one."

"That was indeed what I said. May I come in, Master?"

Jared said, "Of course," and the cub streaked from his hands and jumped up the bookshelves. "We're honored, Warden."

The Warden walked to the table littered with apparatus

and touched an alembic. "Your Era detail is a little . . . eccentric, Jared. But the Sapienti are not so bound by Protocol, of course." He lifted the delicate glassware and raised it so that his left eye, hugely magnified, gazed at them through it. "The Sapienti do as they will. They invent, they experiment, they keep the mind of mankind active even in the tyranny of the past. Always searching for new sources of energy, new cures. Admirable. But tell me, how is my daughter progressing?"

Jared linked his frail fingers. Carefully he said, "Claudia is always a remarkable pupil."

"A scholar."

"Indeed."

"Intelligent and able?" The Warden lowered the glass. His eyes were fixed on her; she looked up and gazed calmly back at him.

"I'm sure," Jared murmured, "that she'll be a success in everything she attempts."

"And she would attempt anything." The Warden opened his fingers and the flask fell. It hit the corner of the desk and smashed, an explosion of glass slivers, sending a raven screeching out through the window.

Jared had leaped back; now he froze. Claudia stood behind him, quite still.

"I am so sorry!" The Warden surveyed the wreckage calmly, then took out a handkerchief and wiped his fingers. "The clumsiness of age, I'm afraid. I hope it didn't contain anything vital?"

Jared shook his head; Claudia caught the faintest glimmer of sweat on his forehead. She knew her own face was pale. Her father said, "Claudia, you'll be pleased to know that Lord Evian and I have finalized the dowry arrangements. You had better begin gathering your trousseau, my dear."

At the door he paused. Jared had crouched and was picking up the sharp, curved fragments of glass. Claudia did not move. She watched the Warden, and his look reminded her, for a moment, of her own reflection as she stared at it in the looking glass each morning. He said, "I won't take lunch after all. I have a lot of work to do. In my study. We seem to have an insect problem."

When the door closed behind him, neither of them spoke. Claudia sat, and Jared dumped the glass into a disposer and switched the monitor on for the tower stairs. Together they watched the Warder's dark angular figure pick a fastidious way through the mouse droppings and hanging webs.

Finally Jared said, "He knows."

"Of course he knows." Claudia realized she was shivering; she pulled an old coat of Jared's around her shoulders. She had the jumpsuit on under her dress, her shoes were on the wrong feet, and her hair was scrunched back in a sweaty tangle. "He came here just to show us that."

"He doesn't believe the ladybugs set the alarms off."

"I told you. The room has no windows. But he won't admit that I got the better of him, and he never will. So we play the game."

"But the Key . . . to bring it away . . ."

"He won't know if he just opens the drawer and looks at it. Only when he tries to pick it up. I can put the original back before then."

Jared wiped his face with one hand. He sat shakily. "A Sapient should not say this, but he terrifies me."

"Are you all right?"

He turned his dark eyes to her, and the fox cub jumped back down and pawed at his knee.

"Yes. But then you terrify me equally, Claudia. Why on earth did you steal it? Did you want him to know it was you?"

She frowned. Sometimes he was too acute. "Where is it?"

Jared looked at her a moment, then made a rueful face. He took the lid from an earthenware crock and dipping a hook in, lifted the Key out of the formaldehyde. The acrid smell of the chemical filled the chamber; Claudia pulled the coat sleeve over her face. "God. Wasn't there anywhere else?"

She had thrust it into his hand and had been too busy dressing to see where he put it. Now he unwrapped it carefully from the protective seal and laid it on the gnarled, singed wood of the workbench. They stared down at it.

It was beautiful. She could see that clearly, its facets catching the sunlight from the window in brilliant rainbow glints. Embedded in its heart the crowned eagle glared out proudly.

But it seemed too fragile to turn in any lock, and its transparency showed no circuitry. She said, "The password to open the drawer was *Incarceron*."

Jared raised an eyebrow. "So you thought . . ."

"It's obvious, isn't it? What else could such a key unlock? Nothing in this house has a key like that."

"We have no idea where Incarceron is. And if we did we couldn't use it."

She frowned. "I intend to find out."

For a moment Jared considered. Then, as she watched, he placed the Key on a small scale and weighed it accurately, took its mass and length, noting the results in his precise script. "It's not glass. A crystal silicate. Also"—he adjusted the scale—"it has a very peculiar electromagnetic field. I would say it's not a key in a strictly mechanical sense but some very complex technology, very pre-Era. It won't just unlock a prison door, Claudia."

She'd guessed that. She sat down again and said thoughtfully, "I used to be jealous of the Prison."

Astonished, he turned, and she laughed.

"Yes. Really. When I was tiny and we were at Court. People flocked to see him—the Warden of Incarceron, the Guardian of the Inmates, Protector of the Realm. I didn't know what the words meant, but I hated them. I thought Incarceron was a person, another daughter, a secret spiteful twin. I hated her." She picked up a pair of compasses from the table and opened them. "When I found out it was a prison, I imagined him going down into the cellars here with a lantern and a huge key—a rusty, ancient key. There would be an enormous door, studded and nailed with the dried flesh of criminals."

Jared shook his head. "Too many gothic novels."

She balanced the compasses on one point and spun them. "For a while I dreamed of the Prison, imagined the thieves and murderers deep under the house, banging on the doors, struggling to get out, and I used to wake up scared, thinking I could hear them coming for me. And then I realized it wasn't that simple." She looked up. "That screen in the study. He must be able to monitor it from there."

Jared nodded and folded his arms. "Incarceron, all the records say, was made and sealed. No one enters or leaves. Only the Warden oversees its progress. Only he knows its location. There is a theory, a very old one, that it lies underground, many miles below the earth's surface, a vast labyrinth. After the Years of Rage half the population were removed there. A great injustice, Claudia."

She touched the Key lightly. "Yes. But none of this helps me. I needed some proof of the murder, not . . ."

A flicker.

A dissolving of light.

She jerked her finger away.

"Amazing!" Jared breathed.

A fingerprint of darkness remained there in the crystal, a circular black opening, like an eye.

Inside it, far off, they saw two glimmers of moving light, tiny as stars.

9

You are my father, Incarceron.
I was born from your pain.
Bones of steel; circuits for veins.
My heart a vault of iron.
—*Songs of Sapphique*

Keiro lifted his lantern. "Where are you, Wise One?"

Gildas had not been in his sleeping cage or anywhere in the main chamber, where the Comitatus had defiantly lit flares in every brazier and were celebrating their victory with raucous song and boasting. It had taken a few clouts of Keiro's fist among the slaves to find someone who had seen the old man, heading for the hovels. Now they had tracked him down to a small cell; he was bandaging a suppurating sore on a slave-child's leg, his mother holding a feeble candle and waiting anxiously.

"I'm here." Gildas glared around. "Bring that lantern closer. I can't see a thing."

Finn came in and saw the light glimmer on the boy, noticing how sickly he looked.

"Cheer up," he said gruffly.

The boy smiled, terrified.

"If you'd only touch him, sir," the mother murmured.

Finn turned. She might once have been pretty; now she was haggard and thin.

"The touch of a Starseer cures, they say."

"Superstitious bloody nonsense," Gildas snorted, tying the knot, but Finn did it anyway, putting his fingers lightly to the boy's hot forehead.

"Not so different to yours, Wise One," Keiro said silkily.

Gildas straightened, wiped his fingers on his coat, and ignored the taunt. "Well, that's the best I can do. The wound needs to drain. Keep it clean."

As they followed him out he growled, "Always more infections, more disease. We need antibiotics, not gold and tinware."

Finn knew him in this mood; the dark gloom that kept him sometimes for days in his cage, reading, sleeping, speaking to no one. The Maestra's death would be tormenting the old man. So, abruptly he said, "I saw Sapphique."

"*What!*" Gildas stopped dead. Even Keiro looked interested.

"He said—"

"Wait." The Sapient looked around hastily. "In here."

It was a dark archway and it led to one of the vast chains that hung in loops from the Den roof. Gildas put his foot in the links and climbed until the darkness hid him; when Finn clambered after him he found the old man on a narrow shelf high in the wall, shoving ancient birdmuck and nests aside.

"I'm not sitting in that," Keiro said.

"Stand then." Gildas took the lantern from Finn and propped it on the chain. "Now. Tell me everything. Each word, exactly."

Finn put his feet over the edge and looked down. "It was a place like this, high up. He was there with me, and I had the Key."

"That crystal? He called it a key?" Gildas looked stunned; he rubbed his stubbly white chin. "That is a Sapient word, Finn, a magic word. A device for unlocking."

"I know what a key is." His voice was angry; he tried to be calm. "Sapphique told me to use it to unlock Time; there was a keyhole in some black, shining rock, but the Key was so heavy I couldn't manage it. I felt . . . devastated."

The old man gripped Finn's wrist, a hard, fierce grip. "What did he look like?"

"Young. Long dark hair. Like the stories."

"And the door?"

"Very small. The rock had light inside, like stars."

Keiro propped himself elegantly against the wall. "Strange dreams, brother."

"Not dreams." Gildas released him; the old man looked incredulous with joy. "I know that door. It has never been opened. It lies about a mile from here, up in Civicry land." He rubbed his face with both hands and said, "Where is this Key?"

Finn hesitated. He had strung it on an old piece of string around his neck, but that had been too heavy, so now it was belted inside his shirt. Reluctantly, he tugged it out.

The Sapient took it reverently. His small hands with their

raised veins explored it; he brought it close to his eyes and gazed at the eagle. "This is what I've been waiting for." His voice was choked with emotion. "The sign from Sapphique." He looked up. "It decides everything. We leave at once, tonight, before Jormanric gets to know what this thing is. Sudden and swift, Finn, we begin our Escape."

"Now wait a minute!" Keiro peeled himself off the wall. "He's not going anywhere. He's sworn to me."

Gildas looked at him in distaste. "Only because he's useful to you."

"And not to you?" Keiro laughed in scorn. "You're a hypocrite, old man. A glass trinket and a few ravings when he's off his head are all you're interested in."

Gildas stood. He barely came to Keiro's shoulder, but his glare was malevolent, his wiry body tense.

"I would be careful, boy. Very careful.

"Or what? You'll turn me into a snake?"

"You're already doing that to yourself."

With a shiver of steel Keiro drew his sword. His eyes were blue and icy.

Finn said, "Stop this." Neither of them even looked at him.

"I've never liked you, boy. I've never trusted you," Gildas said grimly. "You're a preening, arrogant thief who considers only his own pleasures, who would murder if it suited him—as it certainly already has. And you'd like nothing more than to make Finn your twin."

Keiro's face was flushed. He raised the sword so that the sharp tip menaced the old man's eyes. "Finn needs me to protect him from you. I'm the one who looks after him, holds his head when he's sick, watches his back. If we're speaking home truths, I could say that the Sapienti are old fools clutching rags of sorcery—"

"I said that's enough!" Finn stepped between them and shoved the blade aside.

Glowering, Keiro whipped it away. "You're going with him? Why?"

"What's there to stay for?"

"For God's sake, Finn! We're well in here—food, girls, all we want! We're feared, respected—powerful enough to tackle Jormanric any time now. Then we'll be Winglords, both of us!"

"And how long," Gildas sneered, "before two is one too many?"

"Shut up!" Finn turned, furious. "Look at you both! The only friends I have in this hell and all you can do is fight over me. Do either of you care about me? Not the seer, the fighter, the fool who takes all the risks, but me, Finn?" He stood shivering, suddenly bone-weary, and as they stared at him he crouched, hands to his head, his voice breaking. "I can't stand this anymore. I'm dying here, terrified, living between seizures, dreading the next one, I can't bear it anymore, I've got to get out, find out who I am! I have to Escape."

They were silent. Dust fell slowly through the beam of the lantern. Then Keiro sheathed his sword.

Finn tried to stop shivering. He looked up, dreading to see the mockery in Keiro's eyes, but his oathbrother held out a hand and pulled Finn up until they were face-to-face.

Gildas growled, "I care for you, you fool boy."

Keiro's eyes were sharp and blue. "Be quiet, old man. Can't you see he's manipulating us both, as ever? You're so good at that, Finn. You did it to the Maestra and you do it to us." He released Finn's arm and stepped back. "All right. Let's say we try to get out. Have you forgotten how she cursed you? A dying curse, Finn. Can we go up against that?"

"Leave that to me," Gildas snapped.

"Ah yes. Sorcery." Keiro shook his head in disbelief. "And how do we know the Key will open this door? Doors only open if Incarceron wants it."

Finn rubbed his chin. He made himself stand upright. "I need to try."

Keiro sighed. He turned away, gazing down at the fires of the Comitatus, and Gildas caught Finn's eyes and nodded. He seemed quietly triumphant.

Keiro swung back. "All right. But secretly. Then if we fail no one will know."

"You don't have to come," Gildas said.

"If he goes, I go."

As he said it his foot dislodged a scatter of birdmuck from

the ledge; watching it fall, Finn thought he saw a shadow flicker below. He grabbed the chain. "Someone was there."

Keiro stared down. "Are you sure?"

"I thought so."

The Sapient pulled himself to his feet. He looked dismayed. "If it was a spy, if he heard about the Key, we're in trouble. Get weapons and food and meet me in ten minutes at the foot of the shaft." He looked at the Key, its rainbow shimmer. "I'll keep this."

"No you won't." Finn took it back firmly. "It stays with me."

As he turned away with it, he felt a sudden strange warmth in its heaviness, and glanced down. Under the eagle's claw a circle of paleness was fading. Inside it he thought he saw, just for a moment, the shadow of a face, staring at him.

A girl's face.

⌐◦◯◦⌐

"I HAVE to confess that I detest riding." Lord Evian walked between the flowerbeds examining the dahlias attentively. "It all seems such an unnecessarily long way from the ground." He sat next to her on the bench and gazed out at the sunny countryside, the church steeple shimmering in the heat haze. "And then your father wanting to come home so abruptly! I do hope it wasn't some sudden illness?"

"I suppose he must have remembered something," Claudia said carefully.

115

The afternoon light warmed the honey-colored stone of the manor; it glinted on the dark gold waters of the moat. Ducks arrowed toward the floating bread; she threw more for them, shredding it in her fingers.

Evian's reflection showed his smooth face as he leaned over. His mouth said, "You must be a little anxious, as well as eager, about this marriage."

She tossed a crust to a moorhen. "Sometimes."

"I assure you, everyone says you'll manage the Earl of Steen without any problems. His mother dotes on him."

Claudia had no doubt of that. Suddenly she felt weary, as if the whole effort of acting her part was overtaking her. She stood, her shadow darkening the water. "If you'll excuse me, my lord, I have so much to see to."

He didn't look up, reaching his plump fingers to the ducks. But he said, "Sit down, Claudia Arlexa."

His voice. She stared in astonishment at the back of his head. The nasal whine was gone. Instead he sounded strong and commanding. He looked up.

She sat, silent.

"This will come as a shock, I'm sure. I enjoy my disguise, but it can be tiresome." The oily smile was gone too, and that made him look different, his heavily lidded eyes a little tired. Older.

"Disguise?" she said.

"Assumed persona. We all have them; don't we, in this tyranny of Time? Claudia, can we be overheard here?"

"It's safer than the house."

"Yes." He turned on the bench, the pale silk suit rustling, and she caught a waft of the exquisite perfume he doused himself with. "Listen to me now. I have to speak with you, and this may be the only chance. Have you ever heard of the Steel Wolves?"

Danger. There was danger here and she had to be very careful. She said, "Jared is a thorough teacher. The Steel Wolf was the heraldic symbol of Lord Calliston, who was found guilty of plotting treason against the Realm, and was the first Prisoner to enter Incarceron. But that was centuries ago."

"A hundred and sixty years," Evian murmured. "And that's all you know?"

"Yes." It was true.

He glanced quickly across the lawns. "Then let me tell you that the Steel Wolf is also the name of a secret organization of courtiers and . . . shall we say . . . malcontents who long for release from the endless playing at an idealized past. From the tyranny of the Havaarnas. They . . . we . . . would have the Realm ruled by a queen who cared for her people, who would let us live as we want. Who would open Incarceron."

Her heart thudded with fear.

"Do you understand what I'm saying, Claudia?"

She had no idea how to deal with this. Biting her lip she watched Medlicote come out of the gatehouse and look around for them. "I think so. You're one of this group?"

He had seen the secretary too. He said swiftly, "I may be. I'm taking a great chance talking to you. But I think you're not so much your father's daughter."

The secretary's dark figure crossed the drawbridge and strode toward them. Evian waved limply. He said, "Think about it. There are not many who would mourn the Earl of Steen." He stood. "Are you looking for me, sir?"

John Medlicote was a tall man of few words. He bowed to Claudia and said, "I was, my lord. The Warden sends his compliments and begs me to inform you that these dispatches have arrived from Court." He held out a leather satchel.

Evian smiled and took it daintily. "Then I must go and read them. Excuse me, my dear."

Claudia dropped an awkward curtsy, watching the small man stroll beside the grave servant, talking lightly of the prospects for the harvest, tugging documents out to read. She crumbled bread between her fingers in silent disbelief.

There are not many who would mourn the Earl of Steen.

Was he talking about assassination? Was he sincere, or was it some plan of the Queen's to trap her, to test her loyalty? If she reported it or kept silent, either way might be a mistake.

She tossed the bread on the dark water, watching the bigger mallards with their green-sheened necks peck and bully the smaller ones aside. Her life was a labyrinth of plots and pretense, and the only person she could trust in all of it was Jared.

She dusted her fingers together, cold in the sun.

Because he might be dying.

"Claudia." Evian had returned; he held a letter up between plump fingers. "Good news, my dear, of your fiancé." He looked at her, his face unreadable. "Caspar is traveling nearby. He will be here tomorrow."

It shook her. She smiled rigidly and threw the last crumbs onto the water. They floated for seconds. Then they were snatched away.

∞

KEIRO HAD stuffed a pack with plunder—fine clothes, gold, jewels, a firelock. It must have been heavy, but he wouldn't be complaining; Finn knew it would hurt him far more to leave any of it behind. For himself, he had brought one spare set of clothes, some food, a sword, and the Key. That was all he wanted. Looking down at his share of the accumulated riches in the chest had filled him with self-loathing, brought back the Maestra's scorching stare of scorn. He had shut the lid with a bang.

Seeing Gildas's lantern ahead, he ran behind his oathbrother, glancing back anxiously.

Incarceron's night was inky. But the Prison never slept. One of its small red Eyes opened, turned, and clicked as he raced below it, and the sound swept a small shiver of dismay through his skin. But the Prison would watch curiously. It played with its inmates, allowed them to kill, wander, fight, and love until it grew tired and tormented them with Lockdowns, with twisting the very shape of itself. They were its only amusement, and maybe it knew there was no Escape.

"Hurry." Gildas was waiting impatiently. He had brought nothing but a satchel of food and medicines and his staff; he strapped that to his back and glanced up the ladder into the shaft. "We get up to the transitway; the top may be guarded, so I'll go first. From there it's two hours to the door."

"Through Civicry territory," Keiro muttered.

Gildas eyed him coldly. "You can still go back."

"No he can't, old man."

Finn spun, Keiro at his side.

From the sides and shadows of the tunnels the Comitatus swaggered; red-eyed, ket-high, crossbows drawn, firelocks in their hands. Finn saw Big Arko flex his shoulders and grin; Amoz swung his fearsome axe.

Among his bodyguards, glowering and huge, Jormanric stood. Red juice stained his beard like blood.

"No one's going anywhere," he growled. "Neither is that Key."

10

> *The eyes in the corridor were dark and*
> *watchful and there were many of them.*
> *"Come out," he said.*
> *They came out. They were children. They*
> *wore rags and their skin was livid with sores.*
> *Their veins were tubes, their hair wire.*
> *Sapphique reached out and touched them.*
> *"You are the ones who will save us," he said.*
>
> —*Sapphique and the Children*

No one spoke.

Finn stepped away from the ladder; he drew his sword and realized Keiro was already armed, but what use were two blades against so many?

Big Arko broke the tension. "Never thought you'd run out on us, Finn."

Keiro's smile was steely. "Who says we are?"

"The sword in your hand says it."

He lumbered toward them, but Jormanric stopped him with the back of a mailed glove against his chest. Then the Winglord looked beyond Finn and Keiro. "Can there really be a device that will open every lock?" His voice was slurred but his eyes were intent. Finn felt Gildas step down from the ladder.

"I believe so. It was sent to me from Sapphique." The old man tried to push past, but Finn caught hold of his belt and stopped him. Annoyed, Gildas jerked free and pointed a bony finger. "Listen to me, Jormanric. I have given you excellent advice for many years. I've healed your wounded and tried to bring some sort of order into this hellhole you've created. But I come and go when I choose and my time with you is over."

"Oh yes," the big man said grimly. "That's true enough."

The Comitatus exchanged grins. They moved closer. Finn caught Keiro's eye; together they closed around Gildas.

Gildas folded his arms. His voice was rich with contempt. "Do you think I fear you?"

"I do, old man. Under all that bluster, you fear me. And you have cause." Jormanric rolled ket around his tongue. "You've stood behind me at enough hand loppings, tongue splittings, seen enough men's heads spitted on pikes to know what I will do." He shrugged. "And your voice has grated on me of late. I'm sick of being lectured and berated. So here's a proposition for you. Get lost before I cut your tongue out myself. Climb the ladder and join the Civicry. We won't miss you."

That wasn't true, Finn thought. Half the Comitatus owed life and limbs to Gildas. He'd patched them and sewn their wounds after too many fights, and they knew it.

Gildas laughed sourly. "And the Key?"

"Ah." Jormanric's eyes narrowed. "The magic Key and the Starseer. I can't let them go. And no one ever deserts the Comitatus." He turned his stare on Keiro. "Finn will be useful, but you, deserter, the only Escape you'll make is through Death's Door."

Keiro didn't flinch. He stood tall, his handsome face flushed with controlled anger, though Finn sensed the finest tremble in the hand that held the sword. "Is that a challenge?" he snapped. "Because if it's not, I make it one." He looked around, at all of them. "This isn't about some crystal trinket, or about the Sapient. This is about you and me, Winglord, and it's been coming a long time now. I've seen you betray anyone who's threatened you, send them into ambushes, poison them, bribe their oathbrothers, make your warband a sludge of ket-heads without a brain cell between them. But not me. I call you a coward, Jormanric. A fat coward, a murderer, a liar. Worn out, finished. *Old.*"

Silence.

In the dark shaft the words rang as if the Prison whispered them mockingly around and around. Finn's grip on his sword was so tight, the cords scorched him; his heart hammered. *Keiro was crazy. Keiro had finished them.* Big Arko glowered; the girls Lis and Ramill watched avidly.

Behind them he saw the dog-slave, creeping closer on its chain.

Everyone looked at Jormanric.

He moved instantly. He pulled a thick ugly knife and the sword from his back, and was on Keiro before anyone could yell.

Finn leaped away; Keiro's sword flashed up by instinct and the blades clanged.

Jormanric's face was red with rage, the blood pulsing in the thick veins of his neck. Right into Keiro's face he spat, "You're dead, boy." Then he attacked.

The Comitatus howled with delight; they whooped and closed around in a tight ring, clashing weapons, stamping in unison. They loved to see bloodshed and most of them had felt the whiplash of Keiro's arrogance; now they'd see him brought down. Finn was shoved heedlessly aside; he tried to slash a space, but Gildas hauled him away. "Stay back!"

"He'll be killed!"

"If he is, it's no loss."

Keiro was fighting for his life. He was young and fit, but Jormanric was twice his weight, old in warcraft, berserk with a battle frenzy that came on him rarely. He hacked at Keiro's face, at his arms, following up with quick slashes of the knife. Keiro staggered back, colliding with one of the Comitatus, who shoved him heartlessly again into the ring; off balance, he flailed forward, and Jormanric struck.

"No!" Finn yelled.

The blade sliced across Keiro's chest; he whipped his face aside with a gasp. A spatter of blood hit the crowd.

Finn had his own knife ready to throw, but there was no

chance; the fighters were too far and Keiro concentrating too hard to glance away. A hand caught Finn's arm; in his ear Gildas murmured, "Back off toward the shaft. No one will see us go."

Finn was too dismayed to answer. Instead he pulled away and tried to shove into the center of the ring, but a great arm slid around his neck. "No cheating, brother." Arko's breath stank of ket.

Despairing, Finn watched. Keiro could never survive this. He was already cut on the leg and wrist; shallow nicks but bleeding freely. Jormanric's eyes were glazed, his ket-stained teeth set in a bared grin. His onslaught was a barrage of violence; he fought without fear or self-awareness, sparks clashing from the blades.

Breathless, Keiro flicked one look of terror sideways; Finn struggled and kicked to get to him. Jormanric roared, a howl of savagery that set all his men yelling encouragement; he took one step forward and swung his sword in an arc of whipping steel.

And staggered.

For a moment, just a second, he was off balance. Then he fell, a crashing, inexplicable fall, his feet whipped behind him, tangled in a chain that slid between the feet of the crowd, looped around a pair of filthy hands muffled in rags.

Keiro leaped on him. He slammed a bone-crunching blow down on the Winglord's mailed back; Jormanric howled in fury and pain.

The shouts of the Comitatus died abruptly.

Arko let go of Finn.

Keiro was white with strain but he didn't stop. As Jormanric rolled, he stamped on the Winglord's left arm; it cracked, an ominous sound. The knife spilled onto the floor. Jormanric heaved himself up to his knees, head down, groaning over his shattered arm, swaying.

From the corner of his eye Finn saw a commotion in the crowd; the dog-creature was being hauled out. He squirmed toward it as it was kicked and cursed, but even as he got there one of its tormentors fell, doubled up by a blow from Gildas's staff. "I'll deal with this," the Sapient roared. "Stop them before someone dies!"

Finn swung back, in time to see Keiro kick Jormanric full in the face.

The Winglord still clung to his sword, but another callous blow to the head laid him out; he crashed spread-eagle, a pool of blood at nose and mouth.

The crowd was silent.

Keiro flung his head back and screamed with triumph.

Finn stared. His oathbrother was transformed. His eyes were bright, his hair sweat-dark and slicked to his scalp, his hands streaked with blood. He seemed taller, glowing with a sleek and concentrated energy that scorched away all weariness; he raised his head and stared around at them all, a raw, blind unrecognizable stare, seeing nothing, challenging everything.

Then, deliberately, he turned back, put the point of his blade to the vein in Jormanric's neck, and pushed.

"Keiro," Finn's voice was sharp. "Don't."

Keiro's eyes swung to him. For a moment it seemed as if he had to struggle to recognize who had spoken. Then he said hoarsely, "He's finished. I'm Winglord now."

"Don't kill him. You don't want his pitiful little kingdom." Finn held his gaze steadily. "You never did. Outside, that's what you want. Nowhere else is big enough for us."

Down the shaft, as if in answer, a warm breeze drifted.

For a moment Keiro stared at Finn, then at Jormanric. "Give this up?"

"For more. For everything."

"A lot to ask, brother." Looking down, he lifted the sword blade away, slowly. The Winglord took a deep ragged breath. And then with one vicious jerk Keiro stabbed the sword down into Jormanric's open palm.

The Winglord howled and flailed. Pinned to the ground he convulsed with agony and wrath, but Keiro knelt and began to tug the liferings from his fingers, the thick skull-faced bands.

"Leave them!" Gildas's yell came from behind them. "The Prison!"

Finn looked up. Lights exploded on around him, flared red. A thousand Eyes winked open. Alarms broke out into a terrible ululating scream.

It was a Lockdown.

The Comitatus split, pushed, fragmented into a panicking mob, and as the wall slots slid open and light cannon flashed, they were fleeing, Jormanric's bleeding agony ignored. Finn hauled Keiro away. "Forget them!"

Keiro shook his head, shoved three rings inside his jerkin. "Go! *Go!*"

A croak from behind. "Did you think I killed the woman, Finn?"

Finn turned.

Jormanric squirmed in pain. He spat the words like venom. "Not true. Ask your brother. Your stinking, treacherous brother. Ask him why she died."

Laserfire flickered like steel rods between them. For a second Finn couldn't move; then Keiro was back, yanking him down. Sprawled on the filthy floor they crawled toward the shaft. The corridor was a sparking grid of energy; efficiently Incarceron restored order, slammed down grilles and doors, emitted a hiss of foul-smelling yellow gas into the enclosed tunnels.

"Where is he?"

"There." Finn saw Gildas scrambling over bodies; he was dragging the dog-slave, its chains swaying and tripping him. Snatching the sword from Keiro, Finn pulled the creature toward him and hacked at the rusty manacles. The sharp blade severed them instantly. He looked up and saw brown eyes, bright in the ragged bindings around the face.

"Leave it! It's diseased." Keiro shouldered past, flinched at a burst of fire that seared the roof, and jumped for the ladder. In seconds he was racing up the darkness of the shaft.

"He's right," Gildas said heavily. "It will slow us."

Finn hesitated. In the uproar and crashing alarms and falling steel he looked back and the eyes of the leprous slave watched him. But it was the Maestra's eyes he saw, her voice that spoke inside his mind.

I will never dare show kindness to a stranger again.

Instantly he stooped, hauled the creature onto his back, and climbed.

Keiro was clattering above, Gildas a wheezing mutter below. As he dragged himself up the rungs, Finn was soon breathless with the weight on his back; the creature's muffled paws gripped him tight, its heels dug into his stomach. He slowed; after thirty rungs he had to stop, breathless, arms like lead. He clung on, gasping.

In his ear, a voice whispered, "Let me go. I can climb."

Astonished, he felt the creature crawl from him, skitter onto the ladder, and scramble up in the dark. Below, Gildas thumped his foot. "Get on! Quickly!"

Dust billowed up the shaft, and the eerie hiss of gas. He hauled himself on, higher and higher until the muscles in his calves and thighs were weak, his shoulders aching with grabbing upward and raising his own weight.

And then without warning he was in wider space, half falling onto the transitway, Keiro yanking him out. They hoisted Gildas up, and speechless, stared down. Stabs of light flickered far below. Red alarms rang; tendrils of gas made Finn cough. Through watering eyes he saw a panel shoot sideways across the shaft, sealing it with a clang.

And then, silence.

THEY DIDN'T speak. Gildas took the creature's hand and Finn stumbled behind with Keiro, because now the climb and the fight were taking their toll, and Keiro was suddenly exhausted, his cuts dripping a telltale trail of blood on the metallic walkways. They hurried without stopping through the labyrinth of tunnels, past doorways with Civicry markings, barred entrances, squeezing through a portcullis with vast, useless squares. And always they were listening, because if the Civicry found them, they would stand no chance. Finn found himself sweating at each turn of the passage, at each distant clang or echoing whisper, straining his ears at shadows and a scurrying Beetle, sweeping a small chamber in endless circles.

After an hour, limping with weariness, Gildas led them into a passageway that became a sloping gallery lit by rows of alert Eyes, and at its top, far up in the dark, he stopped and slid down against a tiny locked door.

Finn helped Keiro to sit and collapsed beside him. The dog-creature was a huddle on the floor. For a moment the narrow space was racked with painful breathing. Then Gildas roused himself.

"The Key," he croaked. "Before they find us."

Finn took it out. There was a single crack in the door, hexagonal, ringed with speckles of quartz.

He put the Key in the lock and turned it.

11

As for poor Caspar, I pity those who have to put up with him. But you are ambitious and we are bound together now. Your daughter will be Queen and my son King. The price is paid. If you fail me, you know what I will do.

—Queen Sia to the Warden of Incarceron; private letter

"Why here?" Claudia trailed after him, between the hedges.

"Obviously," Jared murmured, "because no one else can find the way through."

Nor could she. The yew maze was ancient and complex, the thick hedges impenetrable. Once when she was small, she had been lost in here for a whole long summer's day, wandering and sobbing with anger, and the nurse and Ralph had organized a search and been almost hysterical with panic before she'd been found sleeping under the astrolabe in the central glade. She didn't remember getting there, but sometimes now, at the edge of her dreams, the drowsy heat came back to her, the bees, the brass sphere against the sun.

"Claudia. You've missed the turn."

She backtracked, and found him waiting, patiently. "Sorry. Miles away."

Jared knew the way well. The maze was one of his favorite haunts; he came here to read and study and discreetly test various forbidden devices. Today it was peaceful after the frantic packing and panic in the house. Threading the mown paths after his shadow, Claudia breathed in the rose-scents, fingering the Key in her pocket.

It was a perfect day, not too hot, a few delicate clouds. A shower of rain was scheduled for three fifteen, but they should be finished by then. As she turned a corner and came suddenly to the central glade, she looked around in surprise.

"It's smaller than I remembered."

Jared raised an eyebrow. "Things always are."

The astrolabe was blue-green copper and apparently decorative; beside it a wrought-iron seat sank elegantly into the turf, a bush of bloodred roses rambling over its back. Daisies studded the grass.

Claudia sat, knees up under her silk dress. "Well?"

Jared put his scanner away. "Seems safe." He turned and sat on the bench, leaning forward, his frail hands nervously folding together. "So. Tell me."

She repeated Evian's conversation quickly, and he listened, frowning. When she'd finished she said, "It may be a trap, of course."

"Possible."

She watched him. "What do you know about these Steel Wolves? Why wasn't I told?"

He didn't look up, and that was a bad sign; she felt a thread of fear unwind down her spine.

Then he said, "I've heard of them. There have been rumors, but no one's sure who is involved, or how real the conspiracy is. Last year an explosive device was discovered in the Palace, in a room where the Queen was expected. Nothing new there, but a small emblem was found too, hanging from the window catch, a small metal wolf." He watched a ladybug scaling a blade of grass. "What will you do?"

"Nothing. Yet." She took the Key out and held it in both hands, letting the sunlight catch its facets. "I'm not an assassin."

He nodded, but seemed preoccupied, staring hard at the crystal.

"Master?"

"Something's happening." Absorbed, he reached out for the Key and took it from her. "Look at it, Claudia."

The tiny lights were back, this time moving deep, a rapid, repeated pattern. Jared placed the artifact quickly on the bench. "It's getting warm."

Not only that, but there were sounds coming from it. She brought her face nearer, heard a clatter and a ripple of musical notes.

Then the Key spoke.

"*Nothing's happening,*" it said.

Claudia gasped and jerked away; wide-eyed she stared at Jared. "Did you . . . ?"

"Quiet. Listen!"

Another voice, older, rasping. "Look closer, fool boy. There are lights inside it."

Claudia knelt, fascinated. Jared's delicate fingers slid silently into his pocket. He took the scanner out and placed it beside the Key, recording.

The Key chimed, a soft sound. The first voice came again, oddly distant and excited. "It's opening. Get back!"

And then a sound came out of the artifact, a heavy clang, ominous and hollow, so that she took a moment to register it, to recognize what it was.

A door. Unlocking.

A heavy, metallic door, perhaps ancient, because it groaned on its hinges, and there was a clatter and smash, as if rust fell, or debris shuddered from its lintel.

Then silence.

The lights in the Key reversed, changed to green, went out.

Only the rooks in the elms by the moat karked. A blackbird landed in the rosebush and flicked its tail.

"Well," Jared said softly.

He adjusted the scanner and ran it over the Key again. Claudia reached out and touched the crystal. It was cold.

"What happened? Who were they?"

Jared turned the scanner to show her. "It was a fragment of conversation. Real-time. A phonic link opened and closed very briefly. Whether you initiated it or they did I'm not sure."

"They didn't know we were listening."

"Apparently not."

"One of them said, 'There are lights inside it.'"

The Sapient's dark eyes met hers. "You're thinking they may have a similar device?"

"Yes!" She scrambled up, too excited to sit, and the blackbird flew off in alarm. "Listen, Master, as you said, this isn't just a key to Incarceron. Maybe it's also a device to communicate!"

"With the Prison?"

"The inmates."

"Claudia . . ."

"Think about it! No one can go there. How else does he monitor the Experiment? Overhear what's happening?"

He nodded, his hair in his eyes. "It's possible."

"Only . . ." She frowned, knotting her fingers together. Then she turned on him. "They sounded wrong."

"You must be more precise in speech, Claudia. How, wrong?"

She searched for the word. When it came, it surprised her. "They sounded scared."

Jared considered. "Yes . . . they did."

"And what would they be scared of? There's nothing to fear in a perfect world, is there?"

Doubtfully, he said, "We may have overheard some form of drama. A broadcast."

"But if they have that . . . plays, films, then they have to know about danger, and risk, and terror. Is that possible? Can you do that if your world is perfect? Would they even be able to create such a story?"

The Sapient smiled. "That is a point we could debate, Claudia. Some people would say your own world is perfect, and yet you know those things."

She scowled. "All right. There's something else too." She tapped the wide-winged eagle. "Is this just for listening? Or can we use it to speak to them?"

He sighed. "Even if we can, we shouldn't. Conditions in Incarceron are strictly controlled; everything was carefully calculated. If we introduce variables, if we open even a tiny key-hole into that place, we may ruin everything. We can't admit germs into Paradise, Claudia."

Claudia turned. "Yes, but . . ."

She froze.

Behind Jared, in the gap in the hedges, her father was standing. He was watching her. For a moment her heart leaped with the terrible shock; then she let the practiced smile slip gracefully over her face.

"Sir!"

Jared stiffened. The Key lay on the bench; he slid out his hand, but it was just out of reach.

"I've been looking everywhere for you both." The Warden's voice was soft, his dark velvet coat an emptiness at the heart of the sunlit glade. Jared looked up at Claudia, white-faced. If he saw the Key . . .

The Warden smiled calmly. "I have some news, Claudia. The Earl of Steen has arrived. Your fiancé is looking for you."

For one cold moment she stared at him. Then she stood, slowly.

"Lord Evian is entertaining him but will only bore him. Are you pleased, my dear?"

He came to take her hand; she wanted to step aside to hide the glittering crystal from him, but she couldn't move. Then Jared gave a murmur and slumped forward slightly.

"Master?" Alarmed, she broke from her father's grip. "Are you in pain?"

Jared's voice was hoarse. "I . . . No . . . Just faint, for a moment. Nothing to worry about."

She helped him to sit up. The Warden stood above them, his face a mask of concern. He said, "I'm afraid you're overdoing things lately, Jared. Sitting out in the sun is not good for you. And so much study, at all hours of the night."

Jared stood shakily. "Yes. Thank you, Claudia. I'm fine now. Really."

"Perhaps you should get some rest," she said.

"I will. I'll go up to my tower, I think. Please excuse me, sir."

He stumbled up. For one terrible second Claudia thought her father would not move. He and Jared stood face-to-face. Then the Warden stepped back, his smile wry. "If you'd like supper sent up, we'll have it seen to."

Jared just nodded.

Claudia watched her tutor walk carefully between the yew hedges. She dared not look at the bench, but she knew it would be empty.

The Warden went and sat down, stretching out his legs and crossing them at the ankles. "A remarkable man, the Sapient."

She said, "Yes. How did you get in here?"

He laughed. "Oh Claudia. I designed this maze before you were born. No one knows its secrets as I do, not even your precious Jared." He turned, one arm over the back of the bench. Quietly he said, "I think you have done something to disobey me, Claudia."

She swallowed. "Have I?"

Her father nodded gravely. Their eyes met.

He was doing what he always did, teasing her, playing games with her. Quite suddenly she couldn't bear it anymore, the plotting, the stupid game. She stood, furious. "All right! It was me who broke into your study." She faced him, her face hot with anger. "You know that, you've known it since you went in there, so why are we pretending! I wanted to see inside, and you never let me. You never let me in. So I broke in. I'm sorry, all right? I'm sorry!"

He stared at her. Was he shaken? She couldn't tell. But she was shaking, all the pent-up fear and rage of years bursting out, the fury that he made her life so false, and Jared's too.

He held up a hand hastily. "Claudia, please! Of course I knew. I'm not angry. Rather, I admire your ingenuity. It will come in useful in your life at the Palace."

She stared. For a moment he had been startled. More than that. Dismayed.

And he had not mentioned the Key.

The breeze rippled the rosebush, bringing a waft of its cloying scent, a silent surprise that he had revealed so much. When he spoke again his voice had its normal acid tone. "I hope you and Jared enjoyed the challenge." He stood abruptly. "The Earl is waiting."

She scowled. "I don't want to see him."

"You have no choice." He bowed and strode toward the gap in the hedge, and she swung around and glared at his back. Then she said, "Why are there no pictures of my mother in the house?"

She had no idea she was going to say it. It came out in a harsh demand quite unlike her own voice.

He stopped dead.

Her heart thudded; she was appalled at herself. She didn't want him to turn, to answer, didn't want to see his face. Because if he showed weakness, she would be terrified; his controlled poise was hateful and yet if it broke, she had no idea what might be underneath.

But he spoke without turning. "Don't go too far, Claudia. Don't try my patience."

WHEN HE was gone she found she was sitting on the bench in a huddle, the muscles of her back and shoulders tight with tension, her hands clenched on the silk of her skirt. She made herself take a slow breath.

Then another.

Her lips were salty with sweat.

Why had she asked him that? Where had it come from? Her mother was someone she never thought of, never even imagined. It was as if she had never existed. Even when she'd been small, looking at the other girls at Court with their fussing mamas, she had had no curiosity about her own.

She gnawed the bitten nails on her fingers. It had been a deadly mistake. She should never, never have said that.

"Claudia!"

A loud, demanding voice. She closed her eyes.

"Claudia, it's no good hiding in all these hedges." Branches swished and cracked. "Talk to me! I can't find the right way!"

She sighed. "So you've finally arrived. And how is my husband-to-be?"

"Hot and irritable. Not that you care. Look, there are five paths here at a meeting point. Which do I take?"

His voice was close; she could smell the expensive cologne he used. Not splashed on, like Evian, but just enough. "The one that looks least likely," she said. "Toward the house."

The peevish mutter became more distant. "Like our engagement, many would say. Claudia, get me out of here!"

She scowled. He was worse than she remembered.

Yew thrashed and snapped.

She stood quickly, brushing down her dress, hoping her face was not as pale as she felt. On her left the hedge shuddered. A sword came through and hacked an opening, and his big silent bodyguard, Fax, stepped through, looked quickly around, then held open the branches. Through them came a thin youth, his mouth sour with dissatisfaction. He glared at her crossly. "Look at my clothes, Claudia. They're ruined. Quite ruined."

He kissed her coldly on one cheek. "Anyone would think you were avoiding me."

"So you've been expelled," she said calmly.

"I left." He shrugged. "Too boring. My mother sends you this."

It was a note, on white thick paper, sealed with the Queen's white rose. Claudia opened it and read.

> *My dear,*
> *You will have heard the good news that your wedding is imminent. After waiting all these years, I'm sure your excitement is as intense as my own! Caspar insisted on coming to escort you here—such a romantic. What a handsome couple you will make. From now on, my dear, you must think of me as your loving mother.*
> *Sia Regina*

Claudia folded it. "Did you insist?"

"No. She sent me." He kicked the astrolabe. "What a bore getting married is going to be, Claudia. Don't you think?"

She nodded, silent.

12

The decay was gradual and we were slow to recognize it. Then, one day, I had been talking with the Prison, and as I left the room I heard it laugh. A low, mocking chuckle.

The sound turned me cold. I stood in the corridor and the thought came to me of an ancient image I had once seen in a fragmented manuscript, of the enormous mouth of Hell devouring sinners.

It was then I knew we had created a demon that would destroy us.

—*Lord Calliston's Diary*

The sound of the unlocking was painful, as if the Prison sighed. As if this was a door that had not been opened for centuries. But no alarms howled. Perhaps Incarceron knew no door could lead them out.

Gildas stepped back at Finn's warning; chunks of debris and a red rain of rust clattered. The door shuddered inward, and stuck.

For a moment they waited, because the narrow slit was dark and a cool, oddly sweet-smelling air moved beyond. Then Finn kicked the rubble aside and put his shoulder to the door. He heaved, and rammed it until it stuck again. But now there was room to squeeze through.

Gildas nudged him. "Take a look. Be careful."

Finn glanced back at Keiro, sitting slumped and weary. He drew his sword and slipped sideways through the gap.

It was colder. His breath frosted. The ground was uneven, and ran downhill. As he took a few steps a strange tinny litter rustled around his ankles; putting a hand down, he felt drifts of crisp stuff, cold and wet, sharp against his fingertips. As his eyes grew used to the deeper gloom, he thought he was standing in a sloping hall of columns; tall black pillars rose to a tangle overhead. Groping to the nearest one, he felt it over with his hands, puzzled. It was icy cold and hard, but not smooth. A mass of fissures and cracks seamed it, knots and swelling growths, and branches of intricate mesh.

"Finn?"

Gildas was a shadow at the door.

"Wait." Finn listened. The breeze moved in the tangle, making a faint silvery tinkle that seemed to stretch for miles. After a moment he said, "There's no one here. Come through."

A few rustles and stirrings. Then Gildas said, "Bring the Key, Keiro. We need to shut this."

"If we do, can we get back?" Keiro sounded worn.

"What's to get back for? Give me a hand." As soon as the dog-slave had slipped through, Finn and the old man shoved and forced the tiny door back into its frame. It clicked quietly shut.

A rustle. A scrape of sound. Light, steadying, in a lantern.

"Someone might see it," Keiro snapped.

But Finn said, "I told you. We're alone."

As Gildas held the lantern high, they looked around at the ominous enclosing pillars. Finally Keiro said, "What are they?"

Behind him, the dog-creature crouched down. Finn glanced at it, and knew it was looking at him.

"Metal trees." The light caught the Sapient's plaited beard, the gleam of satisfaction in his eye. "A forest where the species are iron, and steel, and copper, where the leaves are thin as foil, where fruits grow gold and silver." He turned. "There are stories, from the old times, of such places. Apples of gold guarded by monsters. It seems they're true."

The air was cold and still. It held an alien sense of distance. It was Keiro who asked the question Finn didn't dare to.

"Are we Outside?"

Gildas snorted. "Do you think it's that easy? Now sit before you fall." He glanced at Finn. "I'll deal with his wounds. This is as good a place as any to wait for Lightson. We can rest. Even eat."

But Finn turned and faced Keiro. He felt cold and sick, but he spoke the words stubbornly. "Before we go any further I want to know what Jormanric meant. About the Maestra's death."

There was a second of silence. In the ghostly light Keiro gave

Finn one exasperated glare and crumpled wearily in the rustling leaves, pushing back his hair with blood-streaked hands. "For God's sake, Finn, do you really think I know? You saw him. He was finished. He would have said anything! It was just lies. Forget it."

Finn looked down at him. For a second he wanted to insist, ask again, to silence the nagging fear inside him, but Gildas eased him aside. "Make yourself useful. Find something to eat."

While the Sapient poured water, Finn tipped out a few packages of dried meat and fruit from his pack and another lantern, which he lit from the first. Then he trampled down the icy metal leaves into a clotted mass, spread some blankets on them, and sat. In the shadowed forest beyond the pool of light, small rustles and scrapings disturbed him; he tried to ignore them. Keiro swore viciously as Gildas cleaned his cuts, stripped his jacket and shirt, and rubbed chewed-up herbs of a disgusting pungency onto the wound across his chest.

In the shadows the dog-slave crouched, barely visible. Finn took one of the food packets, opened it, and held some out. "Take it," he whispered.

A rag-bound hand, crusted with sores, snatched it from him. While the creature ate he watched, remembering the voice that had answered him, a low, urgent voice. Now he whispered, "Who are you?"

"Is that thing still here?" Sore and irritable, Keiro pulled his

146

jacket back on and laced it, scowling at the slashes and tears.

Finn shrugged.

"We dump it." Keiro sat, wolfed down the meat, and looked around for more. "It's poxed."

"You owe *that thing* your life," Gildas remarked.

Hot, Keiro glared up. "I don't think so! I had Jormanric where I wanted him." His eyes turned to the creature; then they widened in sudden fury and he leaped up, strode to where it crouched, and snatched away something dark. "This is mine!"

It was his bag. A green tunic and a jeweled dagger spilled out. "Stinking thief." Keiro aimed a kick at the creature; it jerked away. Then, to their astonishment, it said in a girl's voice, "You should be grateful to me for bringing it."

Gildas turned on his heel and stared at the shadow of rags. Then he stabbed a bony finger at it. "Show yourself," he said.

The ragged hood was pushed back, the wrapped paws unwound bandages and gray strips of binding. Slowly, out of the crippled huddle a small figure emerged, crouched up on its knees, a dark cropped head of dirty hair, a narrow face with watchful, suspicious eyes. She was layered with clothes strapped and tied to make humps and bulges; as she tugged the clotted wrappings from her hands, Finn stepped back in disgust at the open sores, the running ulcers. Until Gildas snorted. "Fake."

He strode forward. "No wonder you didn't want me near you."

In the dimness of the metal forest the dog-slave had become a small thin girl, the sores clever messes of color. She stood upright slowly, as if she had almost forgotten how. Then she stretched and groaned. The ends of the chain around her neck clattered and swung.

Keiro laughed harshly. "Well, well. Jormanric was slyer than I thought."

"He didn't know." The girl looked at him boldly. "None of them knew. When they caught me I was with a group—one old woman died that night. I stole these rags from her body and made the sores out of rust, rubbed muck all over myself, hacked off my hair. I knew I had to be clever, very clever, to stay alive."

She looked scared, and defiant. It was hard to tell her age; the brutal haircut made her seem like a scrawny child, but Finn guessed she was not so much younger than himself. He said, "It didn't turn out to be such a good idea."

She shrugged. "I didn't know I'd end up as his slave."

"And tasting his food?"

She laughed then, a bitter amusement. "He ate well. It kept me alive."

Finn glanced at Keiro. His oathbrother watched the girl, then turned away and curled up in the blankets. "We dump her in the morning."

"It's not up to you." Her voice was quiet but firm. "I'm the servant of the Starseer now."

Keiro rolled and stared. Finn said, "Me?"

"You brought me out of that place. No one else would have

done that. Leave me, and I'll follow you. Like a dog." She stepped forward. "I want to Escape. I want to find the Outside, if there is one. And they said in the slavehall that you see the stars in your dreams, that Sapphique talks to you. That the Prison will show you the way out because you're its son."

He stared at her in dismay. Gildas shook his head. He looked at Finn and Finn looked back.

"Up to you," the old man muttered.

He had no idea what to do, so he cleared his throat and said to the girl, "What's your name?"

"Attia."

"Well, look, Attia. I don't want a servant. But . . . you can come with us."

"She has no food. That means we have to feed her," Keiro said.

"Neither do you." Finn nudged the pack of clothes. "Or me, now."

"Then she shares your catch, brother. Not mine."

Gildas leaned back against one of the metal trees. "Sleep," he said. "We'll discuss it when the lights come on. But someone has to keep watch, so first it can be you, girl."

She nodded, and as Finn curled up uneasily in the blankets, he saw her slip into the shadows and vanish.

Keiro yawned like a cat. "She'll probably slit our throats," he muttered.

CLAUDIA SAID, "I said *good night*, Alys," and watched in her dressing table mirror as her nurse fussed over silk garments strewn on the floor.

"Look at this, Claudia, it's ruined with mud . . ."

"Put it through the washing machine. I know you've got one somewhere."

Alys gave her a glare. They both knew the endless archaic scrubbing and beating and starching of clothes was so wearing that the staff had secretly abandoned Protocol long ago. It was probably the same even at Court, Claudia thought.

As soon as the door was closed she jumped up and went over and locked it, turning the wrought-iron key and clicking on all the secrecy systems. Then she leaned her back against it and considered.

Jared had not been at supper. That didn't mean anything; he would have wanted to keep up the pretense, and he hated the Earl's stupidity. For a moment she wondered if he really had been ill in the maze, and whether she should call him, but he had warned her to keep the minicom for emergencies, especially with the Warden in the house.

She tied the belt of her dressing gown and jumped on the bed, reaching up to grope in the canopy of the four-poster.

Not there.

The house was quiet now. Caspar had talked and drunk his way through supper; fourteen courses of fish and finches, capons and swan, eels and sweetmeats. He had talked loudly and peevishly about tournaments, his new horse, a castle he was having built on the coast, the sums he had lost at gambling. His new passion seemed to be boar-hunting, or at least staying well back while his servants trussed a wounded boar for him to kill. He had described his spear, the kills he had made, the tusked heads that adorned the corridors of the Court. And all the time he had drunk and refilled and his voice had grown more and more hectoring and slurred.

She had listened with a fixed smile and had teased him with odd, barbed questions that he had barely understood. And all the time her father had sat opposite and toyed with the stem of his wineglass, turning it on the white cloth between his thin fingers, looking at her. Now, as she jumped down and went over to the dressing table, searching through all the drawers, she remembered that cool look, how it appraised her sitting there, beside the fool she would have to marry.

It wasn't in any of the drawers.

Suddenly chilled, she went to the window and unlatched it, letting the casement swing open, curling herself up in a miserable huddle on the cushions of the window seat. If he loved her, how could he do this to her? Couldn't he see the misery it would be?

The summer evening was warm and smelled sweetly of stocks and honeysuckle and the hedge of musk-roses that curved around the moat. From far over the fields the bell of Hornsely church softly tolled twelve chimes. She watched as a moth fluttered in and swooped recklessly around the flame of the candles; its shadow briefly huge on the ceiling.

Had there been a new edge in his smile? Had that stupid blurted question about her mother sharpened the danger?

Her mother had died. That's what Alys had said, but Alys hadn't been working here then, nor had any of the servants except Medlicote, her father's secretary, a man she rarely spoke to. But maybe she should. Because that question had gone in like a knife, through the Warden's studied armor of grave smiles and cold Period decorum. She had stabbed him and he had felt it.

She smiled, her face hot.

It had never happened before.

Could there be something strange about her mother's death? Illness was rife, but for the rich, illegal drugs could be found. Medicines too modern for this Era. Her father was strict, but surely if he had loved his wife he would have done anything, however illegal, to save her. Could he have sacrificed his wife just because of Protocol? Or was it worse than that?

The moth scuttered on the ceiling. Leaning forward, she looked out of the window at the sky.

The summer stars were bright. They lit the roofs and gables of the manor house with a faint, ghostly glimmer, an owl-light, reflecting the black and silver ripples of the moat.

Her father was implicated in Giles's death. Could he have killed before?

A touch on her cheek made her jump. The moth wings brushed her, whispered, "In the window seat" and were gone, fluttering out toward the faint light in Jared's tower.

Claudia grinned.

She pushed herself up, groped under the cushions, and touched the cold edge of crystal. Carefully, she pulled it out.

The Key took the light of the stars and held it. It seemed to shine with a faint luminescence, and the eagle within it held a sliver of light in its beak.

Jared must have brought it here while everyone was at supper.

She took the precaution of blowing the candles out and closing the window. Tugging the heavy quilt from her bed, she wrapped herself in it and propped the Key on her knees. Then she touched it, rubbed it, breathed on it.

"Speak to me," she said.

⟨∞⟩

FINN WAS so cold he barely had the energy even to shiver.

The metal forest was utterly black; the lantern threw only a tiny pool of light, on Keiro's sprawled hand, on the huddle that was Gildas. The girl was a shadow under a tree; she made no sound and he wondered if she was even asleep.

He reached out cautiously for Keiro's pack. He would pull

one of his oathbrother's fancy jackets over his own. Two, maybe, and if they split Keiro could put up with it.

Tugging the pack over, he put his hand in, and touched the Key.

It was warm.

He lifted it out, very gently, and let his fingers close over it, so that the heat it was generating comforted his cramped fingers. Quietly it said, "Speak to me."

Wide-eyed, Finn glanced at the others.

No one moved.

Carefully, his leather belt creaking in the stillness, he stood up and turned. He managed three steps before the rustling crunch of the metal leaves made Keiro mutter and turn over.

Behind the tree, Finn froze.

He brought the Key up to his ear. It was silent. He touched it, all over, shook it. Then he whispered to it, "Sapphique. Lord Sapphique. Is that you?"

CLAUDIA GASPED.

The answer had come so clearly. She looked wildly around for anything to record this on, saw nothing and cursed. Then she said, "No! No. My name's Claudia. Who are you?"

"Quiet! They'll wake up."

"Who will?"

There was a pause. Then he said, "My friends." He sounded breathless, oddly terrified.

"Who are you?" she said. "Where are you? Are you a Prisoner? Are you in Incarceron?"

HE JERKED his head back and stared at the Key in disbelief.

There was a small blue light in the heart of it; he bent closer so that it lit his skin. "Of course I am. Do you mean . . . Are you . . . Outside?"

There was silence. It lasted so long he thought the link had been broken; he said hurriedly, "Did you hear me?" and at the same time the girl said, "Are you still there?" in awkward collision.

Then she said, "I'm sorry. I shouldn't be speaking to you. Jared warned me about this."

"Jared?"

"My tutor."

He shook his head, and his breath frosted the crystal.

"But look," she said, "it's too late now and I can't believe a few words can damage a centuries-old experiment, do you?"

He had no idea what she was talking about. "You are Outside, aren't you? Outside exists? The stars are there, aren't they?"

He was terrified she wouldn't answer, but after a moment she said, "Yes. I'm looking at them."

He breathed out in amazement; the crystal furred instantly with frost.

"You didn't tell me your name," she said.

"Finn. Just Finn."

Silence. A self-conscious stillness, the Key clumsy in his hands. There was so much he wanted to ask, to know, that he didn't know where to begin. And then she said, "How are you speaking to me, Finn? Is it a crystal key, with the hologram of an eagle inside?"

He swallowed. "Yes. A key."

A rustle, behind him. He looked around the tree, saw Gildas snore and grunt.

"Then we each have a replica of the same device." She sounded quick, thoughtful, as if she was used to solving problems, working out solutions; a clear voice that made him remember suddenly, with the tiniest spark of pain, candles. The seven candles on the cake.

At that moment, with their usual abruptness, the lights of Incarceron came on.

He gasped, saw that he was standing in a landscape of copper and gilt and tawny redness. The forest stretched for miles, sloping down, far down into a wide, undulating landscape. He stared at it in astonishment.

"What was that? What happened? Finn?"

"The lights went on. I . . . . I'm in a new place, a different Wing. A metal forest."

She said oddly, "I envy you. It must be fascinating."

"Finn?" Gildas was on his feet, looking around. For a moment Finn wanted to call him over, and then caution set in. This was his secret. He needed to keep it.

"I have to go," he said hurriedly. "I'll try and speak to you again . . . now we know . . . that is, if you want to. But you have to," he added urgently. "You have to help me."

The girl's answer surprised him. "How can I help you? What can be wrong in a perfect world?"

Finn's hand tightened as the blue light faded. Desperately he whispered, "Please. You have to help me Escape."

13

Walls have ears.
Doors have eyes.
Trees have voices.
Beasts tell lies.
Beware the rain.
Beware the snow.
Beware the man
You think you know.
　—*Songs of Sapphique*

Finn's voice.

As she pulled on the gauntlet and flexed the foil, his voice whispered again inside her mask.

You have to help me Escape . . .

"En garde, please, Claudia." The swordmaster was a small gray man who sweated profusely. His sword crossed hers; he gave signals with the tiny precise movements of a skilled fencer. Automatically she responded, practicing lunges, parries—sixte, septime, octave—as she had done since she was six.

There had been something familiar about the boy's voice.

Inside the warm darkness of the mask she bit her lip,

attacked, took quarte, riposted, hitting the maestro's padded jacket with a satisfying thud.

The accent, the slightly slow vowels. It was how they spoke at Court.

"Feint of straight thrust, disengage, please."

She obeyed, hot now, the glove already softened with sweat, the foil whipping, the small clicks of the familiar exercise comforting, the control of the sword forcing her mind to speed.

You have to help me Escape.

Fear. Fear in the whispering, of being overheard, of saying what he said. And the word *Escape* like a holy thing, forbidden, full of awe.

"Quarte counter quarte, please, Claudia. And keep your hand high."

She took the parries absently, the blades of the foils sliding past her body. Behind the maestro Lord Evian came out of the main door into the courtyard and stood on the steps, taking snuff. He watched her, elegantly poised.

Claudia frowned.

She had so much to think about. The fencing lesson was her own escape. In the house it was chaos; her clothes being packed, the last measurements for the wedding dress, the books she refused to leave behind, the pets she insisted came with her. And now this. One thing—Jared would have to carry the Key. It wouldn't be safe in her baggage.

They were fighting now. She let all thoughts go, concentrated on the hits, the clicked parries, the bending of the foil as she hit once, again, again.

Until finally he stepped back. "Very good, my lady. Your point control remains excellent."

Slowly she took off her mask and shook his hand. Close up, he looked older, and a little sad.

"I'll be sorry to lose such a pupil."

Her hand clenched on his. "Lose?"

He stepped back. "I . . . it seems . . . after your wedding . . ."

Claudia restrained her anger. She released his hand and drew herself up. "After my marriage I will still require your services. Please disregard anything my father has said about this. You will travel with us to the Court."

He smiled, and bowed. His doubt showed; as she turned away and took the cup of water from Alys, she felt the heat of humiliation scorch her face.

They were trying to isolate her. She had expected this; Jared had warned her of it. At Queen Sia's court they wanted her alone with no one to trust, no one to plot with. But she was having none of that.

Lord Evian had waddled over. "Quite wonderful, my dear." His small eyes enjoyed her figure in the fencing breeches.

"Don't patronize me," she snapped. Waving Alys away, she took the cup and jug and stalked to a bench that stood at the edge of the green lawn. After a moment Evian came after her. She turned on him. "I need to talk to you."

"The house overlooks us," he said quietly. "Anyone can see."

"Then wave your handkerchief and laugh. Or whatever it is spies do."

His fingers closed the snuffbox. "You are angry, Lady Claudia. But not, I think, with me."

That was true. But still she glared at him. "What do you want from me?"

He smiled serenely at the ducks on the lake, the small black moorhens in the rushes. "As yet, nothing. Obviously we will make no move until after the wedding. But then, we will need your help. The Queen must be dealt with first—she is the most dangerous. And then, when you are safely Queen, your husband will meet with some accident . . ."

She drank the cold water. Upside-down in the cup she saw Jared's tower reflected, the blue sky behind it, the tiny windows in perfect Protocol.

"How do I know this isn't a trap?"

He smiled. "Does the Queen doubt you? She has no reason."

Claudia shrugged. She only met the Queen at festivals. The first time had been at her betrothal, and that had been years ago. She remembered a slim blond woman in a white dress, sitting on a throne that had seemed to have hundreds of steps up to it, and she had had to climb every one, concentrating, carrying the basket of flowers that was almost as big as she had been.

The Queen's hands, the nails a glossy red.

The cool palm on her forehead.

The words. "How charming, Warden. How sweet."

"You could be recording this," she said. "You could be testing me . . . my loyalty."

Evian sighed, a tiny sound. "I assure you . . ."

"Assure all you like, it could be true." She dumped the cup and picked up the towel Alys had left, wiping her face with its softness. Then she turned. "What do you know about Giles's death?"

It startled him. His pale eyes widened slightly. But he was practiced at deception; he answered without giving anything away. "Prince Giles? He fell from his horse."

"Was it an accident? Or was he murdered?"

If he was recording this, she knew she was finished now.

His stubby fingers folded together. "Really, my dear . . ."

"Tell me. I need to know. Of all people it concerns me most. Giles was . . . we were betrothed. I liked him."

"Yes." Evian looked at her shrewdly. "I see." He seemed uncertain, then, as if he'd made up his mind, he said, "There was something strange about the death."

"I knew it! I told Jared—"

"The Sapient knows about this?" He looked up in alarm. "About me?"

"I would trust Jared with my life."

"Those are the most dangerous people." Evian turned,

watching the house. One of the ducks meandered toward him; he gave a flurried wave and it padded away, quacking.

"We never know where the listeners are," he said quietly, staring after it. "That is what the Havaarna have done to us, Claudia. They have riddled us with fear."

For a moment he seemed almost shaken; then he brushed an invisible crease from his silk suit and said in his changed voice, "Prince Giles rode out that morning without any of his usual attendants. It was a fine spring morning; he was well, in good health, a laughing boy of fifteen years. Two hours later a messenger thundered in on a horse white with sweat; he leaped from it and raced into the hall of the Court, ran up the steps, and threw himself at the Queen's feet. I was there, Claudia. I saw her face when they told her of the accident. She is a pale woman, as they all are, but then she was white. If it was an act, it was expert. They brought the boy back on a hastily made bier of boughs, their coats laid over his face. Grown men were weeping."

Impatient, Claudia said, "Go on."

"They laid him in state. Wearing a great gold robe and a tunic of white silk embroidered with the crowned eagle. Thousands filed past him. Women sobbed. Children brought flowers. How beautiful he was, they said. How young."

He watched the house.

"But there was something odd. A man. His name was Bartlett. A man who had looked after the boy from his earliest years. He was old now, retired and feeble. They allowed him in to see the body late one afternoon, when the people had left. They brought him through the pillars and shadows of the Chamber of State and he climbed the steps with difficulty and looked down at Giles. They thought he would weep and wail and howl with grief. They thought he would tear his clothes with agony. But he didn't."

Evian looked up and she saw his small eyes were shrewd. "He laughed, Claudia. The old man laughed."

⬥

AFTER TWO hours walking through the metallic forest the snow began.

Stumbling over a root of copper and out of a daydream, Finn realized it had been falling for some time; it was already coating the leaf-litter with a fine frost. He looked back, his breath smoking.

Gildas was a little way behind, talking to the girl. But where was Keiro?

Finn turned quickly. All morning he had been unable to stop thinking of that voice, the voice from Outside, where the stars were. Claudia. How had she been able to speak to him? He felt the cold lump of the Key inside his shirt; its awkwardness comforted him. "Where's Keiro?" he said.

Gildas stopped. He planted his staff in the ground and leaned on it. "Scouting ahead. Didn't you hear him tell you?" Suddenly he strode forward and looked hard at Finn, the blue eyes clear as crystal in his small lined face. "Are you well? Is this a vision coming on you, Finn?"

"I'm fine. Sorry to disappoint you." Sickened by the eagerness in the Sapient's voice Finn looked at the girl. "We need to get that chain off you."

She had wrapped it around her like a necklace to stop it swinging. He could see the raw skin under the collar where she had padded it with cloth. She said quietly, "I can manage. But where are we?"

Turning, he stared over the miles of forest. A wind was rising, the metallic leaves meshing and rustling. Far below, the wood was lost under snow clouds, and high above the roof of the Prison was a distant oppression, its lights misted and faint.

"Sapphique came this way." Gildas sounded tense with excitement. "In this forest he defeated his first doubts, the dark despairs that told him there was no way on. Here he began the climb out."

"But the way leads down," Attia said quietly.

Finn looked at her. Beneath the dirt and hacked hair her face was lit with a strange joy. "Have you been here before?" he asked.

"No. I was from a small Civicry group back there. We never left the Wing. This is so . . . wonderful."

The word made him think of the Maestra, and the chill of guilt struck through him, but Gildas pushed past and strode on. "It may appear to lead downhill, but if the theory that

Incarceron is underground is true, we must climb eventually. Perhaps beyond the wood."

Appalled, Finn gazed at the forested leagues. How could Incarceron be so vast? He had never imagined it would be like this. Then the girl said, "Is that smoke?"

They followed her pointing finger. Far off, in the distant mists, a thin column rose and dissipated. It looked like the smoke from a fire, he thought.

"Finn! Give me a hand!"

They turned. Keiro was dragging something out from the thickets of copper and steel; as they ran over to him Finn saw that it was a small sheep, one of its legs crudely repaired, the circuits exposed.

"You're still thieves then," Gildas said acidly.

"You know the rule of the Comitatus." Keiro sounded cheerful. "Everything belongs to the Prison, and the Prison is our Enemy."

He had already cut its throat. Now he looked around. "We can butcher it here. Well, she can. She may as well make herself useful."

None of them moved. Gildas said, "It was stupid. We have no idea of what inmates are here. Or of their strength."

"We have to eat!" Keiro was angry now, his face darkening. He threw the sheep down. "But if you don't want it, fine!"

There was an awkward silence. Then Attia said simply, "Finn?"

166

He realized she would do it if he asked her to. He didn't want to have that power. But Keiro was glowering, so he said, "All right. I'll help you."

Side by side, they knelt and cut the sheep up. She borrowed Gildas's knife and worked efficiently; he realized she had done it often before, and when he was clumsy, she pushed him aside and dissected the raw flesh. They took only a little; they had no way of carrying more or any tinder to cook it on as yet. Only half the beast was organic; the rest was a patchwork of metal, ingeniously put together. Gildas raked over the remains with his stick. "The Prison breeds its beasts less well these days."

He sounded grave. Keiro said, "What do you mean, old man?"

"What I say. I can remember when the creatures were all flesh. Then circuits began to appear, tiny things, threaded instead of vein, of cartilage. The Sapienti have always studied and dissected any tissue we could find. At one time I offered rewards for carcasses brought to me, though the Prison was usually too quick."

Finn nodded. They all knew that the remains of any dead creature vanished overnight; that Incarceron sent its Beetles out instantly and collected the raw material for recycling. Nothing was ever buried here, nothing burned. Even those of the Comitatus who had been killed were left, wrapped in their favorite possessions, decked with flowers, in a place by the abyss. In the morning, they were always gone.

To their surprise Attia spoke. "My people knew this. For a long time now the lambs have been like this, and the dogs. Last year, in our group, a child was born. Its left foot was made of metal."

"What happened to it?" Keiro asked quietly.

"The child?" She shrugged. "They killed it. Such things can't be allowed to live."

"The Scum were kinder. We let all sorts of freaks live."

Finn glanced at him. Keiro's voice was acid; he turned and led the way through the wood. But Gildas didn't move. Instead he said, "Don't you see what it means, fool boy? It means the Prison is running out of organic matter . . ."

But Keiro wasn't listening. He lifted his hand, alert.

A sound was rising in the wood. A low whisper, a rustling breeze. Tiny at first, barely raising the leaves, it stirred Finn's hair, Gildas's robe.

Finn turned. "What is it?"

The Sapient moved, pushing him on. "Hurry. We must find shelter. Hurry!"

They ran between the trees, Attia always at Finn's heels. The wind grew rapidly. Leaves began to lift, swirl, fly past them. One nicked Finn's cheek; putting his hand up to the sudden sting he felt a cut, saw blood. Attia gasped, her hand protecting her eyes.

And all at once they were in a blizzard of metal slivers, the leaves of copper and steel and silver a razor-sharp whirlwind in the sudden storm. The wood groaned and bent, twigs cracked with snaps that rang in the invisible roof.

As he ran, ducking and breathless, Finn heard the roar of the storm like a great voice. It raged at him, picked him up and threw him; its anger crashed him against the metal trees, it bruised him and beat at him. Stumbling, he knew the leaves were its words, arrows of spite, that Incarceron was taunting him, its son, born from its cells, and he stopped, bent over, gasping, "I hear you! I hear you! Stop!"

"Finn!" Keiro yanked him down. He slid, the ground giving way, crumpling into a hollow between the tangled roots of some vast oak.

He landed on Gildas, who shoved him off. For a moment each of them caught breath, listening to the deadly leaves slicing the air outside, the whine and hum. Then Attia's muffled voice came from behind.

"What is this place?"

Finn turned. Behind them he saw a dull rounded hollow, seamed deep under the steel oak. Too low to stand up in, it extended back into darkness. The girl, on hands and knees, crept inside. Foil leaves crackled under her; he smelled a musty, odd tang, saw that the walls sprouted fungi, contorted, spore-dusted masses of flabby growth.

"It's a hole," Keiro said sourly. He drew his knees up, brushed litter from his coat, and then looked at Finn. "Is the Key safe, brother?"

"Of course it is," Finn muttered.

Keiro's blue eyes were hard. "Well, show me."

Oddly reluctant, Finn put his hand into his shirt. He drew the Key out, and they saw the crystal glimmer in the dimness. It was cold, and to Finn's relief, silent.

Attia's eyes went wide.

"Sapphique's Key!"

Gildas turned on her. "What did you say?"

But she wasn't looking at the crystal. She was staring at the picture scratched meticulously onto the back wall of the tree, smeared by centuries of dirt and overgrown by green lichen, the image of a tall, slim, dark-haired man sitting on a throne, in his upheld hands a hexagonal slot of darkness.

Gildas took the Key from Finn. He slotted it into the aperture. Instantly it began to glow; light and heat burned from it, showing them one another's dirty faces, the slanting cuts, brightening the furthest recesses of the hollow.

Keiro nodded. "We seem to be going the right way," he muttered.

Finn didn't answer. He was watching the Sapient; the glow of awe and joy on the old man's face. The obsession. It chilled him to the bone.

14

We forbid growth and therefore decay.
Ambition, and therefore despair. Because
each is only the warped reflection of the
other. Above all, Time is forbidden. From
now on nothing will change.

—*King Endor's Decree*

"I don't think you'll be wanting all this junk." Caspar picked a book out of the pile and opened it. He gazed idly at the bright illuminated letters. "We have books at the Palace. I never bother with them."

"You do surprise me." Claudia sat on the bed and gazed around hopelessly at the chaos. How could she have so many possessions? And so little time!

"And the Sapienti have thousands." He tossed it aside. "You are so lucky, Claudia, that you never had to go to the Academy. I thought I'd die of dullness. Anyway, aren't we going out with the hawks? The servants can do all this. It's what they're for."

"Yes." Claudia was biting her nail; she realized, and stopped.

"Are you trying to get rid of me, Claudia?"

She looked up. He was watching her, his small eyes fixed

in that nerveless stare. "I know you don't want to marry me," he said.

"Caspar . . ."

"It's all right, I don't mind. It's a dynastic thing, that's all. My mother's explained it. You can have any lovers you like, after we've had an heir. I certainly will."

She stared at him in disbelief. She couldn't sit still; she jumped up and paced the disrupted room. "Caspar, listen to yourself! Have you ever thought about what sort of life we'll have together, in that marble mausoleum you call a palace? Living a lie, a pretense, keeping false smiles on our faces, wearing clothes from a time that never existed, posing and preening and aping manners that should only be in books? Have you thought about that?"

He was surprised. "It's always been like that."

She sat next to him. "Have you never wanted to be free, Caspar? To be able to ride out alone one spring morning and set off to see the world? To find adventure, and someone you can love?"

It was too much. She knew it as soon as she had said it. Too much for him. She felt him stiffen and frown, and he glared at her. "I know what all this is about." His voice was harsh. "It's because you'd have rather had my brother. The saintly Giles. Well, he's dead, Claudia, so forget about him." Then his smile came back, sly and narrow. "Or is this about Jared?"

"Jared?"

"Well, it's obvious, isn't it? He's older, but some girls like that."

She wanted to slap him, to get up and slap his sniggering little face. He grinned at her. "I've seen how you look at him, Claudia. Like I said, I don't mind."

She stood, stiff with anger. "You evil little toad."

"You're angry. That proves it's true. Does your father know about you and Jared, Claudia? Should I tell him, do you think?"

He was poison. He was a lizard with a flicking tongue. His smirk was acid. She bent and put her face into his and he moved back.

"If you mention this again, to me, to anyone, I will kill you. Do you understand, my lord Steen? Myself, personally, with a dagger through your weak little body. I will kill you like they killed Giles."

Trembling with wrath she marched outside and slammed the door with a clap that rang down the corridor. Fax, the bodyguard, was lounging outside. As she passed him he stood, with an insolent slowness, and as she ran beneath the portraits to the stairs, she felt his eyes on her back, the cold smile.

She hated them.

All of them.

How could he say that!

How could he even think it! Thundering down the stairs, she crashed through the double doors, maids scattering before her,

her mood like thunder. Such a filthy lie! Against Jared! Jared, who would never dream, never even think of such a thing!

She screamed for Alys, who came running. "What's wrong, lady?"

"My riding coat. Now!"

While she waited she fumed, pacing, staring through the open front door at the eternal perfection of the lawns, the blue sky, the peacocks practicing their eerie cries.

Her anger was warm and a comfort. When the coat came she flung it around her, snapped, "I'm riding out."

"Claudia . . . There's so much to do! We leave tomorrow."

"You do it."

"The wedding dress . . . the final fitting."

"You can tear it to shreds as far as I'm concerned." Then she was gone, running down the steps and across the courtyard, and as she ran, she looked up and saw her father, standing in the impossible window of his study that didn't exist, wasn't even there.

He had his back to her, was talking to someone.

Someone in the study with him?

But no one ever went in there.

Slowing, she watched for a moment, puzzled. Then, afraid he'd turn around, she hurried to the stables and found Marcus already saddled, pawing the ground with impatience. Jared's horse was ready too, a lean rangy creature called TamLin, which was probably some secret Sapient jest she'd never understood.

She looked around. "Where's the Wise One?" she asked Job.

The boy, always tongue-tied, muttered, "Gone back to the tower, lady. He forgot something."

She stared at him. "Job, listen to me. You know everyone on the estate?"

"Pretty much." He swept the floor hastily, raising clouds of dust. She wanted to tell him to stop, but that would have made him even more nervous, so she said, "An old man called Bartlett. Pensioned off, a retainer of the Court. Is he still alive?"

He raised his head. "Yes, my lady. He has a cottage out on Hewelsfield. Just down the lane from the mill."

Her heart thudded. "Is he . . . Is his mind still clear?"

Job nodded, and managed a smile. "He's razor-sharp, that one. But he doesn't say much, not about his days at Court. He just stares if you ask him."

Jared's shadow darkened the doorway and he came in slightly breathlessly. "Sorry, Claudia."

He swung himself up into the saddle, and as she put her foot in Job's linked hands, she said quietly, "What did you forget?"

His dark eyes met hers. "A certain object that I didn't want to leave unguarded." His hand moved discreetly to his coat, the high-necked Sapient robe of dark green.

She nodded, knowing it was the Key.

As they rode off she wondered why she felt so oddly ashamed.

THEY MADE a fire from the dried fungi and some snapping powder from Gildas's pack and cooked the meat while the whirlwind raged outside. No one spoke much. Finn was shivering with cold, and the cuts on his face stung; he sensed that Keiro was still weary too. It was hard to tell about the girl. She sat slightly apart, eating quickly, her eyes watching and missing nothing.

Finally Gildas wiped greasy hands on his robe. "Were there any signs of the inmates?"

"The sheep were roaming," Keiro said carelessly. "Not even a fence."

"And the Prison?"

"How should I know? Eyes in the trees probably."

Finn shivered. His head felt echoey and strange. He wanted them to sleep, to fall asleep so he could get the Key out again and talk to it. To her. The girl Outside. He said, "We can't move on, so we may as well rest. Don't you think?"

"Sounds good," Keiro said lazily. He arranged his pack against the back of the hollow. But Gildas was staring at the image carved in the tree trunk. He crawled closer, reached out, and began to rub at it with his veined hands. Curls of lichen fell. The narrow face seemed to emerge from dinginess and the green fur of moss, its hands holding the Key so carefully drawn, they seemed real. Finn realized that the Key must be linking into some circuitry in the tree itself, and for a moment a blur of vision caught him off guard, a sense that the whole of Incarceron was a great creature in whose entrails of wire and bone they crept.

He blinked.

No one seemed to have noticed, though the girl was staring at him. Gildas was saying, "He's leading us along the way he took. Like a thread through the labyrinth."

"So he left his own picture?" Keiro drawled.

Gildas frowned. "Obviously not. This is a shrine, created by the Sapienti who have followed him. We should find other signs on the way."

"I can't wait." Keiro rolled himself over and curled up.

Gildas glared at his back. Then he said to Finn, "Take the Key out. We need to take care of it. The way may be longer than we think."

Thinking of the vast forest outside, Finn wondered if they would wander in it forever. Carefully he reached up and removed the Key from the hexagon; it came away with a slight click, and instantly the hollow was dim and the whistling splinters of foil blurred the distant Prison lights.

Finn was stiff and uncomfortable, but he kept still, listening. After a long while he knew by the old man's harsh breathing that Gildas was sleeping. He wasn't sure about the others. Keiro had his face turned away. Attia always seemed silent, as if she had learned that keeping still and being overlooked kept her alive. Outside, the forest roared with the storm. He heard the cracking of its branches, the turmoil of its contempt surge from far distances, felt the strength of the wind batter the trees, shudder the iron trunk above him.

They had angered Incarceron. They had opened one of its forbidden doors and crossed some boundary. Perhaps it would trap them here forever, before they had barely begun.

At last, he couldn't wait any longer.

Cautiously, taking infinite pains to keep the rustle of the leaf-litter down, he tugged the Key from his pocket. It was cold, frosted with cold. His fingers left smeared imprints on it, and even the eagle inside was hard to see until he had rubbed condensation from its surface.

He held it tight. "*Claudia,*" he breathed.

The Key was cold and dead.

No lights moved in it. He dared not speak louder.

But just then Gildas muttered, so he took the chance and curled up, bringing it closer. "Can you hear me?" he said to it. "Are you there? Please, answer."

The storm raged. It whined in his teeth and nerves. He closed his eyes and felt despair, that he had imagined all of it, that the girl did not exist, that he was indeed born in some Womb here.

And then, as if out of his own fear, came a voice, a soft remark. "Laughed? Are you sure that's what he said?"

Finn's eyes snapped open. A man's voice. Calm and considering.

He glanced around wildly, afraid the others had heard, and then a girl said, ". . . Of course I'm sure. Why should the old man laugh, Master, if Giles was dead?"

"Claudia." Finn whispered the name before he could stop himself.

Instantly Gildas turned; Keiro sat up. Cursing, Finn shoved the Key into his coat and rolled over to see Attia staring at him. He knew at once that she'd seen everything.

Keiro had his knife out. "Did you hear that? Someone outside." His blue eyes were alert.

"No." Finn swallowed. "It was me."

"Talking in your sleep?"

"He was talking to me," Attia said quietly.

For a moment Keiro looked at them both. Then he leaned back, but Finn knew he was not convinced. "Was he now?" his oathbrother said softly. "So who's Claudia?"

⌐◦◦◦⌐

THEY CANTERED quickly up the lane, the deep green leaves of the oaks a tunnel over their heads. "And you believe Evian?"

"On this I do." She looked ahead at the mill rising at the foot of the hill. "The old man's reaction was all wrong, Master. He must have loved Giles."

"Grief affects people strangely, Claudia." Jared seemed worried. "Did you tell Evian you would find this Bartlett?"

"No. He—"

"Did you tell anyone? Alys?"

179

She snorted. "Tell Alys and it's around the servants' hall in minutes." That reminded her. She slowed the breathless horse. "My father paid off the swordmaster. Or tried to. Has he said anything more to you?"

"No. Not yet."

They were silent while he leaned down and unlatched the gate, easing the horse back to drag it wide. On the other side the lane was rutted, lined by hedgerows, dog-roses twined among nettles and willow-herb, the white umbels of cow-parsley.

Jared sucked at a sting on his finger. Then he said, "That must be the place."

It was a low cottage half obscured by a great chestnut that grew beside it. As they rode closer Claudia scowled at its perfect Protocol, the thatch with holes in it, the damp walls, the gnarled trees of the orchard. "A hovel for the poor."

Jared smiled his sad smile. "I'm afraid so. In this Era only the rich know comfort."

They left the horses tied, cropping lush long grass from the verge. The gate was broken, hanging wide; Claudia saw how it had recently been forced, how the grass blades were dragged back under it, still wet with dew.

Jared stopped. "The door's open," he said.

She went to step past him, but he said, "A moment, Claudia." He took out the small scanner and let it hum. "Nothing. No one here."

"Then we go in and wait for him. I've only got today." She strode up the cracked path; Jared followed quickly.

Claudia pushed the door wider; it creaked and she thought something shuffled inside. "Hello?" she said quietly.

Silence.

She put her head around the door.

The room was dark and smelled of smoke. A low window lit it, the shutter off and leaning against the wall. The fire was out in the hearth; as she came in she saw the blackened cooking pot on its chains, the spit, ashes drifting in the draft down the great chimney.

Two small benches lined the chimney corner; near the window stood a table and chair and a dresser with some battered pewter plates and a jug on it. She picked the jug up and sniffed the milk inside.

"Fresh."

There was a small doorway into the cow byre. Jared crossed to it and looked through, stooping under the lintel.

His back was to her, but she knew, from his sudden, intent stillness, something was wrong. "What?" she said.

He turned, and his face was so pale, she thought he was ill. He said, "I'm afraid we're too late."

She came over. He stayed, blocking her way. "I want to see," she muttered.

"Claudia . . ."

"Let me see, Master." She ducked under his arm.

The old man lay sprawled on the floor of the byre. It was quite obvious that his neck was broken. He lay on his back, arms flung out, one hand buried in the straw. His eyes were open.

The byre smelled of old dung. Flies buzzed endlessly and wasps came in and out through the open doorway; a small goat bleated outside.

Cold with awe and anger she said, "They killed him."

"We don't know that." Jared seemed to come to life all at once. He knelt by the old man, touched neck and wrist, ran the scanner over him.

"They killed him. He knew something about Giles, about the murder. They realized we were coming here!"

"Who could have realized?" He stood quickly, stepped back into the living room.

"Evian knew. My talk with him must have been bugged. Then there's Job. I asked him . . ."

"Job's a child."

"He's scared of my father."

"Claudia, I'm scared of your father."

She looked again at the small figure in the straw, letting her anger loose, clutching her arms around herself. "You can see the marks," she breathed.

Hand marks. Two bruises like the dark traces of thumbs, deep in the mottled flesh. "Someone big. Very strong."

Jared jerked open the cupboard in the dresser and pulled out plates. "Certainly he didn't fall."

She turned.

He slammed the drawer, went to the chimney, and stared up. Then to her astonishment he climbed on one of the benches and reached into the darkness, groping blindly. Soot fell in showers.

"Master?"

"He lived at Court, Claudia. He must have been literate."

For a moment she didn't understand. Then she turned and gazed hurriedly around, found the bed, tipped the mattress up, tore open the lice-ridden straw.

Outside, a blackbird shrieked and flapped.

Claudia stared. "Are they coming back?"

"Maybe. Keep looking."

But as she moved her foot caught on a board that creaked, and when she knelt and pulled at it, it swung up on a pivot with the ease of constant use.

"Jared!"

It was the old man's store of treasures. A battered purse with some copper coins, a broken necklace with most of the stones pried out, two quills, a fold of parchment, and, carefully hidden right at the bottom, a blue velvet drawstring bag, small as her palm.

Jared took the parchment and riffled through it. "Looks like some sort of testament. I knew he would have written it down! If he'd been taught by Sapienti, it's only . . ." He glanced over. She had opened the blue bag. Out of it she slid a small oval of gold, its back engraved with the crowned eagle. She turned it over.

A boy's face looked up at them, his smile shy and direct, his eyes brown.

Claudia smiled back at him, bitter. She looked up at her tutor. "It must be worth a fortune, but he never sold it. He must have loved him very much."

Gently he said, "Are you sure . . . ?"

"Oh yes, I'm sure. It's Giles."

CHAINED,
HAND AND FOOT

15

Sapphique rode out of the Tanglewood and saw the Fortress of Bronze. People were streaming into its walls from all around.

"Come inside," they urged him. "Hurry! Before it attacks!"

He looked around. The world was metal and the sky was metal. The people were ants on the plains of the Prison.

"Have you forgotten," he said, "that you are already Inside?"

But they hurried past and said he was deranged.

—*Legends of Sapphique*

The storm had raged all night before dying away so abruptly that Finn had been woken at once by the silence. It seemed eerie after the wind, but at least it meant they could move now, before the Prison changed its mind. Keiro had scrambled outside and stretched, groaning with cramp. After a minute his voice had come back, unusually muted. "Look at this."

When Finn had pulled himself up, he had seen that the forest was bare. Every leaf, every thin metallic curl of foliage lay heaped in immense drifts.

The trees had broken out into flower. Copper blossoms, scarlet and gold, glimmered up hill and down dale as far as he could see.

Behind him, Attia had laughed. "It's beautiful."

He had turned, surprised, realizing he saw it only as an obstacle. "Is it?"

"Oh yes. But you . . . you're used to color. Coming from Outside."

"You believe me?"

She nodded slowly. "Yes. There's something different about you. You don't fit. And the name you called out in your sleep, this Claudia. You remember her?"

It was what he had told them. He looked up. "Listen, Attia, I need your help. It's just . . . I need sometimes to be alone. The Key . . . it helps the visions. Sometimes I need to be away from Keiro and Gildas. Do you understand?"

She had nodded gravely, her bright eyes fixed on him. "I told you, I'm your servant. Just tell me when, Finn."

He had felt ashamed. Looking at his face, she had said nothing more.

Since then they had hurried through a landscape of jewel-bright color, between plantations of trees that had marched downhill, the forest floor broken and seamed with streams in strange insulated beds, riven with cracks. Insects Finn had never imagined crawled in great drifts of leaves that blocked the path; finding detours around these lost them hours. And high in the bare branches jackdaws hopped and karked in flocks, following the travelers with beady curiosity till Gildas cursed them and waved a fist at them. Then, silently, they all flew away.

Keiro nodded. "So the Sapienti still have some magic after all."

Breathless, the old man glared at him. "I wish it worked on you."

Keiro grinned at Finn.

Finn allowed himself a smile. He felt lighter somehow, and as he trudged after Gildas down the aisles of the wood, he began to sense something that must be like happiness. The Escape had begun. The Comitatus was far behind; all that life of brutal infighting, of murder and lies and fear was over. Things would be different now. Sapphique would show him the way out.

Stepping over a tangle of root he almost felt like laughing aloud, but instead he put his hand inside his shirt and touched the Key.

He jerked his hand away at once.

It was warm.

He glanced at Keiro, pacing ahead. Then he turned. Attia was where she always walked. At his heels.

Annoyed, he stopped. "I don't want a slave."

She stopped too. "Whatever you say." Her eyes watched him with that bruised look.

He said, "There's a stream here, I can hear it. Tell the others I'm getting some water."

Without waiting, he strode off the path deep into a thicket of platinum thorns, then crouched among the undergrowth. Umbels of pliant wire rose around him, hollow reeds where microBeetles worked busily.

Hurriedly he took out the Key.

It was a risk. Keiro might come. But it was hot now in his fingers, and there were the familiar small blue lights deep in the crystal. "Claudia?" he whispered anxiously. "Can you hear me?"

"Finn! At last!"

Her voice was so loud it made him swallow; he glanced around. "Quiet! Be quick please. They'll come looking for me."

"Who will?" She sounded fascinated.

"Keiro."

"Who's he?"

"My oathbrother . . ."

"All right. Now listen. There's a small finger panel at the base of the Key. It's invisible but the surface is slightly raised. Can you find it?"

His fingers groped, leaving dirty smudges. "No," he said, flustered.

"Try! Do you think he has a different artifact?"

The question wasn't for Finn. The other voice answered her, the one he remembered as Jared. "It's almost certainly identical. Finn, use your fingertips. Search the edge, the facets near the edge."

What did they think he was! He scrabbled, his hands sore.

"Finn!" Keiro's murmur was right behind him. He jumped up, shoving the Key back, gasped, "For God's sake! Can't I take a drink in peace?"

His brother's hand shoved him back down into the leaf drift. "Get down and shut up. We've got visitors."

CLAUDIA SAT back on her heels and swore with frustration. "He's gone! Why is he gone?"

Jared went to the window and gazed out at the utter chaos in the courtyard. "It's just as well. The Warden is coming up the steps."

"Did you hear the way he sounded? Again, it was so . . . panicky."

"I know how he feels." Jared tugged a small pad from the pocket of his riding coat and thrust it at her. "This is the full draft of the old man's testament. Read it while we travel."

Doors slamming. Voices outside. Her father's. Caspar's.

"Delete it straight afterward, Claudia. I have a copy."

"We should do something. About the body."

"We weren't there, remember?"

He barely had the words out before the door opened. Claudia calmly slipped the pad down her dress.

"My dear." Her father came in and stood before her. She

stood up to meet him. He wore his usual black frockcoat, the scarf at his neck silkily expensive, his boots the finest leather. But today he wore a small white flower in his buttonhole, as if to mark the occasion, and that was so unlike him she stared at it in surprise.

"Are you ready?" he asked.

She nodded. She was wearing a dark blue traveling dress and cloak, with a special pocket sewn into it for the Key.

"A great morning for the House of Arlex, Claudia. The beginning of a new life for you, for us all." His hair with its streak of silver was tied severely back, his eyes dark with satisfaction. He pulled on his gloves before he took her hand. She looked at him without smiling, and the old dead man in the straw was in her mind, his eyes open.

She smiled and dropped a curtsy. "I'm ready, sir."

He nodded. "I always knew you would be. I always knew you'd never let me down."

Like my mother did? she wondered acidly. But she said nothing, and her father gave Jared the briefest nod and led her out. They swept into the great hall, over the lavender-strewn floor, down between the rows of fascinated servants, the Warden of Incarceron and his proud daughter, setting out for the marriage that would make her a queen. And on a signal from Ralph the staff cheered and applauded and threw sweet irises underfoot; they rang tiny silver bells in honor of the wedding they would never see.

Jared walked behind, a satchel of books under one arm. He shook hands with the servants, and the maids moped over him, pushing tiny packets of sweetmeats at him, promising to keep the tower safe, not to touch any of his precious instruments, feed the fox cub and the birds.

As Claudia took her seat in the coach and looked back, she felt a rueful lump in the back of her throat. They would all miss Jared, his gentle ways, his fragile good looks, his willingness to dose their coughing children and advise their wayward sons. None of them seemed at all sorry to see *her* go.

But then whose fault was that? She had played the game. She was the mistress, the Warden's daughter.

Cold as ice. Hard as nails.

She raised her head and smiled across at Alys. "Four days' traveling. I intend to ride for at least half of it."

Her nurse frowned. "I doubt the Earl will. And he'll probably want you to sit in his coach for some of the time."

"Well, I'm not married to him yet. When I am, he'll soon find out it's what I want that counts." If they thought her hard, she would be hard. And yet, as the horses were mounted and the outriders gathered and the coaches began the slow turn to the gatehouse, all she wanted was to be staying here, in the house where she had lived since she was born, and she leaned out of the window and waved and called out all their names, her eyes stinging with sudden tears. "Ralph! Job! Mary-Ellen!"

And they waved back, a storm of handkerchiefs and the white doves rising from the gables and the bees in the honeysuckle buzzing as the carriage rumbled over the wooden drawbridge. In the dark green waters of the moat she saw the house reflected, saw moorhens and swans arrow over it, and behind her in a great procession the wagons and coaches and riders and hounds and falconers of her entourage, of the household of the Warden of Incarceron, on the day his plans began to come to fruition.

Windblown, she threw herself back in the leather seat and blew hair from her eyes.

Well, maybe.

◇

THEY WERE men and yet how could they be?

They were at least eight feet tall. They walked with an odd angular gait, stalking like herons, ignoring the vast drifts of sharp leaves, crunching straight through them.

Finn felt Keiro's hand grip so tight on his arm it hurt. Then his brother breathed a single syllable in his ear.

"*Stilts.*"

Of course. As one of them paced by he saw them up close, knee-high metallic calipers, and the men walked on them expertly, taking long strides, and he saw too that they used the height to touch certain points of the trees, small knots in the trunks, and that the trees instantly sprouted semi-organic fruits that the men harvested.

Turning his head he looked for Gildas, but wherever the Sapient and the girl were hidden, they were invisible to him.

He watched the line of men work down through the trees. As they moved down the hillside they seemed to shrink, and Finn distinctly saw the man on the end shimmer, as if he passed through some disturbance in the air.

After a while only their heads and shoulders showed. Then they were gone.

Keiro waited a long moment before getting up. He gave a soft whistle and a heap of leaves convulsed nearby. Gildas's silvery head came up. He said, "Gone?"

"Far enough."

Keiro watched Attia scramble hurriedly out, then he turned. Taking one look at his oathbrother he said quietly, "Finn?"

It was happening. Looking at the shimmer in the air had done it. Finn's skin crawled with itches, his mouth was dry, his tongue felt stiff. He rubbed his hand over his mouth. "No," he mumbled.

"Get hold of him," Gildas snapped.

From somewhere distant Keiro said, "Wait."

And then Finn was walking. Walking straight to the place, the emptiness between two great boughs of copper where the air had moved as if dust fell through a column of light there, as if a slot in Time opened there. And when he came to it he stopped, stretching both arms before himself as if he were blind. It was a keyhole out of the world.

Through it, a draft blew.

Small flashes of pain stung him. He struggled through them, feeling, touching the edges, bringing his face close, putting his eye to the sliver of light, gazing through.

He saw a shimmer of color. It was so bright it made his eyes water, made him gasp. Shapes moved there, a green world, a sky as blue as in his dreams, a great buzzing creature of black and amber hurtling toward him.

He cried out and staggered back, felt Keiro grab both arms from behind. "Keep looking, brother. What do you see? What is it, Finn?"

He crumpled. All the strength went from his legs and he collapsed in the leaf-litter. Attia shoved Keiro away. Quickly she poured water into a cup and held it out to Finn; blindly he took it and gulped it down, then closed his eyes and put his head in his hands, dizzy and sick. He retched. Then vomited.

Above him, voices raged. When he could hear, he realized one of them was Attia's.

". . . treating him like that! Don't you see he's sick!"

Keiro's laugh was scornful. "He'll get over it. He's a seer. He sees things. Things we need to know."

"Don't you care about him at all?"

Finn dragged his head up. The girl was facing up to Keiro, her hands gripped into fists at her sides. Her eyes had lost their bruised look; now they blazed with anger.

Keiro kept his mocking grin. "He's my brother. Of course I care about him."

"You only care about yourself." She turned to Gildas. "And you too, Master. You . . ."

She stopped. Gildas obviously wasn't listening. He stood leaning one arm on a metal tree, staring ahead. "Come here," he said quietly.

Keiro put his hand out and Finn took it, pulling himself groggily to his feet. They crossed to the Sapient and stood behind him; looking out, they saw what he saw.

The forest ended here. Ahead a narrow road ran down to a City. It stood behind walls in a fiery landscape of bare plains. Houses clustered together, constructed of patches of metal, towers and battlements built of strange dark wood, thatched with tin and copper leaves.

All along the road to it, in long noisy streams of laughter and shouting and song, in crowds and wagons, carrying children and driving flocks of sheep, hundreds and hundreds of people were streaming.

⋙──◇◇◇──⋘

HER KNEES up on the carriage seat, Claudia read the small pad while Alys slept. The carriage bounced; outside, the green woods and fields of the Wardenry rattled by in a cloud of dust and flies.

My name is Gregor Bartlett. This is my testament. I pray those who find it to keep it safe, and when the time comes, to use it, because a great injustice has been done and only I am alive to know about it.

I worked in the Palace from my early years. I was a stable boy and a postillion, then a house servant. I became trusted, rose to be important. I was Valet of the Chamber to the late King, and I remember his first wife, the frail pretty woman from Overseas that he married when they both were young. When his first son, Giles, was born I was given charge of him. I arranged the wet nurse, appointed maids of the nursery. He was the Heir; nothing was spared for his comfort. As the boy grew I came to love him like my own. He was a happy child. Even when his mother died and the King remarried, he lived in his own wing of the Palace, surrounded by his precious toys and pets, his own household. I have no children of my own. The boy became my life. You must believe that.

Gradually, I sensed a change. As he grew, his father came to him less and less. There was a second son now, the Earl Caspar, a squalling noisy baby petted over by the women of the Court. And there was the new Queen.

Sia is a strange, remote woman. They say the King looked out of his carriage once as he was being driven along a forest road, and there she stood, at the crossroads. They say that as he drove past her he saw her eyes—they are strange eyes, with pale irises—and after that moment he could not stop thinking about her. He sent messengers back, but no one was there. He had the nearby villages and estates searched, issued proclamations, offered rewards to his *noblemen, but no one could find her. And then, weeks later, as he walked in the gardens of the Palace, he looked up and she was there, sitting by the fountain.*

No one knows her parentage, or where she comes from. I believe her to be a sorceress. What became clear soon after her son was born was her hatred for Giles. She never showed it to the King or his Court; to them she was careful to honor the Heir. But I saw it.

He was betrothed at seven years old to the daughter of the Warden of Incarceron. A haughty little girl, but he seemed to like her . . .

Claudia smiled. Glancing at Alys she leaned out of the window. Her father's carriage was behind; he must be sharing it with Evian. She scrolled the text down.

. . . the happiness of his birthday party, a night when we rowed on the lake under the stars and he told me how happy he was. I will never forget his words to me.

The death of his father affected him badly. He became solitary. Did not attend the dances and games. He studied hard. I wonder now if he had begun to fear the Queen. He never said so. Now I will pass to the end. The day before the riding accident I received a message that my sister, who lived at Casa, was sick. I asked Giles for leave to go to her; the dear boy was most concerned, and insisted the kitchens make me up a parcel of delicacies to take her. He also made sure I had a carriage. He waved me off on the steps of the Outer Court. That was the last time I ever saw him.

When I arrived, my sister was in excellent health. She had no knowledge of who had sent the message.

My heart misgave me. I thought of the Queen. I wanted to return at once, but the coachman, who may have been the Queen's man, refused, saying the horses were exhausted. I am no longer a rider, but I saddled a horse from the inn and I rode back, galloping hard, all through the night. I will not try to write the agonies of worry I felt. I came over the hill and saw the thousand pinnacles of the Court, and I saw that from every one of them a black pennant flew.

I remember little after that.

They had laid his body on a bier in the Great Council Chamber, and after it was ready, I asked leave to approach him. A message came from the Queen, with a man to escort me. He was the secretary of the Warden, a tall silent man called Medlicote . . .

Claudia was so surprised she whistled. Alys snored and turned.

. . . I climbed the steps like a broken creature. My boy lay there and they had made him beautiful. I bent to kiss his face with tears blinding my eyes.

And then I paused.

Oh, they had made a good job of it. Whoever the boy was he was the right age and coloring, and the skinwand had been carefully used. But I knew, I knew.

It was not Giles.

I think I laughed. One gasp of joy. I pray no one noticed, that no one knows. I sobbed, retired, played the heartbroken retainer, the broken old man. And yet I know the secret that the

Queen, and perhaps the Warden, wish no one to know.

That Giles is alive.

And where else can he be but in Incarceron?

Alys grunted and yawned and opened her eyes. "Are we nearly at the inn yet?" she asked sleepily.

Claudia stared at the small pad, eyes wide. She looked up at her nurse as if she'd never seen her before. Then she glanced down and read the last sentence again.

And again.

16

Don't defy me, John. And be on your guard.
There are plots in the Court, and conspiracies
against us. As for Claudia, from what you say
she has already seen what she searches for. How
amusing that she did not even recognize it.

—Queen Sia to the Warden; private letter

It was hours before she could get Jared alone. There was the fuss of finding their rooms, the innkeeper bowing and scraping, the supper, endless small talk from Evian, her father's calm watchfulness, Caspar's complaints about his horse.

But finally, well after midnight, she tapped on the door of his attic and slipped in.

He was sitting at the window looking at the stars, a bird pecking bread from his hands. She said, "Don't you ever sleep?"

Jared smiled. "Claudia, this is folly. If they catch you here, you know what they'd think."

She said, "I'm bringing you into danger, I know. But we have to talk about what he wrote."

He was silent a moment. Then he released the bird, closed the window, and turned, and she saw the shadows under his eyes. "Yes."

They looked at each other. Finally she said, "They didn't kill Giles. They imprisoned him."

"Claudia . . ."

"They wouldn't spill Havaarna blood! Or perhaps the Queen was afraid to. Or my father . . ." She looked up. "It's true. My father must know."

The bleakness in her voice shocked them both. She sat on a chair. "And there's something else. This boy Finn. The Prisoner. His voice . . . seems familiar."

"Familiar?" He looked sharply at her.

"I've heard it before, Master."

"You imagine that. Don't make this assumption, Claudia."

She was still a moment. Then she shrugged. "In any case we need to try again."

Jared nodded. He went over and locked the door, clipped a small device to its back and adjusted it. Then he turned.

Claudia had the Key ready. She activated the speech channel, and then the small visual circuit that they had discovered. He stood behind her, watching the hologram of the eagle flap silent wings.

"Did you delete the pad?"

"Of course. Completely."

As the Key began to glow, he said quietly, "They had no problem spilling the old man's blood, Claudia. They may already know we searched his house. They must fear what we found."

"By *they* you mean my father." She looked up. "He won't hurt me. If he loses me, he loses the throne. And I'll protect you, Master, I swear."

His smile was rueful. She knew he didn't believe she could.

Very quietly, the Key spoke. "Can you hear me?"

Claudia said, "It's him! Touch the panel, Finn. Touch it! Have you found it?"

"Yes." He sounded hesitant. "What will happen if I do?"

"We'll be able to see each other, we think. It won't hurt you. Try it, please."

There was a second of dead air, a few crackles. And then Claudia almost jumped back. Out of the key a beam projected silently. It opened to a square, and crouched in the square, startled and dirty, was a boy.

He was tall and very thin, his face famished and anxious. His hair was lank and long, tied back in a knot of string, and his clothes were the drabbest she had ever seen, muddy grays and greens, badly worn. A sword and a rusty knife were stuck in his belt.

He stared at her in astonishment.

FINN SAW a queen, a princess.

Her face was clean and clear, her hair shone. She wore a dress of some lustrous silk, and a pearl necklace that would be worth a fortune if a buyer could ever be found rich enough. He saw at once that she had never been hungry, that her mind was clear and intelligent. Behind her a grave dark-haired man watched, wearing a Sapient's coat that put Gildas's rag to shame.

Claudia was silent so long, Jared glanced at her. He saw she was stricken, probably by the boy's condition, so he said softly, "It seems Incarceron is no paradise then."

The boy glared at him. "Are you mocking me, Master?"

Jared shook his head sadly. "No indeed. Tell us how you came to have this artifact."

Finn glanced around. The ruin was silent and black; Attia's shadow crouched in the doorway, watching the darkness outside. She gave him a small nod of reassurance. He looked back at the holoscreen, afraid that its light would give them away.

As he told them about the eagle on his wrist, he watched Claudia. He was good at reading faces, but hers was difficult, so controlled, so unrevealing, though the faintest widening of her eyes told him she was fascinated. Then he slipped into lies, about finding the Key in a deserted tunnel, obliterating the Maestra, her death, his shame, as if none of it had ever happened. Attia glanced over, but he kept his face away. He told them about the Comitatus, about the terrible fight he had fought with Jormanric, how he had defeated the giant in single combat, stolen three skull-rings from his hands, led his friends out of that hell. About how they were following a sacred trail out of the Prison.

She listened intently, asking brief questions. He had no idea if she believed any of it. The Sapient was silent, once only raising an eyebrow, when Finn talked of Gildas.

"So the Sapienti still survive? But what happened to the Experiment, the social structures, the food supply? How did it all break down?"

"Never mind that," Claudia said impatiently. "Don't you see what the eagle mark means, Master. Don't you see?" She leaned forward eagerly. "Finn. How long have you been in Incarceron?"

"I don't know." He scowled. "I . . . only remember . . ."

"What?"

"The last three years. I get . . . memories, but—" He stopped. He didn't want to tell her about the seizures.

She nodded. Her hands were clasped in her lap, he saw. A diamond ring gleamed on one finger. "Listen, Finn. Do I look familiar to you? Do you recognize me?"

His heart leaped. "No. Should I?"

She was biting her lip. He felt her tension. "Finn, listen to me. I think you may be . . ."

"FINN!"

Attia's scream was stifled. A hand grabbed her and clamped down on her mouth. "Too late," Keiro said gleefully.

Out of the darkness Gildas strode in and looked into the holoscreen. For a second he and Jared shared a startled stare.

Then the screen went blank.

The Sapient breathed a prayer. He turned and looked at

Finn and the obsession was back in his hard blue eyes. "I saw! I saw Sapphique!"

Finn suddenly felt very tired. "No," he said, watching Attia struggle wildly out of Keiro's grip. "It wasn't."

"I saw, fool boy! I saw him!" The old man knelt painfully before the Key. He reached out and touched it. "What did he say, Finn? What was his message to us?"

"And why didn't you tell us you could see people with it?" Keiro snapped. "Don't you trust us?"

Finn shrugged. He, not Claudia, had done most of the talking, he realized. But he had to keep them guessing, so he said, "Sapphique . . . warns us."

"Of what?" Nursing his bitten hand Keiro gave the girl a sour look. "Bitch," he muttered.

"Of danger."

"What sort? The whole place is—"

"From above." Finn muttered it at random. "Danger from above."

Together, they looked up.

Instantly Attia screamed and threw herself aside; Gildas swore. The net collapsed like the web of an uber-spider, each end weighted; it crashed down on Finn, flattening him under its impact, a crumpling of dust and screeching bats. For a moment the breath was knocked right out of him, then he realized Gildas was struggling and tangling next to him, that the two of them were meshed in heavy ropes sticky with an oozing resin.

"Finn!" Attia knelt and pulled at the net; her hand stuck and she pulled it hastily away.

Keiro had his sword out; he pushed her aside and slashed at the cables, but they were threaded with metal and the blade clanged. At the same time a shrill alarm in the ruin began to whine, a high, wailing note.

"Don't waste your time," Gildas muttered. Then, furiously, "Get out of here!"

Keiro stared at Finn. "I don't leave my brother."

Finn struggled to get up but couldn't. For a moment the whole nightmare of being chained before the trucks of the Civicry crashed back into his mind; then he gasped, "Do as he says."

"We can get that thing off you." Keiro looked around wildly. "If we had some sort of pivot."

Attia grabbed a metal strut from the wall. It fell to rust in her hands and she flung it down with a wail.

Keiro hauled at the net. The dark oil blackened his hands and coat; he swore but kept pulling, and Finn heaved from below, but after a second they all collapsed, defeated by the weight.

Keiro crouched at the net. "I'll find you. I'll rescue you. Give me the Key."

"What?"

"Give it to me. Or they'll find it on you and take it."

Finn's fingers closed on the warm crystal. For a moment he saw Gildas's startled gaze through the mesh; the Sapient said, "Finn, no. We'll never see him again."

"Shut your mouth, old man." Furious, Keiro turned. "Give it to me, Finn. *Now*."

Voices outside. The barking of dogs down the track.

Finn wriggled. He squeezed the Key between the oily mesh; Keiro grabbed it and pulled it out, his fingers smearing oil on the perfect eagle. He shoved it inside his jacket, then tugged off one of Jormanric's rings and jammed it on Finn's finger. "One for you. Two for me."

The alarm stopped.

Keiro backed, glancing around, but Attia had already vanished. "I'll find you, I swear."

Finn didn't move. But just as Keiro faded into the night of the Prison, he gripped the chains and whispered, "It will only work for me. Sapphique speaks only to me."

If Keiro heard him, he didn't know. Because just then the doors crashed in, lights were beamed in his eyes, the teeth of dogs were snapping and growling at his hands and face.

━◁◆▷━

JARED LOOKED at her aghast. "Claudia, this is madness . . ."

"It could be him. It could be Giles. Oh yes, he looks different. Thinner. More worn. Older. But it could easily be him. Right age, right build. Hair." She smiled. "Right eyes."

She paced the room, consumed with restlessness. She didn't want to say how the boy's condition had appalled her. She knew that the failure of the Incarceron Experiment was a terrible blow, that all the Sapienti would be rocked by it. Crouching suddenly by the dying fire, she said, "Master, you need to sleep and so do I. Tomorrow I'll insist you travel with me. We can read Alegon's Histories till Alys falls asleep and then we can talk. Tonight, I'll just say this. If he isn't Giles, he could be. We could make a case out that he is. With the old man's testament and the mark on the boy's wrist, there would be doubt. Enough doubt to stop the marriage."

"His DNA . . ."

"Not Protocol. You know that."

He shook his head. "Claudia, I can't believe . . . This is impossible . . ."

"Think about it." She got up and crossed to the door. "Because even if this boy is not Giles, Giles is in there somewhere. Caspar's not the Heir, Jared. And I intend to prove that. If it means taking on the Queen and my father, I'll do it."

At the door she paused, not wanting to leave him in this pain, wanting to say something that would ease his distress. "We have to help him. We have to help all of them in that hell."

He had his back to her, but he nodded. Bleakly he said, "Go to bed, Claudia."

She slipped out into the dim corridor. One candle burned far down in an alcove. As she walked her dress swished the dry rushes on the floor, and at her door she paused and looked back.

The inn seemed silent. But outside the door that must be

Caspar's, a sudden small movement made her stare, and she bit her lip in dismay.

The big man, Fax, was lying there across two chairs.

He was looking straight at her. Ironically, with a leer that chilled her, he waved the tankard in his hand.

17

In ancient statutes Justice was always blind. But what if it sees, sees everything, and its Eye is cold and without Mercy? Who would be safe from such a gaze?

Year by year Incarceron tightened its grip. It made a hell of what should have been Heaven.

The Gate is locked; those Outside cannot hear our cries. So, in secret, I began to fashion a key.

—Lord Calliston's Diary

As he passed under the gate of the City, Finn saw it had teeth.

It was designed like a mouth, gaping wide, fanged with metal incisors that looked razor-sharp. He guessed there was some mechanism that closed it in emergencies, creating an impassible interlocking bite.

He glanced at Gildas, leaning wearily on the wagon. The old man was bruised and his lip swollen from the blow they had given him. Finn said, "There must be some of your people here."

The Sapient scratched his face with his tied hands and said dryly, "If so, they don't command much respect."

Finn frowned. This was all Keiro's fault. The first thing the

Crane-men had done after dragging them out of the trap had been to search Gildas's pack. They had tipped out the powders and ointments, the carefully wrapped quills, the book of the Songs of Sapphique he always carried. None of those mattered. But when they had found the packets of meat, they had looked at one another. One of them, a thin scrawny man, had turned on his stilts and snapped, "So you're the thieves."

"Listen, friend," Gildas had said darkly, "we had no idea the sheep was yours. Everyone has to eat. I'll pay you, with my learning. I am a Sapient of some skill."

"Oh, you'll pay, old man." The man's stare had been level. He had looked at his comrades; they had seemed amused. "With your hands, I would think, when the Justices see this."

Finn had been tied up, so tightly, the cords burned his skin. Dragged outside, he had seen a small cart harnessed to a donkey; the Crane-men leaped up onto it, sliding expertly out of the strange metal calipers.

Roped behind, Finn had stumbled beside the old man along the road that led to the City. Twice he had glanced back, hoping to see Keiro or perhaps Attia, just a glimpse, a brief wave, but the forest was far away now, a distant glimmering of impossible colors, and the road ran straight as an arrow down the long metallic slope, the ground on each side studded with spikes and jagged with chasms.

Amazed at such defenses, he muttered, "What are they so scared of?"

Gildas scowled. "Attack, clearly. They're anxious to be in before Lightsout."

More than anxious. Almost all of the great crowds they had seen earlier were already inside the wall; as they hurried to the gate, a horn rang out in the citadel, and the Crane-men had urged the donkey on fiercely, so that Gildas was breathless with the pace, and almost fell.

Now, safe inside, Finn heard the clang of a portcullis and the rattle of chains. Had Keiro and Attia gotten here too? Or were they out there in the wood? He knew the Crane-men would have found the Key if he'd kept it, but the thought of Keiro having it, perhaps speaking to Claudia with it, made him nervous. And there was another thought that nagged at him, but he would not think of that. Not yet.

"Come on." The leader of the foraging party pulled him upright. "We have to do this tonight. Before the Festival."

As he trudged through the streets, Finn thought he had never seen such a hive of people. The lanes and alleyways were festooned with small lanterns; when the Prison lights went off the world was transformed instantly into a network of tiny twinkling silver sparks, beautiful and brilliant. There were thousands of inmates, setting up tents, bargaining in vast bazaars, searching for shelter, herding sheep and cyberhorses into corrals and market squares. He saw beggars without hands, blinded, missing lips and ears. He saw disfiguring diseases that made him gasp and turn away. And yet no halfmen. Here too it seemed, that abomination was restricted to animals.

The noise of clattering hooves was deafening; the stink of dung and sweat, of crushed straw and the sudden, vivid sweetness of sandalwood, of lemons. Dogs ran everywhere, tugging over food sacks, rummaging in drains, and slyly behind them the small copper-scaled rats that bred so fast slunk into cracks and doorways, their tiny eyes red.

And he saw that images of Sapphique were on every corner, mounted above doorways and windows, a Sapphique who held out his right hand to show the missing finger, who held in the left what Finn recognized, with a silent leap of his heart, as a crystal Key.

"Do you see that?"

"I see it." Gildas sat breathlessly on a step while one of their captors moved into the crowd. "This is obviously some sort of festival. Perhaps in Sapphique's honor."

"These Justices . . ."

"Leave the talking to me." Gildas straightened, tried to adjust his robe. "Don't say a word. Once they know what I am, we'll be released and this whole mess will be sorted. A Sapient will be listened to."

Finn scowled. "I hope so."

"What else did you see, back there in the ruin? What else did Sapphique say?"

"Nothing." He had run out of lies, and his arms ached from

being tied in front of him. Fear was threading into his mind like a cold trickle.

"Not that we'll see the Key again," Gildas said bitterly. "Or that liar Keiro."

"I trust him," Finn said between gritted teeth.

"More fool you."

The men came back. They tugged their prisoners to one side, pushed them through an archway in a wall and up a broad dim staircase that curved to the left. At the top a great wooden door confronted them; by the light of the two lanterns that guarded it, Finn saw that an enormous eye had been carved deep in the black wood; the eye stared out at him and he thought for a moment that it was alive, that it watched him, that it was the Eye of Incarceron that had studied him curiously all his life.

Then the Crane-man rapped on the wood and the door opened. Finn and Gildas were led inside, a man on each side of them.

The room, if it was a room, was pitch-black.

Finn stopped instantly. He breathed hard, hearing echoes, a strange rustle. His senses warned him of a great emptiness, before him, or perhaps to the side; he was terrified of taking another step in case he plummeted into some unknown depths. A faint memory stirred in his mind, a whisper of someplace without light, without air. He pulled himself upright. He had to keep alert.

The men stepped away, and he felt isolated, seeing nothing, touching no one.

Then, not very far in front of him, a voice spoke.

"We are all criminals here. Is that not so?"

It was a low, quiet question, modulated. He had no idea if the speaker was male or female.

Gildas said immediately, "Not so. I am not a criminal, nor were my forebears. I am Gildas Sapiens, son of Amos, son of Gildas, who entered Incarceron on the Day of Closure."

Silence. Then, "I did not think any of you were left." The same voice. Or was it? It came from slightly to the left now; Finn stared in that direction, but saw nothing.

"Neither I nor the boy have stolen from you," Gildas snapped. "Another of our companions killed the animal. It was a mistake but—"

"Be silent."

Finn gasped. The third voice, identical to the first two, came from the right. There must be three of them.

Gildas drew in a breath of annoyance. His very silence was angry.

The central voice said heavily, "We are all criminals here. We are all guilty. Even Sapphique, who Escaped, had to pay the debt to Incarceron. You too will pay the debt in your flesh and with your blood. Both of you."

Perhaps the light was growing, or perhaps Finn's eyes were adjusting. Because now he could make them out; three shadows seated before him, dressed in robes of black that covered their whole bodies, wearing strange headdresses of black that he realized all at once were wigs. Wigs of raven-dark, straight hair. The effect was grotesque because the speakers were ancient. He had never seen women so old.

Their skin was leathery with wrinkles, their eyes milky white. Each of them had her head lowered; as his foot scraped uneasily he saw how their faces turned to follow the sound, and he realized they were blind.

"Please . . ." he muttered.

"There is no appeal. That is the sentence."

He glanced at Gildas. The Sapient was staring at some objects at the women's feet. On the steps in front of the first lay a rough wooden spindle, and from it a thread spilled, a fine silvery weave. It coiled and tangled around the feet of the second woman, as if she never moved from the stool where she sat, and hidden in its skein was a measuring stick. The thread, dirty by now and frayed, ran under the chair of the third, to where a sharp pair of shears leaned.

Gildas looked stricken. "I have heard of you," he whispered.

"Then you will know we are the Three Without Mercy, the Implacable Ones. Our justice is blind and deals only in facts. You have stolen from these men, the evidence is presented." The middle crone tipped her head. "You agree, my sisters?"

One each side, identical voices whispered, "We agree."

"Then let the punishment for thieves be carried out."

The men came forward, grabbed Gildas, and forced him to his knees. In the dimness Finn saw the outline of a wooden block; the old man's arms were pulled down and held across it at the wrist. "No!" he gasped. "Listen to me . . ."

"It wasn't us!" Finn tried to struggle. "This is wrong!"

The three identical faces seemed deaf as well as blind. The central one raised a thin finger; a knife blade glimmered in the darkness.

"I am a Sapient of the Academy." Gildas's voice was raw and terrified. Drops of sweat stood out on his forehead. "I will not be treated like a thief. You have no right . . ."

He was held in a rigid grip; one man at his back, another grasping his tied wrists. The knife blade was lifted. "Shut up, old fool," one of them muttered.

"We can pay. We have money. I can cure illnesses. The boy . . . the boy is a seer. He speaks to Sapphique. He has seen the stars!"

It came out like a cry of desperation. At once the man with the knife paused; his gaze flashed to the crones.

Together they said, "The stars?" The words were an overlapping murmur, a wondering whisper. Gildas, gasping for breath, saw his chance. "The stars, Wise Women. The lights Sapphique speaks of. Ask him! He's a cell-born, a son of Incarceron."

They were silent now. Their blind faces turned toward Finn; the central one held out her hand, beckoning, and the

Crane-man shoved him forward so that she touched his arm and grabbed it. Finn kept very still. The old woman's hands were bony and dried, the fingernails long and broken. She groped down his arms, over his chest, reached up to his face. He wanted to break away, to shudder, but he kept still, enduring the cool, rough fingers on his forehead, over his eyes.

The other women faced him, as if one felt for them all. Then, both hands pressed against his chest, the central Justice murmured, "I feel his heart. It beats boldly, flesh of the Prison, bone of the Prison. I feel the emptiness in him, the torn skies of the mind."

"We feel the sorrow."

"We feel the loss."

"He serves me." Gildas heaved himself up and stood hastily. "Only me. But I give him to you, sisters, I offer him to you in reparation for our crime. A fair exchange."

Finn glared at him, astonished. "No! You can't do that!"

Gildas turned. He was a small shrunken shape in the darkness, but his eyes were hard and crafty with sudden inspiration, his breathing ragged. He looked meaningfully at the ring on Finn's finger. "I have no choice."

The three crones turned to one another. They did not speak, but some knowledge seemed to pass between them. One cackled a sudden laugh that made Finn sweat and the man behind him mutter with terror.

"Shall we?"

"Should we?"

"Could we?"

"We accept." They spoke it in unison. Then the crone on the left bent and picked up the spindle. Her cracked fingers spun it; she took the thread and pulled it out between finger and thumb. "He will be the One. He will be the Tribute."

Finn swallowed. He felt weak, his back sheened with cold sweat. "What tribute?"

The second sister measured the thread, a short span. The third crone took the shears. Carefully she cut the thread and it fell silently in the dust.

"The Tribute we owe," she whispered, "to the Beast."

◁◦◦◦▷

KEIRO AND Attia reached the City just before Lightsout, the last league on the back of a wagon whose driver never even noticed them. Outside the gate they jumped off.

"Now what?" she whispered.

"We go straight in. Everyone else is."

He strode off and she glared at his back, then ran after him.

There was a smaller gate, and to the left a narrow slit in the wall. She wondered what it was for, then she saw that the guards were making everyone walk through it.

She looked back. The road was empty. Far out in the silent plain the defenses waited; high above, what might have been a bird circled like a silver spark in the dim mists.

Keiro pushed her forward. "You first."

As they walked up, the guard ran a practiced eye over them, then jerked his head toward the slit. Attia walked through. It was a dim, smelly passageway, and she emerged in the cobbled street of the City.

Keiro took one step after her.

Instantly, an alarm rang. Keiro turned. A soft, urgent bleep in the wall. Just above, Incarceron opened an Eye and stared.

The guard, who had been closing the gate, stopped. He spun around, drawing his sword. "Well, you don't look like . . ."

With one blow to the stomach Keiro doubled him up; another sent him crashing against the wall. He lay crumpled. Keiro took a breath, then crossed to the panel and flicked the alarm off. When he turned Attia was staring at him. "Why you? Why not me?"

"Who cares?" He strode quickly past her. "It probably sensed the Key."

She stared at his back, at the rich jerkin and the mane of hair he pushed so carelessly back. Quietly, so he couldn't hear her, she said, "So why are you so scared?"

∞

WHEN THE carriage dipped as he climbed in, Claudia sighed with relief. "I thought you'd never come."

She turned from the window and the words died in her mouth.

"I'm touched," her father said dryly.

He pulled off one glove and flicked dust from the seat. Then he laid his stick and a book beside him, and called, "Drive on."

The carriage creaked as the horses were whipped up. In a moment of jangling harness and the swaying turn in the inn-yard Claudia tried to stop herself falling into his trap. But the anxiety was too much. "Where's Jared? I thought . . ."

"I asked him to travel with Alys in the third coach this morning. I felt we should talk."

It was an insult, of course, though Jared wouldn't care and Alys would be thrilled to have him to herself. But to treat a Sapient like a servant . . . She was rigid with fury.

Her father watched her a moment, then gazed out of the window, and she saw that he had allowed a little more gray into his beard, so that his look of grave distinction was stronger than ever.

He said, "Claudia, a few days ago you asked me about your mother."

If he had struck her, she couldn't have been more astonished. Then, instantly, she was on the alert. It was just like him to take the initiative, to turn the game around, to attack. He was a master chess player at the Court. She was a pawn on his board, a pawn he would make a queen, despite everything.

Outside, a soft summer rain was drenching the fields. It smelled sweet and fresh. She said, "Yes I did."

He gazed out at the countryside, his fingers playing with

the black gloves. "It is very hard for me to speak about her, but today, on this journey toward everything I have always worked for, perhaps the time has come."

Claudia bit her lip.

All she felt was fear. And for a moment, just a fragment of time, something she had never felt before. She felt sorry for him.

18

We have paid the tribute of the dearest and best and now we await the outcome. If it takes centuries, we will not forget. Like wolves we will stand guard. If revenge must be taken we will take it.

—*The Steel Wolves*

"I married in middle age." John Arlex watched the heavy foliage of summer shadow the interior of the coach with glints of sunlight. "I was a wealthy man—our family has always been part of the Court—and the post of Warden had been mine from youth. A great responsibility, Claudia. You have no idea how great."

He sighed briefly.

The coach jolted over stones. In the pocket of her traveling coat, she felt the crystal Key tap against her knee, remembered Finn's fear, his starved face. Were they all like that, the Prisoners her father watched over?

"Helena was a beautiful and elegant woman. Ours was not an arranged marriage, but a chance meeting at a winter ball at the Court. She was a Lady of the Chamber to the last Queen, Giles's mother, an orphan, the last of her line."

He paused, as if he wanted her to say something, but she didn't. She felt that if she spoke it would break the spell, that he might stop. He didn't look at her. Softly he said, "I was very much in love with her."

Her hands were clenched together. She made them relax.

"After a short courtship we were married at Court. A quiet wedding, not like yours will be, but there was a discreet banquet later, and Helena sat at the head of my table and laughed. She looked very much like you, Claudia, if a little shorter. Her hair was fair and smooth. She always wore a black velvet ribbon around her neck, with a portrait of us both inside it."

He smoothed his knee absently.

"When she told me she was pregnant I was more happy than I can say. Perhaps I had thought the time was gone, that I would never have an heir. That the care of Incarceron would pass from the family, that the line of the Arlexi would die out with me. In any case, I took even greater care of her. She was strong, but the constraints of Protocol had to be observed."

He looked up. "We had so little time together."

Claudia took a breath. "She died."

"When the child was born." He looked away, out of the window. Leaf shadows flashed over his face. "We had a midwife and one of the most renowned of the Sapienti in attendance, but nothing could be done."

She had no idea what to say. Nothing had prepared her for this. He had never talked to her like this before. Her fingers were knotted back together. She said, "I never saw her then."

"Never." His dark glance turned to her. "And afterward I could not bear to see her image. There was a portrait, but I had it locked away. Now there is only this."

He drew from inside his shirt a small gold locket, tugged the black ribbon over his head and held it out. For a moment she was almost afraid to take it; when she did, it was warm from his body heat.

"Open it," he said.

She undid the fastening. Inside, facing each other in two oval frames were two miniatures, exquisitely painted. On the right, her father, looking grave and younger, his hair a rich brown. And opposite, in a low-cut gown of crimson silk, a woman with a sweet, delicate face, smiling, a tiny flower held to her mouth.

Her mother.

Her fingers trembled; glancing up to see if he noticed, she saw he was watching her. He said, "I will have a copy made for you at Court. Master Alan the painter is a fine workman."

She wanted him to break down, to cry out. She wanted him to be angry, to be scorched with grief, something, anything she could respond to. But there was only his grave calm.

She knew he had won this round of the game. Silently she gave the medallion back.

He slid it into his pocket.

Neither of them spoke for a while. The coach rumbled along

the high road; they passed through a village of tumbledown cottages and a pond where geese rose up and flapped white wings in fright. Then the road ran uphill, into the green shade of a wood.

Claudia felt hot and embarrassed. A wasp blundered through the open window; she waved it out and wiped her hands and face with a small handkerchief, noticing how the brown dust of the road came off on the white linen.

Finally she said, "I'm glad you've told me. Why now?"

"I am not a demonstrative man, Claudia. But only now am I ready to speak of it." His voice was gravelly and hoarse. "This wedding will be the pinnacle of my life. Of hers too, had she lived. We must think of her, of how proud and happy she would have felt." He raised his eyes and they were gray as steel. "Nothing must be allowed to spoil things, Claudia. Nothing must get in the way of our success."

She met his eyes; he smiled his slow smile. "Now. I am sure you would prefer Jared's company to mine." There was an edge to the words that she did not miss. He picked up his stick and thumped on the carriage roof; outside, the coachman gave a low call, drawing the horses to a restless, stamping, snorting halt. When they were still, the Warden leaned over and opened the door. He climbed down and stretched. "What a beautiful view. Look, my dear."

She stepped out beside him.

A great river ran below them, glinting in the summer sunshine. It ran through rich farmlands, the fields golden with the ripening barley, and she saw that butterflies were rising in clouds from the flowery meadows beside the road. The sun was hot on her arms; she raised her face to it gratefully, closing her eyes and seeing only a red heat, smelling the dust and some pungent crushed yarrow in the hedge.

When she opened them again he was gone, walking back to the following coaches, swishing his stick, speaking a pleasant word to Lord Evian, who climbed out and mopped perspiration from his red face.

And the Realm stretched before her to the distant misty heat of the horizon, and she wished for a second that she could run into its summer stillness, escape into the peace of the empty land. Somewhere no one else would be.

Somewhere she would be free.

A movement at her elbow. Lord Evian stood there, sipping from a small wine flask. "Beautiful," he breathed. He pointed a plump finger. "Do you see?"

She saw a glitter miles away in the distant hills. A brilliant diamond-white reflection. And she knew it was the sunlight on the roof of the great Glass Court.

≪◇◇◇≫

KEIRO ATE the last scrap of meat and leaned back, replete. He drank the dregs of beer and looked around for someone to refill the tankard.

Attia was still sitting by the door; he ignored her. The tavern was full; he had to call twice to get attention. Then the alewife came over with a jug and as she filled said, "What about your friend? Doesn't she eat?"

"She's no friend of mine."

"She came in behind you."

He shrugged. "Can't help being followed by girls. I mean, look at me."

The woman laughed and shook her head. "All right, handsome. Pay up."

He counted out a few coins, drank the beer, and stood, stretching. He felt better after the wash, and the flame-red jerkin had always looked good on him. Striding between the tables he ignored Attia as she scrambled up to follow and was halfway down the dim alleyway before her voice made him stop.

"When are we going to find them?"

He didn't turn.

"God knows what's happening to them. You promised . . ."

Keiro swung around. "Why don't you get lost?"

The girl stared back. She was a timid little thing, he'd thought, but this was the second time she'd confronted him, and it was getting annoying. "I'm not going anywhere," she said quietly.

Keiro grinned. "You think I'm going to desert them, don't you?"

"Yes."

Her directness threw him. It made him angry. He turned

and walked on, but she came after him like a shadow. Like a dog.

"I think you want to, but I won't let you. I won't let you take the Key."

He told himself he wouldn't answer her, but the words came out anyway. "You have no idea what I'll do. Finn and I are oathbrothers. That means everything. And I keep my word."

"Do you?" Her voice slid into a sly copy of Jormanric's. "*I haven't kept my word since I was ten and knifed my own brother. Is that how it works, Keiro? Is that how the Comitatus is still with us, inside you?*"

He turned on her then, but she was ready for him. She leaped, scratching his face, kicking and pushing him so that he staggered and crashed back against the wall. The Key fell out, a clatter on the filthy cobbles; they both grabbed for it, but she was quicker.

Keiro hissed with anger. He caught her hair, dragged it back savagely. "Give it to me!"

She screamed and squirmed.

"Let go of it!"

He pulled harder. With a howl of pain Attia threw the Key into the darkness; instantly Keiro let her go and scrambled after it, but as soon as he picked it up, he dropped it with a yell.

It lay on the ground, small blue lights traveling inside it.

Suddenly, with alarming silence, an image field sprang up around it. They saw a girl dressed in a sumptuous dress, her back against a tree, lit by a glorious brilliance of light. She stared at them both. When she spoke, her voice was sharp with suspicion.

"Where's Finn? Who the hell are you?"

⊰⊱

THEY HAD given him a meal of honeycakes and some strange seeds and a hot drink that bubbled slightly, but he had been afraid to taste it in case it was drugged. Whatever he was going into, he wanted a clear head.

They had also given him clean clothes and water to wash in. Outside the door of the room two of the Crane-men stood, leaning against the wall.

He crossed to the window. There was a long drop. Below was a narrow street, crowded with people even now, begging and selling and setting up makeshift camps in the street, sleeping under sacks, their animals wandering everywhere. The noise was appalling.

He put his hands on the sill and leaned out, looking up at the roofs. They were mostly straw, with some metal patched here and there. There was no way he could climb out on them; the house leaned outward as if it would fall, and he certainly would. For a moment he wondered if it might not be better to break his neck here than have to face some nameless creature, but there was still time. Things might change.

He ducked inside and sat on the stool trying to think. Where was Keiro? What was he doing? What plan did he have? Keiro was willful and wild, but he was a great plotter. The ambush of the Civicry had been his idea. He was bound to think of something good. Already Finn missed his brashness, his utter self-certainty.

The door opened; Gildas squeezed in.

"You!" Finn jumped up. "You've got a nerve . . ."

The Sapient held up both hands. "You're angry. Finn, I had no choice. You saw what would have happened to us." He sounded grim, went and sat heavily on the stool. "Besides, I'm coming with you."

"They said only me."

"Silver coins do much." He grunted tetchily. "Most people try to bribe their way out of being taken to the Cave, it seems, not in."

There was only one seat in the room; Finn sat on the floor among the straw and wrapped his arms around his knees. "I thought I was on my own," he said softly.

"Well, you're not. I am not Keiro, and I will not desert my seer."

Finn scowled. Then he said, "Would you desert me if I saw nothing?"

Gildas rubbed his dry hands together, making a papery sound. "Of course not."

They were silent a moment, listening to the babble of the street. Then Finn said, "Tell me about the Cave."

"I thought you knew the story. Sapphique came to the Citadel of the Justices, which must be where we are. He learned that the people here pay a Tribute every month to a being they only know as the Beast—the tribute is a young man or woman of the town. They go into a cave on the mountainside; none ever return."

He scratched his beard. "Sapphique came before the Justices and offered himself in place of the girl whose life was due. They say she wept at his feet. As he went out all the people of the town watched him go, in silence. He entered the Cave alone, without weapons."

Finn said, "And?"

Gildas was silent a moment. When he went on, his voice was lower. "For three days nothing happened. Then, on the fourth, news went around like wildfire that the stranger had emerged from the Cave. The townspeople lined the walls, threw open the gates. Sapphique walked slowly up the road. When he reached the gates he lifted up his hand, and they saw that the index finger on the right was missing, and that the hand bled into the dust. He said, 'The debt has not been paid. There is not enough of me to pay the debt. What lives in the Cave is a hunger that can never be satisfied. An emptiness that can never be filled.' Then he turned and walked away and the people let him go. But the girl, the one whose life he saved, she ran after him, and traveled with him for a while. She was the first of his Followers."

Finn said, "What—?" but the door slammed open before he could finish. The Crane-men beckoned. "Out. The boy must sleep now. At Lightson we leave."

Gildas went, with one swift look. The man threw Finn some blankets; he dragged them around himself and sat huddled against the wall, listening to the voices and singing and barking in the street.

He felt cold and utterly alone. He tried to think of Keiro, of Claudia, the girl the Key had shown him. And Attia, would she forget him? Would they all leave him to his fate?

He rolled over and curled up.

And then he saw the Eye.

It was very tiny, up near the ceiling, half hidden in cobwebs.

It watched him steadily and he stared back, then sat up and faced it. "Speak to me," he said, his voice soft with anger and scorn. "Are you too scared to speak to me? If I was born from you, then talk to me. Tell me what to do. Spring the doors open."

The Eye was a red spark, unblinking.

"I know you're there. I know you can hear me. I've always known. The others forget, but I don't." He was standing now; he came over and reached up, but the Eye was, as always, too high. "I told her about you, the Maestra, the woman that was killed, that I killed. Did you see that? Did you see her fall, did you catch her? Have you got her somewhere, alive?"

His voice was shaking, his mouth was dry; he knew the signs but was too angry and scared to stop.

"I will Escape from you. I will, I swear it. There must be somewhere to go. Where you can't see me. Where you don't exist!"

He was sweating, sick. He had to sit down, lie down, let the dizziness sweep over him, the patchwork of images, a room, a table, a boat on a dark lake. He choked on them, fought them off, drowned in them. "No," he said. "No." The Eye was a star. A red star. It fell slowly into his open mouth. And as it burned inside him, he heard it speak in the faintest of breaths, the murmur of dust in deserted corridors, the scorch of ashes in the heart of the fire.

"*I am everywhere,*" it whispered. "*Everywhere.*"

19

Down the endless halls of guilt
My silver thread of tears is spilt.
My fingerbone the key that broke
My blood the oil that smoothes the lock.
— *Songs of Sapphique*

Claudia stared at the holo-image in dismay. "What do you mean imprisoned? You're all in Prison, aren't you?"

The boy grinned, a soft mockery she already disliked. He sat on the curb of what looked like some sort of dark alleyway and leaned back, gazing at her with a considering scrutiny. "Are we, indeed? And where are you then, Princess?"

She frowned. In fact she had run into the garderobe of the hostelry where the carriages had stopped for lunch, a stinking stone chamber too close to Protocol for comfort. But she wasn't going to waste time explaining. "Listen to me, whatever your name is—"

"Keiro."

"Well, Keiro. It's vital I speak to Finn. How did you get this Key from him anyway? Did you steal it?"

He had very blue eyes, and his hair was blond and long. He was handsome and he certainly knew it. He said, "Finn and

I are oathbrothers, sworn to each other. He gave it to me for safety."

"So he trusts you?"

"Of course."

Another voice said, "Well, I don't."

A girl stepped up behind him; he glared at her hotly and muttered, "Will you shut up?" but she crouched and spoke hurriedly to Claudia.

"I'm Attia. I think he's going to leave Finn and the Sapient and try to Escape as Sapphique did, and he thinks the Key will work for him. You musn't let him! Finn will die."

Bewildered by the names, Claudia said, "Wait. Slow down! Why will he die?"

"They seem to have some sort of ritual in this Wing. He has to face the Beast. Is there anything you can do? Some magic from the stars? You have to help us!"

The girl had the filthiest clothes Claudia had ever seen; her hair was dark and hacked into a rough, jagged cut. She was clearly worried sick. Trying to think, Claudia said, "How can I do anything? You have to get him out of it!"

"What makes you think we can?" Keiro asked calmly.

"You've got no choice." A shout out in the inn-yard made her glance around nervously. "Because Finn is the only one I'll talk to."

"Like him, do you? And who are you anyway?"

She glared. "The Warden of Incarceron is my father."

Keiro snorted. "What Warden?"

"He . . . oversees the Prison." She felt cold. His scorn chilled her. Quickly she went on. "Maybe I can find charts of the Prison, a map of its secret ways, its doorways and corridors that will show you the way out. But I won't tell you a thing until I see Finn."

It was a lie that would have made Jared groan, but she had no choice. She didn't trust this Keiro; he was too arrogant, and the girl seemed angry and scared.

Keiro shrugged. "What's so special about Finn?"

She hesitated. Then she said, "I think . . . I think I recognize him. He's older, he looks different, but there's something about him, his voice . . . If I'm right his real name is Giles, and he's the son of . . . a fairly important person out here." She shouldn't say too much. Just enough to get him to act.

Keiro stared, astonished. "Are you telling me all that guff about coming in from Outside is actually true? That mark on his wrist means something?"

"I've got to go. Just get him."

He folded his arms. "If I can't?"

"Then forget the magic of the stars." She looked at the girl, their eyes meeting briefly. "And this Key will just be a useless lump of crystal. But if you're his brother, you'd want to rescue him."

Keiro nodded. "I do." He nodded toward Attia. "Forget her. She's crazy. She knows nothing." His voice was low and earnest. "Finn and I are brothers and we watch each other's backs. Always."

Attia gazed at Claudia, her face bruised. Doubt moved in her eyes. "Is he related to you?" she asked quietly. "Your brother? Cousin?"

Claudia shrugged. "Just a friend. A friend, that's all." Hurriedly, she switched the field off.

The Key glimmered in the fetid darkness. She shoved it into the pocket in her skirt and ran out, desperate for fresh air. Alys was loitering anxiously in the passageway, servants bustling past her with trays and dishes.

"Oh, there you are, Claudia! Earl Caspar is looking for you."

But Claudia could already hear him, the thin annoying bray of his voice, and to her dismay she saw that it was Jared he was talking to, and Lord Evian, the three of them sitting on benches in the sunshine, the hostel dogs sprawled in an expectant row at their feet.

She came out and crossed the cobbles.

Evian stood immediately and made an ornate bow; Jared moved quietly to make a space for her. Caspar said crossly, "You're always avoiding me, Claudia!"

"Of course not. Why on earth would I do that?" She sat down and smiled. "How nice. All my friends together."

Caspar scowled. Jared shook his head slightly. Beside them Evian hid a smile with his lace-edged handkerchief. She wondered how he could sit there so coolly with the Earl, a boy he was plotting to have murdered. But then, he would probably protest that it wasn't personal, that this was politics, nothing more. The game, always.

She turned to Jared. "I want you to travel with me now. I'm so bored! We can discuss Menessier's *Natural History of the Realm*."

"Why not me?" Caspar tossed a hunk of meat to the dogs and watched them fight over it. "I'm not boring." His small eyes turned to her. "Am I?"

It was a challenge. "Indeed not, Your Grace." She smiled pleasantly. "And of course I'd love you to join us. Menessier has some excellent passages on the fauna in the coniferous forests."

He stared at her in disgust. "Claudia, don't try that wide-eyed innocent junk with me. I told you, I don't care what you get up to. Anyway, I know all about it. Fax told me about last night."

She felt herself go pale, couldn't look at Jared. The dogs growled and fought. One brushed her skirt and she stamped at it.

Caspar stood up, smugly triumphant. He was wearing a garish collar of gold links and a frock coat of black velvet, and he kicked the dogs aside till they yelped. "But I'm warning you, Claudia, you'd better be more discreet. My mother's not as open-minded as I am. If she found out, she'd be furious." He grinned at Jared. "Your clever tutor might find that his illness gets suddenly worse."

She was so angry, she almost leaped to her feet, but Jared's light touch kept her sitting. They watched Caspar stride away across the inn-yard, avoiding the puddles and dung heaps in his expensive boots.

Finally Lord Evian took out his snuffbox. "Dear me," he said quietly. "Now that was a threat if ever I heard one."

Claudia met Jared's eyes. They were dark and troubled. "Fax?" he said.

She shrugged, exasperated with herself. "He saw me coming out of your room last night."

His dismay showed. "Claudia . . ."

"I know. I know. It's all my fault."

Evian sniffed the snuff delicately. "If I may be allowed to comment, that was a very unfortunate thing to happen."

"It's not what you think."

"I'm sure."

"No. Really. And you can drop the act. I've told Jared about . . . the Steel Wolves."

He glanced around quickly. "Claudia, not aloud, please." His voice lost its affectations. "I appreciate you trust your tutor, but—"

"Of course she should have told me." Jared tapped the table-top with his long fingers. "Because the whole plot is foolish, utterly criminal, and almost certain to be betrayed. How could you even think about bringing her into it!"

"Because we can't do it without her." The fat man was

calm, but a film of sweat glistened on his forehead. "You above all, Master Sapient, understand what the iron decrees of the Havaarna have done to us. We are rich, some of us, and live well, but we are not free. We are chained hand and foot by Protocol, enslaved to a static, empty world where men and women can't read, where the scientific advances of the ages are the preserve of the rich, where artists and poets are doomed to endless repetitions and sterile reworkings of past masterpieces. Nothing is new. New does not exist. Nothing changes, nothing grows, evolves, develops. Time has stopped. Progress is forbidden."

He leaned forward. Claudia had never seen him so grave, so stripped of his effete disguise, and it chilled her, as if he were someone else entirely, an older, exhausted, desperate man.

"We are dying, Claudia. We must break open this cell we have bricked ourselves into, escape from this endless wheel we tread like rats. I have dedicated myself to freeing us. If it means my death, I don't care, because even death will be a sort of freedom."

In the stillness the rooks cawed around the trees overhead. Horses in the stable yard were being harnessed, their feet stamping the cobbles.

Claudia licked dry lips. "Don't do anything yet," she whispered. "I may have . . . some information for you. But not yet." She stood quickly, not wanting to say any more, not wanting to feel the raw anguish he had opened in her like a stab wound. "The horses are ready. Let's go."

THE STREETS were full of people, all silent. Their silence terrified Finn; it was so intense, and the hungry way they looked at him made him stumble, the women and the scruffy children, the maimed, the old, the soldiers; cold, curious stares that he dared not meet, so that he looked down, at his feet, at the dirt on the road, anywhere but at them.

The only sound that rang in the steep streets was the steady tramp of the six guards around him, the crack of their iron-soled boots on the cobbles, and far above, circling like an omen, a single large bird screeching mournful cries among the clouds and echoing winds of Incarceron's vault.

Then someone sang back, a single note of lament, and as if it was a signal, all the crowd picked it up and crooned it softly, their sorrow and their fear in one strange soft song. He tried to make out the words, but only fragments came to him . . . the silver thread that broke . . . all down the endless halls of guilt and dreams . . . and like a chorus the haunting, repeated phrase: his fingerbone the key, his blood the oil that smoothes the lock.

Turning a corner, Finn glanced back.

Gildas walked behind, alone. The guards ignored him, but he walked firmly, his head high, and the people's eyes moved wonderingly over the green of his Sapient coat.

The old man looked grim and purposeful; he gave Finn a brief nod of encouragement.

There was no sign of Keiro or Attia. Desperately Finn stared into the crowds. Had they found out what was happening to him? Would they wait outside the Cave?

Had they spoken to Claudia? Anxiety tormented him, and he would not let himself think the thing that he dreaded, that lurked in the dark of his mind like a spider, like Incarceron's mocking whisper.

That Keiro might have taken the Key and gone.

He shook his head. In the three years of the Comitatus, Keiro had never betrayed him. Taunted him, yes, laughed at him, stolen from him, fought with him, argued with him. But he'd always been there. And yet now Finn realized with a sudden coldness how little he knew about his oathbrother, about where he had come from. Keiro just said his parents were dead. Finn had never asked any questions. He'd always been too absorbed in his own agonizing loss, in the memory flashes and the fits.

He should have asked.

He should have cared.

A rain of tiny black petals began to fall on him. Looking up he saw that the people were throwing them, tossing out handfuls that fell on the cobbles and made a fragrant dark carpet on the road. And he saw that the petals had a peculiar quality, that as they touched each other they melted, and that the gutters and streets ran with a sticky, clotted mass that exuded the sweetest of scents.

It made him feel strange. And as if it broke into a dream, it made him remember the voice he had heard in the night.

I am everywhere. As if the Prison had answered him. He looked up now, as they marched under the gaping maw of the gate, and saw a single red Eye in the portcullis, its unblinking gaze fixed on him.

"Can you see me?" he breathed. "Did you speak to me?"

But the gate was behind him and they were out of the City.

The road led straight and it was deserted. The sticky oil trickled along it; behind he heard the gates and doors slam, the wooden bolts drawn across, the iron grilles crash down. Out here under the vault the world seemed empty, the plain swept by icy winds.

The soldiers hastily unshouldered the heavy axes they carried; the one in front also had some sort of device with a canister attached, a flame-throwing machine, Finn guessed. He said, "Let the Sapient catch up."

They slowed, as if now he was not their prisoner but their leader, and Gildas strode breathlessly up and said, "Your brother hasn't shown himself."

"He'll turn up." Saying it helped.

They walked swiftly, closed into a tight group. On either side the ground was seamed with pits and traps; Finn saw the steel teeth gleam in their depths. Glancing back, he was surprised at how the City was already far behind, its walls lined with people, watching, shouting, holding their children up to see.

The guard captain said, "We turn off the road here. Be careful; step only where we step and don't think of running off. The ground is sewn with fireglobes."

Finn had no idea what fireglobes were, but Gildas frowned. "This Beast must be fearsome indeed."

The man glanced at him. "I have never seen it, Master, and don't intend to."

Once off the smooth road the going was rough. The coppery earth seemed to have been scored and clawed into vast furrows; in several places it was burned, carbonized to a charcoal crispness that rose in clouds of dust as they trod on it, or vitrified almost to glass. Enormous heat would have been needed to do that, Finn thought. It stank too, an acrid cindery smell. He followed the men closely, watching their steps with nervous attention; when they paused and he raised his head, he saw that they were far out on the plain, the Prison lights so high above they were brilliant suns, casting his and Gildas's shadows behind them.

Far in the mile-high vault the bird still circled. Once it screeched, and the guards looked up at it. The nearest muttered, "Looking for carrion."

Finn began to wonder how far they would walk. There were no hills out here, no ridges, so where would they find a cave? He had pictured it as some dark aperture in a metallic cliff. Now he was filled with a new apprehension, because even his imagination was betraying him.

"Stop." The guard captain held up a hand. "This is it."

There was nothing there. That was Finn's first idea. Relief flooded him. It was all a pretense. They'd let him go now, run back to the City, spin some gruesome tale about a monster to keep the people quiet.

Then, as he pushed past the men, he saw the pit in the ground.

And the Cave.

—◇◇◇—

JARED SAID, "You promised them maps that don't exist! It was a crazy idea, Claudia. Things are getting so dangerous for us!"

She knew he was deeply worried. She crossed to his side of the carriage and said, "Master, I know. But the stakes are so high."

He looked up and she saw the pain was back behind his eyes. "Claudia, tell me you're not thinking seriously about this folly of Evian's. We are not murderers!"

"I'm not. If my plan works, there'll be no need of it." But she didn't say what she was thinking: that if the Queen really did find out, that if he, Jared, was in any danger at all, she would have them all killed without hesitation, even her father, to save him.

Maybe he knew it. As the carriage jolted he glanced out of the window and his expression darkened, his black hair brushing the collar of the Sapient coat. "Here's our prison," he said bleakly.

And following his gaze she saw the pinnacles and glass towers of the Palace, the turrets and towers festooned with flags and bunting, heard that all the bells were ringing to welcome her, all the doves flapping, all the cannon were being fired in deep booming salute from every mile-high terrace that rose in splendor into the pure blue sky.

20

We have put everything that is left into this.
It is bigger than all of us now.

> —*Project report; Martor Sapiens*

"Take this, and this."

The guard captain thrust a small leather bag and a sword into Finn's hands. The bag seemed so light, it must be empty. "What's in it?" he asked nervously.

"You'll see." The man stepped back and glanced at Gildas. Then he said, "Why not flee, Master? Why waste your life?"

"My life is Sapphique's," Gildas snapped. "His fate is mine."

The captain shook his head. "Suit yourself. But no one else has ever come back." He jerked his head at the Cave entrance. "There it is."

There was a moment of tense silence. The guards gripped their axes tightly; Finn knew that this was the moment they expected him to make some sort of break for freedom, now that he had a sword in his hand and his back to unknown terrors. How many of those brought as Tribute had screamed and fought in panic here?

Not him. He was Finn.

Reckless, he turned and looked down at the crack.

It was very thin, and utterly black. Its edges were burned and scorched, as if the metal of the Prison's structure had been superheated and melted countless times into grotesque twistings and taperings. As if whatever crawled out of these metal lips could melt steel like toffee.

He glanced at Gildas. "I'll go first." Before the Sapient could object, he turned and lowered himself into the slash of darkness, taking one last rapid look into the distance. But the scarred plain was empty, the City a remote fortress.

He slithered his boots over the edge, found a foothold, squeezed his body in.

Once he was below ground level, the darkness closed over him. By feeling with hands and feet he realized that the crack was a horizontal space between tilted strata, and it sloped down into the ground. He had to spread-eagle himself to fit in it, inching forward over a dark slab-like surface littered with debris that seemed to be stones and smooth balls of melted steel that rolled painfully under him. His fingers groped in dust and a lump of rubble that crumbled away like bone. He dropped it hastily.

The roof was low; twice it grazed his back and he began to fear being stuck. As soon as the thought touched him with cold terror he stopped.

Sweating, he gulped a deep breath. "Where are you?"

"Right behind." Gildas sounded strained. His voice echoed; a small shower of dust fell from above into Finn's hair and eyes. A hand grabbed his boot. "Move on."

"Why?" He tried to roll his head to look back. "Why not wait here till Lightsout, then crawl back. Don't tell me those men will wait out there until dark. They've probably gone already. What's to stop us . . . ?"

"Fireglobes are to stop us, fool boy. Acres of them. One wrong step and your foot's blown off. And you didn't see what I saw last night, how they patrol the City walls, how vast searchlights sweep the plain all night. We'd be easily seen." He laughed, a grim bark in the darkness. "I meant what I said to the blind women. You are a Starseer. If Sapphique came here, so must we. Though I fear my theory that the way out leads upward seems doomed to be proved wrong."

Finn shook his head in disbelief. Even in this mess the old man cared more about his theories than anything else. He scrabbled on, digging the toes of his boots in and heaving himself forward.

For the next few minutes he was sure that the roof was dipping so low that it would meet the floor and trap him; then, to his relief, the gap began to widen and at the same time tip leftward and slope more steeply. Finally he could rise to his knees without banging his head on the roof. "It opens ahead." His voice was hollow.

"Wait there."

Gildas fumbled. There was a loud crack and light hissed; one of the crude, smoking flares the Comitatus had used to signal distress. It showed Finn the Sapient lying flat on his stomach dragging a candle from the pack. He lit it from the flare; as the spitting red light died, the small flames flickered, guttering in a draft from somewhere ahead.

"I didn't know you'd brought those."

"Some of us," Gildas said, "thought to bring more than garish clothes and useless rings." He cupped his hand around the flame. "Go quietly. Though whatever it is it will have already smelled and heard us coming."

As if in answer, something rumbled ahead. A low grinding sound, sensed like a vibration under their splayed hands. Finn tugged the sword out and gripped it tight. He could see nothing in the blackness.

He moved on, and the tunnel opened, became a space around him. In the flicker of the tiny candle flame he saw the ridged sides of the metal strata, outcrops of crystal quartzes, strange furrings of oxides that gleamed in turquoises and orange as the light edged past them. He pulled himself to hands and knees.

Ahead, something moved. He sensed it rather than heard it, felt a draft of foul air that caught in the back of his throat. Very still, he listened, every sense straining.

Behind him, Gildas grunted.

"Keep still!"

The Sapient cursed. "Is it here?"

"I think so."

He was becoming aware of the space. As he grew accustomed to the darkness, edges and facades of sloping rock began to separate from shadows; he saw a pinnacle of scorched stone and realized with sudden shock that it was immense, and a long way off, and that the draft was a wind now, blowing in his face, a warm stench like the breathing of a great creature, a terrible acrid stink.

And then in an instant of clarity he knew it was curled all around him, that the black, faceted rock face was its scabbed skin, the vast spurs of stone its fossilized claws, that he was in a cave formed by the ancient, scaly hide of some smoldering beast.

He turned to yell a warning.

But slowly, with a terrible creaking weight, an eye opened.

A red eye, heavily lidded, bigger than he was.

———◦○◇○◦———

ALL THE way through the streets the noise was deafening. Flowers were flung constantly; after a while Claudia found herself flinching at the repeated thud and slither of the impact on the carriage roof, and the scent of the crushed stems grew sweet and cloying. The climb was steep and she was tossed uncomfortably in the seat; beside her Jared looked pale. She took his arm. "Are you all right?"

He smiled wanly. "I wish we could get out. Throwing up on the Palace steps won't make much of an impression."

She tried to smile. Together they sat in silence as the carriage rumbled and clattered through the gateways of the Outer Citadel, under its vast defenses, through its courtyards and cobbled porticoes, and with each twist and turn, she knew she was becoming ensnared deeper and deeper in the life that waited for her here, the mazes of power, the labyrinth of treachery. Slowly the raucous shouts faded; the wheels ran smoothly, and peeping around the curtain she saw that the road was lined with red carpet, expensive swathes of it, and all across the streets garlands of flowers hung and doves flapped between roofs and gables.

There were more people up here; these were the apartments of the courtiers, the Privy Council and the Office of the Protocol, and the cheers were more refined, punctuated by bursts of music from viols and serpents and fife and drum. Somewhere ahead she could hear roars and clapping—Caspar was obviously leaning from the window of his coach to acknowledge his welcome home.

"They'll want to see the bride," Jared murmured.

"She's not here yet."

A silence. Then she said, "Master, I'm afraid." She felt his surprise. "I am, truly. This place scares me. At home, I know who I am, what to do. I'm the Warden's daughter, I know where I stand. But this is a dangerous place, full of pitfalls. All my life I've known it was waiting for me, but now I'm not sure I can face it. They'll want to absorb me, make me one of them, and I won't change, I won't! I want to stay me."

He sighed, and she saw his dark gaze was fixed on the veiled window. "Claudia, you're the bravest person I know."

"I'm not . . ."

"You are. And no one will change you. You will rule here, though it won't be easy. The Queen is powerful, and she will envy you, because you're young and you'll take her place. Your power is as great as hers."

"But if they send you away . . ."

He turned. "I won't go. I am not a brave man, I understand that. Confrontation disturbs me; one look from your father and I'm chilled to the bone, Sapient or not. But they can't make me leave you, Claudia." He sat upright, away from her. "I have looked death in the face for years now, and that gives some sort of recklessness, at least."

"Don't talk about that."

He shrugged gently. "It will come. But we mustn't think so much of ourselves. We should consider whether we can help Finn. Give me the Key and let me work on it a little more. It has complexities I've barely guessed at yet."

As the coach jolted over a threshold she took it from her hidden pocket and gave it to him, and as she did so the wings of the eagle deep in the crystal flickered, as if it flapped them and took off. Jared pulled back the curtain quickly, and the sun caught the gleaming facets.

The bird was flying.

It was flying over a dark landscape, a charred plain. Far below, a chasm gaped in the earth, and the bird swooped and plummeted inside, twisting sideways into the narrow crack, making Claudia hiss with fear.

The Key went black. One single red light pulsed in it.

But even as they stared at it the coach rumbled to a halt, the horses stamping and blowing, and the door was flung open. The Warden's shadow darkened the threshold. "Come, my dear," he said quietly. "They're all waiting."

Without looking at Jared, without even letting herself think, she stepped out of the coach and drew herself upright, her arm in her father's.

Together, they faced the double row of applauding courtiers, the splendor of silk banners, the great stairway leading upward to the throne.

Sitting on it, resplendent in a silver gown with vast ruff, sat the Queen. Even from this distance the redness of her hair and lips were evident, the radiance of the diamonds at her neck. Behind her shoulder, a scowling presence, stood Caspar.

The Warden said calmly, "The smile, I think."

She put it on. The bright, confident smile, as false as everything in her life, a cloak over the coldness.

Then they walked steadily up the stairs.

⚬⚬⚬⚬⚬

IT WAS the ironic stare of his nightmares and he recognized it, his voice hoarse. "*You?*"

Behind, he heard Gildas's gasp. "Strike at it. Strike, Finn!"

The Eye was aswirl. Its pupil was a spiral of movement, a scarlet galaxy. All around it, heaving itself up, the darkness convulsed, and he saw the vast hide of the Beast was studded with objects,

257

bits of jewelry, bones, fragments of rags, shafts of weapons. They were centuries old; skin and hide had grown over them. With a tearing and cracking an outcrop of dark faceted rock became its head and reared up over him; spurs of metal slid out like claws, grasping the shuddering tilting floor of the cavern.

Finn couldn't move. Dust and fumes clouded over him.

"Strike!" Gildas grabbed his arm.

"It's useless. Can't you see . . . ?"

Gildas gave a roar of anger, snatched the sword from him, and thrust it into the clotted hide of the Beast, leaping back as if he expected blood to cascade out in a great gout. Then he stared, seeing what Finn had seen.

There was no wound. The hide opened and dissolved, absorbed the blade, reassembled around it. The Beast was a composite creature, a grinding, swift formation of millions of beings, of bats and bones and beetles, dark clouds of bees, an ever-changing kaleidoscope pattern of rock fragments and metal shards. As it turned and rose into the roof of the chamber, they saw that over the centuries it had absorbed all the terror and the fear of the City, that all the Tribute sent out to placate it had been absorbed, eaten, had only made it grow huger. Somewhere inside it were the billions of atoms of the dead, of the victims and the children dragged out here by decree of the Justices. It was a magnetized mass of flesh and metal, its crumbling tail studded with fingernails and teeth and talons.

It stretched out its head above them and leaned down, bringing the great red Eyes close to Finn's face, making his skin scarlet, his shaking hands look as if they were red with blood.

"Finn," it said, in a voice of deep pleasure, a throaty treacle of huskiness. *"At last."*

He stepped back, into Gildas. The Sapient's hand gripped his elbow. "You know my name."

"I gave you your name." Its tongue flickered in the dark cavern of its mouth. *"Gave it long ago, when you were born in my cells. When you became my son."*

He was shuddering. He wanted to deny it, shout out, but no words would come.

The creature tipped its head, studying him. The long muzzle, dripping bees and scales, fragmented into a cloud of dragonflies and re-formed again. *"I knew you'd come,"* it said. *"I've been watching you, Finn, because you are so special. In all the entrails and veins of my body, in all the millions of beings I enclose, there is no one quite like you."*

The head zoomed closer. Something like a smile formed and broke. *"Do you really think you can escape from me? Do you forget that I could kill you, shut down light and air, incinerate you in seconds?"*

"I don't forget," he managed to say.

"Most men do. Most men are content to live in their prison and think it is the world, but not you, Finn. You remember about me. You look around and see my Eyes watching you, in those nights of darkness you called out to me and I heard you . . ."

"You didn't answer," he whispered.

"But you knew I was there. You are a Starseer, Finn. How interesting that is."

Gildas pushed forward. He was white, his sparse hair wet with sweat. "Who are you?" he growled.

"I am Incarceron, old man. You should know. It was the Sapienti who created me. Your great, towering, overreaching endless failure. Your nemesis." It zigzagged closer, its mouth wide so that they could see the rags of cloth that hung there, smell the oily, oddly sweet stench of it. *"Ah, the pride of the Wise. And now you dare to seek a way free of your own folly."*

It slid back, the red Eyes narrowing to slits. *"Pay me, Finn. Pay me as Sapphique paid. Give me your flesh, your blood. Give me the old man and his terrible desire for death. Then perhaps your Key may open doors you do not dream of."*

Finn's mouth was dry as ash. "This isn't a game."

"No?" The Beast's laugh was soft and slithering. *"Are you not pieces on a board?"*

"People." His anger was rising. "People that suffer. People you torment."

For a moment the creature dissolved to clouds of insects. Then they clotted in abrupt gargoyles, a new face, serpentine and sinuous. *"I'm afraid not. They torment each other. There is no system that can stop that, no place that can wall out evil, because men bring it in with them, even in the children. Such men are beyond correction, and it is my task only to con-*

tain them. I hold them inside myself. I swallow them whole."

A tentacle lashed out and around his wrist. *"Pay me, Finn."*

Finn jerked back, glanced at Gildas. The Sapient looked shrunken, his face drawn as if all his dread had fallen on him at once, but he said slowly, "Let it take me, boy. There's nothing for me now."

"No." Finn stared up at the Beast, its reptilian smile inches from him. "I've already given you one life."

"Ah. The woman." The smile lengthened. *"How her death tears at you. Conscience and shame are so rare. They interest me."*

Something in its smirk made him catch his breath. A jolt of hope hurt him; he gasped, "She's not dead! You caught her, you stopped her fall! Didn't you? You saved her."

The red spiral winked at him. *"Nothing is wasted here,"* it murmured.

Finn stared, but Gildas's voice was a growl in his ear. "It's lying, boy."

"Maybe not. Maybe . . ."

"It's playing with you." Sour with disgust, the old man stared at the swirling confusion of the Eye. "If it is true we made such a thing as you, then I'm ready to pay for our folly."

"No." Finn grabbed him tight. He slid a dull circle of silver from his thumb and held it up, a glittering spark. "Take this for your Tribute instead, *Father.*"

It was the skull-ring. And he was beyond caring.

21

I have worked for years in secret to make a device that is a copy of the one Outside. Now it protects me. Timon died last week and Pela is missing in the riots, and even though I am hidden here in this lost hall, the Prison searches for me. "My lord," it whispers, "I feel you. I feel you crawl on my skin."

— *Lord Calliston's Diary*

The Queen rose graciously.

In the porcelain whiteness of her face her strange eyes were clear and cold. "My dear, dear, Claudia."

Claudia dropped a curtsy, felt the whisper of a kiss on each cheek, and in the tight grip of the embrace sensed the thin bones of the woman, the small frame inside the boned corset and huge hooped skirts.

No one knew Queen Sia's age. After all, she was a sorceress. Older than the Warden perhaps, though beside her he was grave and dark, his silvered beard meticulous.

Brittle or not, her youth was convincing; she looked barely older than her son.

Turning, she led Claudia in, sweeping past Caspar's sullen

stare. "You look so pretty, my sweet. That dress is wonderful. And your hair! Now tell me, is that natural or do you have it colored?"

Claudia breathed out, already irritated, but there was no need to answer. The Queen was already talking about something else. ". . . and I hope you won't consider that too forward of me."

"No," Claudia said blankly into a second of silence.

The Queen smiled. "Excellent. This way."

It was a double wooden door and was flung open by two footmen, but when Claudia was inside, the doors closed and the whole tiny chamber moved soundlessly upward.

"Yes I know," the Queen murmured, holding her close. "Such a breach of Protocol. But it's only for me, so who's to know?"

The small white hands were so tight on her arm, she could feel the nails digging in. She was breathless, as if she had been kidnapped. Even her father and Caspar were left behind.

When the doors opened, the corridor that stretched before her was a vision of gilt and mirrors; it had to be three times the size of the house at home. The Queen led her along it by the hand, between vast painted maps that showed every country in the Realm, adorned in their corners with fantasies of curling waves and mermaids and sea monsters.

"That's the library. I know you love books. Caspar, unfortunately, is not so studious. Really, I don't know if he can read at all. We won't go in."

Escorted firmly past, she looked back. Between each map stood a blue and white china urn that could have hidden a man, and the mirrors reflected each other in such sunlit confusion that she suddenly had no idea where the corridor ended or if it ever did. And the small white figure of the Queen seemed repeated before her and behind and to the side, so that the dread Claudia had felt in the coach seemed to be concentrated in that swift, unnaturally young stride, that sharp, confiding voice.

"And this is your suite. Your father is next door."

Immense.

A carpet her feet sank into, a bed so canopied with saffron silk, she felt it would drown her.

Suddenly she pulled her hand from the Queen's and stood back, knowing the trap. Knowing she was caught in it.

Sia was silent. The empty chatter was gone. They faced each other.

Then the Queen smiled. "You will not need to be warned, I'm sure, Claudia. John Arlex's daughter will be well trained, but I suppose it won't hurt to tell you that many of the mirrors are double sided and the listening devices all over the Palace are most efficient." She stepped closer. "You see, I have heard you were recently a little curious about dear lost Giles."

Claudia kept her face perfectly composed, but her hands were icy. She glanced down. "I've thought about him. If things had been different . . ."

"Yes. And we were all devastated by his death. But even if

the Havaarna Dynasty is over, the Realm must be governed. And I have no doubt, Claudia, that you will do it very well."

"Me?"

"Of course." The Queen turned and sat elegantly on a gilt chair. "Surely you know Caspar is incapable even of ruling himself? Come and sit here, my sweet. Let me advise you."

Surprise was freezing her. She sat.

The Queen leaned forward, her red lips making a coy smile. "Now, your life here can be a very pleasant one. Caspar is a child—let him have his toys, horses, palaces, girls, and he will make no trouble. I have made quite sure he knows nothing about politics. He gets bored so easily! You and I can have such a pleasant time, Claudia. You have no idea how tiresome it gets with just these men."

Claudia stared at her hands. Was this real, any of it? How much of it was the game?

"I thought . . ."

"That I hated you?" The Queen's giggle was girlish. "I need you, Claudia! We can rule together, and you'll be so good at it! And your father will smile his grave smile. So." Her small hands tapped Claudia's. "No more sad thoughts about Giles. He's in a better place, my dear."

Slowly, she nodded and stood, and the Queen stood too, with a rustle of silk.

"There's just one thing."

One hand on the door, Sia turned. "Yes?"

"Jared Sapiens. My tutor. I . . ."

"You won't need a tutor. I can teach you everything now."

"I want him to stay." She said it firmly.

The Queen stared straight back. "He's young for a Sapient. I don't know what your father was thinking of . . ."

"He will stay." She made sure it was a statement, not a question.

The Queen's red lips twitched. Her smile was pleasant. "Whatever you say, my sweet. Whatever you want."

<><><>

JARED PLACED the scanner on the door frame, opened the tiny casement, and sat on the bed. The room was sparse, as perhaps the Court thought a Sapient's cell should be, with wooden floorboards and dark paneling topped with trefoils and crude roses.

It smelled of rushes and damp, and seemed bare enough, but he had already removed two small listening devices and there might be others. Still, he had to take the chance.

He took out the Key and held it, activating the speechlink.

Nothing but darkness.

He touched it again, concerned: The darkness grew to a wide circle but remained dark. Then, very faintly, he saw the edge of a crouching figure in it. "We can't talk," it whispered. "Not now."

"Then listen." Jared kept his voice low. "This may help. A combination of two, four, three, one on the touch panel produces a dampening field. Any surveillance system will lose track of you, completely. You'll disappear from its scanners. Do you understand that?"

"I'm not stupid." Keiro's scornful whisper barely came through.

"Have you found Finn?"

Nothing. They'd switched off.

Jared linked his fingers and swore softly in the Sapient tongue. Outside the window, the voices of people rose up, some fiddlers in the distant gardens scraping a jig.

There would be dancing tonight to welcome the bride of the Heir.

And yet if the old man Bartlett had been right, the real Heir was still alive, and Claudia was convinced it was this boy Finn. Jared shook his head, unfastening the collar of his coat with long fingers. She wanted it so much. His doubts would have to stay silent, because without this hope, she would have nothing. And after all, it was possible, just possible, that her instinct was right.

Wearily, he leaned back against the stiff bolster, took the medication pouch from his pocket, and prepared the dose. It was three grains stronger now, and had been for the last week, but the pain that lived deep in his body seemed still to grow slowly, like a living thing; he sometimes thought that it devoured the drug, that he was feeding its appetite.

He applied the syringe, frowning. These were morbid and foolish ideas.

But when he lay back and slept, he dreamed for a moment that an eye, scarlet as galaxies, had opened in the wall and looked at him.

◄───◊◊◊───►

FINN WAS desperate; he held the ring high. "Take it and let us go."

The Eye zoomed in, examined it closely. *"Do you believe this object is of some value?"*

"It contains a life. Trapped inside."

"How apposite. As all your lives are trapped inside me."

He was shivering. Surely if Keiro was listening, he would act now. If he was here.

Gildas understood. He must have, because he snapped loudly, "Take it! Let us go."

"As I took Tribute from Sapphique? As I took this?" In the clotted hide of the Beast a glimmer of light opened; they saw a tiny frail bone, embedded deep.

Gildas murmured a prayer of awe.

"How small it is!" The Beast considered it. *"And yet how much pain it cost. Let me see this trapped life."*

It slid the tendril closer. Finn gripped the ring in his fist, his sweat making it slippery. Then he opened his hand.

At once, the Eye blinked. It widened, contracted, stared around. From the Beast's throat a whisper slid like oil, a puzzled, fascinated demand.

"How did you do that? Where are you?"

268

A hand clamped over Finn's mouth; as he convulsed around he saw Attia, one finger on her lips in warning. Behind her Keiro stood, the Key held tight in one hand, a flamethrower in the other.

"You are invisible!" The Beast sounded appalled. *"This isn't possible!"*

A mass of tentacles streamed out from it, groping formations of tiny spiders sticky with thread.

Finn stumbled back.

Keiro shouldered the flamethrower. "If you want us," he said calmly, "here we are."

A burst of flame roared across Finn; the Beast howled with rage. In an instant the cavern was an explosion of panicking, screeching birds and bees and bats released from shape and order; they arced and flapped and spiraled high into the cavern roof, beating themselves senselessly against rock.

Keiro whooped with delight. He fired again, a burst of yellow flame, and the Beast was a clattering cascade of fragments, of scorched skin and tumbling rock, its red Eye nothing but a tiny explosion of gnats that split in frenzied fear.

The flames sizzled, hit walls, and rebounded in sudden heat. "Leave it!" Finn yelled. "Let's get out!"

But the roof and floor were tilting, the crack closing around them.

"I may not be able to see you," the Prison remarked acidly through the uproar, *"but you're in here, and I will hold you tight, my son."*

Back to back it forced them together, spiraling in, the cave walls falling, slabs of the roof crashing down. Finn grabbed for Attia's hand in the chaos. "Stay together!"

"Finn." Gildas's voice was choked. "In the wall. Up there."

For a moment Finn had no idea what he meant; then he saw it. A fissure sloping up.

Instantly Attia pulled herself free. She ran and leaped; catching at the jutting facets, she dragged herself above the whipping tentacles, climbing the very scales of the Beast itself.

He shoved Gildas after her; the old man clambered awkwardly but with desperate vigor, lumps of stone and gems rolling and sliding under his hands.

Finn turned.

Keiro had the weapon ready. "Go on! It's searching for us!"

Incarceron was blinded. He saw how parts of the Beast reformed, a claw, a tail, how it groped and lashed in the darkness. It felt them on its skin, sensed the vibrations of their movement. He wanted to ask Keiro how he had done this, but there was no time, so he turned and scrambled after Gildas.

Minute by minute the wall was changing, re-forming and rippling, tilting itself straighter as if the Beast reared up, twisting itself around to tear them from its back. High into the cavernous spaces it took them, hanging on, and as Finn stared up he saw cracks of light up there, pinpricks of brilliance, and for a giddy moment he was among the stars, and then one swiveled over him and it was a searchlight, silvering his hands and face as he gasped, helplessly exposed.

Attia turned, her face a blur. "Slow down! We have to stay near the Key!"

Keiro was climbing far below, the flamethrower cast aside. As the ridged hide rippled he slipped, one foot scraping into space, and maybe the Beast felt that, because it hissed, and the air steamed with sudden fumes.

"Keiro!" Finn turned. "I'll have to go back for him."

Attia squirmed down. "No. He can manage."

Keiro clung tight. He pulled himself back; the Beast quivered. Then it laughed, that sinister chuckle Finn remembered so well. *"So you have some device to mask yourselves with. I congratulate you. But I certainly intend to discover what it is."*

Dust fell; a shaft of light. "Wait!" Finn yelled at Gildas; breathlessly the old man shook his head.

"I can't hang on anymore."

"You can!"

He gave Attia a desperate look; she hauled Gildas's arm over her shoulders and said, "I'll stay with him."

He almost fell down to where Keiro hung, grabbed him with one hand and clung to him. "It's useless! There's no way out."

"There has to be," Keiro gasped. "Don't we have a Key?"

He wriggled it out and Finn's hand caught it; for a moment they were both holding it. Then Finn snatched it and held it away. He pressed every button, jabbed at the eagle, its sphere, its crown. Nothing. As the Beast lashed under them he shook the Key, swore at it, and felt the warmth of it grow suddenly in his hands, overheating with an ominous whine. With a yelp he juggled it; it burned him.

"Use it!" Keiro yelled. "Melt the rock!"

Finn clamped the Key to the cave side. Instantly it hummed and clicked.

Incarceron screamed. A howl of anguish. Rocks clattered down, Attia shouted from above. As Finn stared, a great white slit unzipped in the wall like a rip in the fabric of the world.

∞

THE WARDEN stood with Claudia at the window and looked down on the torchlit revelry. "You did well," he said gravely. "The Queen is pleased."

"Good." Claudia was so tired, she could barely think.

"Tomorrow, perhaps we . . ." He stopped.

A shrill, urgent bleep. Insistent and loud. Startled, Claudia stared around. "What's that?"

Her father stood very still. Then he reached into his waistcoat pocket and took out his watch, and with a click of his thumb, sprang the gold case open. She saw the handsome dial, the time. Quarter to eleven.

But this was no chime. It was an alarm.

The Warden stared. When he looked up, his eyes were cold and gray. "I have to go. Good night, Claudia. Sleep well."

Astonished, she watched him stride to the door. "Is it . . . is it the Prison?" she said.

He turned, his gaze sharp. "What makes you say that?"

"The alarm . . . I've never heard it before . . ."

He was watching her. She cursed herself. Then he said, "Yes. There seems to be an incident. Don't worry. I'll see to it personally."

The doors closed after him.

For a moment she stayed there, frozen. She stared at the wooden panels; then, as if the stillness galvanized her into action, she grabbed a dark shawl, wrapped it around herself, and flung herself at the door, opening it quickly.

He was well down the gilt corridor, walking fast. As soon as he rounded the corner, she ran after him, breathless, silent on the soft carpets. Her image flickered in dim mirrors.

At the side of a great china vase a curtain swirled; slipping behind it she found herself at the top of a dim flight of spiral stairs. She waited, her heart hammering, watching his dark figure descend below, and she saw he was running, a quick, agitated step. Hurriedly she edged down after him, around and around, one hand on the damp rail, until the gilt walls became brick and then stone, the steps hollowed with use, slimed with green lichen.

It was cold down here, and very dark. Her breath clouded. She shivered and wrapped the shawl tight.

He was going to the Prison.

He was going to Incarceron!

Faint, very far ahead, the alarm was bleeping, loud and urgent, a relentless panic.

These were the wine cellars. They were huge chambers, vaulted, piled with barrels and casks, wiring snaking down their walls, hung with white salts that had oozed from the brickwork. If it was Protocol, it was very convincing.

Peering around a stack of casks, she made herself keep still.

He had come to a gate.

It was green bronze, set deep in the wall, glistening with snail trails, corroded with age. Great rivets studded it. Rusted chains hung across it. With a silent leap of her heart she saw the Havaarna eagle, its outspread wings almost lost under layers of verdigris.

Her father glanced around and she ducked back, breathless. Then he tapped a swift combination into the globe the eagle held; she heard a click.

Chains slid and swung, crashing down.

In a shower of spiderwebs and snails and dust, the gate juddered open.

She leaned out, desperate to see what lay behind, to see Inside, but there was only darkness and a smell, a sour, metallic stink, and she had to dive back hastily as he turned.

When she looked again he was gone, and the gate was closed.

Claudia leaned back on the wet bricks and breathed out a soundless whistle of damp breath.

At last. Finally.

She had found it.

THE ALARM screamed in their teeth, in their nerves, in their bones. Finn thought it would bring on a fit; terrified, he scrambled for the slit, against the icy wind that howled through it.

The Beast was gone. Even as Keiro climbed over Finn and grabbed Gildas, it dissolved; suddenly they were all tumbling in a cascade of fragments, and then they slammed against the wall, a chain of bodies held only by Finn's grip.

He yelled with the agony. "I can't hold you!"

"You bloody will!" Keiro gasped.

Terror stretched him. Keiro's hand slid, an agonizing jerk.

He couldn't do it. His hand scorched.

A shadow fell on him. He thought it was the Beast's head, or a great eagle, but as he twisted in despair and stared up, he saw it swoop in through the slit, humming with contained power, a silver ship, an ancient sailing ship, its sails a patchwork of cobweb, its ropes tangled and dangling over the side.

It loomed above them, and very slowly, a hatch opened in its base. A basket was lowered, swaying on four immense cables, and above it a face looked over the side of the ship, a hideous, gargoyle face, deformed by goggles and a bizarre breathing apparatus.

"Get in," it rasped. "Before I change my mind."

How they did it he had no idea, but in seconds Keiro had tumbled into the wildly rocking basket; Gildas hauled after him. Attia leaped, pausing only for a moment, and then Finn let himself drop, his mind so black with relief that he fell without fear, and didn't feel himself land, until a welcome silence exploded into Keiro's yell in his ear. "Get off me, Finn!"

He struggled up. Attia was bending over him, concerned. "Are you all right?"

". . . Yes."

He wasn't, he knew, but he leaned past her to the edge and he looked over, giddy with the swaying, the icy wind.

They were out of the Cave, above the plain, miles above the City. It lay like a toy on the plain, and from this height they could see the scorch marks and the fumaroles around it, as if the land itself was the skin of the Beast that rumbled beneath, fuming with wrath.

Clouds wisped across, vapors of metallic yellow, a rainbow.

Finn felt Gildas grab him, the old man's voice delirious with joy, snatched away by the wind. "Look up, boy! See! There are Sapienti still, with power!"

He twisted his head. And saw, as the silver ship spiraled upward, a tower so narrow and impossibly high that it seemed like a needle balanced upright on a cloud, its top glimmering with light. He felt his breath frost and condense on the rail, crack and splinter, each ice shard polarized by the tower, each crystal aligned as if by a magnet. Gasping in the thin air, he gripped the old man's arm, shaking with cold and fear, not daring to look down again, seeing only the minute landing place at the needle's tip grow bigger, the slowly revolving globe at its apex.

And yet, high as they were, above them for miles and miles, the night of Incarceron extended into the freezing sky.

⋙◆◆◆⋘

THE HAMMERING woke Jared in a cold sweat of fear.

For a moment he had no idea what it was, and then he heard her whisper, "Jared! Quickly, it's me!"

He sat up and stumbled over, tugging the scanner off the frame, fumbling for the latch. As soon as he lifted it, the door flew open, almost hitting him in the face; then Claudia was inside, breathless and dust-smeared, a filthy shawl around her silk dress.

"What is it?" he gasped. "Claudia, has he found out? Does he know we have the Key?"

"No. No." She had no breath; she plumped down on the bed and bent double, clutching her side.

"Then what?"

She raised her hand, making him wait; after a moment, when she could speak and looked up, he saw her face was lit with triumph.

He stepped back, suddenly wary. "What have you done, Claudia?"

Her smile was bitter. "What I've longed to do for years. I've found the door to his secret. The entrance to Incarceron."

A World That Hangs
in Space

22

> "Where are the leaders?" Sapphique asked.
> "In their fortresses," the swan replied.
> "And the poets?"
> "Lost in dreams of other worlds."
> "And the craftsmen?"
> "Forging machines to challenge the darkness."
> "And the Wise, who made the world?"
> The swan lowered its black neck sadly.
> "Dwindled to crones and sorcerers in towers."
>
> —Sapphique in the Kingdom of Birds

Finn carefully touched one of the spheres.

It showed him his own face, swollen grotesquely in delicate lilac glass. Behind him he saw Attia come through the archway and stare around.

"What is this?" She stood amazed among the bubbles that hung from the ceiling, and he saw how clean she was this morning, her hair scrubbed, the new clothes making her seem younger than ever.

"His laboratory. Look in here."

Some of the spheres contained whole landscapes. In one, a colony of small golden-furred creatures slumbered peacefully or dug in sandy hillocks. Attia spread her hands on it, flat on the glass. "It feels warm."

He nodded. "Did you sleep?"

"A bit. I kept waking up because it was so quiet. You?"

He nodded, not wanting to say that his exhaustion had made him fall onto the small white bed and sleep at once, without even undressing. Though when he had woken this morning, he had found that someone had wrapped the blankets around him, and laid clean clothes on the chair in the bare white room. Had it been Keiro?

"Did you see the man on the ship? Gildas thinks he's a Sapient."

She shook her head. "Not without the facemask. And all he said last night was 'Take those rooms and we'll talk in the morning.'" She glanced over. "It was brave, going back for Keiro."

They were silent for a while. He came around and stood next to her, and as they watched the animals scratch and roll, they became aware that beyond this globe was a whole chamber of glass worlds, aqua-green and gold and pale blue, each hanging from a fine chain, some tinier than a fist, others vast as halls, where birds flew, or fish swam, or billions of insects clouded and swarmed.

"It's as if he's made cages for them all," she said quietly. "I hope he hasn't got one for us." Then, catching the sudden jerk of his reflection, "What is it? Finn?"

"Nothing." His hands left hot smears on the sphere as he leaned on it.

"You saw something." Attia's eyes were wide. "Was it the stars, Finn? Are there really millions of them? Do they gather and sing in the darkness?"

Stupidly, he didn't want to disappoint her. He said, "I saw . . . I saw a lake in front of a great building. It was night. Lanterns were floating on the water, little paper lanterns each with a candle inside so they looked blue and green and scarlet. There were boats on the lake and I was in one of them." He rubbed his face. "I was there, Attia. I was leaning over the side and tried to touch my reflection in the water, and yes, there were stars. And they were angry because my sleeve got wet."

"The stars?" She came closer.

"No. The people."

"What people? Who were they, Finn?"

He tried. There was a scent. A shadow.

"A woman," he said. "She was angry."

It hurt. Remembering hurt. It triggered flashes of light; he closed his eyes against them, sweating, his mouth dry.

"Don't." Anxious, she reached out to him, the welts red on her wrists where the chains had chafed the skin. "Don't upset yourself."

He rubbed his face with his sleeve and the room was still with a quiet he had not known since the cell where he had been born. Awkwardly he muttered, "Is Keiro still asleep?"

"Oh him!" She scowled. "Who cares?"

He watched her wander between the spheres. "You can't dislike him that much. You stuck with him in the City."

She was silent, so he said, "How did you manage to follow us?"

"It wasn't easy." She tightened her lips. "We heard rumors about the Tribute, so he said we should steal a flamethrower. I was the one who had to cause a diversion so he could get it. Not that I got any thanks."

Finn laughed. "That's Keiro. He never thanks anyone." Splaying his hands on the sphere, he leaned his forehead on it and the reptiles inside stared back impassively. "I knew he'd come. Gildas said no, but Keiro would never betray me."

She made no answer but he became aware that her silence was charged with an odd tension; when he looked up, she was watching him with something like anger. It burst out of her abruptly. "You're so wrong, Finn! Can't you see what he's like? He would have left you easily, just taken the Key and gone and not even cared!"

"No," he said, surprised.

"Yes!" She faced up to him, the bruises livid in the white skin of her face. "Because it was only the girl's threat that made him stay."

He felt cold. "What girl?"

"Claudia."

"He spoke to her!"

"She threatened him. 'Find Finn,' she said, 'or the Key will be useless to you.' She was really angry with him." Attia shrugged lightly. "It's her you should thank."

He wouldn't believe it.

There was no way he would.

"Keiro would have come." His voice was low and stubborn. "I know how he seems, that he doesn't care about anyone, but I know him. We've fought together. We took the oath."

She shook her head. "You're too trusting, Finn. You must have been born Outside, because you don't fit here."

Then, hearing footsteps, she said quickly, "Ask him for the Key. Ask him. You'll see."

Keiro wandered into the room and whistled. He was wearing a doublet of dark blue, his hair wet, and he was still eating an apple from the plate in their room, the last two skull-rings gleaming on his fingers. "So this is where you are!" He turned a complete circle. "And this is a Sapient's tower. Beats the old man's cage."

"I'm glad you think so." To Finn's dismay one of the largest spheres clicked open and a stranger stepped out, followed by Gildas. He wondered how much they had overheard, and how there could be steps inside the sphere leading down, but before he was sure about that, it clicked shut and was just a glimmer among the hundreds of others.

Gildas wore a Sapient's robe of iridescent greens. His sharp face was washed, his white beard trimmed. He looked different,

Finn thought. Some of the hunger had gone; when he spoke his voice was not querulous but had a new gravity.

"This is Blaize," he said. And then, softly, "Blaize Sapiens."

The tall man bowed his head slightly. "Welcome to my Chamber of Worlds."

They stared at him. Without the breathing mask, his face was remarkable, mottled with sores and spots and acid burns, his thin straggle of hair tied back in a greasy ribbon.

Under the Sapient's coat he wore ancient knee breeches stained with chemicals, and a ruffled shirt that perhaps had once been white.

For a moment no one spoke. Then, to Finn's surprise it was Attia who said, "We have to thank you, Master, for saving us. We would have died."

"Ah . . . well. Yes." He looked at her, his smile lopsided and awkward. "That is indeed true. I thought I had better come down."

"Why?" Keiro's voice was cool.

The Sapient turned. "I don't quite understand . . . ?"

"Why bother? To save us? Do we have something you need?"

Gildas frowned. "This is Keiro, Master. The one with no manners."

Keiro snorted. "Don't tell me he doesn't know about the Key." He bit the apple, a loud crunch in the silence.

Blaize turned to Finn. "And you must be the Starseer." His

eyes looked at Finn with unnerving scrutiny. "My colleague tells me Sapphique sent this Key to you, and that it will lead you Outside. That you believe you came from Outside."

"I did."

"You remember?"

"No. I just . . . believe."

For a moment the man gazed at him, one thin hand absently scratching a sore on his cheek. Then he said, "Regretfully, I have to tell you that you are mistaken."

Gildas turned in astonishment; Attia stared.

Annoyed, Finn said, "What do you mean?"

"I mean you didn't come from Outside. No one has ever come from Outside. Because, you see, there is no Outside."

For a moment the silence in the room was appalled, full of disbelief. Then Keiro laughed softly and threw the apple core on the stone slabs of the floor. He came over, took out the Key, and slapped it down next to the glass sphere. "All right, Wise One. If there's no Outside, what's this for?"

Blaize reached out and picked it up. He turned it carelessly and calmly. "Ah yes. I have heard of such devices. Perhaps the original Sapienti invented them. There is a legend that Lord Calliston made one in secret and died before he could try it. It renders the user invisible to the Eyes, and no doubt has other abilities. But it cannot let you out."

Gently he placed the crystal on the table. Gildas glared at him. "Brother, this is folly! We all know Sapphique himself—"

"We know nothing about Sapphique but a muddle of tales and legends. Those fools down there in the City, whose doings I watch to relieve my boredom, they invent new tales of Sapphique every year." He folded his arms, his gray eyes relentless. "Men love to make stories, brother. They love to dream. They dream that the world is deep underground, and if we could journey up we would find the way out, a trapdoor into a land where the sky is blue and the land breeds corn and honey and there is no pain. Or that there are nine circles of the Prison surrounding its center, and if we go deep into them we find the heart of Incarceron, its living being, and we will emerge through it into another world." He shook his head. "Legends. Nothing more."

Finn was shocked. He glanced at Gildas; the old man seemed stricken, then anger burst out of him. "How can you say this?" he snapped. "You, a Sapient? I thought when I saw what you were, that our struggles would be easier, that you'd understand . . ."

"I do, believe me."

"Then how can you say there is no Outside?"

"Because I have seen."

His voice was so somber and heavy with despair that even Keiro stopped pacing up and down and stared at him. Beside Finn, Attia shivered. "How?" she whispered.

The Sapient pointed to a sphere, a black, empty shell. "There. The experiment took me decades, but I was determined. My sensors penetrated metal and skin, bone and wire. I felt my way through miles of Incarceron, its halls and corridors, its seas, its rivers. Like you, I believed." He laughed harshly, biting the worn nails of his hand. "And yes, I found Outside, in a way." He turned and touched the controls, and the sphere lit. "I found this."

They saw an image in the darkness. A sphere within the sphere, a globe of blue metal. It hung in the everlasting blackness of space, alone, silent.

"This is Incarceron." Blaize jabbed a finger at it. "And we live inside it. A world. Constructed, or grown, who knows. But alone, in a vastness, a vacuum. In nothing. There is Nothing outside." He shrugged. "I am sorry. I do not wish to destroy the dreams of your lifetime. But there is nowhere else to go."

Finn couldn't breathe. It was as if the bleak words drew the life out of him. He stared at the globe and felt Keiro come close behind him, sensed his oathbrother's warmth and energy, and it comforted him. But it was Gildas who surprised them all.

He laughed. A gruff, throaty roar of scorn. Drawing himself upright, he turned on Blaize and glared at him. "And you call yourself Wise! Fooled by the Prison's malice, more like. It shows you lies and you believe them, and live up here above men and despise them. Worse than a fool!" He strode up to the taller man; Finn took a quick step after him. He knew the old man's temper.

But Gildas stabbed the air with his knotty finger, and his

voice was hard and low. "How dare you stand there and deny me my hope and these their chance of life. How dare you tell me Sapphique is a dream, that the Prison is all there is!"

"Because it's true," Blaize said.

Gildas wrenched out of Finn's grip. "Liar! You're no Sapient. And you forget. We've seen Outsiders."

"Yes!" Attia said. "And spoken to them."

Blaize paused. He said, "Spoken to them?"

For a moment it almost seemed his certainty was shaken. He linked his fingers together and his voice was tight. "Spoken to whom? Who are they?"

Everyone looked at Finn, so he said, "A girl called Claudia. And a man. She calls him Jared."

There was a second of silence. Keiro said, "So explain that."

Blaize turned his back. But almost at once he swung around and his face was grave. "I have no wish to upset you. But you've seen a girl and a man. How do you know where they are?"

Finn said, "They're not here."

"No?" Blaize glanced at him quickly, his pocked face tipped sideways. "How do you know? Have you not thought that they also may be in Incarceron? In some other Wing, some distant level where life seems different, where they don't even know they are imprisoned? Think, boy! This quest for Escape will become a folly that will eat up your life. You will spend years in hopeless traveling, searching, and all for nothing! Find a place to live, learn peace instead. Forget the stars."

His voice murmured among the glass spheres, high into the timbered rafters of the roof. Dismayed, barely hearing Gildas's angry outburst, Finn faced the window and stood there, staring out through the sealed glass at the drifting clouds of Incarceron's stratosphere, too high for birds, the icy landscape miles below, the distant hills and dark slopes that might be walls beyond his sight.

His own fear terrified him.

If this was true, there was no Escape, from here or from himself . . .

He was Finn and always would be, with no past and no future and there was nowhere to go back to. No one else that he had once been.

Gildas and Attia were angry; they were arguing, but Keiro's cool comment sliced through the noise and silenced everyone. "Why don't we ask them?" he said. He picked the Key up and touched the controls; turning quickly, Finn saw how adept at it he was.

"There's no point," Blaize said rapidly.

"For us there is."

"Then I will leave you to speak to your friends." Blaize turned. "I have no wish to do so. Feel free to treat the tower as your home. Eat, rest. Think about what I've said."

He walked between the spheres and out of the door, the robe flapping about his stained clothes, a faint scent of acid and something else, something sweet, drifting behind him.

As soon as he was gone Gildas swore, long and bitterly.

Keiro grinned. "You learned something useful from the Comitatus then."

"To think that after all these years I should find a Sapient and he should be so weak!" The old man sounded sick with disgust. Then he thrust out his hand. "Give me that Key."

"No need." Keiro placed it hastily on the table and stepped back. "It's working."

The familiar hum rose; the holo-image sprang out and cleared to a circle of light. Today it seemed even brighter than before, as if they were nearer its source, or its power had grown. Into it, as close as if she were among them, Claudia stepped. Her eyes were bright, her face alert. Finn almost felt he could reach out and touch her.

"They found you," she said.

"Yes," he whispered.

"I'm so pleased."

Jared was with her, one arm leaning against what seemed like a tree. And suddenly Finn realized they were sitting in a field, or a garden, and the light in that place was a glorious gold.

Gildas shouldered past him. "Master," he said curtly. "You are a Sapient?"

"I am." Jared stood and bowed formally. "As are you, I see."

"For these fifty years, son. Before you were born. Now answer me three questions and answer them true. Are you Outside Incarceron?"

Claudia stared. Jared nodded slowly. "Yes."

"How do you know?"

"Because this is a palace, not a prison. Because the sun is above us, and the stars at night. Because Claudia has discovered the gate that leads to the Prison . . ."

"Have you?" Finn gasped.

But before she could answer, Gildas snapped, "One thing more. If you are Outside, where is Sapphique? What did he do when he got out there? When will he return to release us?"

There were flowers in the garden, brilliant red poppies.

Jared looked at Claudia, and in the silence between them a bee buzzed on the petals, a small murmur that made Finn shiver with lost memory.

Then Jared stood and came forward, so close, he and Gildas were face-to-face. "Master," he said courteously. "Forgive me for my ignorance. For my curiosity. Forgive me if this seems a stupid question. But who is Sapphique?"

23

Nothing has changed, or will change.
So we must change it.

—*The Steel Wolves*

Finn thought the bee would come out of the nimbus of gold and land on him. As it buzzed near his hand, he jerked back and it darted away.

He looked at Gildas. The old man had almost staggered; Attia was helping him sit, and Jared was reaching his own hand out as if to help, dismay on his face. He glanced at Claudia; Finn heard his murmur. "I shouldn't have asked. The Experiment . . ."

"Sapphique Escaped." Keiro pulled a bench over and sat in the hologlow, its light rich on his red coat. "He got out. He's the only one that ever did. That's the legend."

"No legend," Gildas snapped hoarsely. He looked up. "You really don't know? I thought . . . that out there he would be a great man . . . a king."

Claudia said, "No. At least . . . Well, we could do some research. He may have gone into hiding. Things here aren't perfect either." She stood quickly. "Perhaps you don't know, but people here believe Incarceron to be a wonderful place. A paradise."

They stared at her.

She saw the startled disbelief in their faces, Keiro's changing almost instantly to an amused, acid grin. "Fabulous," he murmured.

So she told them. She told them about the Experiment, her father, the sealed enigma of the Prison. And then she told them about Giles. Jared said, "Claudia . . ." but she waved a hand at him and went on quickly, pacing on the astonishingly green grass. "They didn't kill him, we know that. They hid him. And I think they hid him in there. I think he's you."

She turned and faced them, and Keiro said, "Are you saying . . ." and then stopped and stared up at his oathbrother. "Finn? A prince?" He laughed, wondering. "Are you crazy?"

Finn hugged himself. He was shaking, he knew, and that rarely lost bewilderment was back in the corner of his mind, glimmers of things gone as fast as shadows in dim mirrors.

"You look like him," Claudia said firmly. "There are no photographs allowed now, it's not Protocol, but the old man had a painting." She held it up, slipping off the blue bag. "Look."

Attia breathed in.

Finn shivered.

The child's hair was shining and his face lit with innocent happiness. Impossible health radiated from him. His tunic was cloth of gold, his skin chubby and pink. A tiny eagle seared his wrist.

Finn stepped closer. He reached out and she lifted the miniature to him, and his fingers closed around the gilt frame; for a moment he felt he had hold of it, that he touched it. And then his fingertips met on nothing and he knew that it was far away, farther than he could imagine. And long ago.

"There was an old man," Claudia said. "Bartlett. He looked after you."

He stared at her. His emptiness scared them both.

"Queen Sia then? Your stepmother, she must have hated you. Caspar, your half brother? Your father, the King, who died. You must remember!"

He wanted to. He wanted to drag them out of the blackness of his mind, but there was nothing there. Keiro was standing and Gildas had his arm, but all he could see was Claudia, her eager, fierce gaze on him, willing him to remember. "We were betrothed. When you were seven there was a big feast. A great celebration."

"Leave him alone," Attia snapped. "Leave him."

Claudia stepped closer. She stretched her hand out and tried to touch his wrist. "Look at it, Finn. They couldn't take it away. It proves who you are."

"It proves nothing!" Attia turned so suddenly, Claudia jerked back. The girl's fists were clenched, her bruised face white. "Stop tormenting him! If you loved him you'd stop! Can't you see it hurts him and he can't remember? You don't really care if it's him, if he's Giles. All you want is not to marry this Caspar!"

In the shocked silence Finn breathed hard. Keiro pushed

him onto the bench; his knees gave way and he sat quickly.

Claudia was pale. She took a step back, but her eyes never left Attia. Then she said, "Actually that's not true. I want the real King. The true Heir, even if he is of the Havaarna. And I want to get you out of that place. All of you."

Jared came close and crouched. "Are you all right?"

Finn nodded. His mind was fogged; he rubbed his face with his hands.

"He gets like this," Keiro said. "And worse."

"It may be the treatment they gave him." The Sapient's dark eyes met Gildas's. "They must have given him drugs to make him forget. Have you tried any antidotes, Master, any therapies?"

"Our medicines are limited," Gildas growled. "I use powdered tumentine and a decoction of poppy. And once harestooth, but it made him sick."

Jared looked politely appalled. Claudia knew by his face that such things were so primitive the Sapienti here had all but forgotten them. All at once she felt furious with frustration; she wanted to reach in and drag Finn out, to break down the invisible barrier. But that was no use, so she made herself say calmly, "I've decided what to do. I'm coming in. Through the gate."

"How does that help us?" Keiro asked, watching Finn.

It was Jared who answered. "I've made a careful study of the Key. From what I can see, our ability to contact each other is changing. The image is becoming clearer and more focused.

This may be because Claudia and I have come to Court; we're nearer to you, and the Key may register this. It may help you navigate toward the gate."

"I thought there were maps." Keiro eyed Claudia. "The Princess here said so."

Claudia sighed, impatient. "I lied."

She looked straight at him; his blue eyes were sharp as ice.

"But," Jared went on hastily, "there are problems. There is a strange . . . discontinuity that puzzles me. The Key takes too long to show us each other; each time it seems to be adjusting some physical or temporal parameter . . . as if our worlds are somehow misaligned . . ."

Keiro looked scornful; Finn knew he thought all this was a waste of time. From the bench he lifted his head and said quietly, "But you don't think, Master, do you, that Incarceron is another world? That it floats free in space, far from Earth."

Jared stared. Then he said gently, "No, I don't. A fascinating theory."

"Who told you that?" Claudia snapped.

"It doesn't matter." Unsteadily, Finn stood. He looked at Claudia. "In this Court of yours, there's a lake, isn't there? Where we floated lanterns with candles inside?"

The poppies around her were red tissue in the sun. "Yes," she said.

"And on my birthday cake, tiny silver balls."

Claudia was so still, she could hardly breathe.

And then as he stared at her in unbearable tension her eyes went wide; she turned, yelled, "Jared! Turn it off! *Turn it off!*"

And in the dark room of spheres instantly there was only darkness, and a strange tilted giddiness, and a scent of roses.

Keiro reached his right hand carefully into the empty space where the holo-image had been. Sparks spat; he jerked back, swearing.

"Something scared them," Attia breathed.

Gildas frowned. "Not something. Someone."

SHE HAD smelled him. A sweet, unmistakable perfume that she realized now had been there for a long time, that she had known but ignored, caught up in the tension of the moment. Now, as she faced the blazing border of lavender and delphiniums and roses, she felt Jared behind her rise slowly to his feet, heard his small breath of dismay as he registered it too.

"Come out," she said icily.

He was behind the rose arch. He stepped from it reluctantly, the peach silk of his suit soft as petals.

For a moment none of them spoke.

Then Evian smiled an embarrassed smile.

"How much did you hear?" Claudia demanded, hands on hips.

He took out a handkerchief and wiped sweat from his face. "Quite too much, I'm afraid, my dear."

"Stop the act." She was furious.

He glanced at Jared and then, curiously at the Key. "That is an amazing device. If we had had any idea it existed, we would have moved heaven and earth to find it."

She hissed out a breath of anger and turned away. To her back he said shrewdly, "You know what it means, if that boy is really Giles."

She didn't answer.

"It means that we have a figurehead for our coup. More than that, a righteous cause. As you so thrillingly said, the true Heir. I gather this was the information you promised me?"

"Yes." She turned and saw his fascinated gaze, and it chilled her as it had before. "But listen, Evian. We're doing this my way. First of all I'm going through that gate."

"Not alone."

"No," Jared said swiftly. "With me."

She shot him a startled look. "Master . . ."

"Together, Claudia. Or not at all."

A trumpet rang out in the Palace. She glanced toward the building in annoyance. "All right. But there's no need for assassinations, don't you see? If the people understand that Giles is alive, if we show him to them, surely the Queen will never be able to deny it . . ."

Her voice trailed off as she looked at them. Jared was playing unhappily with a small white flower from the grass; rubbing its perfume between his fingers. He wouldn't look at her. Evian did, but his small eyes were almost pitying. "Claudia," he said, "are you such an innocent still?" He came over to her, no taller than she was, sweating in the warm sun. "The people will never see Giles. She would not let that happen. You and he would be killed mercilessly, like the old man I spoke of. Jared too, and anyone else they thought knew about the plot."

She folded her arms, feeling her face go hot. She felt humiliated, like a small child being told off kindly, to make it worse. Because, of course, he was right.

"They are the ones who must be killed." Evian's voice was low and hard. "They must be removed. We are decided on that. And we are ready to act."

She stared up at him. "No."

"Yes. Very soon now."

Jared dropped the flower and turned his head. He looked very pale. "You must at least wait until after the wedding."

"The wedding is in two days. As soon as it's over we will move. It's best if neither of you know any details . . ." He raised a hand to forestall her. "Please, Claudia, don't even ask me. If it should go wrong, if you are questioned, this way you can give nothing away. You won't know the time, or the place, or the method. You have no idea who the Steel Wolves are. You cannot be blamed."

By no one but herself, she thought bitterly. Caspar was a greedy little tyrant and would grow worse. The Queen a silky murderess. They would always enforce Protocol.

They would never change. And yet she didn't want their blood on her hands.

The trumpet rang out again, urgent. "I have to go," she said. "The Queen is hunting and I have to be there."

Evian nodded and turned away, but before he had taken two steps she forced the words out. "Wait. One thing."

The peach silk shimmered. A butterfly fluttered at his shoulder, curious.

"My father. What about my father?"

In the beautiful blue sky a flutter of pigeons rose from one of the Palace's thousand towers. Evian did not turn and his voice was so quiet she barely heard it. "He is dangerous. He is implicated."

"Don't hurt him."

"Claudia . . ."

"Don't." She clenched her fists. "He is not to be killed. Promise me now. Swear. Or I go to the Queen this minute and tell her everything."

That made him turn, startled. "You wouldn't . . ."

"You don't know me."

Iron-cold she faced him. Only her stubbornness would keep a knife out of her father's heart. She knew he was her enemy, her subtle foe, her cold opponent over the chessboard. But he was still her father.

Evian flashed a glance at Jared, then breathed out, a long uneasy breath. "Very well."

"Swear." She put her hand out and grabbed his and held it tight; it was hot and clammy. "With Jared as witness."

Reluctant, he let her raise their clasped fingers. Jared put his delicate hand on top.

"I swear. As I am a lord of the Realm and a devotee of the Nine-Fingered One." Lord Evian's small gray eyes were pale in the sunlight. "The Warden of Incarceron will not be killed."

She nodded. "Thank you."

They watched him detach his hand and walk away, wiping his fingers fastidiously with a silk handkerchief, disappearing down the greenness of the lime walk.

As soon as he was gone, Claudia sat on the grass and clutched her knees under the blue dress. "Oh, Master. What a mess."

Jared seemed barely to be listening. He shifted restlessly about, as if he was stiff. Then he stopped so abruptly, she thought a bee had stung him. "Who's the Nine-Fingered One?"

"What?"

"That was what Evian said." He turned, and there was a tension in his dark eyes she knew well, like the burning obsessions that sometimes kept him at his experiments for days and nights. "Have you ever heard of such a cult before?"

Brutally, she shrugged. "No. And I don't have time to care. Listen. Tonight, after the banquet, the Queen holds a meeting of her Council, a great Synod, to prepare the deeds of the wedding and the succession. They'll be there, Caspar and the

Warden and his secretary and anyone of importance. And they won't be able to leave."

"Not you?"

She shrugged. "Who am I, Master? A pawn on the board." She laughed, the laugh she knew he hated, hard and bitter. "So that's when we go into Incarceron. And this time we take no chances."

Jared nodded mildly. His face had fallen, but the edge of excitement still lingered. "I'm glad you said we, Claudia," he murmured.

She looked up. "I'm afraid for you," she said simply. "Whatever happens."

He nodded. "That makes two of us."

They were silent a moment.

"The Queen will be waiting."

But she made no move to go, and when he looked at her, her face was taut and distant. "That girl Attia. She was jealous. She was jealous of me."

"Yes. They may be close, Finn and his friends."

Claudia shrugged. She stood and brushed pollen from her dress. "Well. We'll soon find out."

24

Do you seek the key to Incarceron?
Look inside yourself. It has always been
hidden there.
                        —*The Mirror of Dreams to Sapphique*

The Sapient's tower was odd, Finn thought.

He and Keiro and Attia had taken the man at his word, and spent the day exploring all over it, and there were things about it that puzzled them.

"The food, for instance." Keiro picked a small green fruit from the bowl and sniffed it cautiously. "This is grown, but where? We're miles in the sky and there's no way down. Don't tell me he takes his silver ship to market."

They knew there was no way down because the basement rooms where the beds were had been built on the bare rock. Small stalagmites rose up between the furniture, icicles of calcium hung from the ceiling, sediments laid down over the century and a half of the Prison's life, though Finn had thought it took longer, millennia even, for such things to form.

As he wandered behind Attia from kitchen to storeroom to observatory he let himself slip for a moment into a daydream of fascinating horror; that Incarceron was indeed a world, ancient and alive, that he was a microscopic creature inside it, tiny as a bacterium, and that Claudia too was here, that even Sapphique was a dream dreamed by Prisoners who could not face the dread of there being no Escape.

"And then the books!" Keiro thrust the door to the library open and gazed at them all in disgust. "Who needs so many books? Who could ever be bothered to read them?"

Finn moved past him. Keiro could hardly read his own name, and was proud of it. He had once gotten into a fight about some supposed insult about him scribbled on a wall by one of Jormanric's bullies; Keiro had come out of the fight alive but badly beaten. Finn remembered being unable to tell him that the graffiti was harmless, even grudgingly admiring.

Finn could read. He had no idea who taught him, but he could read even better than Gildas, who muttered the words half aloud and had only seen about a dozen books in his life. The Sapient was here now, sitting at the desk in the library's heart, his knobbly hands turning the pages of a great codex bound in leather, his eyes close to the handwritten text.

Around him, on shelves that reached to the shadowy ceiling, Blaize's library was immense, towers of heavy volumes all numbered in gold and bound in green and maroon.

Gildas raised his head. They had expected him to be in awe, but his voice was acid. "Books? There are no books here, boy."

Keiro snorted. "Your eyes are worse than you think."

Impatiently, the old man shook his head. "These are useless.

Look at them. Names, numbers. They tell us nothing."

Attia took a book from the nearest shelf and opened it, and Finn looked over her shoulder. It was thick with dust, and the edges of the pages were eaten away, so dry they fell into flakes. On the page was a list of names:

MARCION

MASCUS

MASCUS ATTOR

MATTHEUS PRIME

MATTHEUS UMRA

each followed by a number. A long, eight-digit number.

"Prisoners?" Finn said.

"Apparently. Lists of names. Volumes of them. For every Wing, every Level, going back centuries."

Beside each name was a small square image of a face. Attia touched one and almost dropped the book. Finn gave a gasp, which brought Keiro over to the table, kneeling up behind them.

"Well, well," he said.

For each name a series of images blinked rapidly over the page, appearing and disappearing in quick succession, until Attia touched one with her small fingertip and it froze, opening into a full-length picture of a hunchbacked man in a yellow coat that filled the page. When she let go, the pictures rippled again, hundreds of images of the same man, in a street, traveling, talking by a fire, asleep, his whole life catalogued there, his body growing gradually older before their eyes, bending, on a stick now, begging, leprous with some terrible sickness.

And then nothing.

Finn said quietly, "The Eyes. They must record as well as watch."

"So how has this Blaize got all this?" Keiro raised his head in sudden shock. "Do you think I'm in here?" Without waiting for an answer he crossed to the shelf marked *K*, found a long ladder, and set it against the books, climbing easily up. He began to take the books out and shove them back, impatient.

Attia had crossed to the *A* section and Gildas was busy reading, so Finn found the letter *F* and looked for himself.

FIMENON

FIMMA

FIMMIA

FIMOS NEPOS

FINARA

His fingers shook as he turned the page, tracing down until he found it.

FINN

He stared at it. There were sixteen Finns, but his was the last. The number was there, in all its black familiarity, the number that had been on his overalls in the cell, that he had learned by heart. Next to it was a small image, two triangles superimposed, one of them inverted. A star. Feeling almost sick with anxiety, he touched it.

Images rippled. Himself crawling in the white tunnel.

He stopped it instantly.

There he was, looking younger, cleaner, his face a mask of fear and tearful determination. It hurt him to look at it. He tried to turn back, but this was the first image; there was nothing before.

Nothing.

His heart thudded. He scrolled on slowly.

He and Keiro. Images of the Comitatus. Himself fighting, eating, sleeping. Once, laughing. Growing, changing. Losing something. He almost thought he could see it going, the ever-changing images showing himself becoming someone harder, watchful, scowling, always there in the background of Keiro's quarrels and schemes. One image showed him in a fit, and he gazed in horrified disgust at his curled, convulsed body, his contorted face. Quickly he let the pictures run on, almost too fast to see, until he jabbed down and held them still.

The ambush.

He saw himself frozen, half out of the chains, grabbing the Maestra's arm. She must have just realized what a trap she was in; her face was caught in a strange, hurt, almost bruised look, her smile already stiffening.

If there was more he didn't want to see it.

He slapped the book shut, the sound loud in the silent room, making Gildas grunt and Attia look over.

"Find anything?" she said.

He shrugged. "Nothing I didn't know. What about you?" He noticed she had left the *A* section and was up among the *C*'s. "Why there?"

"What Blaize said about no Outside. I thought I'd look up Claudia."

He went cold. "And?"

She was holding the book, a big green volume. She closed it quickly and turned, shoving it back into the shelf. "Nothing. He's wrong. She's not in Incarceron."

There was something subdued about her voice, but before he could think about it Keiro's hiss of wrath jerked him around.

"He's got everything about me in here! Everything!"

Finn knew that Keiro had been orphaned as a baby and had grown up in the gang of filthy urchins that always seemed to be hanging around the Comitatus; warriors' by-blows, children of women they'd killed, kids who nobody knew. It would have been a tooth-and-nail struggle to eat and survive and keep a face as unmarked as Keiro's in that ferocious rabble. Maybe that was why his oathbrother looked so alarmed. He too closed the book with a clap.

"Forget your petty histories." Gildas looked up, his sharp face lit. "Come and read a real book. This is the journal of one Lord Calliston, the one they called the Steel Wolf. He is said to have been the first Prisoner." He turned a page. "It's all here, the Coming of the Sapienti, the first convicts, the establishment of the New Order. They seem to have been relatively few, and they spoke to the Prison in those days as they spoke to each other."

Now he did sound awed.

They crowded around and saw that the book was smaller than the others and the text truly handwritten, with some scratchy pen. Gildas tapped the page. "The girl was right. They set the Prison up as a place to dump all their problems, but there was a definite hope of creating a perfect society. According to this we should have all been serene philosophers long ago. Look here."

He read aloud, in his rasping voice.

"Everything was prepared for, every eventuality covered. We have nutritious food, free education, medical care better than Outside, now that the Protocol rules there. We have the discipline of the Prison, that invisible being that watches and punishes and rules.

"And yet.

"Things decay. Dissident groups are forming; territory is disputed. Marriages and feuds develop. Already two Sapienti have led their followers away to live in isolation, claiming they fear the murderers and thieves will never change, that a man has been killed, a child attacked. Last week two men came to blows over a woman. The Prison intervened. Since then neither of them has been seen.

"I believe they are dead and that Incarceron has integrated them into its systems. There was no provision for the death penalty, but the Prison is in charge now. It is thinking for itself."

In the silence Keiro said, "Did they really think it would work?"

After a moment Gildas turned the page. The whisper was loud in the stillness. "It seems so. He is not clear about what went wrong. Perhaps some unplanned element entered and tipped the balance, by just a remark, a small act, so that the flaw in their perfect ecosystem gradually grew and destroyed it. Perhaps Incarceron itself malfunctioned, became a tyrant—that certainly happened, but was it cause or effect? And then there's this."

He pointed out the words as he read them, and Finn, leaning forward, saw that they were underlined, the page grubby, as if someone else had fingered them over and over.

"*. . . or is it that man contains within himself the seeds of evil? That even if he is placed in a paradise perfectly formed for him he will poison it, slowly, with his own jealousies and desires? I fear it may be that we blame the Prison for our own corruption. And I do not except myself, for I too am one who has killed and looked only to my own gain.*"

In the vast silent room only motes of dust fell through the slant of light from the roof.

Gildas closed the book. He looked up at Finn and his face was gray. "We shouldn't stay here," he said heavily. "This is a place where dust gathers and doubt enters the heart. We should go, Finn. This is not a refuge. It's a trap."

A footstep in dust made them look up. Blaize stood on

the gallery that circled the skylight, gazing down at them, his hands tight on the rail.

"You need rest," he said calmly. "Besides, there is no way down from here. Until I decide to take you."

∞∞∞∞

CLAUDIA HAD been meticulous; scanners pre-placed in all the cellars, holo-images of herself and Jared sleeping peacefully in their beds, a hefty bribe to the under-steward to learn the duration of the debate, the number of clauses in the marriage treaty, the time it would all take.

Finally she had seen Evian and told him to argue about anything. As long as her father remained in the Great Chamber until well past midnight.

Slipping between the casks and barrels in her dark clothes, she felt like a shadow released from the endless banquet upstairs, the polite banter, the Queen's red-lipped cloying intimacies, the way she clutched at Claudia's hand and held it so tightly, thrilling herself with how they would be so happy, the palaces they would build, the hunts, the dances, the dresses. Caspar had glowered at her, drinking too much wine and escaping as soon as he could to meet some serving girl. And her father, grave and poised in his black frockcoat and gleaming boots, had caught her eye once down the long table, a swift glance between the candles and flowers.

Did he guess she had some plan?

There was no time to fret now. As she ducked under a snag

313

of cobweb she straightened up into a tall figure and nearly screamed with shock.

He grabbed her. "Sorry, Claudia."

Jared wore dark clothes too. She glared at him. "God, you gave me a fright! Have you got everything?"

"Yes." He was pale, his eyes dark-shadowed.

"Your medication?"

"Everything." He forced a wan smile. "Anyone would think I was the pupil here."

She smiled back, wanting to cheer him. "It will be all right. We have to look, Master. We have to see Inside."

He nodded. "Hurry then."

She led him through the vaulted halls. Tonight the bricks seemed damper than before, the exhalations of the salted walls a fetid air that clouded their breathing.

The gate seemed higher, and as she came near to it, Claudia saw that the chains were back across, each metal link thicker than her arm. But it was the snails that made her shiver: fat, large creatures, their silvery trails crisscrossing the condensation on the metal as if they had bred down here for centuries.

"Yuck." She pulled one off; it came away with a soft plop and she threw it down. "This is it. He put a combination into the lock."

The Havaarna eagle spread wide wings. In the globe it held were seven small circular hollows; she was about to touch them when Jared caught her fingers.

"No! If the wrong combination goes in, alarms will go off. Or worse, we may be trapped. This must be done carefully, Claudia."

He pulled out the small scanner and began, very gently, to take readings and adjust them, crouching among the rusted chains.

Impatient, she went back, checked the cellars, returned.

"Hurry, Master."

"I can't hurry this." He was absorbed, his fingers moving gently.

After long minutes she was almost sick with impatience. She took the Key out, looked at it behind his back. "Do you think . . . ?"

"Wait, Claudia. I'm almost certain of the first number."

It could take hours. There was a disc on the door; it gleamed greenish bronze, slightly brighter than the surrounding metal. Over his head, she reached out and slid it aside.

A keyhole.

Shaped like the crystal, hexagonal.

She reached out and fitted the Key into it.

Instantly it leaped out of her fingers.

With a great crack that made her screech and made Jared jump back in terror, the Key turned by itself. Chains crashed. Rust fell. The gate shuddered ajar.

Scrambling up, Jared was frantically checking all the alarms; he gasped, "Claudia, that was so stupid!" but she didn't care, she was laughing because it was open, the gate, the Prison. She had unlocked Incarceron.

The last chain slid.

The cellars rang with echoes.

Jared waited until every last whisper of noise was stilled.

"Well?" she said.

"No one coming. Everything up there is normal." He wiped sweat from his forehead with one hand. "We must be too far down for them to hear. More than we deserve, Claudia."

She shrugged. "I deserve to find Finn. And he deserves to be free."

They stared at the dark slit, waiting. She half expected a crowd of Prisoners to burst through.

But nothing happened, so she stepped forward and opened the gate.

And looked Inside.

25

*I remember a story of a girl in Paradise
who ate an apple once. Some wise Sapient
gave it to her. Because of it she saw things
differently. What had seemed gold coins were
dead leaves. Rich clothes were rags of cobweb.
And she saw there was a wall around the
world, with a locked gate.*

*I am growing weak. The others are all
dead. I have finished the key but no longer
dare to use it.*

—Lord Calliston's Diary

It was impossible.

She stood frozen, felt hope shatter inside her.

She had expected dark corridors, a maze of cells, stone passageways running with rats and damp.

Not this.

Behind its oddly tilted entrance the white room was a perfect copy of her father's study. Its machines hummed efficiently, its single desk and chair stood uncluttered in the strip of light from the ceiling.

She let out a breath of despair. "It's exactly the same!"

Jared was scanning carefully. "The Warden is a man of

meticulous tastes." He lowered the device and she saw from his face he was as stunned as she was. "Claudia, now the gate is open, I can tell you that there is no Prison below us, no underground labyrinth. This room is all there is."

Appalled, she shook her head. Then she stepped in.

Immediately she felt the same effect as before; that peculiar blurring and clicking, the floor seeming to even out under her feet, the walls to grow straighter. Even the air seemed different in the room, cooler and drier, not the damp exhalations of the cellars.

Turning back she watched Jared.

"Now that was very strange," he said. "That was a spatial shift. As I said before, as if the room and the cellar are not quite . . . adjacent."

He stepped in after her, and she saw how his dark eyes widened. But she was almost too sick with disappointment to care.

"Why make a copy of his study here?" She stalked over and kicked the desk angrily. "It looks no more used than the other one!"

Jared stared around, fascinated. "Is it exactly the same?"

"In every single detail." She leaned on the desk and said the password Incarceron and the drawer rolled open. Inside, as she'd expected, was a crystal Key the image of their own. "He keeps a Key at home and one here. But the Prison is somewhere else."

318

The bitterness in her voice made Jared give her a worried glance and then come to her side. Quietly he said, "Don't torment yourself . . ."

"I told Finn I'd found the way in!" Disgusted, she turned and hugged her arms around herself. "And what do we do now? Tomorrow I'll be married to Caspar or executed for treason."

"Or you'll be Queen," he said.

She stared at him. "Or Queen. After a bloodbath that will haunt me forever."

She walked away and glared at the humming silver machines. Behind her, she heard Jared say, "Well, at least . . ."

He stopped.

When he didn't finish the sentence she turned, saw him bent over the open drawer with the Key inside. Slowly he straightened and glanced at her sideways. When he spoke his voice was hoarse with excitement.

"It isn't a copy. It's the same room."

She stared.

"Look, Claudia. Come and look."

The Key. It lay in the black velvet and he reached out and touched it, and to her utter shock she saw how his fingers passed through the image onto the soft nap below. It was a holo-image.

The holo-image she had put there.

She stepped back, looked around. Then quickly she dived and scrabbled around the legs of the chair. "If it's the same, there was a . . ." She gasped, then jumped up with a mutter of bafflement. She held a very tiny scrap of metal. "This was lying just there before! But how? How can it be the same room? That was at home. Miles away." She stared at the open door, the dim cellars of the Palace beyond.

Jared seemed to have forgotten his fear. His narrow face was lit; he took the metal scrap and looked at it closely, then slipped a small bag from his pocket and sealed the object inside. He aimed the scanner at the chair. "There's something strange just here. The spatial rift seems stronger." He frowned in frustration. "Ah, if only we had better instruments, Claudia! If only the Sapienti had not been so hampered by Protocol all these years!"

"Have you noticed," she said, "how the chair is fixed to the floor?"

She hadn't seen it before, but there were metal clasps to keep it in position. She walked around it. "And why here? It's too far from the desk. There's just that light above."

They stared up at it. A narrow, faintly blue light, falling on the chair and nothing else. Barely bright enough to read by.

A cold thought chilled her. "Master . . . this is not a place of torture, is it?"

He didn't answer at first, then she was grateful for his measured tone. "I doubt it. There are no restraints, no signs of violence. Do you think your father would need to use such devices?"

She didn't want to answer that. Instead she said, "We've seen all we can. Let's get out." It was past midnight. Her whole body was listening for footsteps.

He nodded, reluctant. "And yet this room holds secrets, Claudia, that I would give worlds to discover. Maybe it is a gateway. Maybe we are not seeing what is here."

"Jared. That's enough."

She crossed to the gate and stepped through. The cellars were still and gloomy. All the alarms were safely in place. And yet she was suddenly shaken by terrors; that dark figures were watching, that Fax was there, that her father stood in the shadows where she had stood, that the bronze gate would slam suddenly and trap Jared inside. She dragged him out so quickly, he almost fell.

Taking the Key, she tugged it out of the keyhole, watched how instantly the gate folded back with barely a clang, the chains linking themselves into place, the snails continuing their relentless slimy progress over the worn wings of the eagle.

She was silent as she followed the Sapient's dark figure through the stacked barrels, silenced by disappointment and bitter failure. What would Finn think of her now?

How Keiro would laugh in scorn and that girl would smirk. And for herself, a day of freedom left.

At the top of the stairs she stopped Jared with a tug of his sleeve. "We should go back separately, Master. We shouldn't be seen together."

He nodded, and in the dark she thought he flushed a little. "You go first. Take care."

She didn't move, her voice bleak. "It's all over, isn't it? Everything's finished. Finn will rot in that place forever."

Jared leaned back on the pillar and took a deep breath. "Don't despair, Claudia. Incarceron is near. I'm sure of that." He took something out of his pocket, and to her surprise she saw it was the tiny flake of metal from the floor in its plastic wrapping.

"What is that?"

"I have no idea. I'll use the Sapients' tower here and try a few investigations tomorrow."

"Lucky you." She turned sourly. "All I have to try is my wedding dress."

She was gone before he could answer, slipping up the stairs into the candlelit corridors, the midnight silences and whispers of the Palace.

Jared turned the tiny scrap between his fingertips.

He pushed back his damp hair and breathed out slowly.

For a moment the strangeness of the room had made him forget the pain. Now it came back, worse, as if to punish him.

⤙◦◦◦⤚

FOR HOURS they saw nothing of Blaize. He seemed to vanish, but Finn had no idea where.

"There's a part of this tower we haven't found yet," Keiro muttered, "and that's the way out." He sprawled on the bed looking up at the white ceiling. "And that guff about the books—I don't believe a word of it."

Blaize had laughed off their questions about the Prison records. "This tower was empty and possibly made only for these books to be stored here," he had said, passing bread across the table that evening. "I found the place and liked it, so I moved in. I assure you I have no idea how the images come to be stored here, and neither the time nor inclination to look at them."

"But you feel safe here," Gildas muttered.

"I am safe. No one can reach me. I removed all the Eyes, and the Beetles can't get in. Of course, Incarceron has many ways of watching and I'm certainly under observation, as my images appear in the book like everyone else's. But not at the moment, though, because of the strange power of your Key. At the moment we are all invisible." He had smiled then, rubbing the scabs on his chin. "Now, if I had a device like that, I could learn much from it. I suppose you wouldn't consider parting with it?"

"He wants it." Keiro sat up now, quickly. "You saw how he looked, when Gildas laughed at him? There was a coldness in his face then, a flicker of something. He wants the Key."

Finn sat on the floor, knees up. "He'll never get it."

"Where is it?"

"Safe, brother." He tapped his coat.

"Good." Keiro lounged back. "And keep your sword with you. This scabby Sapient makes me uneasy. I don't like him."

"Attia says we're his prisoners."

"That little bitch." But Keiro's remark was preoccupied; as Finn watched, he rolled off the bed and stood, snatching a quick look at himself in the faceted window glass. "But don't fret, brother. Keiro has a plan."

He tugged his coat on and went out, peering cautiously around the door.

Alone, Finn pulled the Key out and looked at it. Attia was asleep and Gildas was restlessly searching the books, as he seemed to have been doing since they came here. Quietly Finn closed the door and put his back against it. Then he activated the Key.

It lit quickly.

He saw a chamber strewn with clothes, and there was light there that made his eyes sting; sunlight through a window. Beyond the circle of the Key was a large, heavy wooden bed, hangings, a wall of carved panels. Then, breathless, Claudia.

"You have to give me more warning! They could have seen you!"

"Who?" he asked.

"The maids, the seamstress. For God's sake, Finn!"

She was red-faced, her hair tousled. He realized she was wearing a white dress, the bodice elaborate with pearls and lace. A wedding dress.

For a moment he had no idea what to say. Then she sat next to him, crouched on the rush-strewn floor. "We failed.

We opened the gate, but it didn't lead to Incarceron, Finn. It was all a stupid mistake. All I found was my father's study." She sounded disgusted with herself.

"But your father is the Warden," he said slowly.

"Whatever that means." She scowled.

He shook his head. "I wish I could remember you, Claudia. You, Outside, all of it." He looked up. "What if I'm not really Giles? That picture . . . I don't look like that. I'm not that boy."

"You were once." Her voice was stubborn; she squirmed to face him, the silk rustling. "Look, all I want is not to marry Caspar. Once you're rescued, once you're free, then our engagement . . . well, it doesn't have to happen, that's all. Attia was wrong; it's not just about me being selfish." She smiled wryly. "Where is she?"

"Asleep. I think."

"She's fond of you."

He shrugged. "We rescued her. She's grateful."

"Is that what you call it?" She stared ahead at nothing. "Do people love each other in Incarceron, Finn?"

"If they do, I haven't seen anything of it." But then he thought of the Maestra, and felt ashamed. There was an awkward silence. Claudia could hear the maids chattering in the next chamber; could see beyond Finn a small room with a frosty window, through which glimmered a dim, artificial twilight.

And there was a smell. As she realized, she breathed in sharply, so that he looked at her. A musty, unpleasant smell, metallic and sour, air that was trapped and recycled endlessly. She scrambled to her knees. "I can smell the Prison!"

He stared. "There is no smell. Besides, how—"

"I don't know, but I can!"

She jumped up, ran out of his sight, came back with a tiny glass bottle that she uncorked and sprayed lightly into the sunlight.

Minute drops shimmered in dust.

And Finn cried out, because the smell of it was rich and strong and it sliced into his memory like a knife; he clasped his hands over his mouth and breathed it again and again, closing his eyes, forcing himself to think.

Roses. A garden of yellow roses.

A knife in the cake and he was pushing down, cutting, and it was easy and he was laughing. Crumbs on his fingers. The sweet taste.

"Finn? Finn!" Claudia's voice swayed him back from endless distance. The dryness was in his mouth, the warning prickle crawling in his skin. He shuddered, forced himself to be calm, breathe slower, let the sweat cool his forehead.

She was close to him. "If you can smell it, the drops must be traveling to you, mustn't they? Perhaps you can touch me now. Try, Finn."

Her hand was close. He put his own around it, closed his fingers.

They passed through hers and there was nothing, not a warmth, not a sensation. He sat back, and they were silent.

Finally he said, "I have to get out of here, Claudia."

"And you will." She knelt up, her face fierce. "I swear to you, I won't give up. If I have to go to my father and beg him on my knees, I'll do it." She turned. "Alys is calling. Wait for me."

The circle went dark.

He sat huddled there till he was stiff and the room was unbearably lonely; then he got up, shoved the Key into his coat, and went out, running down the steps into the library, where Gildas was pacing irritably forward and back, Blaize watching him across a table spread with food. When he saw Finn, the thin Sapient stood.

"Our last meal together," he said, spreading a hand.

Suspicious, Finn eyed him. "Then what?"

"Then I take you all to a safe place and let you resume your journey."

"Where's Keiro?" Gildas snapped.

"I don't know. So, you're just letting us go?"

Blaize looked at him, his gray eyes calm. "Of course. My aim was only ever to help you. Gildas has persuaded me that you need to travel on."

"And the Key?"

"I must do without it."

Attia was sitting at the table, her hands clasped together.

Catching Finn's eye, she shrugged slightly. Blaize rose. "I will leave you to make your plans. Enjoy your meal."

In the silence after he was gone Finn said, "We misjudged him."

"I still think he's dangerous. If he's a Sapient, why doesn't he cure that pox he has?"

"What do you know of the Sapienti, ignorant girl?" Gildas growled.

Attia chewed her fingernail, then as Finn reached out for an apple, snatched it first, and bit it. "I taste your food," she said indistinctly. "Remember?"

He was angry. "I'm not the Winglord. You're not my slave."

"No, Finn." She leaned across the table. "I'm your friend. That means a lot more."

Gildas sat down. "Any news from Claudia?"

"They failed. The gate led nowhere."

"As I thought." The old man nodded heavily. "The girl is clever, but we must expect no help from them. We must follow Sapphique alone. Now, there is a story that tells how . . ."

His hand reached to the fruit, but Finn grabbed it. His eyes were fixed on Attia; she half rose, pale, and suddenly choking, the apple stalk dropping from her fingers. As he jerked forward and caught her she crumpled, her fingers tearing at her throat.

"The apple," she gasped. "It's burning me!"

26

You chose rashly. I've warned you before.
She is far too clever and you underestimate
the Sapient.

—*Queen Sia to the Warden; private letter*

"It's poisoned!" Finn clambered over the table and grabbed her; she choked, clutching his arms. "Do something!"

Gildas shoved him aside. "Get my bag of medicines. Hurry!"

It took him precious seconds to find it, and by the time he got back Gildas had Attia lying on her side, writhing in pain. The Sapient grabbed the bag and tore through it, then pulled the cap off a small vial and held it to her lips. Attia struggled.

"She's choking," Finn muttered, but Gildas only swore, forcing it on her so that she drank it and coughed and convulsed.

Then, with a horrible racking sound she was sick.

"Good," Gildas said quietly. "That's it." He held her tight, his quick fingers feeling her pulse, the clammy skin of her forehead. She was sick again, and then slumped back, her face white and mottled.

"Is it out? Is she all right?"

But Gildas was still frowning. "Too cold," he muttered. "Get a blanket." Then, "Close the door and guard it. If Blaize comes, keep him out."

"Why would he . . . ?"

"The Key, fool boy. He wants the Key. Who else would have done this?"

Attia moaned. She was shivering now, a strange blueness on her lips and under her eyes. He obeyed, slamming the heavy door.

"Is it out of her?"

"I don't know. I don't think so. It might have entered the bloodstream almost immediately."

Finn stared at him in dismay. Gildas knew about poisons; the women of the Comitatus had been experts, and Gildas had not been above learning from them.

"What else can we do?"

"Nothing."

The door shuddered; it hit Finn on the shoulder and he turned, drawing the sword with one fierce slash. Keiro stood still.

"What's . . . ?" His quick eyes took in the scene. He said, "Poison?"

"Some corrosive." Gildas watched the girl retching and squirming. He stood slowly, resigned. "There is nothing I can do."

"There has to be!" Finn shoved him aside. "I could have eaten that! It could have been me!" He knelt down next to her, trying to lift her, make her easier, but her mutters of pain made him stop. He felt angry and helpless. "We have to do something!"

Gildas crouched by him. His harsh words cut through the moans. "It's acidic, Finn. Her internal system may be already burned, her lips, her throat. It will be over very soon."

Finn looked at Keiro.

"We go," his brother said. "Right now. I've found where he keeps the ship."

"Not without her."

"She's dying." Gildas forced him to look. "Nothing can be done. It would take a miracle and I don't have one."

"So we save ourselves?"

"That's what she'd want."

They had hold of him, but he shrugged them off and knelt by her. She was still and seemed to be barely breathing, the faded bruises clear in her skin. He had seen death, he was used to death, but his whole soul revolted against this, and the shame he had felt at the Maestra's betrayal came back and swept over him like heat, as if it would overwhelm him. He choked back words, knew tears were filling his eyes.

If it would take a miracle, Attia would get one.

He leaped up and turned to Keiro, grabbing at his hands. "A ring. Give me another of the rings."

"Now wait a minute." Keiro jerked back.

"Give it to me!" His voice was a rasp; he raised the sword. "Don't make me use this, Keiro. You'll still have one left."

Keiro was calm. His blue eyes gave one glance at Attia as she curled in agony. Then he stared back. "You think it will work?"

"I don't know! But we can try."

"She's a girl. She's no one."

"One each, you said. I'm giving her mine."

"You've had yours already."

For a moment they faced each other, Gildas watching. Then Keiro tugged one of the rings over his knuckles and looked down at it. Wordless, he threw it at Finn.

Finn caught it, dropped the sword, and grabbed Attia's fingers, pushing the ring on; it was far too big for her, so he held it there, praying under his breath, to Sapphique, to the man whose life was in the ring, to anyone. Gildas crouched beside him, deeply cynical.

"Nothing's happening. What should happen?"

The Sapient scowled. "This is superstition. You yourself scorned it."

"Her breathing. It's slowing."

Gildas felt her pulse, touched the dirty scars where the chains had been. "Finn. Accept it. There's no . . ."

He stopped. His fingers tightened, felt again.

"What? What—"

"I thought . . . The pulse seems stronger . . ."

Keiro said, "Then pick her up! Bring her. But let's go!"

Finn threw him the sword, crouched, and picked Attia up.

She was so light, he could carry her easily, though her head lolled against him. Keiro already had the door open and was looking out. "This way. Keep quiet."

He led them out.

They ran up a dusty winding stair to a trapdoor; Keiro flung it back and hauled himself into darkness, dragging Gildas quickly after him. "The girl."

Finn passed her up. Then he looked back.

In the stairwell a strange hum seemed to ripple the air. It rose ominously toward him and he climbed hastily, scrambling up and slamming the trapdoor down. Keiro was wrestling with a grid on the wall, Gildas grasping it with his knotted hands.

Attia's eyes flickered, then opened.

Finn stared. "You should be dead."

She shook her head, speechless.

The grid came off the wall with a rattling crash; behind it he saw a great dark hall, and in the center, tethered to the floor by an iron cable, the silver ship, floating free. They ran, Finn with Attia's arm over his shoulder, tiny figures over the smooth gray floor, vulnerable and exposed, like mice under the wide stare of an owl, because in the roof above them a great screen lit, and as Finn stared up it showed him an eye. Not the tiny red Eyes he knew, but a human eye, gray-irised, magnified enormously, as if it stared into a powerful microscope.

Then the ripple in the air came through the floor and threw

them all off their feet, a Prisonquake that made the thin needle of the Sapient's tower vibrate to its top.

Keiro rolled and leaped up. "Over here."

A shimmering rope ladder hung down. Gildas grasped it and began to climb, swaying awkwardly, though Keiro held the end firmly.

Finn said, "Can you get up there?"

"I think so." Attia pushed hair from her face. She was still deathly pale, but the blueness was ebbing. She seemed to be able to breathe.

He looked down at her finger.

The ring was shrunken. A thin brittle hoop, it fractured as she grasped the rope; tiny fragments fell unnoticed. Finn touched one with his foot. It looked like bone. Ancient, dried bone.

Behind them, the trapdoor clanged open.

Finn whirled; he felt Keiro hand him back the sword and draw his own.

Together, they faced the dark square of blackness.

◦◦◦◦◦

"AND SO everything is ready for tomorrow." The Queen placed the last of the papers on the red leather desk and sat back, putting her fingertips together. "The Warden has been so generous. Such a dowry, Claudia. Whole estates, a coffer of jewels, twelve black horses. He must love you very much."

Her nails were painted with gold. It was probably real,

334

Claudia thought. She picked up one of the deeds and glanced over it, but all she was aware of was Caspar, striding up and down on the creaking wooden floor.

Queen Sia looked around. "Caspar. Be quiet."

"I'm bored rigid."

"Then go riding, dear. Or badger-baiting, or whatever it is you do."

He turned. "Right. Good idea. See you, Claudia."

The Queen raised a perfect eyebrow. "Hardly the way the Heir speaks to his fiancée, my lord."

Halfway to the door he stopped and came back. "Protocol is for the serfs, Mother. Not us."

"Protocol keeps us in power, Caspar. Don't forget that."

He grinned and made a low and elaborate bow to Claudia, then kissed her hand. "See you at the altar, Claudia." She stood and curtsied coldly.

"Right. Now I'm off."

He slammed the door and they could hear the thud of his boots down the corridor.

The Queen leaned across the table. "I'm so glad we have this little time alone, Claudia, because I have something to say. I know you won't mind it, my dear."

Claudia tried not to frown, but her lips tightened. She wanted to get away, find Jared. They had so little time!

"I have changed my mind. I have asked Master Jared to leave the Court."

"No!"

It was said before she could stop herself.

"Yes, dear. After the wedding, he will return to the Academy."

"You have no right . . ." Claudia was on her feet.

"I have every right." The Queen's smile was sweet and deadly. She leaned forward. "Let us understand each other, Claudia. There is only one Queen here. I will teach you, but I will not tolerate any rival. And you and I need to understand this, because we are alike, Claudia. Men are weak; even your father can be ruled, but you have been brought up to be my successor. Wait your time. You can learn a lot from me." She leaned back, her fingers tapping the papers. "Sit down, my dear."

There was steely threat in the words. Claudia sat slowly. "Jared is my friend."

"From now on, I will be your friend. I have many spies, Claudia. They tell me much. It really will be for the best."

She stretched out and pulled the bell; a servant came in instantly, in powdered wig and livery. "Tell the Warden I await him."

When he had gone she opened a box of sweetmeats and took a moment to select one, then offered them to Claudia with a smile.

Numb, Claudia shook her head. She felt as if she had picked up a pretty flower and found it rotting away inside, crawling with maggots. She realized she had never seriously thought of Sia as the danger. Her father had always been the one to fear. Now she wondered how wrong she was.

Sia watched her, her red lips in a small smile. She wiped them with a lace-edged kerchief. And as the doors were flung open, she leaned back in the chair and dangled her arm over the side. "My dear Warden. What kept you?"

He was flushed.

Claudia noticed it at once, through the whirl of her dismay. He never hurried, yet now his hair was just a little askew, his dark coat unbuttoned at the top.

He bowed gravely, but his voice had an edge of breathlessness. "I'm sorry, ma'am. Something that required my attention."

—◁◇◇▷—

NOTHING CAME through the trapdoor.

Finn said, "Get up the ladder."

As Keiro turned, the floor rippled again. Finn stared at it. The quake lifted the flagstones as if a wave of water roared under them. Before he had time to move, the whole world shifted. He fell crashing against the floor, then was rolling downhill, down a slope that should not be there. Slamming against a pillar he gasped, pain shooting down his side.

The hall was tilting.

With sickening certainty he thought that the Sapient's tower was falling, that it had been fractured at its spindly base. Then the rope ladder brushed him and he grabbed it. Keiro was already on board, leaning over the silver timbers of the deck. Finn scrambled up; as soon as he could reach, they linked hands.

"I've got him. GO!"

The ship rose. With a howl of fear Finn slid onto the deck; the whole contraption swung and rocked and then it drifted, ropes snapping one by one below it.

There was an opening in the tower wall ahead, the wide shelf where Blaize had landed the craft. But as Gildas hauled with all his wiry strength to spin the spoked wheel, the ship jerked and they all fell, rubble cascading from above onto the deck and sails.

"Something's holding us down!" he roared.

Keiro hung over the side. "God! There's an anchor!"

He clambered back. "There must be a winch. Come on!"

They opened a hatch and scrambled down into the darkness under the deck. Thuds of falling brickwork crashed overhead.

They found a maze of walkways and galleys. Running down and flinging the doors open, Finn saw each cabin was empty; there were no stores, no cargo, no crew. Before he had time to think about it, Keiro yelled from the darkness below.

In the lowest deck it was dark. A circular capstan filled the space; Keiro was jamming the bar into place. "Help me."

Together, they pushed. Nothing moved; the mechanism was stiff, the anchor chain heavy.

Again they heaved, Finn feeling his back muscles crack, and slowly, with a long reluctant groan, the capstan creaked into motion.

Finn gritted his teeth and heaved again, sweat breaking out on his face; beside him he heard Keiro gasp and grunt.

Then another body was there. Attia, still pale, laboring on the bar next to him.

"What . . . good . . . are you?" Keiro growled.

"Good enough," she snapped back, and Finn saw to his surprise that she was grinning, her eyes bright under the tangled hair, color back in her face.

The anchor juddered. The ship swayed, then abruptly, lifted.

"We've got it!" Keiro dug his heels in and pushed, and quite suddenly the capstan was turning quickly under their weight, the great chain of the anchor rasping up through the floor and looping obediently as they forced it around.

When they had it all in and the mechanism ground to a stop Finn raced up the steps of the companionway, but as he burst out onto the deck he stopped with a yell of fright.

They were sailing in a cloud. It wisped around him, opening to give glimpses of Gildas swearing at the wheel, the great billowing sails, a bird below them in a patch of light.

"Where are we?" Attia muttered behind him.

Then the ship dropped out of the mist, and they saw they were in an ocean of blue air, the tilted tower of the Sapient already far behind.

Breathless, Keiro leaned on the rail and whooped with delight.

Finn stood next to him, looking back. "Why didn't he try to stop us?" Reaching into his jacket, he touched the crystal sharpness of the Key.

"Who bloody cares!" his oathbrother said.

And then he turned and punched Finn hard in the stomach.

Attia screamed. Finn collapsed, all breath gone, the pain an amazement inside him, an airless blackness that loomed over his sight.

From the wheel Gildas yelled something, his words snatched away.

Slowly, the agony ebbed. When Finn could gasp in air he looked up and saw Keiro with both arms spread on the rail, looking down at him with a grin.

"What . . . ?"

Keiro held out a hand and pulled him up, staggering, face-to-face. "That'll teach you not to draw a sword on me again," he said.

27

Sapphique strapped the wings to his arms and flew, over oceans and plains, over glass cities and mountains of gold. Animals fled; people pointed up. He flew so far, he saw the sky above him and the sky said, "Turn back, my son, for you have climbed too high."

Sapphique laughed, as he rarely did. "Not this time. This time I beat on you until you open."

But Incarceron was angered, and struck him down.

—Legends of Sapphique

"She's said that Jared has to leave." She turned and glared at her father, wanting to ask if it was his doing.

"I told you. It was bound to happen." The Warden walked past her and sat on the chaise near the window of his room, gazing out at the pleasure gardens, where parties of courtiers walked in the evening cool. "I think you will have to comply, my dear. It's a small price to pay to gain a kingdom."

She was ready to burst out in temper, but he turned and looked at her, that cold measuring look she so dreaded.

"Besides, we have something more important to discuss. Come and sit down."

She didn't want to. But she crossed to the chair by the gilt table and sat.

He glanced at his watch, then clicked the lid shut and kept it in his hand.

He said quietly, "You have something that belongs to me."

She felt her skin prickle with danger. For a moment she thought she couldn't speak at all, but then her voice came, surprisingly calm.

"Do I? What could that be?"

He smiled. "You are truly remarkable, Claudia. Even though I've created you, you always surprise me. But I've warned you before about pushing me too far." He put the watch in his pocket and leaned forward. "You have my Key."

She drew in a breath of dismay. He leaned back, crossing one leg over another, the leather of his boots gleaming. "Yes. You don't deny it, and that's wise. It was ingenious to place an image of the Key in the drawer, quite ingenious. I suppose I have Jared to thank for that. When I checked my study that day the alarms went off, I rolled the drawer open and glanced inside; I didn't think to pick up the Key. And the ladybugs—what a creative touch! What a fool you must both have thought me."

She shook her head, but he stood abruptly and paced to the windows. "Did you talk about me with Jared, Claudia? Did you laugh together because you had stolen it from me? I'm sure you must have enjoyed that."

"I took it because I had to." She clutched her hands together. "You kept it from me. You never told me."

He stopped and looked at her. He had smoothed his hair back now, and his gaze was as calm and considering as ever. "About what?"

She stood up slowly, and faced him. "About Giles," she said.

She had expected astonishment, a moment's startled silence. But he was not at all surprised. She knew, with sudden certainty, that he had been waiting for that name, that by saying it she had fallen into some trap.

He said, "Giles is dead."

"No he isn't." The jewels around her neck tickled; with a sudden fury, she tugged them off and flung them on the floor, then folded her arms and all the pent-up words burst out of her. "His death was faked. You and the Queen faked it. Giles is in Incarceron, locked away. You took his memory so he doesn't even know who he is. How could you do that?" She kicked a footstool aside; it fell and rolled. "I can understand why she did it, why she wanted her useless son to be King, but you! I was already engaged to Giles. Your precious plan would have worked out anyway. Why did you do that to us?"

He raised an eyebrow. "Us?"

"Don't I count? Didn't the fact that I would end up with Caspar mean anything to you? Did you ever think about me?"

She was trembling. All the anger of her life was coming out, frustration for all the times he had driven away and left her for months, had smiled down at her and not touched her.

He rubbed his stubbly beard with thumb and forefinger. "I did think of you." His voice was quiet. "It was obvious you liked Giles. But he was a stubborn boy, too kind, too honorable. Caspar is a fool and will make a poor King. You will be able to rule him far more effectively."

"That's not the reason you did it."

He looked away. She saw his fingers tapping on the fireplace. He picked up a dainty china figurine and examined it, then put it down. "You're right."

He was silent; she wanted him to speak so much, she could have screamed. It seemed an age before he went back to the chair and sat and said calmly, "I'm afraid the real reason is a secret you will never learn from me."

Seeing her astonishment, he raised his hand. "I know you despise me, Claudia. I'm sure you and your Sapient think me a monster. But you are my daughter and I have always acted in your interests. Besides, Giles's imprisonment was the Queen's plan, not mine. She forced me to agree."

She snorted in scorn. "Forced! She has power over you!"

He whipped his head up and hissed, "Yes. And so do you."

For a second the venom in his voice stung her. "Me?"

His hands were fists on the wooden armrests. He said, "Let it go, Claudia. Let it be. Don't ask, because the answer may destroy you. That's all I'm going to say." He stood, tall and dark, and his voice was bleak. "Now, about the Key. Nothing you have done with it has escaped me. I know about your search for Bartlett, about your communication with Incarceron. I know about this Prisoner you believe is Giles."

She stared in amazement and he laughed his dry laugh. "There are a thousand million Prisoners in Incarceron, Claudia, and you believe you've found the right one? Time and space are different there. This boy could be anyone."

"He has a birthmark."

"Does he now! Let me tell you something about the Prison." His voice cruel now, he came up to her and stared down at her. "It's a closed system. Nothing enters. Nothing leaves. When Prisoners die their atoms are reused, their skin, their organs. *They are made from each other.* Repaired, recycled, and when the organic tissues are not available, they are patched with metal and plastic. Finn's eagle means nothing. It may not even be his. The memories he thinks he sees may not be his."

Horrified, she wanted to stop him, but no words would come. "The boy is a thief and a liar." He went on, remorseless. "One of a gang of cutthroats that preyed on others. I suppose he's told you that?"

"Yes," she snapped.

"How very honest. Has he told you that in order to get his copy of the Key an innocent woman was thrown to her death down a precipice? *After* he had promised her she was safe?"

She was silent.

345

"No," he said. "I thought not." He stood back. "I want all this nonsense to cease. I want the Key. Now."

She shook her head.

"Now, Claudia."

"I haven't got it," she whispered.

"Then Jared—"

"Leave Jared out of this!"

He caught hold of her. His hand was cold and he gripped her wrist like iron. "I want the Key or you will regret defying me."

She tried to shake him off, but he held tight. She glared at him through her tumbling hair. "You can't hurt me. I'm all you've got to make your plan work and you know it!"

For a moment they stared at each other. Then he nodded, and let her go. A white circle of bloodless skin looped her wrist like the mark of a manacle.

"I can't hurt you," he said hoarsely.

Her eyes widened.

"But there is this Finn. And there is Jared."

She stepped back. She was shaking, her back cold with sweat. For a moment they looked at each other. Then, not trusting herself to speak, she turned and ran to the door, but his words caught her there and she had to hear them.

"There is no way out of the Prison. Bring me the Key, Claudia."

She slammed the door behind her. A passing servant stared in surprise. In the mirror opposite Claudia saw why;

her reflection showed a tousled, red-faced creature, scowling with unhappiness. She wanted to howl with rage. Instead she walked to her room and closed the door, and threw herself on the bed.

She thumped the pillow and buried her head in it, curling up small, arms hugging her body. Her mind was a maze of confusion, but as she moved, paper crinkled on the pillow and she raised her head and saw the note pinned there. It was from Jared. *I need to see you. I've discovered something incredible.*

As soon as she'd read it, it dissolved to ash.

She couldn't even smile.

⊰∞∞⊱

PERCHED IN the rigging of the ship, Finn held on tight, seeing far below lakes of sulfurous yellow liquid, viscous and evil-smelling. On the landscape slopes, animals grazed, odd gawky creatures from here, the herd splitting and fleeing in terror as the shadow of the ship fell on them. Beyond were more lakes, small scrubby bushes the only things that grew near them, and away to the right a desert stretched as far as he could see into the shadows.

They had been sailing for hours. Gildas had steered first, at random, high and steady until he had yelled irritably for someone to relieve him and Finn had taken a turn, feeling the strangeness of the craft below, its buffeting by drafts and breezes. Above him the sails had flapped; the winds catching and sloughing the white canvas. Twice he had sailed the ship through cloud. The second time the temperature had dropped alarmingly and by the time they had emerged from the tingling grayness, the wheel and deck around him had been frosted with needles of ice that fell and clattered on the boards.

Attia had brought him water. "Plenty of this," she'd said, "but no food."

"What, nothing?"

"No."

"What did he live on?"

"There's only some scraps Gildas has." As he'd drunk, she'd taken the wheel, her small hands on the thick spokes. She'd said, "He told me about the ring."

Finn wiped his mouth.

"It was too much to do for me. I owe you even more now."

He'd felt proud and grumpy both at once; he'd taken the wheel back and said, "We stick together. Besides, I didn't think it would work."

"I'm amazed Keiro gave it."

Finn shrugged. She was watching closely. But then she had looked into the sky. "Look at this! This is so wonderful. All my life I lived in a little dark tunnel lined with shanties and now all this space . . ."

He said, "Do you have any family?"

"Brothers and sisters. All older."

"Parents?"

"No." She shook her head. "You know . . ."

He knew. Life in the Prison was short and unpredictable. "Do you miss them?"

She was still, gripping the wheel tight. "Yes. But . . ." She smiled. "It's odd how things work out. When I was captured, I thought it was the end of my life. But instead it led to this."

He'd nodded, then said, "Do you think the ring saved you? Or was it Gildas's emetic?"

"The ring," she said firmly. "And you."

He hadn't been so sure.

Now, looking down at Keiro lazing on the deck, he grinned. Called to take his turn, his oathbrother had taken one look at the great wheel and gone below for some rope; then he'd lashed it and seated himself next to it, feet up. "What can we possibly hit?" he'd said to Gildas.

"You fool," the Sapient had snarled. "Just keep your eyes open, that's all."

They had passed over hills of copper and mountains of glass, whole forests of metal trees. Finn had seen settlements cut off in impenetrable valleys where the inhabitants lived in isolation; great towns; once a castle with flags flying from its turrets. That had scared him, thinking of Claudia. Rainbows of spray arched over them; they had flown through strange atmospheric effects, a reflected island, patches of heat, flickering blurs of purple and gold fire. An hour ago a flock of long-tailed birds had suddenly squawked and circled and dive-bombed the deck, making Keiro duck. Then just as suddenly they had vanished, a mere drift of dimness on the horizon. Once, the ship had drifted very low; Finn had leaned out over mile on mile of stinking hovels, the people running from haphazard dwellings of tin and wood, lame and diseased, their children listless. He had been glad when the wind had lifted the ship away. Incarceron was a hell. And yet he possessed its Key.

He took it out and touched the controls. He'd tried it before, but nothing had happened. Nothing happened now either, and he wondered if it would ever work again. But it was warm. Did that mean they were traveling in the right direction, toward Claudia? But if Incarceron was so vast, how many lifetimes might it take to travel to the exit?

"Finn!"

Keiro's yell was sharp. He looked up.

Ahead, something flickered. He thought at first it was the lights; then he saw that the dimness was not the usual gloom of the Prison but a dark bank of storm clouds, right across their path. He scrambled down, rasping his palms to heat on the cables.

Keiro was hastily untying the wheel.

"What is that?"

"Weather."

It was black. Lightning flickered inside it. And as they sailed closer, thunder, a low rumble, an amused, dark chuckle.

"The Prison," he whispered. "It's found us."

"Get Gildas," Keiro muttered.

He found the Sapient below, poring over charts and maps under the creaking lamp. "Look at these." The old man glanced up, his lined face shadowed in the lamplight.

"How can it be this vast? How can we hope to follow Sapphique through all this?"

Appalled, Finn stared at the heap of charts slithering off the table, covering the floor. If these showed the extent of Incarceron, they could journey through it forever. "We need you. There's a storm ahead."

Attia ran in. "Keiro says hurry."

As if in response the ship heeled over. Finn grabbed the table as the charts slid and rolled. Then he climbed back up on deck.

Black clouds reared up over the masts, the silver pennants flapping and snapping. The ship was almost lying on her side; he had to hang on to the rail and scramble across to the wheel by grabbing anything within reach.

Keiro was sweating and swearing. "This is the Sapient's sorcery!" he yelled.

"I don't think so. It's Incarceron."

The thunder rumbled again. With a scream the gale hit them; they both held the wheel and hung on, crouching behind its meager shelter. Objects flapped against them, shards of metal, leaves, fragments of debris rebounding like hail. And then a snow of tiny white grit, ground glass, bolts, stones that tore through the sails.

Finn turned.

He saw Gildas lying flat behind the main mast, clinging on, one arm around Attia. "Stay there!" he yelled.

"The Key!" Gildas's yell was snatched away by the wind. "Let me take it below. If you're lost . . ."

He knew. And yet he hated the thought of parting with it.

"Do it," Keiro growled without turning.

Finn let go of the wheel.

Instantly he was flung back, buffeted, tumbling, over the deck. And the Prison swooped. He felt it zoom in on him, and rolling over, he screamed in terror.

From the heart of the storm, an eagle plummeted from the sky, black as thunder, its talons crackling with lightning. It stretched out for the Key, ready to snatch him and it.

Finn threw himself to one side. A tangle of ropes slammed into him; he grabbed the nearest and whipped it up, whirling it around, the heavy tarred end so close to the bird's breast that it swerved and swept past, flying high to turn and swoop again.

He dived past Gildas into the shelter of the deck.

"It's coming back!" Attia screamed.

"It wants the Key." Gildas ducked. Rain lashed them; thunder rumbled again, and this time it was a great voice, a murmur of anger far away and high above.

The eagle dived. Keiro, exposed by the wheel, curled up small. They saw how it circled and screeched angrily, its beak wide. Then, quite suddenly, it turned to the east and flew away.

Finn tugged out the Key. He touched it and instantly Claudia was there, wet-eyed, her hair rumpled. "Finn," she said, "Listen to me. I've—"

"You listen." He grabbed tight as the ship rolled and swayed. "We need help, Claudia. You have to speak to your father. You have to get him to stop the storm or we'll all die!"

"Storm?" She shook her head. "He's not . . . He won't help. He wants you dead. He's found out everything, Finn. He knows!"

"Then—"

Keiro yelled. Finn looked up and what he saw made his fingers clutch on the Key, so that seconds before the image flicked off, Claudia saw it too.

A great solid metal wall. The Wall at the End of the World.

Rising from unknown depths it soared into the hidden reaches of the sky.

And they were heading straight for it.

28

*Entry is through the Portal. Only the Warden will
have a key, and this will be the only way to leave.
Though every prison has its chinks and crannies.*

—Project report; Martor Sapiens

It was late; the bell in the Ebony Tower was chiming ten. In the summer dusk, moths flitted in the gardens and a distant peacock cried as Claudia hurried down the cloister. Servants passed her and struggled to bow, loaded down with chairs and tapestries and great haunches of venison. The whole bustle of the feast preparations had been under way for hours. She frowned, annoyed, not daring to ask one of them where Jared's room was.

But he was waiting.

As she turned a dank corner by a fountain of four stone swans, his hand came out and clutched her. Tugged through an archway she stood breathless as he closed the oaken door almost shut and put his eye to the slit.

A figure strode past. She thought she recognized her father's secretary.

"Medlicote. Is he following me?"

Jared put a finger to his lips. He looked paler and more drawn than usual, and there was a nervous energy about him that worried her. He led her down some stone steps, across a neglected courtyard, into a pathway overarched with yellow hanging laburnum. Halfway down he paused and whispered, "There's a folly down here I've been using. My room is bugged."

A great moon hung over the Palace. The scars of the Years of Rage pockmarked its face; its silvery sheen lit the orchard and glasshouses, reflected on diamond-paned casements that hung open in the heat. A small burst of music drifted from a room, with voices and laughter and the chink of plates. Jared's dark figure slipped between two pillars where stone bears danced, through bushes that smelled of lavender and lemon balm, to a small structure built into a wall, in the most neglected corner of the walled garden. Claudia glimpsed a turret, a ruined parapet overgrown with ivy.

He unlocked the door and ushered her in.

It was black, and stank of damp soil. Light flickered over her; Jared had a small torch; he pointed it at an inner door. "Quickly."

The door was mildewed with age, the wood so soft it crumbled. Inside the dim room, the windows had been blocked with ivy; as Jared lit lamps, Claudia stared around. "Just like home." He had set up his electron microscope on a rickety table, unpacked a few boxes of instruments and books.

He turned; in the flame light his face was haggard. "Claudia, you must look at this. It changes everything. Everything."

His anguish scared her. "Calm down," she said quietly. "Are you well?"

"Well enough." He leaned over the microscope, his long fingers adjusting it deftly. Then he stepped back. "You remember that scrap of metal I took from the study? Take a look at it."

Puzzled, she put her eye to the lens. The image was blurred; she refocused very slightly. And then she went very still, so rigid that Jared knew she had seen, and in that instant, had understood.

He went and sat wearily on the floor, among the ivy and nettles, the Sapient robe wrapped around him, its hem trailing in the dirt. And he watched her as she stared.

⬥〰⬥

IT WAS the Wall at the End of the World.

If Sapphique had truly fallen down it from top to bottom, it must have taken years. As Finn gazed up he felt the wind rebound from its immensity, making a slipstream that roared before them. Debris from the heart of Incarceron was blasted upward and then plummeted in an endless maelstrom; once trapped in that wind nothing would escape.

"We need to turn!" Gildas was staggering to the wheel; Finn scrambled after him. Together they squeezed beside Keiro, hauling, trying to make the ship veer before she struck the updraft.

With the thunder, Lightsout came.

In the blackness Finn heard Keiro swear, felt Gildas struggle around him, holding on tight. "Finn. Pull the lever! In the deck."

His hand groped, found it, and he tugged.

Lights blinked on, two beams of light horizontal from the bow of the ship. He saw how close the Wall was. The discs of light played on huge rivets, bigger than houses, the bolted panels immense, battered by the impact of fragments, immeasurably cracked and scarred and corroded.

"Can we back out?" Keiro yelled.

Gildas threw him a glance of scorn. And in that instant they fell. Plunging down, spilling beams and spars and ropes, the ship dropped down the side of the Wall like a great silvery angel, the sails its flailing wings, shredding in seconds, until just as they thought she would break, the slipstream caught them. Mast snapping, the silver craft shot upward again, spinning uncontrollably, the headlights wheeling on the Wall, darkness, a rivet, darkness. Tangled in the ropes Finn clung on, grabbing an arm that might have been Keiro's. The raging wind hurtled them high, the up-current welling from a roaring darkness, and as they rose the air thinned, the clouds and storm left far below, the Wall a sheer nightmare that sucked them close. They were so near, Finn could see its pitted surface was webbed with cracks and tiny doors, openings where bats gusted out and navigated the gale with ease. Scoured by the collision of a billion atoms the metal gleamed in the headlights.

The ship rolled. For a long second Finn was sure it would

roll right over; he held on to Keiro and closed his eyes, but when he opened them it had righted, and Keiro was crashing against him, flailing in the ropes.

The stern swung around. There was a great slither, a tremendous jerk.

Gildas roared. "Attia! She's let the anchor go!"

Attia must have gone below and pulled the pins from the capstan. The ascent slowed, the sails shredding. Gildas hauled himself up and pulled Finn close. "We have to get right into the Wall, and jump."

Finn stared, blank. The Sapient snapped, "It's the only way out! The ship will fall and rise and tumble forever! We have to drive her in there!"

He pointed. Finn saw a dark cube. It jutted out from the beaten metal, a hollow opening of darkness. It looked tiny; their chance of entering it remote.

"Sapphique landed on a cube." Gildas had to hold on to him. "That has to be it!"

Finn glanced at Keiro. Doubt flickered between them. As Attia came up the hatchway and slid toward them, Finn knew his oathbrother thought the old man was crazy, consumed with his quest. And yet what choice did they have?

Keiro shrugged. Reckless, he spun the wheel and headed the ship straight at the Wall. In the headlights the cube waited, a black enigma.

CLAUDIA COULD not speak. Her astonishment, her dismay were too great.

She saw animals.

Lions.

She counted them numbly: six, seven . . . three cubs. A pride. That was the word, wasn't it . . . ? "They can't possibly be real," she murmured.

Behind her, Jared sighed. "But they are."

Lions. Alive, prowling, one roaring, the rest snoozing in an enclosure of grass, a few trees, a lake where water birds waded.

She drew back, stared at the microscope, looked again.

One of the cubs scratched another; they rolled and fought. A lioness yawned and lay down, paws flat.

Claudia turned. She looked at Jared through the mothy lamplight and he looked back, and for a moment there was nothing to be said, only thoughts she didn't dare to think, implications she was too horrified to follow through.

Finally she said, "How small?"

"Incredibly small." He bit the ends of his long dark hair. "Miniaturized to about a millionth of a nanometer . . . Infinitesimal."

"They don't . . . How do they stay . . . ?"

"It's a gravity box. Self-adjusting. I thought the technique was lost. It seems to be an entire zoo. There are elephants, zebra . . ." His voice trailed off; he shook his head. "Perhaps it was the prototype . . . trying it first on animals. Who knows?"

"So this means . . ." She struggled to say it. "That Incarceron . . ."

"We've been looking for a huge building, an underground labyrinth. A world." He stared ahead into the darkness. "How blind we've been, Claudia! In the library of the Academy there are records that propose that such things—trans-dimensional changes—were once possible. All that knowledge was lost in the War. Or so we thought."

She got up; she couldn't sit still. The thought of the lions tinier than an atom of her skin, the grass they lay on even smaller, the minute ants they crushed with their paws, the fleas on their fur . . . it was too difficult to take in. But for them the world was normal. And for Finn . . . ?

She walked in nettles, not noticing. Made herself say, "Incarceron is tiny."

"I fear so."

"The Portal . . ."

"A process of entering. Every atom of the body collapsed." He glanced up and she saw how ill he looked. "Do you see? They made a Prison to hold everything they feared and diminished it so that its Warden could hold it in the palm of his hand. What an answer to the problems of an overcrowded system, Claudia. What a way to dismiss a world's troubles. And it explains much. The spatial anomaly. And there might be a time difference too, a very tiny one."

She went back to the microscope and watched the lions roll and play. "So this is why no one can come out." She looked up. "Is it reversible, Master?"

"How do I know? Without examining every—" He stopped dead. "You realize we have seen the Portal, the gateway? In your father's study there was a chair."

She leaned back against the table. "The light fixture. The ceiling slots."

It was terrifying. She had to walk again, pace up and down, think about it hard. Then she said, "I have something to tell you too. He knows. He knows we have the Key."

Without looking at him, not wanting to see the fear in his eyes, she told him about her father's anger, his demands. By the time she had finished, she found herself crouched beside him in the lamplight, her voice down to a whisper. "I won't give the Key back. I have to get Finn out."

He was silent, the coat collar high around his neck. "It's not possible," he said bleakly.

"There must be some way . . ."

"Oh, Claudia." Her tutor's voice was soft and bitter. "How can there be?"

Voices. Someone laughing, loud.

Instantly she leaped up, blew the lamps out. Jared seemed too dispirited to care. In the dark they waited, listening to the revelers' drunken shouts, a badly sung ballad fading away through the orchard. Claudia felt her heart thudding so loudly in the hush, it almost hurt. Faint bells chimed eleven in the clock towers and stables of the Palace. In one hour her wedding day would dawn. She would not give up. Not yet.

"Now that we know about the Portal and what it does . . . could you operate it?"

"Possibly. But there's no way back."

"I could try." She said it quickly. "Go in and look for him. What have I got here? A lifetime with Caspar . . ."

"No." He sat up and faced her. "Can you even begin to imagine life in there? A hell of violence and brutality? And here—if the wedding doesn't happen, the Steel Wolves will strike at once. There will be a terrible bloodshed." He reached over and took her hands. "I hope I've taught you always to face facts."

"Master—"

"You have to go through with the wedding. That's all that's left. There is no way back for Giles."

She wanted to pull away, but he wouldn't let her. She hadn't known he was so strong. "Giles is lost to us. Even if he's alive."

She slid her hands down and held his, tight with misery. "I don't know if I can," she whispered.

"I know. But you're brave."

"I'll be so alone. They're sending you away."

His fingers were cool. "I told you. You have far too much to learn." In the darkness he smiled his rare smile. "I'm going nowhere, Claudia."

THEY COULDN'T do it. The ship wouldn't hold steady, even with all of them hauling at the wheel. Her sails were rags, her rope trailed everywhere, her rails were smashed, and still she yawed and zigzagged, the anchor swinging and the bow oscillating toward the cube, away from it, above, below.

"It's impossible," Keiro growled.

"No." Gildas seemed lit with joy. "We can do it. Keep strong." He gripped the wheel and stared ahead.

Suddenly the ship dropped. The headlights picked out the cube's opening; as they closed on it, Finn saw it was filmed across with a strange viscosity like the surface of a bubble. Rainbows of iridescence glimmered on it.

"Giant snails," Keiro muttered. Even now he was able to joke, Finn thought.

Nearer, nearer. Now the ship was so close, they could see the reflection of her lights, swollen and distorted. So close that the bowsprit touched the film, indented it, pierced it so that it popped with soft abruptness, vanishing into a faint puff of sweet air.

Gradually, fighting the upstream, the ship slewed into the dark cube. The buffeting slowed. Vast shadows overwhelmed the headlights.

Finn stared up at the square of blackness. As it opened as if to swallow him, he felt that he was very tiny, was an ant crawling into a fold of cloth, a picnic cloth laid on the grass far away and long ago, where a birthday cake with seven candles lay half eaten, and a little girl with brown curly hair was handing him a golden plate, so politely.

He smiled at her and took it.

The ship cracked. The mast splintered, toppled, wood showering around them. Attia fell against him, scrabbling after a crystal glitter that slid from his shirt. "Get the Key," she yelled.

But the ship hit the back of the cube and darkness crashed down on him. Like a finger crushing the ant. Like a main mast falling.

THE LOST PRINCE

29

> *Despair is deep. An abyss that swallows dreams.*
> *A wall at the world's end. Behind it I await*
> *death. Because all our work has come to this.*
> —Lord Calliston's Diary

The morning of the wedding dawned hot and fine.

Even the weather had been planned; the trees were in full blossom and the birds sang, the sky was a cloudless blue, the temperature perfect, the breeze gentle and sweetly scented.

From her window Claudia watched the sweating servants unloading the carriage-loads of gifts, saw even from up here the glint of diamonds, the dazzle of gold.

She put her chin on the stone sill, felt its gritty warmth.

There was a nest just above, a swallow that dipped in and out regularly with beakfuls of flies. Invisible chicks cheeped urgently as the parents came and went.

She felt heavy-eyed and bone-weary. All night she had lain awake and looked up into the crimson hangings of the bed, listening to the silence of the room, her future hanging over her like a weighty curtain ready to fall. Her old life was finished—the freedom, the studying with Jared, the long rides and tree-climbing, the carelessness of doing as she liked. Today she would be Countess of Steen, would enter the war of scheming and treachery that was the life of the Palace. In an hour they would come to bathe her, do her hair, paint her nails, dress her like a doll.

She looked down.

There was a roof far below, the slope of some turret. For a dreamy moment she thought that if she tied all the sheets of the bedclothes together, she might let herself down, slowly, hand over hand till her bare feet touched the hot tiles. She might scramble down and steal a horse from the stables and ride away, escape just as she was, in her white nightdress, into the green forests on the far hills.

It was a warming thought. The girl who disappeared. The lost Princess. It made her smile. But then a call from below jerked her back; she glanced down and saw Lord Evian, resplendent in blue and ermine, gazing up at her.

He called something; she was too high to hear what, but she smiled and nodded, and he bowed and walked away, his small heeled shoes clacking.

Watching him, she knew that all the Court was like him, that behind its perfumed and elaborate facade lurked a web of hatreds and secret murders, and her own part in that would begin very soon, and to survive it she must be as hard as they were. Finn could never be rescued. She had to accept that.

She got up, sending the swallow off in panic, and walked to the dressing table.

It was laden with flowers, tussy-mussies, nosegays, and bouquets. They had been arriving all morning, so that the room smelled exquisite and sickly. Behind her, on the bed, the white gown lay spread in its finery. She looked at herself.

All right. She would marry Caspar and become Queen. If there was a plot, she would be part of it. If there were killings, she would survive them. She would rule. No one would tell her what to do ever again.

She opened the dressing table drawer, took out the Key, and placed it on the tabletop. It glimmered, its crystal facets catching the sunlight, its eagle splendid.

But first she would have to tell Finn. Break it to him that there was no escape.

Tell him their engagement was over.

She reached out to it, but just as she touched it, there was a low knock on the door and instantly she slid it smoothly into the drawer and picked up a brush. "Come in, Alys."

The door opened. "Not Alys," her father said.

He stood, dark and elegant, framed by the gilt lintel. "May I come in?"

"Yes," she said.

His coat was new, a deep black velvet, a white rose in the lapel, his knee breeches satin. He wore shoes with discreet buckles and his hair was caught in a black ribbon. He sat gracefully, flipping the tails of the coat. "All this finery is rather a bother. But one has to be perfect on such a day." Glancing at her plain dress, he took his watch out and opened it, so that the sun caught the silver cube that hung on the chain. "You have only two hours, Claudia. You should dress now."

She leaned her elbow on the table. "Is that what you came to tell me?"

"I came to tell you how proud I am." His gray eyes held hers, and the light in them was keen and sharp. "Today is the day I have planned and schemed for for decades. Long before you were born. Today the Arlexi come to the heart of power. Nothing must go wrong." He stood up and strode to the window, as if tension would not let him keep still. He smiled. "I confess I have not slept, thinking of it."

"You're not the only one."

He looked at her closely. "You must have no fear, Claudia. Everything is arranged. Everything ready."

Something in his tone made her glance up. For a moment she looked at him and saw under the mask, saw a man driven so fiercely by his dream of power that he would sacrifice anything to achieve it. And with a cold shiver she saw that he would not share it. Not with the Queen, or Caspar. "What do you mean . . . everything?"

"Just that things will turn out in our favor. Caspar is nothing but a stepping-stone."

She stood. "You know, don't you? About the assassination plan . . . the Steel Wolves. Are you one of them?"

He crossed the room in one step and grabbed her arm so tightly, she gasped. "Keep quiet," he snapped. "Do you think there aren't listening devices even here?"

He led her to the window and flung it open. Strains of lute and drum floated upward, the shouts of a guard commander drilling his men. Under cover of the noise his voice was low and husky. "Just do your part, Claudia. That's all."

"And then you kill them." She tugged away.

"What happens after doesn't concern you. Evian had no right to approach you."

"Doesn't it? How long before I'm in your way too? How long before I fall off my horse?"

She had shocked him. "That will never happen."

"No?" Her scorn was acid; she wanted it to burn him. "Because I'm your daughter?"

He said, "Because I have come to love you, Claudia."

There was something there that struck her. Something odd. But he turned away. "Now. The Key."

She frowned, then went to the dressing table and opened the drawer. The Key gleamed; she took it out and laid it on the top, among the clustered flowers.

The Warden came and looked down at it. "Not even your precious Jared could have discovered all the mysteries of this device."

"I want to say good-bye," she said, stubborn. "To Finn, and

the others. To explain to them. Then I'll give you the Key. At the wedding."

His eyes were cold and clear. "You always have to try my patience, Claudia."

For a moment she thought he would just take it. But he walked to the door.

"Don't keep Caspar waiting too long. He gets so . . . sulky."

She locked the door after him and sat down, holding the Key in both hands. *I have come to love you.* Perhaps he even thought that was true.

She switched the field on.

Then she jumped back, so fast that the Key fell with a clatter onto the floor.

Attia was in her room.

"You have to help us," the girl said at once. "The ship has crashed. Gildas is hurt."

The field widened; she saw a dark place, heard a distant howling as of wind. Petals blew off the flowers on her table, as if a gale from that place moved here.

Attia was shoved aside; Finn said, "Claudia, please. Can Jared help . . . ?"

"Jared's not here." Helpless, she saw the wreckage of a strange craft littering the floor. Keiro was tearing a piece of sail into strips and binding Gildas's arm and shoulder; she saw blood already seeping through. "Where are you?"

"The Wall." Finn looked weary. "I think we've come as far

as we can. This is the End of the World. There's a passageway beyond, but I don't know if he can travel . . ."

"Of course I bloody can," Gildas snapped.

Finn pulled a face. "Not for long. We must be close, Claudia, to the gate."

"There is no gate." She knew her voice was flat.

He looked at her. "But you said—"

"I was wrong. I'm sorry. It's all over, Finn. There is no gate and there is no way out. Not ever. Not from Incarceron."

◦○◦

JARED WALKED into the Great Hall. It was thronged with courtiers and princes, ambassadors, Sapienti, dukes, and duchesses. It was a bewilderment of colored satins and the smell of sweat and powerful fragrances, and it made him feel a little weak. There were seats along the wall; he made for one and sat, leaning his head back against the cool stone. All around him, the guests at Claudia's wedding chattered and laughed. He saw the bridegroom, with a gang of his wild young friends, already drinking, laughing uproariously at some joke. The Queen was not present yet, nor the Warden.

A crinkle of silk beside him made him turn. Lord Evian bowed. "You look a little tired, Master."

Jared stared back. "A sleepless night, sir."

"Ah yes. But soon now, all our worries will be over." The fat man smiled, and fanned himself with a small black fan. "Please give Claudia all my best wishes."

He bowed again and turned. Jared said suddenly, "One moment, my lord. The other day . . . when you made a certain promise . . ."

"Yes?" Evian's smug manner was gone; he looked guarded.

"You mentioned the Nine-Fingered One."

Evian glared. He grabbed Jared's arm and hauled him into the crowd, moving so fast, people stared as they were pushed aside. Out in the corridor he hissed, "Never say that name aloud. It is a sacred and a holy name for those who believe."

Jared tugged his arm free. "I have heard of many cults and beliefs. Certainly all the ones the Queen allows. But this—"

"This is not the day to discuss religion."

"Yes it is." Jared's eyes were sharp and clear. "And we have very little time. Does he have another name, this hero of yours?"

Evian breathed out angrily. "I really can't say."

"You will say, my lord," Jared said pleasantly, "or I'll make such an outcry right now about your assassination plan that every guard in the Palace will hear it."

Evian's brow prickled with sweat. "I think not."

Jared glanced down; the fat man had a dagger in his hand, the blade hard against Jared's stomach. With an effort, he met the man's eyes. "Either way, my lord, you would be discovered. All I ask is a name."

For a moment they were face-to-face. Then Lord Evian said,

"You are a brave man, Sapient, but don't cross me again. As for the name, yes, indeed there is one, hidden in time, lost in legend. The name of the One who claimed to have escaped from Incarceron. In the most mysterious of our rites he is known as Sapphique. Does that satisfy your curiosity?"

Jared stared at him for a split second. Then he shoved him aside. And ran.

—◦◇◦—

KEIRO WAS wild with anger; he and Gildas were yelling at her. "How can you abandon us?" the Sapient scorched. "Sapphique Escaped! Of course there is a way out!"

She was silent. She was looking at Finn. He sat huddled up against a smashed angle of decking, stiff with misery. His jacket was torn and there were cuts on his face, but now more than ever she was sure he was Giles. Now that it was too late.

"And you're marrying him," he said quietly.

Gildas swore. Keiro gave his oathbrother a scathing look. "What does it matter who she marries! Perhaps she decided she likes him better than you." He turned, hands on hips, and faced her arrogantly. "Is that it, Princess? Was this all a little diversion for you, a pretty game?" He jerked his head. "Such lovely flowers! Such a sweet dress!"

He came up so close to her that she almost felt he would reach out and grab her, but then Finn said, "Shut up, Keiro." He got up and faced her. "Just tell me why. Why is it so impossible?"

She couldn't. How could she tell them that? "Jared found some things out. You have to believe me."

"What things?"

"About Incarceron. It's finished, Finn. Please. Make a life for yourself there. Forget the Outside . . ."

"And what about me?" Gildas snapped. "I've spent sixty years planning my Escape! I scoured the Prison for a lifetime before I found a Starseer, and I'll never find another! We have traveled to the End of the World, girl! I will not give up my dreams of a lifetime!"

She stood up and stalked toward him, furious. "You use him like my father uses me. All he is to you is a way out; you don't care about him! Any of you!"

"That's not true!" Attia hissed.

Claudia ignored her. Looking hard at Finn she said, "I'm sorry. I wish things could have been different. I'm sorry."

There was some sort of commotion outside her door; she turned and yelled, "I won't see anyone! Send them away!"

Finn said, "Do you know what I'm escaping from? From not knowing myself. Having this darkness inside me, this emptiness. I can't live with that. Don't leave me here, Claudia!"

She couldn't bear it anymore. Not Keiro's anger, not the fierce old man, not him. He was hurting her, and none of this was her fault, none of it. She reached out for the Key. "This is good-bye, Finn. I have to give up the Key. My father knows about everything. It's over."

Her fingers closed on the link. Voices argued outside the door.

And then Attia said, "He's not your father, Claudia."

They all turned to her.

She was sitting on the floor, arms around her knees. She didn't get up or say anything more but just sat there in the shocked silence she had created, her narrow face grimy and calm, her dark hair greasy.

Claudia came right up to her. "What?" Her own voice sounded small and unfamiliar.

"I'm afraid it's true." Attia was cool and distant. "I wouldn't have told you, but now you're forcing me to, and it's time you knew. The Warden of Incarceron is not your father."

"You lying little bitch!"

"No, it's true."

Keiro grinned.

Claudia felt as if the world had shaken. Suddenly the hubbub outside was too much; turning her back on them, she hauled open the door. Jared was there, and two guards holding him back.

"What is this?" Her voice was steel. "Let him through."

"Your father's orders, lady—"

"My father," she screamed, "can go to hell!"

Jared pushed her back into the room and slammed the door. "Claudia, listen—"

"Please, Master! Not now!"

He saw the lightfield. Claudia stalked back to it. "All right. Tell me," she said.

For a moment Attia said nothing. Then she stood up, brushing dirt from her bare arms. "I never liked you. Haughty, selfish, spoiled. You think you're so tough—you wouldn't last ten minutes in here. And Finn is worth ten of you."

"Attia," Finn growled, but Claudia said sharply, "Let her speak."

"Back there in the Sapient's tower we found lists of all the Prisoners who have ever been in this place. They all looked for their own names, but I didn't." Attia came close to Claudia. "I looked for yours."

Finn turned, chilled. "You said it wasn't there."

"I said she wasn't in Incarceron. But she has been."

He felt so cold. Looking at Claudia, he saw her face was white; it was Jared who said quietly, "When?"

"She was born here, and she lived here for one week. Then, nothing. She vanishes from the records. Someone took a week-old baby girl out of the Prison, and there she is, look, the daughter of the Warden. He must have been very desperate for a daughter. And there must have been one who died, or he would have chosen a son."

Keiro said, "You recognize her from a photo of a baby? That's—"

"Not just a baby." Attia kept her eyes on Claudia. "Someone put paintings of her into the book. Images, just like us. Of

378

her growing up. Of her having everything she wanted, clothes, toys, horses. Of her . . ."

"Getting betrothed?" Keiro said slyly.

Finn turned with a gasp. "Was I there? Was I in that image too? Attia!"

Her lips set. "No."

"Are you sure?"

"I'd tell you if you were." She turned earnestly. "I would tell you, Finn. It was just her."

He looked at Claudia. She seemed stunned with shock. He glanced at Jared, who muttered, "I have also found the name of Sapphique here. It seems he truly did Escape."

Gildas spun around and the two Sapienti exchanged glances. "You see what this means." The old man was triumphant. He was bleeding and limping, but his whole body was charged with energy. "They took her out. Sapphique got out. There is a way. Perhaps if we brought both the Keys together, we could unlock it."

Jared frowned. "Claudia?" he said.

She couldn't move for a moment. Then her head jerked up and she looked Finn hard in the eyes and he saw her gaze was fierce and bitter. "Keep the Key switched on, all the time," she said. "When I get Inside, I'll need to find you."

30

All my years to this moment
All my roads to this wall.
All my words to this silence
All my pride to this fall.

—*Songs of Sapphique*

She paced the study floor anxiously, dressed in dark trousers and jacket. "Well?"

"Five minutes." Jared worked on the controls without looking up. He had already placed a handkerchief on the chair and operated the device; the handkerchief had disappeared, but he couldn't get it back.

Claudia stared at the door.

She had torn up her wedding dress in a fury that had amazed even herself, shredding the lace and ripping the flouncy skirt wide open. All that was over. Protocol was over. She was at war now. Racing down here through the dark cellars, she had run through anger and bewilderment and the emptiness of a wasted past.

"All right." Jared looked up. "I think I understand what's what, but where this machine will take you, Claudia . . . ?"

"I know where it takes me. Away from him." The knowledge

that he was not her father still rang in her head like a great blare of sound, endlessly echoing, so that she felt she would never hear anything else but that girl's quiet, devastating words.

Jared said, "Sit in the chair."

She grabbed her sword and walked over and stopped. "What about you? When he finds out . . ."

"Don't worry about me." He took her arm gently and made her sit. "It's about time I stood up to your father. I'm sure it will be good for me."

Her face clouded. "Master . . . if he hurts you . . ."

"All you need to worry about is finding Giles and bringing him back. Justice must be done. Good luck, Claudia." He raised her hand and kissed it formally. For a moment she was stricken with the thought that she would never see him again; all she wanted to do was jump up and hug him, but he moved away to the panel of instruments and looked up. "Ready?"

She couldn't speak. She nodded. And then, just before his fingers touched the panel, she said hurriedly, "Good-bye, Master."

He pressed the blue square, and it happened. From the ceiling slots a cage of white light fell, so blindingly brilliant and so quick that it was gone as soon as it had come, and all he could see was the black aftermath imprinted on his retina.

He brought his hands away from his face.

The room was empty. He could smell a faint sweetness.

"Claudia?" he whispered.

Nothing. For a long moment he waited in the silence. He

wanted to stay, but he had to get out of the study; the Warden must not know what had happened for as long as possible, and if they found him here . . . Hurriedly he slammed the controls back, slid out through the great bronze door, and locked it behind him.

All the way up through the cellars Jared sweated with fear. There must be some alarm he had overlooked, some screaming trigger his scanner had failed to detect. At every step he expected to hurtle into the Warden or a posse of Palace guards, and by the time he came up to the formal corridors, he was pale and shivering and had to lean in an alcove and take deep, careful breaths, a passing maid staring at him curiously.

In the Great Hall, the crowd's noise was louder. As he threaded among them he sensed the growing tension, the expectation heightened almost to hysteria. The staircase that Claudia should descend was in full view, lined by footmen in powdered wigs. As he slipped into a seat by the fireplace he saw the Queen, glorious in cloth of gold and a tiara of diamonds, flicker an irritated glance at it.

But brides were always late.

Jared leaned back and stretched out his legs. He was light-headed with fear and fatigue and yet he felt something else that surprised him: a strange peace. He wondered how long it would last.

Then he saw the Warden.

Tall and grave, the man who was not Claudia's father. Jared

watched as the Warden smiled, nodded, exchanged graceful small talk with the waiting courtiers. Once he took out his watch and glanced at it, held it to his ear as if in all the hub-bub he needed to check it was going. Then he put it away and frowned.

Impatience grew, slowly.

The crowd murmured. Caspar came over and said something to his mother, she spoke to him sharply, and he went back to his supporters. Jared watched the Queen.

Her hair was swept up elaborately, her lips red in the whitened pallor of her face, but her eyes were cool and shrewd and he recognized the growing suspicion in them.

She crooked a finger and the Warden moved to her side. They spoke briefly. A servant was called, a smooth silver-haired steward, and he bowed and vanished discreetly.

Jared rubbed his face.

It must be panic up there in her rooms, the maids searching for her, fingering the dress, terrified for their own skins. Probably they had all fled. He hoped Alys wouldn't be there—the old nurse would be blamed.

He leaned back against the wall and tried to summon up all his courage.

He didn't have long to wait.

There was a disturbance on the stairs. Heads turned. Women craned to see, a rustle of dresses and faint applause that petered out into bewilderment, because the silver-haired servant was racing down, breathless, and in his hands he had the dress, or rather what was left of it. Jared wiped sweat from his lip. He had never seen Claudia so furious as when she had torn it to shreds.

Confusion erupted.

A scream of anger, orders, the clash of weapons.

Slowly, Jared stood.

The Queen was white-faced; she turned on the Warden. "What is this? Where is she?"

His voice was icy. "I have no idea, madam. But I suggest . . ."

He stopped. His gray eyes met Jared's through the agitated crowd.

They looked at each other and in the sudden growing hush the crowd noticed and fell back between them, as if people feared to stand in that corridor of anger.

The Warden said, "Master Jared. Do you know where my daughter is?"

Jared managed a small smile. "I regret I cannot say, sir. But I can say this. She has decided against the wedding."

The crowd was utterly silent.

Her eyes glittering with wrath, the Queen said, "She's jilted my son?"

He bowed. "She has changed her mind. It was sudden, and she felt she could not face either of you. She has left the Palace. She begs your indulgence."

Claudia would hate that last, he thought, but he had to be so careful. He steeled himself for the reaction. The Queen gave a laugh of pure venom; she turned on the Warden. "My dear John, what a blow for you! After all your plans and schemes! I have to say I never thought it a very good idea. She was so . . . unsuitable. You chose your replacement so badly."

The Warden's eyes never left Jared's, and the Sapient felt that basilisk stare slowly petrify his courage. "Where has she gone?"

Jared swallowed. "Home."

"Alone?"

"Yes."

"In a carriage?"

"On horseback."

The Warden turned. "A patrol after her. At once!"

Did he believe it? Jared wasn't sure.

"Of course I pity your domestic troubles," the Queen said cruelly, "but you realize that I will never suffer an insult like this again. There will be no wedding, Warden, even if she comes back crawling on her hands and knees."

Caspar muttered, "Scheming ungrateful bitch," but his mother silenced him with a look.

"Clear the chamber," she said sharply. "I want everyone out."

As if it was a signal, an uproar of voices burst out, excited questions, shocked whispers.

Through it all Jared stood still, and the Warden stood watching him, and there was a look in those eyes the Sapient could not bear now. He turned away.

"You stay." John Arlex's order was hoarse and unrecognizable.

"Warden." Lord Evian pushed up close to them. "I have just heard . . . such news . . . is it true?"

His affectations were gone; he was pale with intensity.

"True. She's gone." The Warden spared him one grim glance. "It's over."

"Then . . . the Queen?"

"Remains the Queen."

"But . . . our plan . . . "

The Warden silenced him with a flash of anger. "Enough, man! Don't you hear what I say? Go back to your puffs and perfumes. It's all we have now."

As if he could not understand what had happened, Evian clawed restlessly at his tight ruffled suit, tugging a button loose. "We can't let it end like this."

"We have no choice."

"All our dreams. The end of Protocol." He reached his hand inside the coat. "I can't. I won't."

He moved in before Jared realized what was happening, the knife flashing out, slashing down at the Queen. As she turned, it caught her high on the shoulder; she screamed in shock. Instantly the cloth of gold was running with blood, small spatterings and trickles that welled up as she gasped and clawed at Caspar, stumbling into the arms of courtiers.

"Guards!" the Warden cried. He whipped out his sword.

Jared turned.

Evian was staggering back, the pink suit smeared with blood. He must have seen he had failed; the Queen was hysterical but not dead, and there was no chance to strike again. At least not at her. Soldiers ran in, their sharp pikes forcing him back in a ring of steel. He stared at Jared without seeing him, at the Warden, at Caspar's pale terror.

"I do this for freedom," he said calmly. "In a world that offers none."

With a swift accuracy he turned the knife and with both hands thrust it into his heart. He crumpled over it, crashed down, juddered a moment and was still. As Jared pushed past the guards and bent over him, he saw death had been almost instant; blood was still slowly welling through the silk cloth.

He gazed down, horrified, at the plump face, the staring eyes.

"Stupid," the Warden said behind him. "And weak." He reached down and hauled Jared up, turning him roughly.

"Are you weak, Master Sapient? I have always thought so. We'll see now if I was right." He looked at the guard. "Take the Master to his room and lock him in. Bring me any devices that are there. Post two men outside. He is not to leave, and will receive no visitors."

"Sire." The man bowed.

The Queen had been hustled out and the crowd scattered; all at once the great Chamber seemed empty. The garlands of flowers and orange blossom drifted slightly in the breeze from the open windows. As Jared was led to the door he stepped on spilled petals and sticky sweetmeats; the detritus of a wedding that would never happen.

Just before they pushed him out, he looked back and saw the Warden standing with both hands on the high fireplace, leaning over the empty hearth. His hands were clenched fists on the white marble.

◄◦◦◦►

NOTHING HAPPENED but a white light. When Claudia opened her eyes, they stung; her sight was watery, and small dark spots floated there for a minute, dimming the walls of the cell.

It was certainly a cell. It stank. The smell was so strong, she retched and then tried not to breathe again, the reek of damp and urine and rotting bodies and straw.

The straw was all around her; she was sitting in it, and a flea jumped out of it onto her hand. With a hiss of disgust she jumped up and shook it off, shivering and scratching.

So this was Incarceron.

It was just as she'd expected.

The cell was stone-walled and the stones were carved with ancient names and dates, filmed with milky lichens and a fur of algae. Above, the groined vault was lost in darkness. There was one window, high in the wall, but it seemed to be covered. Nothing else. But the cell door was open.

Claudia took another breath, trying not to cough. The cell was silent, a heavy, oppressive silence that was cold and clammy. A listening silence. And in the corner of the cell, she saw an Eye. A small red Eye that watched her impassively.

She felt normal. No tingling or sickness. She looked at herself, her hands clutching the Key. Was she really so minute? Or was any notion of size relative—was this normality and the Realm outside a place of giants?

She crossed to the door. It had not been locked for a long time. Chains hung from it, but they were corroded into a mass with rust, and the hinges were eaten away so that the door hung at an angle. She ducked under it, into the passageway.

It was stone-flagged and filthy, and it stretched into darkness.

She looked at the Key, operated the imager. "Finn?" she whispered. Nothing happened. Only, far off down the corridor, something hummed. A low-pitched whine, like a machine being activated. She flicked the Key off hastily, her heart thudding. "Is that you?"

Nothing.

She took two steps, then stopped. The sound came again, just ahead, a soft, oddly questing sound. She saw a red Eye open, turn slowly through a half circle, then stop and swivel back toward her. She kept very still.

"I see you," a voice said softly. *"I recognize you."*

Not Finn's. Not anyone she knew.

"I never forget any of my children. But you haven't been here for a while. I'm not sure I understand that."

Claudia wiped her cheek with a grimy hand. "Who are you? I can't see you."

"Yes you can. You're standing on me, breathing me."

She stepped back, staring down, but there was only the stone floor, the darkness.

The red Eye watched her. She breathed a sickening breath. "You're the Prison."

"I am." It sounded fascinated. *"And you are the Warden's daughter."*

She couldn't speak. Jared had said it was an intelligence, but she hadn't realized it would be like this.

"Shall we help each other, Claudia Arlexa?" The voice was calm and had a slight echo. *"You are looking for Finn and his friends. Isn't that right?"*

"Yes." Should she have said that?

"I will lead you to them."

"The Key will do that."

"Don't use the Key. It interferes with my systems."

Was she mistaken, or had that been hurried, almost annoyed? She began to walk on slowly, into the dark corridor. "I see. And what do you want in return?"

A sound. It could have been a sigh, or a soft laugh. *"Not a question I have been asked before. I want you to tell me what is Outside. Sapphique promised faithfully that he would come back and tell me, but he never has. Your father does not speak of it. I begin to wonder, in my heart of hearts, if there even is an Outside, or whether Sapphique passed only into death and you live in a place here I am unable to detect. I have a billion Eyes and senses, and yet I cannot see out. It is not only the inmates who dream of Escape, Claudia. But then, how can I escape from myself?"*

She came to a corner. The passageway forked in two, both dark and dripping, and identical. She frowned and held the Key tightly. "I don't know. It's pretty much what I'm trying to do. All right. Take me to Finn. And as we go I'll tell you what's Outside."

Lights flickered on ahead. *"This way."*

She paused. "You do really know where they are? This isn't a trick?"

Silence. Then, *"Oh Claudia. How angry your father will be with you. When he finds out."*

31

He fell all day and all night. He fell into a pit of darkness. He fell like a stone falls, like a bird with broken wings, like an angel cast down. His landing bruised the world.

—*Legends of Sapphique*

"It's changed." Keiro looked intently at the Key. "The colors."

Finn lifted the crystal into a glimmer of light. The red lights were humming, flickering into a muted rainbow. The Key seemed warmer in his hand.

"Maybe she's Inside."

"Then why doesn't she talk to us?"

Ahead, Gildas turned, a limping shadow in the darkness. "Is this the way? Finn?"

He had no idea. The wreckage of the ship was far behind; the cube had become a funnel, narrowing as they hurried into it, the sides and roof closing in, becoming black faceted stone, the familiar obsidian glint of walls.

"Keep close to me," he muttered. "We don't know how far the protective field goes."

Gildas barely heard. Since he had spoken to Jared the feverish possession of his quest had come over him again; anxiously he limped ahead, examining faint scratches on the walls, muttering to himself. He seemed to ignore his injuries, but Finn guessed they were more serious than he let on.

"The old fool's losing it," Keiro muttered in disgust. He turned. "And then there's her."

Attia hung back. She seemed to be walking deliberately slowly; in the shadows she seemed deep in thought.

"That was some stunt she pulled." Keiro walked on. He gave a sharp glance at Finn. "A real blow under the belt."

Finn nodded. Claudia had gone so still. Like someone stabbed with a deep wound keeps still, so as not to feel the pain.

"But," Keiro said, "it means there's a way out. So we can get out too."

"You're heartless. You only ever think about yourself."

"And you, brother." His oathbrother glanced around, alert. "If there is an Outside and you're some sort of king out there, then I'm guarding you like gold. Prince Keiro sounds good to me."

"I'm not sure I can do that . . . be that."

"You can. It's all pretense. You're a master of lies, Finn." Keiro looked at him sidelong. "You'll be a natural."

For a moment they shared a look. Then Finn said, "Can you hear something?"

A murmur. It drifted down the corridor, a gust of soft voices. Keiro drew his sword. Attia closed up. "What is it?"

"Something ahead." Keiro listened intently, but the sound

did not come again. Standing still, one hand against the wall, Gildas whispered, "Maybe it's Claudia. She's found us."

"Then she was very quick about it." Keiro walked on softly. "Stay together. Finn, go at the back, and keep the Key safe."

Gildas snorted but took his place between them.

It was a voice. It was speaking somewhere ahead, and as they crept toward it, the passageway became cluttered; great chains lay across it, manacles and shackles, scattered heaps of tools, a broken Beetle on its back. They passed small cells, some with the doors locked, and through the grille in one Finn saw a tiny dark room with rats clambering over an empty plate, a filthy pile of rags in one corner that might have been a body. Everything was still. He felt that this was a place forgotten even by its makers, a corner of itself even Incarceron had overlooked for centuries. Had it been somewhere like this that the Maestra's people had found the Key, with the desiccated bones of the man who had made it, or stolen it?

Stepping around a great pillar he realized he was beginning to forget her. Already it seemed so long ago, and yet the clatter of the bridge, her single look, were still inside him, waiting for him to sleep, to think he was safe. And her pity.

Attia grabbed him; he realized he had been walking past them.

"Stay awake, brother." Keiro's hiss was fierce.

Heart thudding, he tried to clear his head. The prickling in his face subsided. He took deep breaths.

"All right?" Gildas whispered.

He nodded. The fit had nearly crept up on him. It made him feel sick.

Peering around the corner, he stared.

The voice was speaking in a language he had never heard, of clicks and squeaks and stilted syllables. It was addressing Beetles and Sweepers and Flies, and the metallic rats that came out of the walls to carry off corpses. Millions of them crouched motionless on the floor of a great hall, lined ropes and aerial walkways, all of them facing one brilliant star that shone like a spark in the darkness. Incarceron instructed its creatures and the words it spoke were a patchwork of sounds, a poetry of cracks and rumbles.

"Can they hear?" Keiro whispered.

"It's not just words." It was a vibration too, deep in the heart of the darkness, a sound like a vast heart beating, a great clock chiming.

The voice stopped. At once the machines turned and filed away, moving in silent rows into the darkness till the last one was gone, barely making a sound.

Finn moved, but Keiro grabbed him tight.

The Eye still watched. Its light lit the empty hall. Then the voice said softly, *"Have you got the Key with you, Finn? Shall I take it now?"*

He gasped. He wanted to run, but Keiro's grip said no. Biting his lip, he heard the Prison's low amused chuckle. *"Claudia* is Inside. Did you know that? Of course I intend to keep you both apart. I am so vast, it will be only too easy. Won't you speak to me, Finn?"

"It's not sure we're here," Keiro muttered.

"It sounds sure to me."

He had an irrational urge to step out from the Key's protection, to open his arms and go out. But Keiro wouldn't let go, and wriggled around to Attia. "Back. Quickly."

"Of course I am only a machine," Incarceron said acidly. "Unlike you. Or are you? Are you all so pure? Perhaps I should try a little experiment of my own."

Keiro shoved him, panicking. "Run!"

It was too late. There was a hiss and a crack. The sword flew out of Keiro's hand and clanged against the wall, held there upside down.

And Finn was hauled back, slammed against the stones, the Key in his belt pinning him there, the dagger he held whipping his arm flat with enormous power.

"Ah. Now I feel you, Finn. Now I feel your fear."

He couldn't move. For a moment of terror he thought he was being sucked into the very fabric of the wall; then Gildas was there tugging at him, and he let go of the knife and his hand came free, and he realized the wall had become a magnet. Scraps of iron, flakes of bronze were flying in a fierce horizontal blizzard; the wall became clotted instantly with tools, chainwork, vast links. Finn ducked, cursing, as one clanged right next to his ear. "Get me off!" he screamed.

His body was crushed between the Key and the magnet.

Gildas already had hold of the crystal; the old man dug his heels and gasped, "Help me," and Attia's small hands grabbed tight. Slowly, as if they were tugging it away from invisible fingers they pulled the weight of the Key from him and he fell forward, stumbling.

"Go. *Go!*"

Incarceron laughed its deep laugh. *"But you can't go. Not without your brother."*

Poised to flee, he stopped.

Keiro was standing by the wall. He had one hand oddly propped against it, the back of his hand to the black surface. For a moment Finn thought he was trying to pry away the sword and yelled "Leave that!" but then Keiro turned and gave him a look of cold fury.

"It's not the sword."

Finn caught his oathbrother's arm and pulled.

It was held tight.

"Let go."

"I'm not holding anything," Keiro said. He turned his face away. Finn looked closer.

"But . . ."

His brother twisted to look at him and Finn was shocked by the anger in his eyes. "It's me, Finn. Don't you realize? Are you that stupid? Me!"

The fingernail of his right forefinger. It was tight to the wall, and when Finn grabbed his hand and pulled on it, it stayed there, a small shield held to the magnet with an attraction nothing could break.

"Shall I let him go?" the Prison said slyly.

Finn looked at Keiro and Keiro looked back. "Yes," he whispered.

With a violence that made them all wince, every piece of metal fell from the walls in one resounding crash.

CLAUDIA STOPPED. "What was that?"

"What?"

"That noise!"

"There are always noises in the Prison. Please do go on about the Queen. She sounds so—"

"It came from down there." Claudia stared down the dim archway she was passing. She saw a low passageway, barely head-high, roped with spiderwebs.

Incarceron laughed, but there was a note of anxiety in its humor. *"To find Finn you must go straight on."*

She was silent. Suddenly she sensed its tense presence all around her, as if it did not breathe, was waiting. She felt small and vulnerable. She said, "I think you're lying to me."

For a moment, nothing. A rat ran up the passage, saw her, and slunk around. Then the voice said thoughtfully, *"Your idea of Finn is a foolishly romantic one; the lost Prince, the imprisoned hero. You remember a little boy and want it to be him. But even if Finn is really Giles, that was a lifetime away and a world ago and he is not the same now. I have changed him.”*

She stared up into the darkness. “No.”

“Oh yes. Your father was right. To survive here men descend to the depths of their beings. They become beasts, not caring, not even seeing the pain of others. Finn has stolen, perhaps killed. How can such a man return to a throne, and govern others? How can he ever be trusted again? The Sapienti were wise, but they made a system without release, Claudia. Without forgiveness.”

Its voice was chilling her. She didn't want to listen, to be drawn into its persuasive doubts.

She activated the Key, turned into the low passage, and began to run.

Her shoes slithered on the rubble that littered the floor, bones and straw, a dead creature so desiccated, it collapsed as she jumped over it.

“Claudia. Where are you?”

It was all around her, before her, under her.

“Stop. Please. Or I will have to stop you.”

She didn't answer. Ducking under an arch, she found three tunnels that met, but the Key was so hot now, it almost scorched her hand, and she plunged into the left-hand tunnel, racing past cell doors that hung open.

The Prison rumbled. The floor rippled, rose up under her like a carpet. She gasped as it flung her up; she landed with a cry, one leg bloodied, but picking herself up, she raced on, because it couldn't be sure where she was, not with the Key.

The world rocked. It tipped from side to side. Darkness closed in, noxious smells seeped from the walls, bats swirled in clouds. She wouldn't scream. Clawing the stones, she pulled herself on, even when the passageway lifted itself up and became a hill, a steep, slippery slope, and all the rubble that lay on it slid down on her.

And then, just as she wanted to let go and slither back, she heard voices.

KEIRO FLEXED his fingers. His face was flushed and his eyes would not meet Finn's. It was Gildas who broke the silence. "So I've been traveling with a halfman."

Keiro ignored him. He looked at Finn, who said, "How long have you known?"

"All my life." His oathbrother's voice was subdued.

"But you. You were the one who hated them most. Despised them . . ."

Keiro shook his head in irritation. "Yes. Of course. I hate them. I have more cause to hate them than you. Don't you see that they scare me stiff?" He flung a glance at Attia, then yelled out at the Prison, "And you! I swear if I could ever find your heart, I'd slice it open!"

Finn didn't know how he felt. Keiro was so perfect, all he

had ever wanted to be. Handsome, bold, without flaw, alive with that zestful confidence he had always envied.

He was never scared stiff.

"All my sons think that," Incarceron said slyly.

Keiro slumped against the wall. A fire seemed to have gone out of him. He said, "It scares me because I don't know how far it goes." Lifting up his hand, he flexed his finger. "It looks real, doesn't it? No one can tell. And how do I know how much more of me is like that? Inside me, the organs, the heart. How do I know?" There was a sort of agony in the question, as if it had been asked silently a million times before, as if behind the bravado and arrogance was a fear he had never revealed.

Finn looked around. "The Prison could tell you."

"No. I don't want to know."

"It doesn't matter to me." Finn ignored Gildas's snort and glanced at Attia.

Quietly she said, "So we're all flawed. Even you. I'm sorry."

"Thanks." Keiro was scornful. "The pity of a dog-girl and a Starseer. That really makes me feel better."

"We're only—"

"Save it. I don't need it." He brushed away Finn's outstretched hand and pulled himself upright. "And don't think it changes me. I'm still me."

Gildas limped past. "Well, you get no pity from me. Let's get on."

Keiro stared at his back with a rigidity of hatred that made

Finn move in; his oathbrother snatched up the sword from the floor, but as he took one step after the Sapient, the Prison shivered and shuddered.

Finn grabbed the wall.

When the world stopped moving, the air was thick with dust; it hung like a fog, and there was a ringing in his ears. Gildas was hissing in pain. Attia scrambled over; she pointed through the miasma. "Finn. What's that?"

For a moment he had no idea. Then he saw it was a face. A face that was oddly clean, with bright clever eyes and a tangle of hastily tied hair. A face that was staring at him out of the mists of the past over the tiny flames of candles on a cake that he leaned over and blew out with one exhausting breath.

"Is that you?" she whispered.

He nodded, silent, knowing this was Claudia.

32

You will thank us for this. Energy will not be wasted on frivolous machines. We will learn to live simply, untroubled by jealousies and desires. Our souls will be as placid as the tideless seas.

—King Endor's Decree

The soldiers came after two hours.

Jared had been waiting for them; he had lain on the hard bed in the silent room and listened to the sounds of the Palace through the open casement; the galloping horses far below, the coaches, the scurry, the shouts. It was as if Claudia had taken a stick to a nest of ants and now they were in a swarming panic, their Queen injured and their peace gone.

The Queen. As he sat up stiffly and gazed at the men, he hoped he wouldn't have to face her fury.

"Master." The liveried servant seemed embarrassed. "Would you come with us, sir."

Always the Protocol. It saved them from facing the truth. As they led him down the stairs, the guardsmen fell in discreetly behind, their halberds held like staffs of office.

He had already gone through all the emotions. Terror, bluster, despair. Now all that was left was a sort of dull resignation.

Whatever the Warden would do to him had to be borne. Claudia had to have time.

To his surprise they took him past the state rooms, where anxious envoys argued and messengers ran in and out, down to a small room in the east wing. When they ushered him in he saw it was one of the Queen's private drawing-rooms, cluttered with fragile gilt furniture, an elaborate clock on the mantelpiece heaped with cherubs and simpering shepherdesses.

Only the Warden was here.

He was not sitting at a desk, but standing, facing the door. Two armchairs were arranged at easy angles by the hearth, where a great bowl of potpourri sat in the empty fireplace.

It still felt like a trap.

"Master Jared." The Warden indicated one chair with a long finger. "Please sit."

He was glad to. He felt breathless and light-headed.

"A little water." The Warden poured it and brought the goblet over. As he drank from it Jared felt Claudia's father . . . no, not her father . . . watching him acutely.

"Thank you."

"You haven't eaten?"

"No . . . I suppose . . . in all the fuss . . ."

"You should take more care of yourself." The voice was hard. "Too many hours working at these forbidden devices."

He waved a hand. Jared saw that the table near the window was covered with pieces of his experiments, the scanners, the imagers, the devices to block alarms. He said nothing. "Of course you understand that all these are illegal." The Warden's eyes were ice-cold. "We have always allowed the Sapienti a certain leeway, but you seem to have been taking great advantage." Then he said, "Where is Claudia, Master?"

"I told you—"

"Don't lie to me. She is not at home. There are no horses unaccounted for."

"Perhaps . . . she may be on foot."

"I do believe she is." The Warden sat opposite him, his black satin breeches creasing elegantly. "And perhaps you thought you were not lying when you said home?"

Jared put the cup down. They faced each other.

"How did she find out?" John Arlex said.

Jared decided, quite suddenly, to tell the truth. "The girl in the Prison told her, Attia, Finn's friend. From some records she had discovered."

The Warden nodded in slow appreciation. "Ah yes. How did she take it?"

"She was . . . very shocked."

"Furious?"

"Yes."

"I would expect nothing else."

"And upset."

The Warden shot him a keen glare, but Jared returned it

calmly. "She had always been so secure as your daughter, sir. Known who she was. She . . . cares for you."

"Don't lie to me." The sudden snarl shocked him with its anger. The Warden got up and paced down the room. "There has only ever been one person Claudia has cared for in her life, Master Sapient. And that is you."

Jared sat still. His heart hammered. "Sir . . ."

"Did you think I was blind?" The Warden turned. "No indeed. Oh, she had her nurses and her waiting women, but Claudia is far above their level and she knew it early. Every time I came home I saw how she and you laughed and talked, how she fussed with your coat if it was cold, sent for possets and sweetmeats, how you had your private jokes, your shared studies." He folded his arms and stared out of the window. "With me she was distant, reserved. She didn't know me. I was a stranger, the Warden, a great man at Court, someone who came and went. Someone to be wary of. But you, Master Jared, you were her tutor and her brother and more her father than I have ever been."

Jared was cold now. Behind the Warden's iron control was a blazing hatred; he had never sensed the depth of it before. He tried to breathe calmly.

"How do you think that felt, Master?" The Warden swung around. "Did you think I didn't feel it? Do you think I didn't suffer, not knowing what to do, how to change it? Aware that with every word I spoke I was deceiving her;

every day, just by being there, by letting her think she was mine."

"She . . . that is what she will not forgive."

"Don't tell me how she thinks!" John Arlex came and stood over him. "I have always been jealous of you. Is that not foolish? A dreamer, a man without family, so fragile a few blows would kill him. And the Warden of Incarceron is sick with envy."

Jared managed to say, "I . . . am very fond of Claudia . . ."

"You know, of course, there are rumors about you." The Warden swung away abruptly and sat down again. "I don't believe them; Claudia is willful but not stupid. However, the Queen does, and let me tell you Jared, at the moment the Queen is screaming for revenge. On anyone. Evian is dead, but the plot obviously included others. You, for one."

He shivered. "Sir, you know well that is not so."

"You knew about it. Didn't you?"

"Yes, but . . ."

"And you did nothing. Told no one." He leaned forward. "That is treason, Master Sapient, and could easily have you hanged."

In the silence someone called outside. A fly buzzed in and droned around the room, hitting the glass and fumbling against it.

Jared tried to think, but there was no time. The Warden snapped, "Where's the Key?"

He wanted to lie. To make something up. Instead he kept silent.

"She's taken it with her, hasn't she?"

He didn't answer. The Warden swore. "The whole world thinks Giles is dead. She could have had everything, the Realm, the throne. Did she think I would let Caspar get in her way?"

"You were in the plot?" Jared said slowly.

"Plot! Evian and his naive dreams of a world without Protocol! There has never been a world without Protocol. I would have let the Steel Wolves deal with the Queen and Caspar, and then had them executed, simple. But now she has turned against me."

He was staring blankly across the room. Jared said gently, "The story you told her . . . about her mother."

"That was true. But when Helena died the baby was sickly and I knew it would die too. And what then of my plans? I needed a daughter, Master. And I knew where to get one." He sat in the armchair opposite. "Incarceron is a failure. A hell. The Wardens have long known that, but there is no remedy, so we keep it secret. I thought I would rescue one soul from that, at least. In the depths of the Prison I found a woman who was so desperate she was willing to part with her newborn girl. I paid well. Her other children survived because of it."

Jared nodded. The Warden's voice had sunk; he seemed to be talking to himself, as if he had justified this endlessly to himself over the years.

"No one realized, except the Queen. That sorceress took one look at the child and knew."

A sudden understanding came to Jared. Fascinated, he said, "Claudia always wondered why you agreed to the plot against Giles. Was it because the Queen . . ." He stopped, not knowing the words, but the Warden nodded without looking up.

"Blackmail, Master Sapient. Her son was to be the one to marry Claudia. If I had not agreed, she taunted me that she would tell Claudia publicly who she was, disgrace her before the whole Realm. I could not have borne that."

For a moment there was a wistful distance in him, a still-ness. Then he raised his head and saw Jared's look and his face went cold. "Do not feel sorry for me, Master. That's something I do not need." He stood. "I know she's gone into Incarceron. For this Finn. There's nothing for you to betray. And she has taken the Key." He laughed bitterly. "It's as well she took it. There's no way out without it."

Suddenly he stalked to the door. "Follow me."

Startled Jared stood, fighting down a shard of fear, but the Warden stepped out into the corridor and waved the guards away impatiently. The men looked at each other.

One said uneasily, "Sir, the Queen has issued orders that we stay with you. For your protection."

The Warden nodded slowly. "My protection. I see. Then please remain here and guard this door after I enter. Allow no one to follow us down."

Before they could argue he had opened a hidden door in the wainscoting and led the way down some dank steps into the cellars. Halfway down, Jared looked back. The men were watching curiously through the slit.

"It appears the Queen suspects me too," the Warden said calmly. He took a lantern from the wall and lit the candle inside it. "We will have to work quickly. The study, as you've no doubt realized, is the same room here as at home. A space halfway between this world and the Prison, a Portal, as the inventor Martor called it."

"Martor's writings are lost," Jared said, hurrying after him.

"I have them. They are classified." His dark figure paced down quickly, holding the lantern high, its shadows flickering down the wall. He glanced back at Jared's astonishment and allowed himself a smile. "You will never see them, Master." Between the casks the darkness lay deep; far above, the guards' voices seemed to whisper in confusion.

At the bronze gate he jabbed the combination in swiftly; the gate shuddered open and as they passed through, Jared felt that odd shiver of displacement he had felt before.

The white room adjusted itself. Everything was exactly as he had left it. He had a sudden pang of anxiety. What was happening to Claudia? Was she safe?

"You sent her through with no idea of the danger." The Warden flicked the control panel out and touched sensors. "Entering the Prison is hazardous, physically and psychologically."

Shelves slid back. The screen lit.

On it, Jared saw a thousand images. They flickered, a checkerboard of tiny squares, of empty rooms, bleak oceans, far towers, dusty corners. He saw a street packed with people, a hideous den of stunted children, a man beating a strange beast, a woman tenderly breastfeeding a baby. Bewildered, he stepped up below the images, watching them flicker, the pain, the hunger, the unlikely friendships, the savage bargainings.

"This is the Prison." The Warden leaned against the desk. "All the images seen by the Eyes. It's the only way to find Claudia."

Jared felt a terrible misery soak him. In the Academy the Experiment was considered one of the glories of the ancient Sapienti, the noble sacrifice of the world's last reserves of energy to save the unredeemable, the poor, the despised. And it had ended in this.

The Warden watched him, a silhouette against the rippling images. "You see, Master, what only the Warden has ever seen."

"Why didn't . . . Why weren't we told . . . ?"

"There is not enough power. They can never be brought back, all those thousands of people. They are lost to us." He took out his watch and gave it to Jared, who took it numbly and then looked down at it. The Warden indicated the silver cube on the chain.

"You are like a god, Jared. You hold Incarceron in your hands."

He felt the pain inside him throb. His hands shook. He

wanted to put it down, to step back, step away. The cube was tiny, he had seen it a thousand times on the watch chain and barely noticed it, but now it filled him with awe. Was it possible it contained the mountains he saw, the forests of silver trees, the cities of ragged people preying on each other's poverty? Sweating, he held it tightly and the Warden said softly, "Afraid, Jared? It takes strength to see a whole world. Many of my predecessors never dared look. They hid their eyes."

A soft bell.

They both looked up. The screen had stopped flashing; as they stared, the pictures started to flick off, and one in the bottom right-hand corner grew, pixel by pixel, until it filled the whole screen.

It was Claudia.

Jared put the watch chain shakily down on the table.

She was talking to the prisoners. He recognized the boy Finn, and the other one, Keiro, who was leaning back against a stone wall, listening. Gildas crouched nearby; Jared saw at once that the old man was hurt, Attia standing next to him.

"Can you speak to them?"

"I can," the Warden said. "But first we listen."

He flicked a switch.

33

What use is one key among a billion prisoners?
—*Lord Calliston's Diary*

"It tried to stop me finding you," Claudia said.

She walked toward him down the gloomy corridor.

"You should never have come Inside." Finn felt awed. She was so out of place, bringing a scent of roses and strange fresh air that tantalized him. He felt he wanted to scratch at some itch in his mind; instead he rubbed a hand wearily over his eyes.

"Come back with me now." She held out her hand. "Come quickly!"

"You just wait a minute." Keiro stood. "He goes nowhere without me."

"Or me," Attia muttered.

"All of you can come then. It must be possible." Then her face fell.

Finn said, "What is it?"

Claudia bit her lip. She suddenly realized she had no idea how to do this. There had been no portal on this side, no chair or control panel; she had simply found herself in that empty cell. And she didn't know the way back there, even if the place was important.

"She can't do it," Keiro said. He came and stared closely at her, and though it annoyed her, she stared calmly back.

"At least I have this." She took the Key from a pocket and held it out. They saw it was identical to the one they knew, though its workmanship seemed better, the eagle perfect in its stillness.

Finn put his hand to his pocket. It was empty. Alarmed, he turned.

"It's here, fool boy." Gildas grabbed at the wall and pulled himself upright. He was gray, his face clammy. He held the Key so tightly in his knotted hands that the skin around his knuckles was white as the bone beneath.

"Are you really from the Outside?" he breathed.

"I am, Master." She walked toward him and reached out her hand for him to feel. "And Sapphique did Escape. Jared discovered that he has followers out there. They call him the Nine-Fingered One."

He nodded, and they saw there were tears in his eyes. "I know that. I have always known that he was real. This boy has seen him in visions. Soon I will see him."

His voice was gruff but there was a quaver in it Finn had never heard before. Oddly scared he said, "We need the Key, Master."

For a moment he thought the Sapient would not let go; there was a brief interval when both his and Gildas's fingers grasped the crystal. The old man looked down. "I have always trusted you, Finn. I never believed you were from Outside, and I was wrong in that, but your visions of the stars have led us to Escape, as I knew they would, ever since the first day I saw you lying curled up on that cart. This is the moment I have lived for."

His fingers opened; Finn felt the weight of the Key.

He looked at Claudia. "Now what?"

She took a deep breath, but it was not her voice that answered. Attia was in the shadows behind Keiro; she did not come forward, but her words were sharp. "What happened to the pretty dress?"

Claudia scowled. "I shredded it."

"And the wedding?"

"Off."

Attia's arms were wrapped around her thin body. "So now you want Finn."

"Giles. His name is Giles. Yes, I want him. The Realm needs its King. Someone who's seen outside the Palace and the Protocol. Someone who has been right down into the depths." She let her annoyance out in her words, channeled it into anger. "Isn't that what you want too? Someone who can end the misery of Incarceron because he knows what it's like?"

Attia shrugged. "It's Finn you should ask. You might just be taking him out of one prison into another."

Claudia stared at her and Attia stared back. It was Keiro's cool laugh that broke the silence. "I suggest we sort all this out in the brave new world Outside. Before the Prison quakes again."

Finn said, "He's right. How do we do this?"

She swallowed. "Well . . . I suppose we . . . use the Keys."

"But where's the gate?"

"There is no gate." This was hard; they were all staring at her. "Not . . . as you think."

"So how did you get here?" Keiro asked.

"It's . . . difficult to explain." As she spoke her fingers moved on the hidden controls of the Key; it hummed, lights moved inside it.

Keiro jumped forward. "Oh no, Princess!" He snatched it from her; she jerked after it, but he had his sword drawn and pointed at her throat. "No tricks. We all go together or not at all."

Furious, she said, "That's the plan."

"Put the weapon down," Gildas snapped.

"She's trying to take him. And leave us here."

"I'm not—"

"Stop talking about me as if I was some object!" Finn's snarl silenced them all. He rubbed a hand through his hair; his scalp was wet and his eyes prickled. His breath seemed short. A fit now would be impossible, but his hands were shaking and he felt it creeping over him.

And then he knew he was falling into it, he must be, because behind Gildas the wall shivered away, and looking out of it, huge and shadowy, was Blaize.

The Sapient's gray eyes surveyed them; his image was enormous in a white room of clean walls. "I'm afraid," he said, "that

Escape is not as easy as my daughter seems to think."

They were still. Keiro lowered the sword. "So that's it," he said. "And look how pleased she is to see you."

Finn watched Claudia turn to the image. He saw now that though the Warden's face was familiar, the scabs had left it; it was thinner, and there was a refined tension about the eyes.

Claudia looked up at it. "Don't call me your daughter." Her voice was hard and cold. "And don't try to stop me. I'm bringing them all out and you—"

"You can't bring them all out." The Warden held her eyes. "The Key will bring only one person out. Their copy, if it works, will do the same. Touch the black eye of the eagle. You will disappear, and reappear here." He smiled calmly. "That is the gate, Finn."

Appalled, she stared at him. "You're lying. You brought me out."

"You were a baby. Tiny. I took a chance."

There was a voice in the room; he turned, and Claudia saw Jared behind him, standing pale and tired.

"Master! Is it true?"

"I have no way of knowing, Claudia." He looked unhappy, his dark hair tangled. "There's only one way to find out, and that's to try."

She looked at Finn.

"Not you." It was Keiro who moved. "Finn and I are going first, and if it works I'll come back for the Sapient." He whipped up his sword as Claudia drew hers. "Drop that, Princess, or I'll cut your throat."

She gripped the leather hilt tight, but Finn said, "Do it, Claudia. Please."

He was looking at Keiro; as she lowered the blade she saw him step closer and say, "Do you really think I'd go and leave them? Give her back the Key."

"No way."

"Keiro . . ."

"You're stupid, Finn. Can't you see this is a setup! You and she would vanish and that would be it. No one would bother coming back for the rest of us."

"I would."

"They wouldn't let you." Keiro stepped up to him. "Once they had their lost Prince, why bother about the criminal Scum? The dog-girl and the halfman? Once you're back in your palace, why think of us?"

"I swear I'd come back."

"Sure. Isn't that what Sapphique said?"

In the stillness Gildas sat down abruptly, as if his strength had gone. "Don't leave me here, Finn," he muttered.

Finn shook his head, utterly weary. "We can't keep Claudia here, whatever the rest of us decide. She came to rescue us."

"Tough." Keiro's blue eyes were relentless. "She was a Prisoner once—she can be again. I go first. To find out what's waiting out there. And if it works, like I said, I'll come back."

"Liar," Attia snapped.

"You can't stop me."

The Warden laughed softly. "Is this the hero you think is Giles, Claudia? The man to govern the Realm? He can't even control this rabble."

Instantly Finn moved. He tossed the Key to Claudia; catching Keiro off guard, he grabbed for the sword. Anger roared in him; anger at all of them, at the Warden's smirk, at the fear and weakness in himself. Keiro staggered back; recovering fast, he whipped the blade up and they both had it; then Finn had torn it from his grip.

Keiro didn't flinch as the blade flickered in his face. "You won't use that on me."

Finn's heart pounded. His chest heaved. Behind him Attia hissed, "Why not, Finn? He killed the Maestra. You know that, you've always known it! He had the bridge cut. Not Jormanric."

"Is it true?" He barely recognized his own whisper.

Keiro smiled. "Make up your own mind."

"Tell me."

"No." His oathbrother held the Key in one fist. "It's your choice. I don't justify myself to anyone."

His heartbeat was so loud, it hurt. It filled the Prison, thudded down all the corridors, in all the cells.

He flung the sword down. Keiro dived for it, Finn kicked it away. Suddenly they were fighting, all Finn's breath gone in a vicious punch to his stomach, Keiro's ruthless skill flooring him. Claudia was shouting, Gildas roaring in anger, but he didn't care now; scrambling up, he flung himself on Keiro, grabbing for the Key. Hindered by the fragile crystal Keiro ducked and then punched again; Finn had him around the waist and down, but as he closed in, Keiro gave a kick that sent him reeling back.

Keiro rolled, picked himself up. Blood welled on his lip. "Now we'll see, brother," he hissed. He touched the black eye of the bird.

A light.

It was so brilliant, it burned their eyes.

It widened around Keiro, it swallowed him, and there was a noise in it, a whine that was painful, a sharp discordant note that cut off instantly.

The light spat out.

And Keiro was still there.

In the shattered silence the Warden's laugh was cool and regretful. "Ah," he said. "I'm afraid that means it won't work for you. Probably the metal components in your body render the process invalid. Incarceron is a closed system; its own elements can never leave."

Keiro stood stock-still.

"Never?" he breathed.

"Not unless the components are removed."

Keiro nodded. His face was grim and flushed. "If that's what it takes." He stepped toward Finn and said, "Get your knife."

"What?"

"You heard."

"I can't do that!"

Keiro laughed sourly. "Why not? Keiro the Nine-Fingered. I always wondered what Sapphique's sacrifice was all about."

Gildas groaned. "Boy, are you suggesting—"

"Maybe more of us are born of the Prison than we thought. Maybe you are, old man. But I won't let one finger keep me here. Get the knife."

Finn didn't move, but Attia did. She brought a small blade she always wore and held it out to him. He took it slowly. Keiro laid his hand on the floor, the fingers spread out. The metallic nail looked just the same as the others. "Do it now," he said.

"I can't . . ."

"You can. For my sake."

They looked at each other. Finn knelt. His hand was shaking. He put the edge of the blade to Keiro's skin.

"Wait," Attia snapped. She crouched. "Think! It may not be enough. As you said, none of us know what we are made of inside. There must be another way."

Keiro's eyes were blue and blank with desperation. He hesitated.

For a long moment he stood there unmoving, and then he closed his hand and nodded slowly. He looked down at the Key and held it out to Finn.

"Then I'll have to find it. Enjoy your kingdom, brother. Rule well. Watch your back."

Finn was too shaken to answer. A distant hammering made them all look up.

"What's that?" Claudia asked.

Jared said quickly, "It's here. Evian made his attempt and is dead. The Queen's guards are at the door."

She stared at her father. He said, "You must come back, Claudia. Bring the boy. I need him now."

"Is he really Giles?" she asked harshly.

The Warden's smile was wintry. "He is now."

As his words ended the screen went blank. A ripple of movement ran down the corridor; Finn looked around anxiously. Bricks clattered from the vault.

Then he looked up and saw the tiny red Eye whirr and click on him.

"Oh yes," the voice said softly. "You have all forgotten about me. And why should I let any of my children go?"

34

He woke and found them all around him.
The old, lame, the diseased, the half-made
men. He hid his head and was filled with
shame and anger. "I have failed you," he said.
"I have journeyed so far and I have failed."

"Not so," they answered. "There is a door
we know, a tiny, secret door. None of us dare
crawl through, in case we die there. If you
promise to come back for us, we will show you."

Sapphique was lithe and slender. He looked
at them with his dark eyes. "Take me there," he
whispered.

—Legends of Sapphique

"What happened?" Jared gasped.

"The Prison has interfered," the Warden hissed with fury. His fingers moved swiftly over the controls.

"Well, stop it! Order it to—"

"I cannot make Incarceron obey me." The Warden glared at him. "No one has done that for centuries. The Prison rules, Master. I have no power over it." Then in a voice so low Jared barely heard, "It laughs at me."

Appalled, Jared stared at the blank screen. Outside, a fist pounded again on the bronze doors. A voice thundered, "Warden! Open this! The Queen demands your presence."

"Evian made a poor job of his assassination," the Warden said. He glanced up. "Don't fear, they won't get in. Even with axes."

"She thinks you were involved."

"Maybe. It is a good excuse to be rid of me. There will be no marriage now."

Jared shook his head. "Then we're all finished."

"In that case, Master, I could do with your help." The gray eyes were fixed on him. "For Claudia's sake we need to work together."

Jared nodded slowly. Trying to ignore the furious banging, he came around to the controls and examined them carefully. "This is so old. Many of the symbols are in the Sapient tongue." He looked up. "Let's try talking to Incarceron in the language of its makers."

⊸✦⊷

THE PRISONQUAKE was swift and sudden. The floor buckled; walls crashed down. Finn grabbed Keiro; together they fell back against a door that gave under their weight, flinging them inside.

Claudia scrambled after them, but Attia said, "Help me with him!" She had Gildas doubled up, gasping. Hurriedly Claudia climbed back, wriggled his arm over her shoulders, and they struggled with him to the cell, where Finn hauled them in and slammed the door tight, he and Keiro wedging it with a split timber.

Outside, rubble cascaded down and they listened to it in dismay. The corridor was surely blocked.

"But you do not think you can lock me out, I hope?" Incarceron laughed its rumbling laugh. *"No one can do that. I am inescapable."*

"Sapphique Escaped." Gildas's voice was a rasp of pain, but he spat the words out. His hands clutched his chest; they shook uncontrollably. "How did he do that then, without a Key? Is there another way out, that only he discovered? A way so secret, so amazing, you can't block it? A way needing no gate and no machinery? Is that it, Incarceron? Is that what you fear, always watching, always listening?"

"I fear nothing."

"Not what you told me," Claudia snapped. She was breathing hard; she glanced at Finn. "I must go back. Jared's in trouble. Will you come?"

"I can't leave them. Take the old man with you."

Gildas laughed: his body convulsed into wheezing gasps. Attia gripped his hands; then she turned her head. "He's dying," she whispered.

"Finn," the Sapient croaked.

Finn crouched down, sick with the prickling behind his eyes. Whatever injuries Gildas had were internal, but the shiver of his hands, the sweat and pallor of his face were only too clear.

425

The Sapient brought his mouth close to Finn's ear. "Show me the stars," he whispered.

Finn looked at the others. "I can't . . ."

"Then allow me," the Prison said. The glimmer of light in the cell went out. One red Eye was a spark in the corner of the wall. *"Look at this star, old man. This is the only star you will ever see."*

"Stop tormenting him!" Finn's howl of rage startled them all. And then to Claudia's amazement he turned back to Gildas and clasped his hand. "Come with me," he said. "I'll show you."

The dizziness of his mind swept over him and he let it. He walked deliberately into its darkness and dragged the old man with him, and all around them the lake glimmered under its floating lanterns, blue and purple and gold, and the boat rocked beneath him as he lay in it and stared up at the stars.

They blazed in the summer night. Like silver dust they lay across the cosmos as if a great hand had scattered them, and their mystery enchanted the velvety blackness.

Beside him, Finn felt the old man's awe.

"These are the stars, Master. Whole worlds, far away, seeming tiny, but really huger than anything we know."

Lake water lapped.

Gildas said, "So far. So many!"

A heron rose from the water with a graceful flap. On the shore the music sounded sweet; voices laughed softly.

The old man said hoarsely, "I have to go to them now, Finn.

I have to go and find Sapphique. He won't have been content, you know, just to be Outside. Not once he had seen this."

Finn nodded. He felt the boat unmoor beneath him, the lilt and slip of the swell. He felt the old man's fingers loosen in his. And as he stared at them, the stars grew and burned, became flames, tiny flames on the tips of tiny candles, and he was blowing them out, blowing at them with his whole breath, all his energy.

They vanished, and he laughed, a great laugh of triumph, and all the people around laughed with him, the King in his red coat, and Bartlett, and his pale new stepmother, and all the courtiers and nurses and musicians, and the little girl in the pretty white dress, the girl who had come that day, that they said would be his special friend.

She was looking at him now. She said, "Finn. Can you hear me?"

Claudia.

◅◦◦◦▻

"IT'S READY." Jared looked up. "You speak, and the translation will be instant."

The Warden had been pacing, listening to the voices outside; now he came and stood by the desk, his arms folded.

"Incarceron," he said.

Silence. Then, on the screen, a small red point of light. It was tiny, like a star. It gazed out at them. It said, *"Who is this speaking the old tongue?"*

427

The voice was uncertain. It seemed to have lost some of its echoing rumble.

The Warden glanced at Jared. Then he said quietly, "You know who this is, my father. This is Sapphique."

Jared's eyes widened, but he stayed silent.

There was another silence. This time the Warden broke it. "I speak to you in the language of the Sapienti. I order you not to harm the boy Finn."

"He has the Key. No prisoner is allowed to Escape."

"But your anger may injure him. And Claudia." Had the Warden's voice changed as he spoke her name? Jared wasn't sure.

A moment of stillness. Then, *"Very well. For you, my son."*

The Warden made a sign to Jared to cut communications, but as his finger reached out to the panel, the Prison said softly, *"But if you are indeed Sapphique, we have spoken often before. You will remember."*

"That was long ago," the Warden said cautiously.

"Yes. You gave me the Tribute I required. I hunted you and you thwarted me. You hid in holes and stole my children's hearts. Tell me, Sapphique, how did you Escape from me? After I struck you down, after the terrible fall through darkness, what doorway did you find that I had overlooked? Through what crevice did you crawl? And where are you now, out there in the places I cannot even imagine?"

The voice was wistful; the Warden looked up at the steady

Eye on the screen. He was hushed as he answered. "That is a mystery I cannot reveal."

"A pity. You see, they did not give me any way to see outside myself. Can you imagine, Sapphique, you the wanderer, the great traveler, can you even dream of how it is to live forever trapped in your own mind, watching only the creatures that inhabit it? They made me powerful and they made me flawed. And only you, when you return, can help me."

The Warden was still. Dry-mouthed, Jared flicked the switch. His hands were shaky and damp with sweat. As he watched it, the Eye faded.

⌖

FINN'S SIGHT was blurred and his whole body had emptied. He lay crooked; only Keiro's arm kept his head off the floor. But for a moment, before the Prison stench crept back, before the world surged in, he knew he was a prince and the son of a prince, that his world was golden with sunlight, that he had ridden into a dark forest one morning in a fairy tale and never ridden out again.

"Drink some of this." Attia gave him water; he managed a swallow and coughed and tried to sit up.

"He gets worse," Keiro was saying to Claudia. "This is what your father has done to him."

She ignored it and bent over Finn. "The Prisonquake has stopped. It just went quiet."

"Gildas?" Finn muttered.

"The old man's gone. He doesn't have to worry about Sapphique anymore." Keiro's voice was gruff. Turning, Finn saw the Sapient lying in the rubble, his eyes closed, his body curled, as if he slept. On his finger, loose and dull, as if Keiro had pushed it there in some vain effort to save him, shone the last skull-ring.

"What did you do?" Claudia asked. "He said . . . odd things."

"I showed him the way out." Finn felt raw, scraped clean. He didn't want to talk about it now, not to tell them what he thought he had remembered, so he sat up slowly and said, "You tried the ring on him?"

"It didn't work. He was right about that too. Maybe none of them ever worked." Keiro pushed the Key into his hands. "Go. Get out now. Get the Sapient to design a key to spring me. And send someone back for the girl."

Finn looked at Attia. "I'll come back myself. I swear."

Attia smiled, wan, but Keiro said, "See you do. I don't want to be stuck with her."

"And for you too. I'll get all the Sapienti in my kingdom on it. We made a vow, brother. Do you think I've forgotten?"

Keiro laughed. His handsome face was grimy and bruised, his hair dull with dirt, his fine coat ruined. But he was the one, Finn thought, who looked like a prince. "Maybe. Or maybe this is your chance to be rid of me. Maybe you're afraid I'd kill you and take your place. If you don't come back, believe me, I'll do it."

Finn smiled. For a moment they looked at each other across

the tilted cell, across the spilled manacles and shackles.

Then Finn turned to Claudia. "You first."

She said, "You will come?"

"Yes."

She looked at him, then the others. Quickly she touched the eye of the eagle and was gone, in a brilliance that made them all gasp.

Finn looked down at the Key he held. "I can't," he said.

Attia smiled brightly. "I trust you. I'll be waiting."

But his finger didn't move, paused above the eagle's dark eye, so she reached over and pressed it for him.

CLAUDIA FOUND herself sitting in the chair amidst an uproar of voices and hammering. Outside the gate Caspar was shouting, ". . . under arrest for high treason. Warden! Can you hear me?" The bronze resounded to frenzied blows.

Her father took her hand and raised her to her feet. "My dear. So where is our young Prince?"

Jared was watching the bronze gate buckle inward. He flashed a quick, glad glance at Claudia.

Her hair was tangled, her face dirty. A strange smell hung around her. She said, "Right behind me."

FINN WAS sitting in a chair too, but this room was dark, a small cell, like the one he remembered from long ago, ancient, the walls greasy with carved names.

Opposite him sat a slim dark-haired man. For a moment he thought this was Jared, and then he knew who it was.

He looked around, confused. "Where am I? Is this Outside?"

Sapphique was sitting against the wall, knees drawn up. He said quietly, "None of us have much idea where we are. Perhaps all our lives we are too concerned with where, and not enough with who."

Finn's fingers were tight on the crystal Key. "Let me go," he breathed.

"It's not me who's stopping you." Sapphique watched Finn and his eyes were dark and the stars were points of light deep inside them. "Don't forget us, Finn. Don't forget the ones back there in the dark, the hungry and the broken, the murderers and thugs. There are prisons within prisons, and they inhabit the deepest."

He stretched out his hand and took a length of chain from the wall; it clanked, rust flaking off. He slipped his hands inside the links. "Like you, I went out into the Realm. It wasn't what I'd expected. And I made a promise too." He dropped the metal on the floor, an enormous crash, and Finn saw the maimed finger. "Maybe that's what's imprisoning you."

He turned sideways and beckoned. A shadow rose from behind him and walked forward, and Finn stifled a cry, because it was the Maestra. She had the same tall, lanky walk, the red hair, the scornful eyes. She stood looking down at Finn and he felt that a chain bound him, fine and invisible and she held the end of it, because he could not move hand or foot.

"How can you be here?" he whispered. "You fell."

"Oh yes, I fell! Through realms and centuries. Like a bird with a broken wing. Like an angel cast down." He could barely tell if it was her whisper or Sapphique's. But the anger was hers. "And that was all your fault."

"I . . ." He wanted to blame Keiro, or Jormanric. Anyone. But he said, "I know."

"Remember it, Prince. Learn from it."

"Are you alive?" He was struck with the old shame; it made it hard to speak.

"Incarceron doesn't waste anything. I'm alive in its depths, in its cells, the cells of its body."

"I'm sorry."

She wrapped her coat about her with the old dignity. "If you are, that's all I ask."

"Will you keep him here?" Sapphique murmured.

"As he kept me?" She laughed calmly. "I don't need a ransom for my forgiveness. Good-bye, scared boy. Guard my crystal Key."

The cell blurred and opened. He felt as if he were dragged through a blinding concussion of stone and flesh; that huge wheels of iron rumbled over him, that he was opened and closed, riven and mended.

He stood up from the chair and the dark figure held out a hand to steady him.

And this time it was Jared.

35

I have walked a stair of swords,
I have worn a coat of scars.
I have vowed with hollow words,
I have lied my way to the stars.
—*Songs of Sapphique*

The gate shuddered.

"Don't worry. It will never break." Calm, the Warden surveyed Finn. "So this is the one you think is Giles."

She glared at him. "You should know."

Finn stared around. The room was so white it hurt, the glare of the lights making his eyes ache. The man he recognized as Pxize laughed lightly, folding his arms. "Actually, it doesn't matter whether he is or not. Now you have him, you will have to make him Giles. Because only he stands between you and disaster." Curious, he stepped closer to Finn. "And what do you think, Prisoner? Who do you think you are?"

Finn felt shaky and filthy; suddenly he knew that his skin was grimed with dirt, that he stank in this sterile room. "I . . . think I remember. The betrothal . . ."

"Are you sure? Or might it not be that these are memories

someone else had, that are now buried in you, filaments of thought trapped in borrowed tissue, that the Prison built into you?" He smiled his cold smile.

"Once we could have found out," Claudia snapped. "Before Protocol."

"Yes." The Warden turned to her. "And that problem I will leave to you."

Finn saw how pale she was, how angry. She said, "All my life you let me believe I was your daughter. And it was all a lie."

"No."

"Yes! You selected me, you educated me, you formed me . . . you even told me all that! Created a creature that would be just what you wanted, that would be pliant and marry whom you said and be what you wanted. What would have happened to me afterward? Would poor Queen Claudia have met with an accident too, leaving only the Warden to be Regent? Was that the plan?"

He met her eyes, and his were clear and gray. "If it was, I changed it because I grew to love you."

"Liar!"

Jared said unhappily, "Claudia, I . . ." but the Warden held up his hand.

"No Master, let me explain. I chose you, yes, and I freely admit at first you were a means to an end. A squalling infant that I saw as rarely as possible. But as you grew, I came . . . to look forward to seeing you. To the way you curtsied to me, showed me your work, were shy with me. And you have become dear to me."

She stared at him, not wanting to hear this, or believe it. She wanted to keep her anger bright, newly minted like a coin.

He shrugged. "I was not a good father. For that I am sorry."

In the stillness between them the hammering broke out again, even louder. Jared said urgently, "It hardly matters, sir, what you did or who this boy is. We are all condemned now. There is no escape from death unless we all enter the Prison."

Finn muttered, "I have to go back for Attia." He held out his hand to Claudia for the other Key; she shook her head. "Not you. I'll go back." Reaching out, she took the crystal copy from him and compared the two. "Who made this?"

"Lord Calliston. The Steel Wolf himself." The Warden stared at the crystal. "I had often wondered if the rumors were true, whether a copy existed, somewhere in the depths of the Prison."

She moved her finger toward the panel, but he stopped her. "Wait. First we must ensure our own safety, or the girl will be better where she is."

Claudia looked at him. "How can I ever trust you again?"

"You must." He put a finger to his lips and nodded. Then, striding across the white cell, he touched the door control and stood back.

Two soldiers fell headlong into the room. Behind them, the ram on chains swung at empty air. Swords were drawn, sharp whispers of steel.

"Do please enter," the Warden said graciously.

The Queen herself was there, Claudia saw with shock, wearing a dark cloak. Behind his mother Caspar glared at her. "I'll never forgive you," he snarled.

"Be quiet." His mother stalked past him into the room, paused at the strange shiver of energy at the threshold, then gazed around. "Fascinating. So this is the Portal."

"Indeed." The Warden bowed. "I am happy to see you so well."

"I very much doubt that." Sia stopped before Finn. She looked him up and down and her face paled. She pressed her red lips tight.

"Yes," the Warden said softly. "Unfortunately a Prisoner has escaped."

Furious, she turned on him. "Why have you done this? What treachery are you planning?"

"None. We can all come out of this safely. All of us. With no secrets spilled, no assassinations. Watch me."

He strode to the control desk, touched a combination of controls, and stood back. Claudia stared, because the wall blanked and showed an image that she took a moment to recognize. In a vast room courtiers crowded in a buzz of scandal. Half-eaten food lay ignored on huge tables. Servants gossiped in anxious huddles.

It was her wedding feast.

"What are you doing?" the Queen snapped, but it was too late. The Warden said, "Friends." Every head in the room turned. Talk dried into a stillness of astonishment.

After a hundred years of Protocol the vast screen behind the throne had probably been forgotten; now Finn stared out at the Court through a fringe of cobwebs, a film of grime.

"Please forgive all the unfortunate confusions of the day," the Warden said gravely. "And I beg all of you, ambassadors from Overseas, and courtiers, dukes and Sapienti, ladies and dowagers all, to overlook this breach of Protocol. But a great day has dawned, and a great wrong has been righted."

The Queen seemed too astounded to speak; Claudia almost felt the same. But she moved; she grabbed Finn's arm and hauled him close to her. They stood together facing the bewildered, fascinated faces of the Court as her father said, "Behold. The Prince we thought was lost, the heir of his father, the hope of the Court, Giles, has returned to us."

A thousand eyes stared at Finn. He looked back, seeing in each one the pinpoint of light, feeling their intense curiosity, their doubt, descend right into his soul. Was this how it would be, to be King?

"In her great wisdom the Queen found it necessary to conceal him in safe exile against a conspiracy against his life," the Warden said smoothly. "But at last, after many years, this danger is ended. The plotters have failed, and are arrested. Everything is calm again."

He glanced once at the Queen; fury was in every inch of her upright back, but when she spoke, her voice was pleasant with happiness. "My friends, I am so delighted! The Warden and I have worked so hard to counter this threat. I want you to prepare the banquet now, for the Prince's coming. Instead of a wedding, a great homecoming, but still a wonderful day, just as we planned."

The Court was silent. Then, from the back, a ragged cheer began.

She jerked her head; the Warden touched the panel. The screen dimmed.

She took a deep breath. "I will never, never forgive you for this," she said evenly.

"I know." John Arlex flicked another switch idly. He sat, and crossed one leg over another, his dark brocaded coat shimmering, and then he reached out and took both Keys from where Claudia had placed them and held them glinting in his hands.

"Such small bright crystals," he murmured. "And such power contained in them! I suppose, Claudia, my dear, that if one cannot be the master of one world, one should find another world to conquer." He glanced at Jared. "I leave her to you, Master. Remember our talk."

Jared's eyes widened; he cried, "Claudia!" but she already knew what was happening. Her father was sitting in the chair of the Portal—she knew she should run forward, dart forward and snatch the Keys from him, but she couldn't move, as if the power of his terrible will kept her frozen.

Her father smiled. "Do excuse me, Majesty. I think I would

be a specter at this feast." His fingers touched the panel.

A brilliance exploded in the room, making them all flinch; then the chair was empty, spinning slightly in the white room, and as they stared at it a spark spat in the controls, then another. Acrid smoke rose; the Queen clenched her fists and screamed at the emptiness, "You can't do this!"

Claudia was staring at the chair; as it imploded into flame, Jared tugged her hastily back. She said bleakly, "He can. He has."

Jared watched her. Her eyes were overbright, her face flushed, but her head was high. The Queen raged with anger, stabbing every button and causing only explosions. As she swept out with Caspar running at her heels, Jared said, "He'll come back, Claudia. I'm sure . . ."

"It's nothing to me what he does." She turned to Finn, who was staring aghast at her.

"Attia," he whispered. "What about Attia? I promised to go back for her!"

"It's not possible . . ."

He shook his head. "You don't understand. I have to! I can't leave them there. Especially not Keiro." He was appalled. "Keiro will never forgive me. I promised."

"We'll find a way. Jared will find one. Even if it takes years. That's my promise to you." She grabbed his hand and pushed the frayed sleeve up to show the eagle mark. "But you must think about this now. You're here. You're Outside and you're free. Of them, of all of that. And we have to make this work, because Sia will always be there, plotting behind our backs."

Bewildered, he stared at her and realized she had no idea of what he had lost. "Keiro is my brother."

"I'll do all I can," Jared said quietly. "There must be another way. Your father came and went as Blaize. And Sapphique found it."

Finn raised his head and gave him a strange look. "Yes. He did."

Claudia took his arm. "We have to go out there now," she said quietly. "You have to lift your head up and be a prince. It won't be like you expect. But everything is acting here. A game, my father calls it. Are you ready?"

He felt the old fear wash over him. He felt he was walking into a great ambush that had been set for him. But he nodded.

Arm in arm, they walked out of the white room, and Claudia led him up through the cellars and the stairs. He passed through chambers of crowding, staring people. She opened a door and he cried out in delight, because the world was a garden and above it, brilliant and blazing, hung the stars, millions of them, higher and higher, above the pinnacles of the Palace, and the trees, and the sweet beds of flowers.

"I knew," he whispered. "I always knew."

LEFT ALONE, Jared gazed around at the ruins of the Portal. The Warden's sabotage looked only too thorough. He had spoken kindly to the boy, but in his heart he felt a deep dread, because to find a way back through this destruction would take time, and how much time did he have?

"You were too much for us, Warden," he murmured aloud.

He climbed up after them, weary now, his chest aching. Servants ran past him; talk echoed in every chamber and hall. He hurried, stepping out into the gardens, glad of the evening cool, the sweet scents.

Claudia and Finn stood on the steps of the building. The boy looked as if he was blind with the glory of the night, as if its purity was an agony to him.

Beside them, Jared slipped his hand into his pocket and brought out the watch. Claudia stared. "Isn't that . . . ?"

"Yes. Your father's."

"He gave it to you?"

"You might say that." And he held it in his delicate fingers, and she noticed, as if for the first time, that there was a tiny silver cube hanging on its chain, a charm that twisted and glittered in the starlight.

"But where are they?" Finn asked, tormented. "Keiro and Attia and the Prison?"

Jared gazed at the cube thoughtfully. "Closer than you think, Finn," he said.

◄◦►